A TIME
TO KEEP

AND OTHER STORIES

BY GEORGE MACKAY BROWN

Poems
Fishermen with Ploughs
Loaves and Fishes
The Year of the Whale
Winterfold
Selected Poems
Voyages

Short stories
A Time to Keep and Other Stories
A Calendar of Love
A Time to Keep
Hawkfall
The Sun's Net
Andrina

Plays
A Spell for Green Corn
Three Plays: The Well, The Loom of Light,
The Voyage of St Brandon

Novels
Greenvoe
Magnus
Time in a Red Coat

Essays
An Orkney Tapestry
(Gollancz)
Letters from Hamnavoe
(Gordon Wright Publishing)
Under Brinkie's Brae
(Gordon Wright Publishing)

Non-fiction
Portrait of Orkney
(with photographs by Werner Forman)

For children
The Two Fiddlers
Pictures in the Cave
Six Lives of Fankle the Cat

A TIME TO KEEP

AND OTHER STORIES

by

George Mackay Brown

THE VANGUARD PRESS

NEW YORK

Library of Congress Cataloging-in-Publication Data
Brown, George Mackay.
   A time to keep and other stories.
   1. Orkney—Fiction.   I. Title.   II. Title: Time to
keep.
[PR6052.R59T54   1987]   823'.914   86-22484
ISBN: 0-8149-0929-9

Designer: Tom Bevans
Manufactured in the United States of America.

CONTENTS

CONTENTS

FOREWORD

The stories in this book are nearly all set in a little group of islands off the north coast of Scotland, called Orkney—"the islands of the whale."

Some of them seek back into the history of Orkney for their themes. That is a fortunate thing for me, because the islands have been continuously lived in for upwards of five thousand years: the oldest inhabited house in Europe has lately been excavated in the island of Papay. Stone-Age Orcadians built the magnificent stone circles at Brodgar and Stenness and the still more wonderful burial chamber of Maeshowe, a hymn in stone to death and resurrection. The midwinter sun enters fleetingly to touch the wall of one tomb with a yellow-as-cornstalks finger.

A Celtic people—one of many—sailed across the turbulent Pentland Firth, and settled, and built impregnable stone castles— "brochs"—to defend themselves from sequent tribes, or perhaps to lord it over a subject race. The drift of the peoples, in those times before history, seemed always to be west and out through the Mediterranean gate; then north.

Those mysterious tribes, the Picts, came, and left a few carvings in stone.

But Orkney's golden age arrived with the Vikings from Norway: a complex people, proud of their strength and cunning, exulting over the hoards of gold and silver taken by war or piracy; yet they had a rough-hewn law code; they were marvellous navigators; they had laughter and a deep enjoyment of life, believing it was better to go into the darkness young and strong than to die "a straw death"....In the end they gave us their rarest treasure, the saint and martyr Magnus, whose bones lie in a pillar of St. Magnus Cathedral at Kirkwall in the heart of the islands. According to the medieval hymn, "like blazing gold his bones endured the fire"....

Orkney, in Norse times, was one of the famous earldoms of

medieval Europe. The grandfather of Magnus, Earl Thorfinn, ruled nine earldoms in Scotland; he was a kinsman of the Scottish king, Macbeth. The story of the Orkney earls, their friends and enemies, their battles and feuds and stratagems and voyages, is told in a marvellous anthology of stories, the *Orkneyinga Saga*. But the greatest art of the Norsemen by far was narrative. There are echoes of the sagas in many of the stories that follow.

Norse influence waned, after three centuries. Orkney was drawn into the orbit of Scotland. All magnificence was drained from the island story, to be replaced by dust of law books, merchants' and lairds' ledgers, the scrolls of vain and cruel upstarts. But the Scottish gift for narrative breaks the centuries-long gloom and oppression in one great ballad, *The Lady Odivere*, and a great midwinter ritual chant, *The New Year Song*, sung from farm to farm under the boreal star wheel.

Orkney is a quiet place now, far removed from the trade routes and centers of power: inhabited by 18,000 people of very mixed descent: Celts, Norse, Scots, with a centuries-long leavening of wrecked mariners and Indian women brought back from the Hudson Bay (where hundreds of Orkneymen went to work in the nineteenth century), and, more recently, hundreds of English people in flight from cities and urban values.

A quiet place and a quiet people, mostly farmers and seamen and fishermen. The slow sure earth rhythms, ploughtime to harvest, and the perilous rhythms of the sea—cross-textures of fish and cornstalk, plough and net—are bound to work themselves into the writings of a modern Orcadian storyteller or poet. Speaking for myself, I find them immensely stimulating.

There is one inexhaustible quarry to be worked. I am thinking of the dark age of our history, between the time of the death of King Hakon in Orkney after the defeat of his Norwegian fleet at Largs in southwest Scotland in 1263, and the emancipation of the crofters a century ago, when gradually they began to take over the land they tilled; and so a little light was let into our history once more. Those dark centuries were thronged, all the same, with smugglers, ministers, lairds, witches, merchants, whalers, Hudson Bay men, the press gangs of the French wars, gangrels, all touched (as well as the farmers and fishermen) by an earth steadfastness and the perilous magic of ocean. But mostly

A TIME
TO KEEP

AND OTHER STORIES

A CALENDAR OF LOVE

The fisherman Peter lived in a tarred hut above the rocks with his boat, his creels, his Bible.

Jean Scarth lived with her father (men called him Snipe) in the pub at the end of the village. Snipe lay in bed now all the time. The doctor said he would never see another New Year.

Thorfinn Vik the crofter lived in a new wooden house at the edge of the moor. His father and mother were dead now. His married sister lived in Canada.

Jean opened the pub at six o'clock. Peter was standing outside with three haddocks in his hand. He didn't come in, he gave Jean the fish and walked off into the darkness. He had his black suit on, the one he wore to the gospel meetings.

Thorfinn came at half past six. His face was gaunt and grey after the New Year drinking. He asked for beer and stood over the counter drinking it. Other men from the hill came in. Seatter of Stark and Eric Weyland came in and began to play draughts. Three tinkers came in.

Jean said to Thorfinn, "Peter from the shore was here tonight. He's a good man, that."

"Give me a whisky," said Thorfinn. "I must keep my strength up for the ploughing."

"He had three fish but he never uttered a word," said Jean.

The men from the hill went out, then the tinkers. Seatter of Stark and Eric Weyland sat over the draughtboard.

Thorfinn said. "The croft's still empty, up by."

Jean said, "I have a pub to work and a sick man to nurse. I can't come."

"I love thee well," said Thorfinn.

"And I think well of you," said Jean. "But I think little of your drinking and carry-on."

1

Seatter of Stark and Eric Weyland began to grumble at each other over the draughtboard.

"It's past nine," said Jean. "Drink up and go."

Thorfinn finished his whisky and went out. After a time Jean followed him to the door. The black footprints went off into the snow-brimmed village.

From the door of the Mission Hall opposite Peter stood watching her. The prayer meeting was over. His black Bible was in his hand.

FEBRUARY

After the gale in the second week of February there was much sea for days. Peter sat over his stove with the evangelical magazines. The ten lost tribes of Israel were not lost at all! They were here, in the islands of Britain, and Peter was one of them, Peter was an Israelite! He read on and on.

The van cost Thorfinn fifty pounds second-hand. Now he could go to dances in the farthest parishes and see new women. He had not passed the driving test, he had neither license nor insurance, but he took the risk, driving at night, with no I-plates.

The old man, who had been so patient and carefree since he took to his bed, now began to summon Jean a hundred times a day. She would have to leave her beer-tap running and go up to him. He had become like a child. He wept and prayed in the darkness... "Don't bury me beside Mary Ann," said Snipe, "nor yet beside my father and mother. There must be a new grave, and I want a granite stone with an anchor on it."

Thorfinn was in the bar. "A sheep was run over, up for Birsay the way, last night. It was me," he said. "If the police come, you must say I was here, alone in the parlour, drinking till closing time."

"I won't tell them any such thing," said Jean. "That would be a lie."

"There's a well-like lass in Birsay," said Thorfinn. "I saw her last week at the dance. Sadie Flett, that's her name."

"I wish you luck of her," said Jean, "and would you drink up, for it's closing time."

The thin cry came from upstairs. "Jean...Jean..."

At midnight the old man was still not sleeping. He was remembering ships and men from sixty years ago, and every memory was a torture.

"For God's sake and for God's sake go to sleep," whispered Jean against the wall, "for the strength and the patience are nearly out of me."

There was a gentle knock at the outer door. Peter stood there in the moonlight.

"I saw the light in your father's room," he said.

"He's far from well," said Jean. "The old bad things are troubling him."

"I'll sit with him till the morning," said Peter.

The night passed.

In the morning Jean found them as she had left them at midnight, Peter awake in the chair and Snipe in bed, but sleeping now as quiet as a stone.

"A morning for haddocks," said Peter. "I'll sleep in the afternoon. I'll watch again tonight.... And as for thee," he went on, "thu must get out in the fresh air. Thu're as pale as a candle."

MARCH

"I love thee," said Thorfinn, "I love thee well."

"I love thee too," said Jean.

Through the van window was the island of Gairsay, and birds, and a flowing sea. It was a Sunday evening—the police were presumably all at home.

The last of winter, a hard grey lump of snow, blocked the ditch. Silently, imperceptibly, the little rill of ditch-water unwove the stubborn snow, carried it off, a cold shining music, down to the loch and the swans.

For a long time they did not speak.

"Throw everything...all they sins...thy weaknesses...in the arms...of the eternal...the everlasting..." said Peter earnestly and hopelessly over the shape in the bed.

"No, but listen," said Snipe. "It was in Montevideo they all got drunk and the next morning the skipper mustered the crew and eight were missing and the same morning the South American police came aboard and said they had seven of them in jail and to bail them out would cost a hundred and eight quid so the skipper—"

"Mr. Scarth," said Peter, "O man, you're *dying*. Are you not sorry before Almighty God?"

"—because he *had* to sail," said Snipe, "that very day. So he paid up, or rather the consul paid. And it was a month before Jock Slater was dragged out of the harbour. He was the eighth one but they didn't have to pay a penny for him—"

"Listen," cried Peter, "in Revelation it says—"

But soon Snipe was out on his own, in a place beyond scriptures and seaports and bad foreign hooch.

Peter met Jean on the stair, "Thy father's dead," he said.

Later, beside the fire, he said, "Bury thy father and sell this bad place. I love thee."

"You're a good man, Peter," said Jean.

She went once more to look at the dead face. She came back crying. "O Thorfinn," she said.

"Thorfinn!" said Peter. "Do you want that badness all over again? Your father died speaking of drink. God help him, that's the truth. Do you want to go on living that way?"

"No," said Jean, "and you're a good man."

"Do you want to go on staying in this place?" said Peter.

"No," said Jean, and kissed him gently. And again.

He took her in his hard religious arms.

In the grey of morning Peter went out and knocked at the undertaker's door and went on home.

He went down on his knees among the nets and oars, and prayed.

APRIL

A stone went up in the churchyard:

In memory of
JOHN SCARTH

4

Inn-Keeper in this Parish
Formerly a Seaman
1880–1962
*"May There Be No Moaning Of The Bar
When I Put Out To Sea"*

Carved anchors, dolphins, waves, sailing ships, tumbled after each other round the edge of the white marble.

"There should have been barrels of sour beer too, and naked women," said Thorfinn.

And later he said, "Many a poor bloody drunkard's last shilling went to pay for that stone."

And to Jean he said, "It's a credit to you, the stone you put up to Snipe...."

"Where are you going in the van tonight?" said Jean.

"Nowhere," said Thorfinn.

"Tell me," said Jean, "so I won't need to hear it from the gossip-mongers."

"I'm going to Holm," said Thorfinn.

"To Hazel Groat," said Jean.

Thorfinn drank his whisky down and went out.

Peter didn't come near the village now, not even for the gospel meetings. He bought his provisions from the grocery van.

"That's a fine stone they've raised for Snipe Scarth in the kirkyard," said Josiah of the Shore to Peter across a black stretch of net.

"I never saw it," said Peter.

"Tell me now," said Josiah, "would you say Snipe's in Heaven or in Hell?"

"It's not for me to say," said Peter.

"Just so," said Josiah. "Poor man.... And he has a daughter."

"He has," said Peter.

"The business is being carried on," said Josiah. "She has a sharp tongue in her head, that one. She'll comb the head of some poor man. Ay."

"There's another tear in the net," said Peter. "What's needed here is a good woman that knows how to mend things, and to clean and to cook. The price of a good woman is above rubies...."

MAY

Jean, dreaming, walked on a green hill. There were swans in the water below her, and clouds like swans in the sky above.

A man walked along the road from the sea. He was all wet from a shipwreck. "Gideon's fleece is not more glorious," Peter said (for it was Peter). He was walking not towards her but towards Thorfinn who was having difficulty in ploughing a field with the axle of a car.

Thorfinn turned and hewed at Peter with his plough-axle but it buckled on Peter's shoulder like cardboard. He touched Thorfinn with his black book. Formally, gently, Thorfinn fell across the furrow.

Jean was carrying a vase. She knelt to put it in a small grave in the corner of the field but a bird looked out of it, a blue bird with sweet frightened eyes. She gathered it in her hands. Its wings were cold. It was a bird of ice.

She was going into a church with a broken arch, where a service was going on. It was night. Her hands were cut and bleeding—inside she would find a cure. O, her hand was a thorn, a flame, such agony! Peter in a black cloak stood at the arch. He looked at her with blank eyes.

Farther in, hidden from her, voices were singing among cold, bright images.

Jean woke with a cry in the dawn.

Peter was walking down the beach, loaded with creels, towards his dinghy. Josiah walked five paces behind him, loaded with creels. It was a good morning for the lobsters.

All that month Thorfinn's van had been probing in another direction, out towards Orphir. The girl there was called Myra Stanger. After the dance he had made her drunk with gin. She sat in the van beside him now, singing in an ugly slack way. Thorfinn drove fast, to be home before the police were stirring. "I love thee," he said to Myra.

At Glengoes he stopped the van. He climbed through a fence and came back later with a dead dangling chicken. He threw it in the back of the van. Myra was asleep. He drank some gin.

Then he started the engine again and drove on into the growing light.

Thorfinn said to Jean, "Ann Johnston. And Sadie Flett. And Hazel Groat. And Myra Stanger. And Agnes Sinclair.... But thee I love."

Jean said to Peter, "So now I see it was only to save the soul of a bad old man you came visiting here."

Peter said to Thorfinn," "Thu're a thing of lust, "Thu're a thing of lust and drunkenness, and I have a strong inclination to drag thee like a rat through the ditch. I can't find in my soul one drop of love for thee, not one, God help me."

Thorfinn said to Peter, "I'll give thee five shillings for that skate, for not only salted does skate put a powerful thirst in the throat, but boiled it sends a man raging after women in the darkness of night, both in dreams and in reality."

Peter said to Jean, "I'm a poor man but strong in my body. I believe my election is sealed. I pray that grace will fall on thee also. I wish to see no woman but thee standing in my door every day when I haul the dinghy ashore after the fishing."

Jean said to Thorfinn, "This is what is wrong with me, this is why I have the darkness under my eyes and my mouth is full of sharp words, that I think I'm...O, go away....It's closing time!"

JULY

On the last day of the Carnival Week in Stromness, Thorfinn drove his unlicensed van past two policemen at the north end of the town and parked it in the square. In the Britannia Bar he drank whisky and beer. There were not many people in the town yet.

That day, Saturday, Peter did not go to the creels. In the afternoon he put on his white shirt and black suit. He took the Bible under his arm. He caught the bus to Stromness at the smithy.

Jean said to James Firth, "I'll give thee a pound to serve at the bar tonight, and thu can have a double whisky before thu opens the door and another when the last customer has gone. Will thu do that? For I must go to Stromness...." James Firth agreed to do that, on those terms. Jean gave him the key.

Thorfinn left the Britannia Bar and went to the Hamnavoe Bar. He drank whisky. Andrew of Feadale came in. Andrew drank vodka, and stood Thorfinn a glass of vodka too. "It has a queer taste, vodka," said Thorfinn, "like sweet paraffin, and the Russians must be a barbarous bloody nation to drink stuff like that. ..." Through the window they could see the parish buses coming in for the Carnival, one after the other.

Peter got off the bus and went to the house of William Simpson the butcher and evangelist. William Simpson did not believe that the British nation comprised the ten lost tribes of Israel. They argued the matter gravely over the ham-and-eggs, quoting texts and authorities. Afterwards they planned the order of the open-air service that was to take place at the Pierhead at seven o'clock, D.V.

Jean got off the bus and went to the doctor's surgery.

Thorfinn drank another glass of vodka with Andrew. Then he drank a glass of rum by himself, and then some whisky and beer. He bought a half-bottle of whisky and went back to the Britannia. There were many people in the street now. In the Britannia he met Sam of Biggings and Freddy and Jock and Archer and Tom.

Peter said to William Simpson that the New Dispensation of Grace began in the year 1917, on the day General Allenby walked into Jerusalem, was abundantly proved by certain texts in Daniel and Revelation, namely... At this point, four more evangelists came in carrying Bibles.

Jean stood on one of the stone piers and watched the fishing boats riding at anchor. It was quiet here, and clean. The doctor had uttered six or seven words. It was lonely here. So the hunted animal carries her wound away to a secret water, and waits patiently for death or renewal.

*

8

Thorfinn drank whisky with the boys. The pub was so full now they decided to go through to the cocktail bar. The cocktail bar was full too. They stood against the wall and drank whisky. There were many girls in the cocktail bar. Freddy took a bottle of whisky out of his coat and passed it round the boys.

Peter stood with eleven others in a ring bedside the fountain. They sang, "Count Your Blessings," "There is a Fountain," "The Hallelujah Lifeboat." Peter read out of Isaiah and Galatians. William Simpson preached. The Carnival—drunkenness, lechery, violence—raged all round that shining circle. Inside was Sion, the promise, the everlasting courts of the King.

The floats went by, one after another, bearing Stone Age men, mermaids, a surgical theatre, a shebeen, a schoolroom, Hell, a Turkish harem, a moon-ship. Then walking clowns, Hawaiian girls, Victorians, Cossacks. Red Indians, Chinamen, Martians. Jean stood in the door of the pharmacy and watched the procession cleaving the crowd, spreading behind a wide wake of cheers, shouts, ribaldry.

"I'll buy thee a drink. I love thee," said Thorfinn at a table where two girls he didn't know and two young men were sitting.

"No," said the girl.

Thorfinn fell across their table and slithered on to the floor in a ruin of gin and beer and broken glass.

Then he found himself outside.

He had never seen so many faces.

He fell on the street. Cars hooted all round. A great walking pelican straddled him.

"Anyone who thinks that is a fool," said William Simpson. "He is a liar and the truth is not in him."

"*I* think that," said Peter.

"Then," said William Simpson severely, "if the cap fits, you can wear it."

They were having black puddings and tea in William Simpson's parlour after the open-air meeting.

From the street below came Carnival cries, songs, laughter, from the hordes of the lost.

"You would like to dictate. You think you have the whole

9

truth. In your pride you think you're God's chosen man in this island," said Peter.

The ten other evangelists listened in a dark silence.

"If it comes to that," said William Simpson with great deliberation, "I have never consorted *with publicans and sinners...*" He munched at his bread. Three of the evangelists looked at Peter accusingly.

Nearly everybody on the street was drunk now. Jean struggled to get to the last bus through the ebbing crowds. She was desperately tired. Vivid images glowed and faded in her mind— three fish, a nautical gravestone, a winter cradle, a bird in a vase, Thorfinn at the plough, Thorfinn at the dartboard, Thorfinn helpless on a mad street....

Round the corner, near the bus stance, a jazz band began to play, and the coloured lights came on.

Thorfinn found himself at the wheel of his van A strange girl was sitting beside him, stroking his head. How had he got here?

He kissed the girl.

He felt in his hip pocket for the whisky. It wasn't there.

"I'll drive thee home," said Thorfinn.

"Yes," said the girl. She went on combing his hair with her fingers.

Solemnly Thorfinn turned the van and drove through the crowd, out of the town.

The police sergeant was standing at the Bank gate. He looked searchingly at Thorfinn. Solemnly and slowly Thorfinn drove past him.

Peter, his Bible askew under his arm, hurriedly crossed the street in front of the van. Thorfinn blasted him with the horn.

"I love thee," said Thorfinn to the girl. "Where does thu live?"

Peter, having missed the last bus, decided to walk home.

He was finished with that crowd in Stromness. He would never go to their meetings again. Never.

He could have taken William Simpson, and broken him, so angry had he been!... By God's help, he had managed to control himself.

But this was the end. He had been to his last gospel meeting in Stromness. Never again.

A green van careered past him.

As Peter walked home, the Carnival rockets rushed up the darkening sky, one after another. Out of their ruin, silent globes of light blossomed and floated, yellow and green and red, to die suddenly on the midnight....

Jean took the key from James Firth and gave him a pound. She locked the door and put out the light. Alone in the darkness she felt for a moment she wanted to pray, but she could think of nobody to pray for except the pelican guiser who had lifted Thorfinn out of the gutter...and maybe the burden inside her that already filled her with such weariness and shame—the pilgrim—the stranger—the lawless dancer.

AUGUST

Three among hundreds of advertisements one week in the *Orcadian,* the local newspaper:

THE TEN LOST TRIBES OF ISRAEL—*where are they?* They inhabit the British Isles *today!* We are THE CHOSEN PEOPLE in a world *hastening to its end!* Those who would like to know more about this *undoubted fact* are invited to a public meeting in Ingsevay Community Centre on (D.V.) 15 August, at 8 p.m.

Experienced full-time *barman* wanted for Ingsevay Inn. Wages £8 10s. per week. Apply Miss Jean Scarth, The Inn, Ingsevay.

FOR SALE—A Green Morris van, 1945, in first-class running order. Can be seen. Apply Box No. 3124.

SEPTEMBER

The oatfield of Helliar was almost cut. Thorfinn had never been so tired. Since before dawn six of them, men and girls, had been working in the field. For this one harvest day the sun had stored up all the heat and glare of a dull summer. It burst suddenly out of the early morning mist and laid an unclouded flame on the hillside. The wind and rain of the previous week had laid and tangled the corn, so that it was hard to cut. Girls and men toiled together, gathering and binding. The reaper jolted along like a huge clogged purposeful insect. About noon the men had taken off their shirts. Thorfinn's back, aflame with the sun, was mottled in addition with insect bites.

They ate their dinner under the south wall—chicken and bannocks and home-brewed ale.

"Where are the clouds of July and August?" said Thorfinn, taking his arm across his sweat-silvered brow. Sam cursed sun, oats, reaper, sweat, women, dogs, the Fall of Man. Ann and the other girls laughed, packing away the plates and bottles.

Thorfinn finished his ale and rose groaning into the hot blue afternoon. Freddy climbed once more into the reaper.

They moved forward, step by step. The corn fell with long hot sighs. The girls followed, gathering and binding the sheaves. The heat accelerated, the insects moved in from the heather. All afternoon the hillside was lapped by pitiless flame. But now at last the harvesters had found a perfect rhythm—faultlessly, effortlessly, they moved through the corn, stooping, rising, burdening and disburdening themselves as in some ritual of birth and death. Sun blistered, insects troubled and stung, limbs were heavy and sore, but the great shining ceremony went on through the afternoon. The bread and ale were secure for another year.

At six o'clock the field was all cut and the harvesters went home.

Peter was gathering limpets from the rocks at low tide, out beyond the Point of Ramness. Slowly he went along the beach, a tin pail in one hand and a blunt knocking-stone in the other. Slowly and surely he moved among the clusters of limpets, knocking them into his ringing bucket.

The tide was at full ebb, the beach was heaped with layer upon layer of tangle. And there, in those brown wastes, a sudden bright swathe!

He went nearer, keeping his balance with difficulty in the slippery weed.

It was long blonde hair.

Peter pulled back the mantling seaweed. A cold dead face looked up at him.

He stood among the seaweed, shocked.... Who could it be? There was that paragraph in the *Orcadian* a fortnight ago about the Hoy woman who was missing....But could the sea have carried her over all this way, from Hoy? She was young.

Peter bent down and lifted her in his arms. Water slopped out of her clothes. Staggering, he carried her up the beach and laid her on a flat sloping rock. The seat streamed from her over the hot stone.

It was a long way from the tents in the deserts of Sinai to this salt pool. It was a long way from the terrible mercy of Jehovah to the wearing doubts and despairs of a corrupt perverse Godless generation.

He walked the mile back to the village. At the shop he got three pennies for a threepenny bit. He phoned the police at Kirkwall.

The body lay on the rock, guarded by a gull and a pail of limpets.

Up among the hills, seven miles from Ingsevay, the tinkers were sleeping in their tent.

"Would you stop muttering to yourself," said old Ezra to the thin huddle beside him, "and go to sleep."

"I'm praying," said Williamina, "and don't say another word till I'm done."

"What are you praying for when the hill's full of rabbits?" said Ezra.

"I'm praying for that girl Jean in Ingsevay. She's going to have a bairn. She's like a ripe apple. She's the shape of an egg."

"Hurry up then," said Ezra, "for it's a hot night, and I want to sleep."

Williamina asked the Virgin and St. Magnus and all the other bright saints of Heaven to pray for Jean who had retreated into the darkness, out of folks' sight, with her precious shameful burden—Jean, who had always been good to the tinkers and given them beer and bread whenever they were passing through in the old poor destitute days before National Assistance.

She touched her crucifix among the straw and prayed for Jean.

"Who is the father of this child?" said Ezra in a sleepy voice.

"A man," said Williamina.

She crossed herself, finishing her prayer. Then she slept.

Peter hesitated, bit his lip, looked up and down the road and between the houses, then walked straight into the pub and up to the bar.

Seatter of Stark and Eric Weyland looked at him as if he were a ghost. So the elders might look at them some Sabbath morning, if ever they stepped doucely into the kirk.

"I want to speak to Miss Scarth," said Peter to James Firth, who had been permanent barman now for two months.

"Jean's not seeing anybody," said James Firth.

"Tell her *I'm* here," said Peter.

"It wouldn't matter a damn if I told her the Archbishop of Canterbury or the Dalai Lama was here, she wouldn't see them," said James Firth.

"Give me a piece of paper," said Peter, "I'll write her a note."

Jean—from study of scripture and multiplying signs I make it that this world is near an end. Woe then unto them that have turned aside. It were better for them, etc. I desire to save thee.
This thy house Rimmon is a house marked for quick destruction. Come to where I live bedside the sea and thou shalt be looked after, both thee and thy unborn child. Tarry here and thou shalt taste of the bitterness of loss. I am they servant, Peter.

Having folded it and handed it to James Firth for delivery, Peter went out again past those two gaping thirsts, Seatter of Stark and Eric Weyland.

He hadn't been gone five minutes when Thorfinn came in.

"Give me a pint," said Thorfinn, "and tell me am I in the horrors with drink, or did that holy fisherman, the damnation-monger, walk out of this place two minutes ago?"

"He did," said Seatter and Eric together.

"It *must* be near the end of the world then," said Thorfinn. To James Firth he said, "I want to see Jean."

James Firth said, "She isn't seeing anybody."

"Tell her it's me," said Thorfinn.

"It wouldn't matter," said James Firth, "if you was Robbie Burns, Casanova and Don Juan all in one."

"Let's see a piece of paper then," said Thorfinn.
He wrote:

My dear Jean—I've said to a hundred lasses, one time or another, "I love thee." All lies. But to thee I say, "I love thee" and "I love thee" and "I love thee"—When will I see you? Thorfinn.

Upstairs Jean read the two letters and put them both on the fire. She tried to retrieve Thorfinn's but the flame beat her. Flake by black flake, they drifted up the chimney.

NOVEMBER

The first snowflake of winter.

At five past five, Josiah summoned up courage to say, "I doubt, Peter, thu've made a miscalculation."

In Peter's hut were gathered Josiah, Josiah's wife Bella, Josiah's cousin Hedda from the quarry, and Josiah's children Aaron and Rebecca. Aaron and Rebecca had been crying, their faces were stained with tears, but now they were quiet again, as if they realized that a great crisis was safely past.

Josiah began again, "I doubt, Peter—"

"Yes," said Peter sadly, "you can all go home now."

It was to have been the end of the world. Peter had calculated it as being due to take place at four-ten that afternoon, and so he had invited Josiah and his dependents (as well as several others who had not come) to assemble in his hut, to the end that all true believers in the parish might be together when the terrible and glorious event took place. But nothing had happened.

"It won't be today," said Peter, and opened the door. "I must have made a miscalculation."

The two children ran shouting into the darkness.

Then the heavens did give a sign. As Peter stood in the lighted doorway, the sky opened and released the first snowflake of winter.

Thorfinn sold the van at last to a Kirkwall docker, and undertook to deliver it on Thursday afternoon at Kirkwall pier.

Unlicensed, uninsured, untested, Thorfinn climbed into the green van for the last time. (He had partially covered the number plates with a careless drapery of sacking.) The darkness was coming down.

At Kiln Corner, on the edge of Kirkwall, a policeman flashed his torch at Thorfinn, signaling him to stop. Thorfinn pressed his foot on the accelerator. The van rushed forward. Sweating, Thorfinn turned it into Bridge Street and eased it into the dark corner of the car park. He got out quickly, whipped the sacking from the number plates, and walked up Bridge Street and along Albert Street. There, opposite the Big Tree, the policeman was, and one of his colleagues with him. They were waiting for a green van to pass. Thorfinn endured their scrutiny and walked on. They hadn't recognized him.

He turned down Castle Street, along Junction Road, and walked down the long pier. There, loading barrels of whisky with a score of other dockers, was his man. Thorfinn told him where the van was parked, then walked back up the pier. The pubs were just opening. He drank three glasses of rum, and went home on the bus at half past six.

Agnes Sinclair was on the bus. She signaled to him, made room for him on her seat. He sat by himself in the front.

At the Dykes he got off the bus. He walked up the long miry road to Helliar. Beyond the peat-stack the police van was parked. When they saw Thorfinn coming the two policemen climbed out of their black van and the Kirkwall docker followed them.

The first policeman called to Thorfinn to stop.

Thorfinn stopped. His fists swelled in the pockets of his raincoat. Would he rush them now, or take them one by one at the gate?

The first snowflake of winter trembled in the air above the henhouse. It eddied and shimmered in the wind. Then it fell lightly and sweetly on to Thorfinn's hot clenched fist, a kiss of peace.

Grinning, he walked forward to meet the interrogators.

Jean sat alone at the top window of the Ingsevay Inn. Through the window, the hill darkened. The sky was grey.

For four months she had lived in this room. She had neither shown herself outside nor in the bar below. She was dedicated to loneliness.

She sewed in a chair beside the window. She waited.

The days darkened around her.

In her womb the slow shameful inexorable dance went on.

But now the shame had died. She was simply indifferent. Indifference lay on her like a heavy stone.

Down below, an argument broke out. It flared, then faded into muttered imprecations and reproaches. Jean recognized the voices of Seatter of Stark and Eric Weyland. James Firth was not good at controlling such outbursts.

Let them carry on. She didn't really care now.

The hill darkened.

Suddenly she saw the first snowflake. It fluttered over the rose bush in the garden. It climbed the air, circled, meandered down the wind. Then surely, gently, chastely, it drifted on to the window and clung there, shimmering.

This as beautiful!

Startled, she looked at the frail grey thing on the windowpane. The dead stone lifted inside her.

And then suddenly everything was in its place. The tinkers would move forever through the hills. Men would plough their fields. Men would bait their lines. Comedy had its place in the dance too—the drinking, the quarreling, the expulsion, the return in the morning. And forever the world would be full of youth and beauty, birth and death, labour and suffering.

The child moved inside her in a wind of light....

The snowflake lived on her window for five seconds, then died into a glistening drop of water.

The hill darkened. A hundred snowflakes fell, a thousand, the wind crammed them against the pane. The hill was lost.

Down in the bar the voices rose again, Seatter of Stark and Eric Weyland.

Jean went quickly downstairs and opened the door into the bar. They were arguing across a draughtboard. Eric screeched, Seatter growled, their flaming faces set close together.

"Out," said Jean quietly, and pointed to the door.

17

They hastened to be gone, like men caught with their trousers down. They almost fell over each other in the door. They were gone.

The awkward silence lasted only for a second.

"Jean, lass," said Sam of Biggings, "we haven't seen thee this long while, and we've missed thee, and we're glad to see thee again."

"And I'm glad to see thee, Sam," said Jean. "And thee, Andrew. And thee, Freddy. And thee, Jock. And Ezra and Williamina from the hill...James," she said to the barman, "whisky on the house for all here, to warm us for the winter."

Out on the road, Seatter of Stark was saying to Eric Weyland, "That's the last drink I buy in that place."

"The impudence, putting *us* out, her best customers!" said Eric. "And her with that great pirate cargo in her!"

"A shameless slut!" said Seatter of Stark.

The cold wind blew them over the hill helter-skelter.

It was snowing faster now.

DECEMBER

"Turn her," said Peter. Josiah leant on the tiller. A wave broke against the *Bethel,* involved them in its ruin, lurched on.

With the blizzard they could see nothing. They might be out in the Sound, they might be under the Black Crag, they might be among the Kirk Rocks.

The engine coughed and snored.

With the blizzard, wind and sea had risen. They were on a broken perilous stair, climbing and falling blindly.

"Watch this wave," said Peter. The wave licked at them coldly, shrugged on.

"Is it an inshore wave, or a wave of the Sound?" said Peter.

"It's more of an inshore wave," said Josiah. "God preserve us."

"Turn her," said Peter. Josiah leant on the tiller. The *Bethel* slipped into a trough between green waves, shuddering.

"Steady," said Peter. The second waved rolled over them, almost rolled them over. The boat took much water.

They could see nothing. Out of a circular wall of blackness

the snow came at them, from all directions. Under the wild-wove shroud at the bottom of the boat there were shapes of fish. The oilskins of the men were black behind, white in front.

The engine coughed. Another salt spasm set the *Bethel* shuddering from stem to stern.

"Turn her," said Peter.

Josiah leant on the rudder. "I never wanted to come out this morning," he said. "It was foolishness."

Peter, bent over the engine, said nothing.

"Now we're in God's hands," said Josiah.

"What better hands could we be in?" said Peter.

A wave came at them. The *Bethel* rose against it. They met, coughing and snarling, tore each other, and passed on.

Peter's hands were blue, heavy, lifeless as he bent over the engine, probing. He didn't like the sound it was making. Maybe they would have to hoist the sail.

Snow came at them from all directions.

Josiah screamed, "O Christ, a rock!"

The black rock rose twenty yards away. The sea was breaking white on it. It was Braga.

"Thank God," said Peter. Now he knew exactly where they were. "Turn her," he said.

Josiah leant on the rudder. His face was a mask of snow.

A new wave threw them forward.

The village was isolated. Through four hushed days and nights the snow had fallen, and spread a vast monotony.

On the fifth day the wind got up. It worked on the blank parish and everywhere altered its contours. It laid white drifts across the roads into Ingsevay, it dragged down the telegraph wires, it buried folds and fences and fishing boats in the noust.

And still the snow fell.

Seatter of Stark and Eric Weyland went into the pub at noon. It was empty.

They stamped their feet and beat on the counter with their knuckles. Nobody answered.

They knew that James Firth would not be there, the roads were blocked. But where was Jean? The door was open. The fire was lit.

19

They set out the draughts on the window seat and waited.

Ezra and Williamina came in. Their faces shone for a minute in the open door, like people transfigured.

"Where's Jean?" said Williamina.

The draught-players shook their heads.

The tinkers stood at the fire, stamping their feet.

"I'll go and draw two pints," said Ezra. "We can pay when she comes in."

"Maybe she's at the well," said Eric Weyland.

Williamina said, when their glasses were half empty, "Maybe her time's come."

"Ah," said Ezra, "drink up. We'll have two more pints while we're waiting."

Seatter of Stark heard the noise first, it came from upstairs, a thin flutter and a cry, like a winged duck in a marsh. He said nothing, but his eyes bulged.

The noise came again, and this time they all heard it.

"It's Jean," said Williamina.

Seatter of Stark and Eric Weyland knocked over the draught-board in their hurry to be gone. They left the door swinging on its hinges. A flurry of snow wet the blue stoned floor of the pub.

"We better get the doctor," said Ezra, though he knew the telephone lines were down and the road was blocked.

"I've taken a hundred bairns into the world," said Williamina. She drank off her beer and went upstairs.

Ezra shut the door and put the iron bar across it. He put three lumps of coal on the fire. Then he went behind the bar and lowered a singing rope from the brandy bottle into a half-pint glass.

Thorfinn woke late to find Helliar half-buried in snow.

His throat was dry after the whisky last night with Sam of Biggings. He put on his coat and set off towards the village for beer.

Beyond Voar, the drifts were high. The road wandered away into a white blank.

He tried to get round by the field above, and came back half an hour later, sodden and red in the face.

He knocked on the window of Voar and asked for a shovel to clear a way through.

"The snow's too deep," said Bella of Voar.

He dug for an hour into the towering whiteness and blankness.... It was impossible.

The four spinsters of Voar called him in to drink tea.

"Ah," said Maggie, "and how much did they fine you in the Sheriff Court?"

"Fifty pounds," said Thorfinn, "with the option of three months' imprisonment. And I'm disqualified from driving for two years.... To obstructing the police in the lawful exercise of their duty, charge not proven."

They looked at him in reprobation and admiration, and put more scones and tea in front of him.

The women of Voar were plain and stout. None of them was ever married. Their names were Bella, Maggie, Betsy and Isa. They spoke in the old-fashioned way.

Thorfinn got to his feet. "I must get through to the village," he said.

"For drink?" said Isa disapprovingly.

"For drink," said Thorfinn. "Give me the shovel. I'll try once more."

The snow had stopped now. He took the spade and went out again. Bella went to the henhouse. Maggie went to the byre. Betsy sat at the spinning wheel. Isa moved about the kitchen, between the fire, the cupboard, the table, seeing to the dinner.

The four women of Voar assembled for their soup at two o'clock. Through the window they could see a small black figure in the snow, like a wingless legless fly on a vast tablecloth.

He would never, never get through.

The spade was striking at the drift in a slow dull mechanical rhythm. Thorfinn was beaten. But he went on digging.

"No man digs like that for drink," said Maggie.

"It's for the woman," said Betsy.

"Yes," said Isa, "it's for Jean."

"They say here time's near," said Betsy, "and the father is said to be that gospel fisherman Peter, but be that as it may, it's a good job old Snipe's lying in the kirkyard away from it all."

21

Thorfinn was still digging. They watched him through the window with pity and amusement.

"The phone," said Bella.

Betsy said, "The line's down."

"We can try," said Isa.

Maggie dialed the Ingsevay Inn and got through at once. A drunk tinker voice spoke from the other end. Maggie couldn't make out what he was saying. Sometimes he sang. He mentioned trout and bagpipes. Finally he said, "I'm drunk with the brandy."

Maggie said severely, "Please tell us how Jean is ... Miss Scarth."

"There's a new landlord at the Inn since an hour ago," said the black reeling old voice, "and may he grow up to be a kinder landlord ... than old Snipe his grandfather ... him that's lying out there in the kirkyard ... under the falling snow ... and never once in his life ... gave a poor tinker ... as much as a thimbleful...." The voice died away into a long musical sigh, "I'm drunk ... with the brandy...."

Outside, Thorfinn was sitting on the edge of the drift, with the spade across his knees and his head in his hands. He was beaten. He would never get through.

They sent out Betsy to tell him the news. Bella raked the fire. Maggie took from the cupboard a full bottle of whisky and five glasses.

THE SELLER OF SILK SHIRTS

I crossed yesterday to the island of Quoylay to sell silk shirts to the people. I am a Sikh boy. My name over here is Johnny.

First was the boatman. He says to another man in the stern, in a voice that goes up and down like singing:

"Do what you like, says I,
But when in future
You want a loan of two pounds,
Don't come, says I, to my door,
Inga,
After what you said and did in the village on Saturday
night."

At the croft above the pier a man was building a new pigsty. He was carrying stones from the beach. A boy was carrying stones from the beach. A girl also was carrying stones from the beach. The girl stopped and made tea.... Those pigs have the expectation of living in a beautiful little house made of stones that have been under the sea.

There is a house where is a telephone and also a shop. Going to such a place I have made a mistake, they also sell shirts though coarse of cotton and wool, not silk shirts. This is strange, also they sell tobacco, sugar, rope, many things. The lady there was most fat and most kind.

I have gone then to a house on a hill. Many hens promenade at the door. I have much fear of the dog but there are words in the inside darkness that say, *"Down, Laddie, down."* What an old lady dusts the chair for my backside to sit! What an old man of words! His wrists were ornamented with blue anchors. Their ale was such that I might have fallen asleep on the chair. I have sold a silk scarf to the lady, that she will wear to the agricultural show next week, I am thinking.

Now did the next big house prove to be the minister's house.

23

There are many unused rooms, none but the minister and his woman, what shame, a hundred of my people might live and sleep there. He has made remarks about bathing in the holy River Ganges that show signal knowledge. No refreshment, neither tea nor ale nor cigarettes, though I have complimented him on the immense number and blackness of his books.

Here is a beautiful girl living alone in a place with broken windows beside the loch. I make myself delightful to this girl. There is no dog. There is no old person behind the door angry. Instead there is a new round cake smoking on the table. This girl says, "Lucky you have come today. At the week-end I had no money, my national assistance was spent. On Saturday night by hard means I got money in the village. Lucky you have come, I must buy a birthday present for Tom the boatman, a silk shirt would be beautiful."

Yet she has not enough money for a silk shirt. Yet I have sold her one cheap, a bargain, a yellow silk shirt spread out wide like a sleeping butterfly on the little flowered bed she sleeps in.

Such was the beautiful poor girl I sold a shirt to, beside the loch. Her name was called Inga. Even so with the cheapness of the sale I had thirty-five per cent profit. Pretty was Inga.

Three things troubled me crossing the field to the hospitable farm of Greengyres. First, I entered inadvertently my foot into a rabbit hole. Second, I was threatened by a female cow with horns. Third, needing to pass water I was faced wherever I turned by near and distant windows. Yet at the delightful farm of Greengyres were met all my difficulties. There I sold no less than one shirt, four pairs sox, six handkerchiefs, all articles silken.

The schoolmistress was forbidding and in a mood to send me away till I have told her of my graduation from the University of Bombay with B.A. degree and the imminence of my Ph.D. studying at the University of Edinburgh in October on a thesis, "The Topography of the Mystical Books of William Blake." She has graduated from that same university. She is not like Inga, pretty. She has long black hairs on her lip, and a wart.

Much walking I did on that island.

On the other side of the hill were three spreading peats, a man and two women, in the sun. Here was much mirth. I say to the man, "You have no shirt, therefore you must buy one of my silk shirts." All laid down their implements with laughter. A woman said, "Nobody wears a silk shirt cutting peats." We laughed greatly. I then responded with this remark, "Yet when the peats are cut and brought home, then will come the hour of celebration that will necessitate the wearing of a silk shirt!" There I stayed with merriment for five-and-twenty minutes, drinking tea from a flask and smoking two cigarettes. Truly these were merry peat-cutters.

In the evening at the stipulated hour I returned to the boat. The boatman was saying to another man in the stern, but really with the speech of those islanders it seems like singing:

> *"So then, what could I say?*
> *For my birthday*
> *Had she not baked a small*
>   *cake*
> *And brought on her arm*
> *A shirt yellow as buttercups*
>   *this very afternoon?*
> *That way*
> *All our troubles ended."*

In the island of Quoylay I have sold seven shirts, three pairs of sox, twenty-one handkerchiefs, five scarves, and to Inga I have given a free headsquare depicting the dance called "The Shake," though I have told her it was the god Krishna among milkmaidens.

THE STORM WATCHERS

A PLAY FOR VOICES

A long shore. Darkness. Seven women standing.

ANNA: I am Anna. The name of my man is Ally. He worked among the hills with a plough and horses. I did not know him then, with the clay on his boots. There came a summer of black corn.

THE WOMEN: The rock is black and cold tonight. The holy rock, Hellyan.

MERRAG: Merrag is my name—an old woman with a grey rope of hair. I never suffered the kisses and foolish words of any man. On account of James my brother I haved sour chaste hands.

THE WOMEN: The rock is long and cold tonight. Hellyan, the kirk rock.

MARGET: I am Marget. "Who are you, Marget?" said Robbie, "to be twisting wet shirts for five brothers? Who are you to be stirring oatmeal for them three times a day above a blink of fire?...But come," he said, "I have a boat and a net and a white lonely place above the shore."

THE WOMEN: Hellyan is the name of this rock. A place of seals and saints and gannets. But fishermen avoid it.

KITTAG: Kittag they call me. My proper name is Catherine. I can write words and I have read a book called *Prudence* and another called *Fortitude*. I have three bonnets that I wear to the kirk, one for each season. Catherine he called me when he courted me, this Peter.

THE WOMEN: Here the gulls sit, on Hellyan, head into the wind, winter and summer.

KIRSTY: Kirsty, that's myself. One morning my father said, "Stir yourself today, a visitor is coming from the island of Westray to take your sister Mary away." I scrubbed the board white and the floor blue. My mother put lupins in the window. Then the stranger came and sat at the board. They called him Josh. He carried the smell of the sea with him. My sisters put oakcakes and cheese and whisky before him.

THE WOMEN: Sailors steer by that landmark. A good rock on a summer day, Hellyan.

RUTH: Ruth is my name. A storm gave my Tors to me. They brought him from the tooth of the sea, a peerie black sodden man. They filled his foreign throat with whisky. They trussed him in a grey blanket. All that winter I taught him English words.

THE WOMEN: Tonight the rock is loud and cold, and dark, Hellyan.

SEENY: I am Seeny. I live with Mansie that men call the blue stallion. I am not married to him, but my three sons are his. Mansie has a lonely, barren, Bible-reading wife in the island of Hoy.

THE WOMEN: Hellyan is loud tonight. The rock of saints and grief and drowning.

ANNA: There came the summer of black corn. Ally left his father's croft and came down to the shore for limpets and seaweed. Anna is my name. The people of the hill were hungry that year, and the sea full of fish. My father put an oat in Ally's hand.

THE WOMEN: A knock at the door for us, near midnight.

MERRAG: On account of James my brother I have faded hands. That one has spoken to no woman for forty winters, not to me even, though he mumbles long to God over the broken bread. Yet this morning he said. "The west is rough." And at the door he said, "We are poor people, we must fish." My name is Merrag. James has a thousand shillings, white and grey, in a box under his bed. Then he turned and walked down to the shore.

THE WOMEN: Yet we were not asleep.

MARGET: "I have a boat," said Robbie, "and a net, and a white lonely place above the shore." The way he would turn a bit of tarry twine in upon itself with his witty fingers, and knot it, and throw the ordered holes out in every direction to be a trap for fishes, a net, a dark shroud! Marget they call me. Stars swarmed across my bride window like sillocks.

THE WOMEN: We lit oil lamps in the window.

KITTAG: Catherine he called me when he courted me, this Peter. Catherine is my proper name. Then one morning in March he said, "Kathy, put the cuithes in salt," and a summer day he filled my white hands with cod's liver: "Kittag, squeeze the oil into the lamps." Before a year was out I had more kicks than kisses from him, and the only words I had time to read for baking, brewing, spinning, darning, gutting fish, was the shorter catechism. This Peter was an elder. And "Kittag, Kittag, Kittag," the neighbours called me all along the shore. But Catherine is my proper name.

THE WOMEN: We put shawls on our heads.

KIRSTY:They laid oatcakes, cheese and whisky before Josh. "Over there by the fire is our eldest daughter, Mary," said my father, but it was me Josh looked at, breaking his oatcake. "Here now is our second daughter, Sarah, at the kirn," said my mother, but Josh looked only at me, cutting his cheese.... "Peerie Kirst is too young for a man," they said both together, but Josh drank his whisky and bent forward till the light from his grey eyes fell on me alone in all that clucking house.

THE WOMEN: We tugged at our shaking doors.

RUTH: All that winter I taught my Tors to speak English words. The children would run in terror from his foreign face; the fishermen were surly at him, till the day he brought the *Solan* home, crammed with haddocks, through a blind snowstorm. Ruth they call me. One night my father put our hands together, Tors with Ruth, and my brother sailed across the Sound next morning with a wedding fee to the minister.

THE WOMEN: Shorewards we leaned, one by one.

SEENY: The blue stallion has a barren Bible-reading wife in the island of Hoy. We must be gentle and not complain too much. I trust that woman in Hoy is praying for Mansie this dark morning. And for me too. I do not wish to be an enemy of God. It is true I am a whore and a bad woman. I am on my knees here, watching the dark waters for sight of bodies. I am no friend of God and this morning he is no friend of mine.

Yet I wish the friend of God would pray for me, and for
Mansie, and for all the men on the boat and for the women
on the shore. I am afraid of the noise out there, at the rock,
where wind and ebb are meeting with a black noise.

THE WOMEN: The night was dark, a shut oyster.

The bodies come ashore. One by one the women kneel down.

ANNA: The people from the hill will come now, Ally, and carry
you back, and lay you among their old corn dead. What it is,
one cold sea kiss! I think I will not forget Ally, whose ploughman's hand was clumsy with hook and oar.

THE WOMEN: Lord, have mercy on us.

MERRAG: What do you want me to do now, sew your thousand
shillings in your shroud? For forty years you said not a word.
Now you'll be quiet all time. And I thought you said too many
words last morning, you drowned old silent man, James my
brother.

THE WOMEN: Lord, have mercy on us.

MARGET: All I can do for you now, Robbie, is carry you up the
beach and through the door and lay you on the flagstones and
take the seaweed out of your hair and strip the oozing clothes
from you and wash the salt from your body and put the long
grey shirt on you and set out the whisky bottle and twelve
glasses for the mourners and send word to the gravedigger
and sing to the cradled bairn, "Sleep on, your father's late
tonight, he's out beyond Hoy where the mermaids are, and
the whales, and the drowned ships."

THE WOMEN: Lord, have mercy on us.

KITTAG: Thank goodness, I have decent black clothes in the kist
and a black hat with a black ribbon on it. Out of the insurance
money Peter will get a black coffin and a deep black grave
and a stone with black letters on it. What a black company
will follow the hearse over the hill! Is it better to be the
widow-woman Catherine than Kittag the fisherman's wife?
It's doucer, a respectable thing, and I'll never once put my
hands in salt again, no never.

THE WOMEN: Lord, have mercy on us.

KIRSTY: Josh, you named the seven stars for me. You showed me
the kittiwake's hall in the crag. "Here," you said, "seal-women
sang to my father."
Wanderings of whale and gannet were secrets between us,
And how the lobsters put on their hard blue coats in
summer,
And cuithe come, legions long, to drink the May flood.
"There," you said, "Is a good flat stone to weigh a creel."
You showed me how to mend a broken net. Many good things
you told me, Josh. But you did not tell me death is like
this.

THE WOMEN: Lord, have mercy on us.

RUTH: Six bodies here, among the seaweed, at first light. All the
shore women but myself, Ruth, has her man. The body of
Tors has not come ashore. The sea is a wild lover, she'll strip
Tors to the skeleton, out there in the shifting beds. I kneel
on the shore, alone of seven, at a grey rock in the first light.

THE WOMEN: Lord, have mercy on us.

SEENY: I pray for Magnus, the blue sea stallion, a trouble to many
women.
I pray for James with his two hoards of silver, fish and
florins.
I pray for Robbie who spread his nets on a white wall.
I pray for Peter who taught Catherine the school-mistress
to bake and scrub, things needful for a woman to know.
What but hunger brought Ally down from the hill? Love
kept him. I pray for that quiet horseman.
I pray for Tors, the foreign skipper—twice the sea took
him and once gave him back.
I pray for Josh, gentle as seals, fierce as gannets.

THE WOMEN: Lord, have mercy on them.
Lord, have mercy on us.
Eternal Fish in the salt net between the drowned and the
hungry, feed our griefs.

THE BALLAD OF THE ROSE BUSH

Margaret was the name of a girl who lived in Dale with her mother and two brothers. This girl was dumb from birth. They kept her indoors; few men ever saw her; maybe Clod the shepherd and the tinkers and the men who came to the hill in summer to shoot.

Sometimes, very early, Margaret would go out by herself to the well for a bucket of water. Once she was seen up at the hill, spreading peats to dry at the peat bank.

She was said to excel at embroidering linen cloths. Other women could make little patterns of flower and shell on their cloths, but this girl sewed fish, hawks, plough-horses, so that when there was a draught between the spread cloth and the wall it seemed that the animals moved and danced on the wind.

One day in summer the women of Dale said, "It is time for some of our peats to be taken home."

Tom said it was impossible that particular day, because he had promised to fleece the sheep at Feolquoy where Simon the farmer was confined to bed with a broken leg.

Sand said, "Perhaps tomorrow. Cuithe and mackerel are thick in the Sound. By tomorrow they will be gone."

Margaret said nothing but took the straw basket on her back and went out.

The woman of Dale said, "There should be somebody with her."

Tom took his shears from the wall and went out, singing.

Later she said, "I heard music in the hills last night. The tinkers are camped there. Mick, the young tinker, has made a new reel called 'The Rose Bush.'"

Sand pushed his boat down over the stones.

Clod the shepherd crossed the hill at noon.

That night Tom came home with a shilling from Simon of Feolquoy for fleecing six sheep.

Tom said, "Where's the girl?"

"She hasn't come back from the peat bank," said the old woman.

Sand came home with wet boots. He hung the gutted cuithes in the chimney-piece among grey smoke.

"Where's Margaret?" he said.

"She isn't home yet," said the woman of Dale.

Later she said, "Mick the young tinker went down by with two dogs in the afternoon, going to the ale-house."

"We will look for her now," said Tom.

They searched for a long while. Then it got dark. They went on searching. They groped through the quarry and put their arms in the cold burn. Then the moon got up. At midnight Sand found her near the well of Kellyan. There was blood round her mouth and her clothes were torn. Sand lifted her over his shoulder. "Maybe she'll still be alive when I get her home," he said to Tom. "Where will you go?"

"To the tinkers' camp," said Tom.

The tinkers were sitting round a peat fire, singing among the broken light. "Where did you get those peats?" said Tom to the old tinker. He lifted a peat and broke it. It opened blue-black and dry.

"Mick found them on the hill," said the old tinker.

"They're our peats," said Tom. "Where is Mick?"

"Drunk," said the old tinker. "He went to sell a tin pail at the Manse to get money for more rum. He lost his fiddle on the hill."

Tom turned away into the darkness. The tinkers began to sing where they had left off.

Tom met Mick on the road between the Manse and the ale-house. He had a half-empty bottle in one pocket and some coppers in his fist. He was going more in the ditch than on the road.

"You have blood on your jacket," said Tom.

"That's no wonder at all," said Mick. "The rabbit in the snare was soaked in blood when I lifted it out this morning."

"Did you meet anybody on the hill today?" said Tom.

"I met Clod the shepherd," said Mick. "He's a desperate dull man. We went round each other in a wide circle."

"Where did you get the Dale peats?" said Tom.

"The whole hillside was scattered with them," said Mick. "A fine treasure on a black cold night."

Then Tom took hold of Mick and twisted his arms behind him and tied them with a piece of rope. "It would give me pleasure to kill you myself," he said, "but why should I, when there's a hangman paid for doing that job."

Tom dragged Mick down to the smithy. There Grund the blacksmith helped him to frogmarch the tinker to the laird's house, a mile further on.

And before morning the sheriff-clerk in Kirkwall was writing out the crime on long curling parchment.

Meanwhile Sand carried Margaret home. "There's no saying whether she'll live or die," he said to the old woman. "But someone will pay for this, no doubt."

They laid the girl on her bed. For three days she neither moved nor ate. On the fourth day she sat an hour by the fire and took some warm milk.

"She'll live," said Sand.

"And that's a pity," said the old woman, "For now everything's turned sour on her." She led the girl back to her bed.

They hanged Mick the tinker at Gallowsha in Kirkwall three days before Christmas. He was nineteen years old that winter.

There was snow on the ground. Mick hung from the gallows a day and a night. Before dawn on the second morning the tinkers came and cut him down. They buried him in a secret place among the hills.

The girl Margaret never went out again. She was not able to work properly from the day they found her near the well of Kellyan, neither to churn nor brew nor bake nor spin. She never stirred to fetch water from the well. She did not weep one tear when the old woman died.

She lived twenty years after that. The winter of her death she took linen and needles and thread and she sat beside the fire a whole day sewing. She sewed black thorns with a red rose in the heart of the bush. Then she put aside the cloth, and soon after midnight she moaned and lay down on her bed. She was dead before Sand put the brandy to her mouth.

All the men of the district came to the funeral, standing round the open coffin and against the walls and crowding in the door. They stood silent, waiting for the minister.

Then the tinkers came.

The old tinker said to Tom, "I've come here out of grief for your sister, in spite of the trouble that has been between our people in the past. I hope you will not take offense."

"The debt was paid," said Sand.

"We take no offense," said Tom. "You're welcome."

The minister came and the funeral service began.

They carried Margaret round the shore to the kirkyard. After the burial all the mourners returned with Tom and Sand to the house for whisky and oat cakes. Only the tinkers did not come; they turned aside among the hills. The old tinker said to Tom at the cross-roads, "They never found the fiddle. But there's always music in the hills now. You must have noticed it yourself."

"I never noticed," said Tom.

Then the tinkers went away.

"Men from every family in the district were at Margaret's burying," said Grund the blacksmith to Tom and Sand. "Your sister was well honoured."

"Clod the shepherd wasn't there," said Tom.

"It's too late now to create trouble," said Sand. "In any case, the debt has been paid."

Now they reached Dale and the mourners all took off their grey caps and went inside one by one. A stone jar of whisky stood on the table.

"That debt was paid a long time ago," said Tom. "We will say no more about it."

"No," said Sand. "Clod the shepherd is an old man. We are not young ourselves. There should be no trouble at this date."

"It's known for a certainty where the tinkers buried Mick after they cut him down from the rope," said Grund. "They buried him in a quiet place on the side of Kringlafiold, and now there's a rose bush growing out of his grave."

"Very likely indeed," said Sand.

"That's a good place for him to be," said Tom, "but I think a man like Mick would sooner be leading his pony along the road, going to the Dounby Market on a fine morning."

Sand carried the stone jar to the first of the mourners.

CELIA

The Norwegian whaler *Erika* tied up at the pier in the middle of Monday afternoon, and when the pubs opened at five o'clock all six of the crew went into the Hamnavoe Bar. Per Bjorling the skipper was with them, but about seven o'clock he bought a full bottle of vodka and left them drinking their whiskies and lagers and went outside. It was getting dark. He walked along the street till he came to an opening that descended step by step to a small pier with a house on it. From inside the house came the thwack of a hammer driving nails into leather. One room of the house had a lamp burning in the window but the other room next the sea was dark. Per Bjorling was about to knock at the door when it was opened from inside. He smiled and raised his sailor's cap and went in.

"What kind of a man is it this time?" shouted a voice from the lighted room. "Is it that bloody foreigner?..." All the people in the neighbouring houses could hear what was being said. Maisie Ness came to the end of her pier and stood listening, her head cocked to one side.

The hammer smacked on leather, a rapid tattoo.

The seaward room remained dark; or rather, the window flushed a little as if a poker had suddenly woken flames from the coal.

"Yes," yelled the shoemaker, "a bloody drunken foreign sailor."

Then silence returned to the piers and one by one the lights went on in all the houses round about.

2

The *Erika* and three other Norwegian whalers caught the morning tide on Tuesday and it was quiet again in the harbour. In the house on the small pier the shoe-repairing began early, the leisurely smack of the hammer on the moulded leather in between periods of quiet stitching. At ten o'clock Maisie Ness from the next close came with a pair of shoes to be soled. She walked straight in through the open door and turned into the room on the left next the street. The shoemaker sat on his stool, his mouth full of tacks. Maisie laid her shoes on the bench, soles upward.

"Celia isn't up yet, surely. I don't hear her," she said.

"Celia's a good girl," said the shoemaker.

"I don't believe you've had your breakfast," cried Maisie Ness, "and it's past ten o'clock. You need your food, or you'll be ill same as you were in the winter-time."

"I'll get my breakfast," said the shoemaker. "Just leave the shoes on the bench. All they need is rubber soles and a protector or two in the right heel to keep it level. You're an impudent woman. Ignorant too. Could you read the deep books that Celia reads? I don't believe you can sign your name. I'll get my breakfast all right. Celia's a good girl. Just keep your tongue off her."

Maisie Ness went up the steps of the pier shaking her head. She managed to look pleased and outraged at the same time.

"Celia," the shoemaker called out, "I'll make you a cup of tea. Just you lie in bed for an hour or two yet."

3

It was early spring. Darkness was still long but the light was slowly encroaching and the days grew colder. The last of the snow still scarred the Orphir hills. One sensed a latent fertility; under the hard earth the seeds were awake and astir; their long journey to blossom and ripeness was beginning. But in Hamnavoe, the fishermen's town, the lamps still had to be lit early.

On Tuesday night every week Mr. Spence the jeweler paid his visit. He would hesitate at the head of the close, look swiftly right and left along the street, then quickly descend the steps.

The shoemaker heard his precise footsteps on the flagstones outside and immediately took down from the shelf the draughtboard and the set of draughtsmen. He had the pieces arranged on the board before Mr. Spence was at the threshold.

"Come in, Mr. Spence," he shouted, "come in. I heard your feet."

And Mr. Spence, without a single glance at the dark seaward

window, went straight into the work-room on the left, bending his head under the lintel and smiling in the lamplight. "Well, Thomas," he said.

They always played for about an hour, best of three games. Mr. Spence generally lost. Perhaps he was a poor player; perhaps he was nervous (he shuffled and blinked and cleared his throat a good deal); perhaps he genuinely liked to give the shoemaker the pleasure of winning; perhaps he was anxious to get this empty ritual over with. They played this night without speaking, the old man in his leather apron and the middle-aged bachelor in his smart serge tailor-made suit. The shoemaker won two games right away, inside half an hour, so that there was no need that night to play a decider.

"You put up a very poor show tonight," said the shoemaker.

"I'm not in the same class as you, Thomas," said Mr. Spence.

He went over to his coat hanging on a peg and brought a half-bottle of whisky out of the pocket. "Perhaps, Thomas," he said, "you'd care for a drink."

"You know fine," said the shoemaker, "I never drink that filthy trash. The poison."

"Then," said Mr. Spence, "perhaps I'll go and see if Miss Celia would care to have a little drink. A toddy, seeing it's a cold night."

"No," said the shoemaker anxiously, "I don't think you should do that. Or if you do, only a very small drop."

But Mr. Spence was already tiptoeing along the lobby towards the dark room, carrying the half-bottle in his hand. He tapped on the door, and opened it gently. The girl was bending over the black range, stabbing the coal with a poker. At once the ribs were thronged with red and yellow flames, and the shadow of the girl leapt over him before she herself turned slowly to the voice in the doorway.

"My dear," said Mr. Spence.

4

"How are you, Thomas?" said Dr. Wilson on the Wednesday morning, sitting down on the bench among bits and scrapings of leather.

"I'm fine," said the shoemaker.

"The chest all right?"

"I still get a bit of a wheeze when the wind's easterly," said the shoemaker, "but I'm not complaining."

There was silence in the room for a half-minute.

"And Celia?" said Dr. Wilson.

"Celia's fine," said the shoemaker. "I wish she would eat more and get more exercise. I'm a nuisance to her, I keep her tied to the house. But she keeps her health. She's fine."

"I'm glad to hear it," said Dr. Wilson.

"Celia's a good girl," said the shoemaker.

"I know she's a good girl," said Dr. Wilson. Then his voice dropped a tone. "Thomas," he said, "I don't want to worry you, but there are complaints in the town."

"She's a good girl," said the old man, "a very good girl to me."

"Complaints," said Dr. Wilson quietly, "that this is a house of bad repute. I'm not saying it, for I know you're both good people, you and Celia. But the scandal-mongers are saying it along the street. You know the way it is. I've heard it twenty times this past week if I've heard it once. That all kinds of men come here, at all hours of the night, and there's drinking and carrying-on. I don't want to annoy you, Thomas, but I think it's right you should know what they're saying in the public, Maisie Ness and the other women. All this worry is not good for your lungs."

"*I* don't drink," said the shoemaker. "How do I know who comes and goes in the night? That Maisie Ness should have her tongue cut out. Celia has a sweetheart, Ronald Leask of Clett, and she's applied to be a member of the Kirk. The minister's coming to see her Friday evening. She's a good girl."

"Perhaps I could see Celia for a minute?" said Dr. Wilson and got to his feet.

"No," said the shoemaker, "she's sleeping. She needs her rest. She's sleeping late. Celia is a very good girl to me. If it wasn't for Celia I know I'd have died in the winter time."

"Good morning, Thomas," said Dr. Wilson. "I'll be back next Wednesday. You have plenty of tablets to be getting on with. Tell Celia I'm asking for her. Send for me if you need me, any time."

5

"Go away," said the shoemaker to Mr. William Snoddy the builder's clerk. "Just you go away from this house and never come back, never so much as darken the door again. I know what you're after. I'm not a fool exactly."

"I want you to make me a pair of light shoes for the summer," said Mr. Snoddy. "That's all I want."

"Is it?" said the shoemaker. "Then you can go some other place, for I have no intention of doing the job for you."

They were standing at the door of the house on the pier. It was Wednesday evening and the lamp was burning in the work-room but the room next the sea was in darkness.

"Last Saturday," said Mr. Snoddy, "at the pier-head, you promised to make me a pair of light shoes for the summer."

"I didn't know then," said the shoemaker, "what I know now. You and your fancy-women. Think shame of yourself. You have a wife and three bairns waiting for you in your house at the South End. And all you can do is run after other women here, there and everywhere. I'm making no shoes for whore-mastering expeditions. You can take that for sure and certain."

"You've been listening," said Mr. Snoddy, "to cruel ground-less gossip."

"And I believe the gossip," said the shoemaker. "I don't usu-ally believe gossip but I believe this particular piece of gossip. You're an immoral man."

"There's such a thing as a court of law," said Mr. Snoddy, "and if ever I hear of these slanders being repeated again, I'll take steps to silence the slanderers."

"You'll have your work cut out," said the shoemaker, "because you've been seen going to this house and that house when the men have been away at the fishing. I've seen you with my own two eyes. And if you want names I'll supply them to you with pleasure."

"Let's go inside," said Mr. Snoddy in a suddenly pleasant voice, "and we'll talk about something else. We'll have a game of draughts."

The shoemaker stretched out foot and arm and blocked the door.

"Stay where you are," he said. "Just bide where you are. What's that you've got in the inside pocket of your coat, eh?"

"It's my wallet," said Mr. Snoddy, touching the bulge at his chest.

"It's drink," said the shoemaker, "it's spirits. I'm not exactly so blind or so stupid that I can't recognize the shape of a half-bottle of whisky. I allow no drink into this house. Understand that."

"Please, Thomas," said Mr. Snoddy. "It's a cold night."

"Forby being a whore-master," said the shoemaker, "you're a drunkard. Never a day passed that you aren't three or four times in the pub. Just look in the mirror when you get home and see how red your nose is getting. I'm sorry for your wife and children."

"I mind my own business," said Mr. Snoddy.

"That's fine," said the shoemaker. "That's very good. Just mind your own business and don't come bothering this house. There's one thing I have to tell you before you go."

"What's that?" said Mr . Snoddy.

"Celia is not at home," shouted the old man. He suddenly stepped back into the lobby and slammed the door shut. Mr. Snoddy stood alone in the darkness, his mouth twitching. Then he turned and began to walk up the pier slowly.

From inside the house came the sound of steel protectors being hammered violently into shoes.

Mr. Snoddy's foot was on the first step leading up to the street when a hand tugged at his sleeve. He turned round. It was Celia. She had a gray shawl over her head and her hair was tucked into it. Her face in the darkness was an oval oblique shadow.

"Celia," said Mr. Snoddy in a shaking voice.

"Where are you off to so soon, Billy boy?" said Celia. "Won't you stop and speak for a minute to a poor lonely girl?"

Mr. Snoddy put his hands round her shoulders. She pushed him away gently.

"Billy," she said, "If you have a little drink on you I could be doing with it."

The loud hammering went on inside the house.

Mr. Snoddy took the flask from his inside pocket. "I think,

G.M. BROWN

dear," he said, "where we're standing we're a bit in the public eye. People passing in the street. Maybe if we move into that corner…"

Together they moved to the wall of the watchmaker's house, into a segment of deeper darkness.

"Dear Celia," muttered Mr. Snoddy.

"Just one little mouthful," said Celia. "I believe it's gin you've gone and bought."

6

Ronald Leask closed the door of the tractor shed. The whole field on the south side of the hill was ploughed now, a good day's work. He looked round him, stretched his aching arms, and walked slowly a hundred yards down to the beach. The boat was secure. There had been southwesterly winds and high seas for two days, but during that afternoon the wind had veered further west and dropped. He thought he would be able to set his lobster-creels the next morning, Friday, under the Hoy crags. The *Celia* rocked gently at the pier like a furled sea bird.

Ronald went back towards his house. He filled a bucket with water from the rain barrel at the corner. He stripped off his soiled jersey and shirt and vest and washed quickly, shuddering and gasping as the cold water slapped into his shoulders and chest. He carried the pail inside and kicked off his boots and trousers and finished his washing. Then he dried himself at the dead hearth and put on his best clothes—the white shirt and tartan tie, the dark Sunday suit, the pigskin shoes. He combed his wet fair hair till it clung to both sides of his head like bronze wings. His face looked back at him from the square tarnished mirror on the mantelpiece, red and complacent and healthy. He put on his beret and pulled it a little to one side.

Ronald wheeled his bicycle out of the lobby on to the road, mounted, and cycled towards Hamnavoe.

He passed three cars and a county council lorry and a young couple out walking. It was too dark to see their faces. As he freewheeled down into the town there were lights here and there in the houses. It would be a dark night, with no moon.

Ronald Leask left his bicycle at the head of the shoemaker's

42

close and walked down the steps to the house. The lamp was lit in the old man's window but Celia's room, as usual, was dark. He knocked at the outer door. The clob-clob-clobbering of hammer against leather stopped. "Who's that?" cried the old man sharply.

"It's me, Ronald."

"Ronald," said the shoemaker. "Come in, Ronald." He appeared at the door. "I'm glad to see thee, Ronald." He took Ronald's arm and guided him into the workroom. "Come in, boy, and sit down."

"How are you keeping, Thomas?" said Ronald.

"I'm fine, Ronald," said the shoemaker, and coughed.

"And Celia?" said Ronald.

"Celia's fine," said the shoemaker. "She's wanting to see thee, I know that. It's not much of a life for a girl, looking after a poor old thing like me. She'll be glad of your company."

"Last time I came, last Thursday, I didn't get much of a reception," said Ronald.

"Celia wasn't well that day," said the shoemaker. "She likes thee more than anybody, I can assure thee for that." He went over to the door and opened it and shouted across the lobby, "Celia, Ronald's here."

There was no answer from the other room.

"She's maybe sleeping," said the shoemaker. "Poor Celia, she works too hard, looking after me. What she needs is a long holiday. We'll go and see her."

The old man crossed the lobby on tiptoe and opened the door of Celia's room gently. "Celia," he said, "are you all right?"

"Yes," said Celia's voice from inside.

"Ronald's here," said the shoemaker.

"I know," said Celia. "I heard him."

"Well," said the shoemaker sharply, "he wants to speak to you. And I'm taking him in now, whether you want it or not. And I'm coming in too for a minute."

The two men went into the room. They could just make out the girl's outline against the banked-up glow of the fire. They groped towards chairs and sat down.

"Celia," said the shoemaker, "light your lamp."

"No," said Celia, "I like it best this way, in the darkness.

Besides, I have no money for paraffin. I don't get many shillings from you to keep the house going, and bread and coal and paraffin cost dear."

"Speak to her, Ronald," said the shoemaker.

"I can't be bothered to listen to him," said Celia. "I'm not well."

"What ails you?" said the shoemaker.

"I don't know," said Celia. "I'm just not well."

"Celia," said Ronald earnestly, "there's an understanding between us. You know it and I know it and the whole of Hamnavoe knows it. Why are you behaving this way to me?"

"That's true," said the shoemaker. "You're betrothed to one another."

"Not this again," said Celia, "when I'm sick." Then she said in a low voice, "I need something to drink."

"Drink!" said the old man angrily. "That's all your mind runs on, drink. Just you listen to Ronald when he's speaking to you."

"Celia," said Ronald, "it's a year come April since I buried my mother and the croft of Clett has stood there vacant ever since, except for me and the dog."

"And a fine croft it is," said the shoemaker. "Good sandy soil and a tractor in the shed and a first-rate boat in the bay."

"I'm not listening," said Celia.

"It needs a woman about the place," said Ronald. "I can manage the farm work and the fishing. But inside the house things are going to wrack and ruin. That's the truth. Celia, you promised six months ago to come to Clett."

"So that's all you want, is it?" said Celia. "A housekeeper."

"No," said Ronald, "I want you for my wife. I love you."

"He does love you," said the shoemaker. "And he's a good man. And he has money put by. And he works well at the farming and the fishing. He's a fellow any girl would be proud to have for a man."

"I'm not well tonight," said Celia. "I would be the better of a glass of brandy."

"And what's more," said the shoemaker, "you love him, because you told me with your own lips not a fortnight ago."

"I do not," said Celia.

Ronald turned to the shoemaker and whispered to him and

put something in his hand. The shoemaker rose up at once and went out. He banged the outer door shut behind him.

"Celia," said Ronald.

"Leave me alone," said Celia.

They sat in the growing darkness. The only light in the room was the dull glow from the range. Ronald could see the dark outline of the girl bedside the fire. For ten minutes they neither moved nor spoke.

At last the door opened again and the old man came back. He groped his way to the table and put a bottle down on it. "That's it," he said to Ronald and laid down some loose coins beside the bottle. "And that's the change."

"Celia," said Ronald, "I'm sorry to hear you aren't well. I've got something here that'll maybe help you. A little brandy."

"That's kind of you," said Celia.

She picked up the poker and drove it into the black coal on top of the range. The room flared wildly with lights and shadows. The three dark figures were suddenly sitting in a warm rosy flickering world.

Celia took two cups from the cupboard and set them on the table and poured brandy into them.

"That's enough for me," said Ronald, and put his hand over the cup next to him.

Celia filled the other cup to the top. Then she lifted it to her mouth with both hands and gulped it like water.

"Good health," said the shoemaker. "I'm saying that and I mean it though I'm not a drinking man myself. The very best of luck to you both."

Ronald raised his cup and drank meagerly from it and put it down again on the table. "Cheers," he said.

Celia took another mouthful and set down her empty cup beside the bottle.

"Are you feeling better now, Celia?" said the shoemaker.

"A wee bit," said Celia. She filled up her cup again. "I'm very glad to see you," she said to Ronald.

"That's better," said the shoemaker, "that's the way to speak."

Celia took a drink and said, "Ronald, supposing I come to live at Clett what's going to become of Thomas?"

"I'll be all right," said the shoemaker, "don't worry about me.

45

I'll manage fine."

"He'll come and live with us," said Ronald. "There's plenty of room,"

"No," said Celia, "but who's going to walk a mile and more to Clett to get their boots mended? We must think of that. He'll lose trade."

"Don't drink so fast," said the shoemaker.

"And besides that," said Celia, "he'll miss his friends, all the ones that come and visit him here and play draughts with him. What would he do without his game of draughts? Clett's a long distance away. I'm very pleased, Ronald, that you've come to see me."

"I'm pleased to be here," said Ronald.

"Light the lamp," said the shoemaker happily.

"I love you both very much," said Celia. "You're the two people that I love most in the whole world."

Celia filled up her cup again. This time half the brandy spilled over the table.

"I don't know whether I'll come to Clett or not," said Celia. "I'll have to think about it. I have responsibilities here. That's what makes me feel ill, being torn this way and that. I can't be in two places, can I? I love you both very much. I want you to know that, whatever happens."

She suddenly started to cry. She put her hands over her face and her whole body shook with grief. She sat down in her chair beside the fire and sobbed long and bitterly.

The two men looked at each other, awed and awkward.

"I'll put a match to the lamp," said the shoemaker. "Then we'll see what's what."

Celia stopped crying for a moment and said, "Leave the bloody lamp alone." Then she started to sob again, louder than ever.

Ronald got to his feet and went over to Celia. He put his arm across her shoulder. "Poor Celia," he said, "tell me what way I can help thee?"

Celia rose to her feet and screamed at him. "You go away from here, you bastard," she shouted. "Just go away! I want never to see you again! Clear off!"

"Celia," pleaded the old man.

"If that's what you want, Celia," said Ronald. He picked up

his beret from the chair and stood with his back to the cupboard. "Good night, Thomas," he said.

"Come back, Ronald," said the shoemaker. "Celia isn't herself tonight. She doesn't mean a word of what she says."

The flames were dying down in the range. Celia and Ronald and the shoemaker moved about in the room, three unquiet shadows.

"Good night, Celia," said Ronald from the door.

"I hate you, you bastard," she shrieked at him.

The last flame died. In the seething darkness the girl and the old man heard the bang of the outer door closing. Celia sat down in her chair and began to cry again, a slow gentle wailing.

Half-way up the steps of the close the shoemaker caught up with Ronald. "This is the worst she's ever been," he said. "You know the way it is with her—she drinks heavily for a week or so, anything she can get, and then for a month or six weeks after that she's as peaceable as a dove. But this is the worst she's ever been. God knows what will come of her."

"God knows," said Ronald.

"It started on Monday night," said the shoemaker. "That Norsky was here with foreign hooch."

"Don't worry, Thomas," said Ronald. "It'll turn out all right, like you say."

"She'll be fine next time you come back," said the shoemaker. "Just you wait and see."

Ronald got on to his bicycle at the head of the close.

The shoemaker went back slowly into the house. As she opened the door Celia's low voice came out of the darkness. "God forgive me," she was saying gently and hopelessly, "O God forgive me."

7

"No," said Celia to the minister, "I don't believe in your God. It's no good. You're wasting your time. What the Hamnavoe folk are saying is true, I'm a bad woman. I drink. Men come about the place all hours of the night. It isn't that I want them fumbling at me with their mouths and their hands. That sickens me. I put up with it for the drink they have in their pockets. I must drink.

"You're not a drinking man, Mr. Blackie. I know that. I *had* to buy this bottle of wine from the licensed grocer's. It gives me courage to speak to you. Try to understand that. And we're sitting here in the half-darkness because I can speak to you better in this secrecy. Faces tell lies to one another. You know the way it is. The truth gets buried under smiles.

"I drink because I'm frightened. I'm so desperately involved with all the weak things, lonely things, suffering things I see about me. I can't bear the pity I feel for them, not being able to help them at all. There's blood everywhere. The world's a torture chamber, just a sewer of pain. That frightens me.

"Yesterday it was a gull and a water rat. They met at the end of this pier. I was pinning washing to the line when I saw it. The gull came down on the rat and swallowed it whole the way it would gulp a crust of bread, then with one flap of its wing it was out over the sea again. I could see the shape of the rat in the blackback's throat, a kind of fierce twist and thrust. The bird broke up in the air. It screamed. Blood and feathers showered out of it. The dead gull and the living rat made separate splashes in the water.

"It seems most folk can live with that kind of thing. Not me— I get all caught up in it...."

Stars slowly thickened and brightened in the window that looked over the harbour. The rising tide began to lap against the gable ends of the houses.

"Mr. Blackie," said Celia, "an earthquake ruined a town in Serbia last week. The ground just opened and swallowed half the folk. Did your God in his mercy think up that too? The country folk in Viet Nam, what kind of vice is it they're gripped in, guns and lies and anger on both sides of them, a slowly tightening agony? Is your God looking after them? They never harmed anybody, but the water in the the rice fields is red now all the time. Black men and white men hate each other in Chicago and Cape Town. God rules everything. He knew what was going to happen before the world was made. So we're told. If that's goodness, I have another name for it. Not the worst human being that ever lived would do the things God does. Tell me this, was God in the Warsaw ghetto too? I just want to know. I was reading about it last week in a book I got out of the Library.

"I know you don't like this darkness and the sound of wine being poured in the glass. It's the only way I can speak to you and be honest. . . .

"I remember my mother and my father. They were like two rocks in the sea. Life might be smooth or rough for one—there was hunger every now and then when the fishing was poor—but the two rocks were always there. I knew every ledge and cranny. I flew between them like a young bird.

"We were poor, but closer together because of that. We gave each other small gifts. I would take shells and seapinks into the house for them. My father always had a special fish for me when he came in from the west, a codling or a flounder as small as my hand. Then my mother would bake a small bannock for me to eat with it at teatime, when I was home from school.

"I was twelve years old. One morning when I got up for school my mother was standing in the door looking out over the harbour. The fire was dead. She told me in a flat voice I wasn't to go to school that day, I was to go back to my room and draw the curtain and stay there till she called me. An hour later I heard feet on the pier. I looked through the edge of the curtain. Four fishermen were carrying something from the boat into the house. The thing was covered with a piece of sail and there was a trail of drops behind it. My father was in from his creels for the last time.

"We knew what real poverty was after that. My mother was too proud to take anything from the Poor Fund. "Of course not," she said, 'my grandfather was schoolmaster in Hoy.' . . . But in the middle of February she swallowed her pride and went to the Poor Inspector. One night I woke up and heard voices and came downstairs and I saw Thomas Linklater the shoemaker having supper beside the fire. A month after that my mother married him in the registry office. He came and sat in my father's chair and slept in my father's bed. He carried a new smell into our house, leather and rosin, like an animal of a different species.

"I hated him. Of course I smiled and spoke. But in my room, in the darkness, I hated the stranger.

"Three years went past. Then it was my mother's turn. I watched her changing slowly. I didn't know what the change was, nor why Dr. Wilson should trouble to come so often. Then I heard Maisie Ness saying 'cancer' to the watchmaker's wife at the end of the close. My mother was a good-looking woman. She was a bit vain and she'd often look long in the mirror, putting her hair to rights and smiling to her reflection. The change went on in her all that summer. She looked in the mirror less and less. Every day though she did her housework. The room had to be swept and the dishes put away before Dr. Wilson called. Half a ghost, she knelt at the unlit fire and struck a match. That last morning she laid three bowls of porridge on the table. She looked at her withered face in the mirror. Then she groped for her chair and sank into it. She was dead before I could put down my spoon. The shoemaker hurried away to find Dr. Wilson. The body slowly turned cold in the deep straw chair.

"I heard the shoemaker crying in his room the day before the funeral.

"'Blessed are the dead which die in the Lord'—that's what you said at the graveside. It was a poor way to die. It was ugly and degrading and unblessed, if anything ever was.

"We were alone in the house together then, a girl and an old cobbler. It was the beginning of winter. We spoke to each other only when it was needful. He gave me the housekeeping money every Friday and it was never enough. 'There'll be more soon,' he would say, 'It's hard times, a depression all over the country. So-and-so owes five pounds for two pairs of shoes and I had a bill from the wholesale leather merchant for twenty pounds odds.' ... I wanted cake on the table at the week-end but there was never anything but the usual bread and oat-cakes and margarine.

"Christmas came. I wanted a few decorations about the house, a tree, paper bells, some tinsel, a dozen cards to send to my special friends—you know the way it is with young girls. 'We can't afford nonsense like that,' the shoemaker said. 'We should be thankful to God for a roof over our heads.' ... And so the walls remained bare.

"That Christmas I hated him worse than ever.

"'Celia,' he said at Hogmanay, just before it struck midnight, 'I'm not a drinking man. But it's bad luck not to drink a health to the house at this time of year. We'll take one small dram together.'

"He brought a half-bottle of whisky out of the cupboard.

"The clock struck twelve. We touched glasses. I shuddered as the whisky went down. It burned my mouth and my stomach and it took tears to my eyes. 'He's doing this deliberately to hurt me,' I thought. My eyes were still wet when the door opened and Mr. Spence the jeweler came in. He had a bottle of whisky in his hand to wish us a good New Year. He poured three glasses and we toasted each other. The cobbler merely wet his lips. I drank my whisky down quickly to get it over with.

"It's hard to explain what happened next. I knew who I was before I took that drink—a poor girl in an ordinary house on a fisherman's pier. I stood there holding an empty glass in my hand. A door was opening deep inside me and I looked through it into another country. I stood between the two places, confused and happy and excited. I still wore Celia's clothes but the clothes were all a disguise, bits of fancy dress, a masquerade. You know the ballad about the Scottish King who went out in the streets of Edinburgh in bonnet and tradesman's apron? I wore the clothes of a poor girl but I was wise, rich, great, gentle, good.

> *Then doon he let his duddies fa',*
> *And doon he let them fa'*
> *And he glittered a' in gold*
> *Far abune them a'.*

"The world was all mine and I longed to share it with everybody. Celia was a princess in her little house on the pier. She pretended to be poor but she had endless treasures in her keeping, and it was all a secret, nobody knew about it but Celia. A wild happiness filled the house.

"I bent down and kissed the old shoemaker.

"Mr. Spence, I remember, was pouring another whisky into my glass. The confusion and the happiness increased. I felt very tired then, I remember. I went to bed wrapped in silks and swan feathers.

"It was Celia the poor girl who woke up next morning. There was a hard gray blanket up at her face. She had a mouth like ashes. The wireless when she switched it on downstairs told of people dying of hunger in the streets of Calcutta, drifting about like wraiths and lying down on the burning pavements. And a plane had fallen from the sky in Kansas and forty people were dead on a hillside.

"She cried, the poor princess, beside the dead fire.

"The next Friday out of the housekeeping money I bought a bottle of cheap wine.

"That's all there is to tell, really. You've heard the confession of an alcoholic, or part of it, for the bad fairy tale isn't over yet.

"Once a month, maybe every six weeks, the fisher girl craves for news of the lost country, the real world, what she calls her kingdom. For a week or more I enchant myself away from the town and the pier and the sound of cobbling. When I have no more money left I encourage men to come here with drink. I'm shameless about it now. Everybody who has a bottle is welcome, even Mr. Snoddy. At the end of every bout I'm in deeper exile than the time before. Every debauch kills a piece of Celia—I almost said, kills a part of her soul, but of course I don't believe in that kind of thing any more.

"And so the bad fairy tale goes on and the fisher girl who thinks that somehow she's a princess is slowly fitted with the cold blood and leathery skin and the terrible glittering eye of a toad.

"This kingdom I've had a glimpse of, though—what about that? It *seemed* real and precious. It seemed like an inheritance we're all born for, something that belongs to us by right.

"If that's true, it should be as much *there* as this pier is in the first light of morning. Why do we have to struggle towards it through fogs of drink? What's the good of all this mystery? The vision should be like a loaf or a fish, simple and real, something given to nourish the whole world.

"I blame God for that too."

There was no sound for a while but the lapping of harbour water against stone as the tide rose slowly among the piers and slipways. The huge chaotic ordered wheel of stars tilted a little westward on its axis.

"The bottle's nearly empty," said Celia, "and I haven't said what I meant to say at all. I wonder if the licensed grocer would sell me another bottle? No, it's too late. And besides, I don't think I have enough money in my purse. And besides, you don't want to listen to much more of this bad talk.

"All the same, you can see now why I could never be a member of your church. All I could bring to it is this guilt, shame, grief for things that happen, a little pity, a sure knowledge of exile.

"Will Christ accept that?"

There was another longer silence in the room.

"Celia," said the Reverend Andrew Blackie, a little hopelessly, "you must try to have faith."

The girl's window was full of stars. The sky was so bright that the outlines of bed and chair and cupboard could be dimly seen, and the shapes of an empty bottle and a glass on the table.

"I want to have faith," said Celia. "I want that more than anything in the world."

8

Ronald Leask worked his creels with Jock Henryson all that Saturday afternoon along the west coast. They hauled eighty creels under Marwick Head and Yesnaby. In the late afternoon the wind shifted round to the northwest and strengthened and brought occasional squalls of rain. They decided to leave their remaining score of creels under the Black Crag till morning and make for home before it got dark. They had a box of lobsters and half a basket of crabs, a fair day's work. As Ronald turned the *Celia* into Hoy Sound he saw three Norwegian whalers racing for the shelter of Hamnavoe on the last of the flood tide. Another squall of rain hit them. Ronald put on his sou'wester and buttoned his black oilskin up to the chin. Jock Henryson was at the wheel now, in the shelter of the cabin.

"It's going to be a dirty night," said Jock.

They delivered their lobsters and crabs at the Fishermen's Society pier. Then Jock said he must go home for his supper. "You come too," he said to Ronald. "The wife'll have something in the pot."

"No," said Ronald, "I think I'll go along for a drink."

It was raining all the time now. The flagstones of the street shone. Ronald stopped for a few seconds at the head of the shoemaker's close, then he walked on more quickly until he came to the lighted window of the Hamnavoe Bar. He pushed open the door. Bill MacIsaac the boatbuilder was at the bar drinking beer with Thorfinn Vik the farmer from Helliar. Sammy Flett the drunk was in too—he was half stewed and he was pestering the barman to give him a pint, and Drew the barman was refusing him patiently but firmly. A half-empty bottle of cheap wine stuck out of Sammy Flett's pocket.

"Here's Ronald Leask, a good man," said Sammy Flett, going up to Ronald unsteadily. "Ronald, you're a good friend of mine and I ask you to accept a cigarette out of my packet, and I'm very glad of your offer to furnish me with a glass of beer for old time's sake."

"A glass of whisky," said Ronald to Drew the barman.

"Absolutely delighted, old friend," said Sammy Flett.

"It's not for you," said Drew the barman to Sammy Flett. "You're not getting nothing, not a drop. The police sergeant was here this morning and your father with him and I know all about the trouble you're causing at home, smashing the chairs and nearly setting fire to the bed at the week-end. This place is out of bounds to you, sonny boy. I promised the sergeant and your old man. You can push off any time you like."

"That's all lies," said Sammy Flett. "Just give me one pint of ordinary beer. That's not much for a man to ask."

"No," said Drew the barman.

"I demand to see the manager," said Sammy Flett.

Ronald Leask drank his whisky at one go and put down his empty glass and nodded to Drew. The barman filled it up again.

"No water?" said Bill MacIsaac the boatbuilder, smiling across at Ronald.

"No," said Ronald, "no water."

"Men in love," said Thorfinn Vik of Helliar, "don't need water in their drink." Vik was in one of his dangerous insulting moods.

Sammy Flett went into the toilet. They heard the glug-glug of wine being drunk, then a long sigh.

The door opened and Mr. William Snoddy the builder's clerk came in out of the rain. He looked round the bar nervously. "A small whisky," he said to Drew the barman, "and put a little soda in it, not too much, and a bottle of export, if you please...." He wiped his spectacles with his handkerchief and owled the bar with bulging naked eyes and put his spectacles on again. Then he recognized the man he was standing beside

"Why, Ronald," he said. "It isn't often we see you in the bar. It's a poor night, isn't it?"

Ronald stared straight ahead at the rank of bottles under the bar clock. He put back his head and drank the remains of his second glass of whisky.

"Ronald, have a glass of whisky with me," said Mr. Snoddy, taking his wallet out of his inside pocket. "It'll be a pleasure."

"Same again," said Ronald to the barman. "And I'll pay for my own drink with my own money."

Mr. Snoddy flushed till his brow was almost as pink as his nose. Then he put his wallet back in his inside pocket.

Sammy Flett emerged from the toilet, smiling.

Bill MacIsaac and Thorfinn Vik began to play darts at the lower end of the bar.

"Oh well," said Mr. Snoddy, "I don't suppose you can force a person to speak to you if he doesn't want to." He drank his whisky down quickly and took a sip of beer.

Suddenly Sammy Flett came up behind Mr. Snoddy and threw his arm round his neck. "If it isn't my dear friend Mr. Snoddy," said Sammy Flett. "Mr. Snoddy, accept a cigarette, with my compliments."

"Go away," cried Mr. Snoddy. "Go away. Just leave me alone."

"Mr. Snoddy," said Sammy Flett, "I'll take the whisky that Mr. Leask refused to accept for reasons best known to himself."

"I come in here for a quiet drink," said Mr. Snoddy to the barman, trying to disengage his neck from Sammy Flett's arm.

"And you shall have it, dear Mr. Snoddy," said Sammy Flett. "Accompany me to the gentleman's toilet. We shall have a drink of wine together. Mr. Snoddy is always welcome to have a drink from Sammy."

"Leave Mr. Snoddy alone," said Drew the barman.

The door opened and six Norwegian fishermen came in. "Six double scotches, six Danish lagers," Per Bjorling said to the barman. The Norwegians shook the rain from their coats and leaned against the bar counter. A row of six blond heads shone with wetness under the lamps.

"I know what they're saying about you, Mr. Snoddy," said Sammy Flett. "They say you're going with other women. They say you're unfaithful to Mrs. Snoddy. It's an evil world and they'll say anything but their prayers. But I don't believe that, Mr. Snoddy. You and me, we're old friends, and I wouldn't believe such a thing about you. Not Sammy. Never."

Mr. Snoddy looked about him, angry and confused. He left his half-empty glass standing on the counter and went out quickly, clashing the door behind him.

"Mr. Snoddy is a very fine man," said Sammy Flett to the Norwegians.

"Is so?" said one of the Norwegians, smiling.

"Yes," said Sammy Flett, "and he's a very clever man too."

"Interesting," said another Norwegian.

"I'm no fool myself," said Sammy Flett. "I didn't sail up Hoy Sound yesterday in a banana skin. Sammy knows a thing or two."

Dod Isbister the plumber came in and Jimmy Gold the postman and Andrew Thomson the crofter from Knowe. They went to the upper-end of the bar and ordered beer. They emptied a box of dominoes on the counter and began to play.

The dart players finished their game and stuck their darts in the cork rim of the board. Thorfinn Vik was a bit drunk. He came over and stood beside Ronald Leask and began to sing:

> *I was dancing with my darling at the Tennessee waltz*
> *When an old friend I happened to see,*
> *Introducing him to my sweetheart and while they were*
> *   dancing*
> *My friend stole my sweetheart from me.*

"No singing," said Drew the barman sternly. "No singing in this bar. There's guests in the lounge upstairs."

Thorfinn Vik turned to Ronald Leask. "That's a song that you'll appreciate, Mr. Leask," he said. "I sang it specially for you. A song about disappointed love."

"Same again," said Ronald Leask to the barman.

"A beautiful song," said Sammy Flett from the middle of the Norwegian group. He had a glass of whisky in one hand and a glass of lager in the other that one of the whalers had bought for him. "Very delightfully sung. Have you got songs in Norway as good as that? I daresay you have. Silence now for a Norwegian love song."

"No singing," said Drew.

"We sing only on our boat," said Per Bjorling. "We respect your rules. Please to give us seven double scotches and seven Danish lagers...." To Sammy Flett he said, "There will be singings later on the *Erika*—how you say?—a sing-song."

"You are the true descendants of Vikings," said Sammy Flett.

"No," said a young Norwegian, "they were cruel men. It is best to forget such people, no? We are peaceable fishermen."

"Such is truthfully what we are," said another Norwegian.

The door opened quietly and Mr. Spence the jeweler tiptoed in. He shook his umbrella closed and went up to the bar. "One half-bottle of the best whisky, to carry out," he murmured to Drew the barman. He laid two pound notes discreetly on the counter.

"Mr. Spence," cried Sammy Flett from the center of the Norwegian group. "My dear friend."

"Leave Mr. Spence alone," said Drew. "He doesn't want anything about you."

"I am content where I am," said Sammy Flett, "in the midst of our Scandinavian cousins. But there's nothing wrong in greeting my old friend Mr. Spence."

Mr. Spence smiled and picked up his change and slid the half-bottle into his coat pocket.

"I think I know where you're off to with that," said Sammy Flett, wagging a finger at him.

Mr. Spence smiled again and went out as quietly and quickly as he had come in.

"Yes," said Thorfinn Vik of Helliar, "we all know where he's going...." He winked across at the domino players. "Mr. Leask knows too."

"I want no trouble in here," said Drew the barman.

"Same again," said Ronald Leask and pushed his empty glass at the barman. His face was very red.

"Is clock right?" said Per Bjorling.

"Five minutes fast," said Drew. "It's twenty minutes to ten."

Sammy Flett drank first his whisky and then his lager very quickly. The huge adams-apple above his dirty collar wobbled two or three times. He sighed and said, "Sammy is happy now. Sammy asks nothing from life but a wee drink now and then."

"I am happy for you," said the Norwegian boy. "I will now buy you other drink."

"No," said Sammy Flett, "not unless you all promise to partake of a little wine with me later in the gentlemen's toilet. At closing time Sammy will show you the pleasures of Hamnavoe. Sammy knows all the places."

"Here is pleasures enough," said the oldest Norwegian, "In the pub."

"No," said Sammy, "but I will take you to girls."

"Girls," said the old man. "Oh no no. I am grandfather."

"I have little sweetheart outside of Hammerfest," said the boy. "Gerd. She is milking the cattles and makes butter, also cheese from goats."

"Also I am married," said another Norwegian, "and also is Paal and Magnus and Henrik. No girls. All are committed among us but Per."

"Is true," said Per Bjorling gravely.

"Per is liberty to find a girl where he likes," said the old man. "Per is goodlooking, is handsome, there is no trouble that Per our skipper will find a beautiful girl."

The other Norwegians laughed.

"He's like a film star," said Sammy Flett. "Thank you most kindly, I'll have a glass of whisky and a bottle of beer. No offense. Per has a profile like a Greek hero."

"Has found a beautiful girl already," said the boy, smiling, "in Hamnavoe."

"One bottle of vodka," said Per Bjorling to Drew, "for outside drinking."

Drew the barman took down a bottle of vodka from the shelf and called out, "Last orders, gentlemen."

"Double whisky," said Ronald Leask.

Sammy Flett said to Per Bjorling, "Are you going to visit this young lady now with your bottle of vodka?"

"A gift to her," said Per Bjorling. "Is a good girl. Is kind. Is understanding, intelligent. I like her very much."

"What is the name of this fortunate young lady, if I might make so bold as to ask?" said Sammy Flett. "Listen, Ronald. Per Bjorling is just going to tell us the name of his Hamnavoe sweetheart."

Per Bjorling said, "Celia."

For about five seconds there was no sound in the bar but the click of dominoes on the counter.

Then Ronald Leask turned and hit Per Bjorling with his fist on the side of the head. The lager glass fell from Per Bjorling's hand and smashed on the floor. The force of the blow sent him back against the wall, his hands up at his face. He turned to Ronald Leask and said, "Is not my wish to cause offense to any man present."

"Cut it out," cried Drew the barman. "That's enough now."

Ronald Leask stepped forward and hit Per Bjorling again, on the mouth. A little blood ran down Per Bjorling's jaw and his cap fell on the floor. He turned and hit Ronald Leask in the stomach and Ronald Leask flapped against the counter like a shiny black puppet. A score of glasses fell and smashed and a rapid pool of whisky and beer formed on the floor. Ronald Leask and Per Bjorling splintered and splashed through it, wrestling with each other. Ronald Leask clubbed down his fist on Per Bjorling's eye and Per Bjorling thrashed him across the jaw with the back of his hand. Ronald Leask went down on all fours among the beer and the broken glass.

"I am sorry for this," said Per Bjorling and held out his hand.

Ronald Leask got slowly to his feet. His trouser knees were sopping wet and the palms of his hands cut and bleeding. A small bubble of blood grew and burst at his right nostril.

"Get out of here," said Drew the barman, taking Ronald Leask by the sleeve of his oilskin, "and never come back again. That applies to you too," he said to Per Bjorling.

"So this is your Scotch hospitality," said the Norwegian called Paal, "to strike a man without reason. This we will not forget."

"Remember this too," said Thorfinn Vik, and struck Paal on the ear. "This is our bar where we come to enjoy ourselves and this is our town and our women live in it."

Drew picked up the telephone and his forefinger juggled in the dial.

"This is cowardice," said the Norwegian boy. He stepped forward and took Thorfinn Vik by the throat. They lurched violently, locked together, between the seats and the bar counter. Half a dozen more glasses went over and smashed. Bill MacIsaac the boatbuilder tried to prize Thorfinn Vik and the young Norwegian apart. Andrew Thomson of Knowe put down his dominoes and began to take off his jacket slowly. "I don't like fighting," he said, "but I'll fight if there's fighting to be done."

"Gentlemen, gentlemen," piped Sammy Flett from the fringe of the fight. Then he noticed an unattended glass of whisky on the bar counter and made for it. He was hidden behind a welter of heaving backs.

"You are bad man," said the old Norwegian to Ronald Leask and slapped him magisterially across the face.

"Enough," cried Per Bjorling.

Two policemen stood in the door.

Dod Isbister with a bottle in his hand and the Norwegian called Magnus with a glass in his hand were circling each other at the top end of the bar. Ronald Leask lashed out at Paal with his foot and missed and kicked Henrik on the elbow. Thorfinn Vik and the young Norwegian went over on the floor with a thud that made the bottles reel and rattle and clink. Dod Isbister threw the bottle he was holding and it missed Magnus's head and smashed into the lamp bulb. The light went out. The pub was a twilight full of grunting, breathing, slithering, cursing shadows.

"All right, gentlemen," said the voice of Drew the barman, "you can break it up. The law is here."

The two policemen beamed their torches slowly over the wreckage. The fighters disengaged themselves. One by one they got to their feet.

"So this is the way it is," said the sergeant. "You'll have to come along to the station. We have accommodation for gentry like you. You haven't heard the last of this, I'm afraid. The sheriff will be wanting to see you all next Tuesday."

"Not me, sergeant," said Sammy Flett. "Sammy never laid a finger on anybody."

"You too," said the sergeant. "I wouldn't be surprised if you weren't at the bottom of this, Flett."

Later, in the Black Maria going to the police station, Sammy Flett said, "That was the best fight since the Kirkwall men threw Clarence Shaw into the harbour last carnival week."

"Shut up, drunkard," said Thorfinn Vik sleepily from the corner of the van.

"No, Thorfinn," said Sammy Flett, "but I want to reassure everyone, especially our Norwegian guests. The beds in the lock-up are very comfortable. The sergeant's wife will give us a cup of tea and toast in the morning. I know, because I've had bed and breakfast at Her Majesty's expense on twenty-two occasions—no, this makes it twenty-three. Everybody is very nice."

"The little Gerd," said the young Norwegian miserably. "I am thinking of her so very much."

The Black Marie jolted to a stop. They had arrived.

9

In the shoemaker's room the lamp was turned down low. It threw a feeble pool of light in one corner. The shoemaker was in his iron bed; he leaned back on three pillows and struggled for breath. Every inhalation was hard-won and shallow; the slack strings of his throat grew taut to force a passage for it, and his whole torso laboured to expel it again. His breathing slowly thickened and roughened, came in a quick spasm, and then he turned over on the pillows in a storm of feeble importunate coughing.

Celia came quickly through from the other room. She sat down on the edge of the bed and took the shoemaker's damp hand in both hers. "You'll be all right," she said. "Just take it easy."

The coughing stopped and the old man lay back on his pillows with his mouth open. Celia wiped his face with her apron. Then she lifted a small brown bottle from the table and shook a tablet out and poured some water in a cup. "You've to take a tablet every four hours, Dr. Wilson says," she said. "It stops the coughing." She put the tablet in his mouth and raised his head and gave him a sip of water.

"If only I could sleep," whispered the shoemaker. He lay back on the pillows with his eyes shut. "I'm a very poor old sick man."

"I won't leave you," said Celia.

"Tell me one thing," said the shoemaker, "then maybe I can get to sleep. Is there any man or drink in the room next door?"

"No," said Celia.

"Tell me the truth," he whispered sternly. "The truth, mind. I heard someone at the door."

"Snoddy came at half-past eight," said Celia. "I sent him away. I told him you were ill. What's more, I told him I didn't want his drink."

"Till the next time," said the shoemaker.

"I suppose so," said Celia.

The shoemaker's breath slowly roughened as new threads of phlegm spun themselves into a thick cord in his chest. Then suddenly he was possessed by spasm after spasm of futile coughing. He drew himself up in the bed and Celia put her arms round his thin body and held him close to her until the tough cord of phlegm broke and the coughing stopped. She took a bowl from the bedside chair and he managed to spit into it. The effort exhausted him. Celia laid him back on his pillows. Then she wiped his face in her apron.

"If only I could sleep," said the shoemaker. "I was dropping off to sleep an hour and more ago and then I was wakened first by Snoddy and then by a terrible noise along the street."

"There was fighting in the Hamnavoe Bar," said Celia. "So Snoddy said. That's what you heard. Drew had to get the police."

"It sounded like an earthquake," said the shoemaker.

Celia stroked his chest outside his gray flannel shirt. "Try to sleep now," she said. "I'll stay beside you till you go to sleep...." After a time she felt his chest grow quiet under her hand. His eyes were shut and his breath came deep and even through slightly parted lips. Celia knew that he wasn't asleep, but he was pretending to sleep so that she could get back to her bed.

Outside the rain slanted darkly. A sudden gust of wind caught the downpour and threw it against the window till all the panes surged and throbbed. Through the onset Celia heard a discreet tapping at the outside door.

"Don't let him in," said the shoemaker, opening his eyes.

It was Mr. Spence the jeweler. "Celia," he said.

"The old man isn't well," said Celia in a low voice. "The doctor was here in the afternoon. I'll have to be up with him all night."

"Perhaps if I could just come in," said Mr. Spence.

"Please go home," said Celia, "Please."

Mr. Spence took the flask of whisky from his coat pocket. "We will just have one little toddy," he said. "Thomas won't mind me being in the house. He tells me I can come whenever I like. You know that. A little dram for a damp night, eh?"

"Not tonight," said Celia, "I'm sorry."

The rain slanted all about Mr. Spence, a diagonal bright-dark nagging susurration on the flagstones of the pier. The gutters bubbled. Celia could smell the wetness from his clothes.

"Celia," said Mr. Spence in a hurt voice, "I am a very lonely man."

"Everyone is lonely," said Celia gently. "We're all prisoners. We must try to find out a way to be pardoned."

She shut the door and drew the bar across it. She was just about to turn into her own seaward room when she heard the shoemaker speaking aloud to himself in the room with the dim light and the noise of rain in it. She stood in the lobby and listened.

"And so it'll be all right once we're settled in Clett. Ronald has a small room I can bide in. It doesn't matter about me, I won't live that long. But Celia, she'll be happy at last. She'll soon learn to look after the cow and the few hens, yes, he'll get a pot of soup when he comes in cold from the fishing. She'll be a good wife to Ronald. And I tell you this, Ronald won't allow all them bottles in his cupboard, no, and no bloody foreigners'll get within a stone's throw of the place, and as for Snoddy, the dog of Clett'll tear the arse off the likes of him. Mr. Spence, he can come as usual twice a week for a game of draughts, I'm sure Ronald won't object to that. We'll be fine once we're settled in Clett. Not that Ronald Leask's conferring any favour on Celia, not a bit of it, he's a lucky chap to be getting the likes of Celia for a wife. She can cook and sew and wash as well as any woman in Hamnavoe. I'll maybe be a burden to them for a winter or two, but Ronald said I could come, and by that time they'll likely have another burden, a bairn in the cradle, but a sweet burden, not an old done man. Once Celia's settled in Clett she'll have a new life entirely, there'll be no more drink and no more poverty and no more stray men in the night. An end to this darkness."

Celia went softly into the room. The shoemaker closed his eyes quickly and pretended to be asleep. But another rope of phlegm was beginning to rasp in his chest. There was a smell too, all about the bed. Celia sat beside him and wiped his face with her apron. He opened his eyes and said, "I'm sorry. I think I've messed the bed up." He was ashamed and his eyes were wet.

"I know," said Celia. "Don't worry. I'll get you cleaned up before anything else. There's a kettle of hot water on the range. Plenty of clean sheets in the cupboard."

She opened the window to let the smell out. Rain and wind swirled in and the shoemaker began to cough. She closed the window again quickly.

For the next twenty minutes Celia washed the old man and dried him and put a clean shirt on him and stripped the bed and put clean sheets on it and set the soiled stinking sheets in a tub of disinfected water in the lobby.

"You'll feel better now," said Celia. "I'm going to make a cup of tea for the two of us."

The shoemaker was racked with a violent spasm of coughing. She held him till the tough cord of phlegm shore in his throat and he spat it out. She laid him back exhausted on the pillows.

"Fighting along the street a while ago," said the shoemaker wearily. "It's always them foreigners."

"It's all quiet now," said Celia. "Time you had another tablet though."

She took a yellow tablet out of the bottle on to her hand and put it on his tongue. She laid her arm round his shoulders and raised him and put the cup of water to his mouth.

"They don't seem to help me, them tablets," said the shoemaker.

"They will," said Celia. "Give them time. Dr. Wilson's tablets always work, you know that."

"Maybe I'll get a sleep now," said the shoemaker.

"Try," said Celia.

But the hoarseness was in his chest again. He coughed and spat out thick phlegm. But as always when this sickness was on him, he had hardly torn the purulent fungus from his bronchial tree when a new growth rose about it, blocking and strangling his breath.

"I'm a terrible nuisance to you," he said, "a silly awkward old man."

"You're not," said Celia, "and you'll be better tomorrow. And there's a fine shed at Clett where you can mend boots. I'll ask Ronald to put a stove in it."

The shoemaker was suddenly asleep, the way sleep comes to the very young and the very old. His cheeks flushed like two withered apples. He breathed as quietly as a child.

"Thank God," said Celia.

She drew the blankets up to his chin and kissed him on the forehead.

The window paled with the end of the night.

The rain had stopped, as it often does before dawn. Celia closed the door of the shoemaker's room softly and unbarred the outer door and went out on to the pier. The first seagulls were screaming along the street, scavenging in the bins. She breathed the clean air of early morning. She stood at the pier wall and watched the sea moving darkly against the weeded steps and slipways. A rat in the seaweed squinnied at her and twitched its whiskers and went into the water with a soft plop. The sun had not yet risen, but light was assembling in broken colours over the Orphir hills. The first blackbird in the fuchsia bush under the watchmaker's wall faltered into song and then was silent again. Celia could see the boats in the harbour now and at the farm across the harbour black ploughed squares among green grass and brown heather. It would be a beautiful morning.

Then the sun rose clear of the Orphir hills and folded the girl in the light of a new day.

A TIME TO KEEP

1

We came down through the fields, Ingi and I.

The wedding was still going on in her father's house in Osmundwall, ten miles over the hill.

There were lacings of snow across the valley and the upper hills were white.

We saw our house in front of us, a clean new house of sea-washed stones. There was no earth-weathering on the walls yet. I had built the house myself between harvest and Christmas. Fires had been lit to burn the dampness out of it, but there was no fire yet for food and companionship. Beside the dwelling-house were byre and barn and stable that the mason had built the winter before. The thatch on the four roofs were new springy heather, covered with wire-netting and weighted with stones.

Ingi went alone into the house. I went into the byre to see that the two cows were all right. There was a sheep here and a sheep there on the field above, seven sheep in all on the hill. One sheep wandered across a line of snow, gray against white.

A new plough leaned against the wall of the barn. The blacksmith must have delivered it that afternoon. I took it inside, a gray powerful curve.

This was our croft, Ingi's and mine. I turned back towards the house. Blue smoke was rising from the roof now. The first true fire had been lit.

2

I was in the firth most days that month, though it was winter. My boat was new also. I had made her with my own hands in the month of June, the dry bright month when work can be carried on late into the night, after the croft work is over. I called the boat *Susanna* after the laird's wife, a red-faced generous woman. I thought a name like that would bring us luck.

I generally got up as soon as it was light. I left Ingi in our bed and I ate a piece of bannock and drank a mouthful of ale. Then I put on my sea-boots and my woolen cap and went down to the beach.

The other crofters who were fishermen also were always there before me that winter, and they kept apart from me. I was like a stranger in the valley.

I launched *Susanna* alone. I didn't feel the need of anyone except Ingi.

That winter the other crofter-fishermen avoided me. Neither the old ones nor the young unmarried ones came near me. They had liked me well enough the summer before but now, since the marriage, I was, it seemed, unpopular. The men of Two-Waters especially kept to their own side of the bay.

I fished alone.

And alone I carried the haddocks up over the fields to the croft. Always the smoke was rising out of the roof, sometimes gray smoke, sometimes blue, sometimes black. But the flame beat in the hearth, the house was alive. And always when I reached the door Ingi stood there before me.

3

One night there was a storm from the south. None of the boats was in the firth next morning. The clouds pressed on the face of the hills and it was too wet to plough, though it was the time of ploughing.

I lay long in the box-bed, my face to the wall. Ingi was up soon after it was light.

I heard her going about her work. Her poker stirred a new flame out of the embers in the hearth. The door opened. She came in with her apron full of peats. The door opened again. Now she was carrying pails of new water from the burn. They rang like bells as she set them down on the flagstones. She turned some fish that were smoking in the chimney. Then her small fists beat on the table as she kneaded the dough. She poured water into a black pot. And the door kept slamming against the wall as she went out and in, louder because of the storm. "For God's sake," I said, "be quiet."

I fell asleep for a while then.

When I woke up the storm was still prowling about the house. But the door was shut tight and the house was warm and full of the smells of new bannocks and boiled fish.

"Get up," Ingi said, "or we'll eat up everything, the dog and myself. You've been sleeping a night and a day." She said a small quiet prayer over the food.

Ingi and I sat at the table and ate. She had not yet learned to cook properly—the fish was raw and the bannocks full of soda. She had been busy at more than food while I was sleeping. The stone floor was still half wet from her scrubbing and she had tried to mend the four broken creels with twine. Ingi was not a valley girl. She had spent her life behind the counter of her father's shop in Osmundwall, but she was doing her best to please me. It grew dark while we were eating.

Ingi put down her bread and took a box of matches from the mantelpiece and lit the paraffin lamp. The flame came up squint— she still didn't know how to trim a wick.

We dipped the last of our bread in the fish brew. "I hope this gale doesn't last," said Ingi. "Our fish is nearly done."

The flame sank in the hearth.

"Tomorrow," said Ingi, "I will make ale, though I've never made it before. There isn't much malt left either. And I'll tell you what I need badly, a pair of black shoes for the kirk on Sundays."

I rose from my chair and blew out the lamp.

Outside the storm prowled between the sea and the hills, restless as a beast.

Ingi put a black peat over the red embers so that the fire would stay alive till morning.

We leaned towards each other then and kissed in the darkness.

4

I dug out a new field at the side of the house—because no one on God's earth could plough such a wilderness—and all the while I was tearing up stones and clumps of heather I thought to myself, "What a fool! Sure as hell the laird will raise your rent for this day's work." And my spade rang against stones or sank with a squelch into a sudden bit of bog.

I looked up once and saw a dozen women trooping across the fields to the school.

It was Good Friday.

I looked up another time and saw a horseman riding between the hills. It was the laird. He turned his horse towards the school also. The Easter service was being held there.

Two of my lambs had been born dead that morning. They lay, red bits of rag, under the wall. I would bury them afterwards.

There was one stone in the new field that just showed a gray curve through the heather. I took the biggest hammer in the barn and was an hour breaking it up and tearing the sharp bits out of the ground.

That was enough labour for one day. The sun was going down. I turned for home.

Ingi was not in. The house was dead. The pot sat black upon a black fire. My shoulders ached with the misery and foolishness of increasing my own rent. I was very hungry too.

Ingi was at the service with the laird and the other women, listening to the story of the lash and the whins and the nails and the last words. All the women were there sitting before the missionary with open mouths, listening to that fairy tale. I and a few others in the island knew better. Mr. Simpson, B.Sc., from Glasgow had not been our schoolmaster four winters for nothing.

I spent the rest of the day in the ale-house with half a dozen other ploughmen.

And how I got home to the croft again I do not know. I woke up in the morning on the rack of my own bed, with all my clothes on.

There was a jam jar with new daffodils in it in the window.

Ingi heard my awakening, a groan and a creak.

She rose up quickly from the chair where she was peeling potatoes and put her cold hand on my forehead. "You'll be fine now," she said. "Bella had two lambs in the night, such bonny peedie things! Your throat must be dry. I'll get you some water."

Bella was the old ewe. None of her lambs, so I had been told when I bought her, ever died.

"You listen to me," I said to Ingi. "You spend too much money every Wednesday at that grocery van. Don't you buy any more jars of jam, and sponge cakes from the bakehouse in Hamnavoe. We're poor people. Remember that."

The daffodils in the window were like a dozen old women shawled in brightness.

The fire burned high in the hearth and the kettle sang.

I closed my eyes.

5

The old field was ploughed and the new field was completely drained and dug. When I turned for home grey smoke was rising over the chimney-head.

There were eleven sheep on the hill now and three cattle in the field, the two cows and a small black bull calf. I went into the house and Ingi was emptying the new ale out of the kirn into stone jars. "You'll bide at home after this," Ingi said. "No more of that ale-house."

But the stuff was flat. She hadn't yet mastered the craft of brewing. Until she did I would have to keep visiting the ale-house.

One day I would come in from the firth with lobsters and another day with haddocks. I got two huge halibut one morning that I could hardly carry up over the fields. She was ready with the stone jar of salt and the knife in the threshold.

I walked between the hills to pay the rent on term day. "You've broken out land," said the factor, "and therefore I think it only fair you should pay ten shillings more rent come Martinmas. Furthermore you have no right to graze sheep on the hill without permission from the laird, who is not giving his permission this year. See to it."

"Did you never hear of the Crofters' Act of 1888?" I said.

He gave me a black look. Then he licked a stamp and thudded

it on the receipt and signed his name across it. "You'll be hearing from the lawyer in Hamnavoe," he said.

I had more kindness than usual from Ingi when I got back from that interview.

And every Sabbath she would be at the holy meeting with the old women. She was away all morning, while I sat at home reading *The Martyrdom of Man*, one of the six books in the cupboard (not counting the Bible). And after the service she would come in at the door and sit in her black clothes in the chair at the other side of the fire and she would say, "We should be very thankful.... But," she said one Sunday, "my shoes are not fit to be seen in God's house."

We were at the peat cutting a whole day that month. We came home stung with clegs, blistered by the sun, and too sore to eat or to make love. But one thing was sure: the red heart of the house would beat all next winter, for we had a great hoard of peats scattered over the hillside to dry. Ingi kissed me once and then I went to sleep in the chair till morning.

I sowed the field with oats. Then I went home in the twilight to bread and ale and the warm fire. There was a little improvement in her brewing, but still the stuff was too thick and sweet.

One morning Ingi was very sick.

6

I was sorting my catch on the beach and so were all the other fishermen when Peter of Two-Waters walked across the stones to me. John and Howie his two sons were behind him. Anna his daughter hovered in the background. "You hauled some of my lobster creels," Peter of Two-Waters said.

"I did not," I said.

"Under the Kame you hauled a dozen lobster creels belonging to me," said Peter of Two-Waters.

"That's not true," I said.

"Don't do it again," said Peter of Two-Waters. "That's thieving. In Kirkwall there's a court and a sheriff and a jail."

"I'm not a thief," I said, "but you're a liar."

"Don't call my father a liar," said John of Two-Waters. "If you call my father a liar again I'll smash you. I will."

"Careful," said Howie of Two-Waters to John. Howie had always been my friend. We had sat together at the same desk in the school and afterwards we had fished together a few times and we had got drunk in each other's company in the ale-house. "Careful now," said Howie to his brother.

"Somebody has been hauling my creels," said old Peter of Two-Waters. "There'll be trouble unless it stops."

"I fish my own lobsters," I said.

Then I put my basket of fish on my shoulder and walked home.

The truth is, I had good catches of lobster that summer, and I shipped them to Billingsgate and got good money for them. I was at home on the sea. Everything I did there was right.

The men of Two-Waters, on the other hand, were poor fishermen. They were good enough crofters but old women could have fished better. They should never had gone on the sea. They hardly knew the bow of a yawl from the stern. The weather made them nervous too—they kept near the shore if there was one cloud in the sky or a whisper of wind.

"No," said Ingi when I got home, "you are not a thief. But don't get into any fights. That Howie of Two-Waters is so strong, he could kill an ox. Besides that, Anna of Two-Waters is my best friend in this valley, and I don't want there to be any trouble between us. This valley is too small for bad blood."

She blew up the fire to heat a pot of ale. Then she knelt and drew off my sea boots.

7

I was baiting a line with mussels at the end of the house when I saw the black car coming between the hills and stopping where the road ended at the mouth of the valley. It was the first car ever seen in the island, a Ford.

A small, neat man with a beard and a watch-chain across his belly got out and came stepping briskly up our side of the valley.

"Ingi," I shouted, "your father's here."

She was baking, going between the table, the cupboard, and the fire, a blue reek all about her.

But now all thought of bread was forgotten. She let out a cry of distress. She threw off her mealy apron, she filled a bowl of water and dipped face and hands in it and wiped herself dry with the towel. She put the text straight on the wall. She covered my six rationalist books with a cloth. She fell to combing her hair and twisting it into a new bright knot at the back of her head. All the same, the house was full of the blue hot reek of baking. And the bed was unmade. And there was a litter of fish-guts and crab toes about the door. She tried hard, Ingi, but she was not the tidiest of the croft women.

Ingi came and stood at the door.

As for me, I went on with my lines. I was not beholden to him.

Mr. Sinclair, merchant in Osmundwall—and forby kirk elder, Justice of the Peace, chairman of the district council—stood at the corner of the barn.

"Father," said Ingi.

"My girl," said Mr. Sinclair. He touched her gently on the arm.

"Well, Bill," he said to me.

"Well," I said.

"Father, I'm glad to see you," said Ingi.

"No happier than I am to see you," said Mr. Sinclair. "Ingi," said he, "you're not looking well. Not at all well. What way is it that we haven't seen you for three whole months, eh? Ingi, I doubt you're working too hard, is that it?"

"On a croft," I said, "everybody must work."

"Is that so, Bill?" said Mr. Sinclair. "Maybe so. At the present moment I'm speaking to Ingi, to my daughter. I'll be wanting to speak to you later, before I go."

"Say what you have to say now," I said, "for I have work to do."

"Bill," said Ingi unhappily.

"Work to do, is that it, work to do," said Mr. Sinclair. "Then if you have so much work to do, why don't you give my daughter enough money for her to live on? Eh? Just answer me. Why don't you do that? Last month you cut down on her money. The van man told me. She couldn't buy jam or paraffin. Don't imagine I don't hear things."

"Father," said Ingi, "please."

73

"We have debts," I said, "to the mason for the barn and to the fishmonger for twine and oilskins and to the dealer in Hamnavoe for the seven sheep and the two cows. The laird, your friend and fellow elder, is threatening to raise our rent. There was furniture and implements to pay for."

"You and Ingi had a hundred pounds from me the week before you married," said Mr. Sinclair quietly. "One hundred pounds sterling, a cheque for that amount."

"You'll get it back," I said, "every penny."

"Bill," said Ingi. "Father."

"It was a present," said Mr. Sinclair, "to see my daughter through her first year or two in comfort. Yes, in the kind of comfort she was used to before she came to this place. Ingi is not a strong girl. She needs looking after."

"All the same," I said, "you'll be paid back. Ingi and I, we don't want your money."

"I think we should go inside," said Mr. Sinclair. "The whole valley's listening to what we say."

It was true enough. A half-dozen old women were at the end of their houses, waiting like hens for scraps of scandal.

"Let them listen," I said. "The truth never hurt anybody."

"Yes, come inside, *please*," said Ingi.

"No," I said. "Can't you see I'm working? I must bait this line and get the boat out before the tide turns."

"Very well," said Mr. Sinclair, "the truth as you say will bear hearing wherever it's uttered. There are other matters to be discussed besides."

Ingi went inside, covering her eyes with the new apron she had put on in honour of her father's arrival. From time to time I could hear a slow hard sob from inside the house.

"For example," Mr. Sinclair said, "it has come to my ears that hardly a night passes but you're in the ale-house. Hardly a night. Yes. The ale-house. But when are you seen at the Sunday service? Never once. No, but in the ale-house when you have a few drams in you there's nothing too vile for you to say against God and his holy Bible. I did not think I was marrying my daughter to a drunkard and an atheist."

I went on baiting my line. I could hear Ingi crying continuously inside the house.

"Listen to her, the poor girl," said Mr. Sinclair. "She does well to cry. For Ingibiorg Sinclair was a happy girl before she met up with the likes of you. She was that. And look at the shame and the misery and the poverty you've brought on her. I got her letter. She's a very unhappy girl."

I opened a few more mussels with my knife.

"I've come here today," he said, "to take her home where she'll be looked after."

I never answered.

I heard him stumping into the house. I went on with the baiting. Coil by coil the haddock line was baited. They spoke low and urgently to each other inside. Then minutes passed. The half-dozen old women still stood at the end of the crofts. I opened a score of mussels and threw the empty blue shells on the grass among the buttercups. The gulls that had been standing along the shore all morning stirred themselves and rose seawards in tumult upon tumult of yelling circles. Down at the rock Howie of Two-Waters was stowing his creels on board. (The fool—it was not a lobster day.) I heard the door opening and a small sob out of Ingi and the brisk feet of Mr. Sinclair on the threshold.

"You haven't heard the last of this," he shouted to me.

"There's never an end to anything," I said, "and it's a fine morning for the haddocks."

I waited till I heard the black Ford coughing among the hills and the old women were inside and the last hook was baited and coiled. Then I rose and went in through the door.

Ingi sat among the half-baked bannocks, dabbing her eyes.

"Ingi," I said, "here's what you're going to get, a pair of new black shoes and a coat and a hat for the kirk on Sabbath. We're going to Hamnavoe on the Saturday boat, the two of us, to the shops."

8

A new wave fell into the *Susanna* and kept the score of dying haddocks alive.

I was trying to get home before the day got worse.

It had been a fine morning. I had left Ingi in bed before the sun rose and eaten my bannock and ale standing. Then I put on thigh boots and put the oilskin over my arm.

There was sun and a blue sea when I got to the beach. The other fishermen were there too, busy around their boats. "First the haddocks," I said to myself, "then the lobsters as I come home in the afternoon."

The gulls encouraged us, white congregations drifting out in the firth, circling and dipping and crying.

I set a line and looked back at the valley. It was like a green open hand among the hills. The cliffs stood near and far, red, gray, black. In the valley chimneys began to smoke, one of them mine. Ingi was up. A green offering hand, our valley, corn-giver, fire-giver, water-giver, keeper of men and beasts. The other hand that fed us was this blue hand of the sea, which was treacherous, which had claws to it, which took more than ever it gave. Today it was peaceable enough. Blue hand and green hand lay together, like praying, in the summer dawn.

I drew in a score of haddocks, middling things.

I felt hungry after that, and had a few corn-beef sandwiches and a flask of milk.

Time for the lobsters.

I found myself drifting among three strange boats. They were Highland fishermen, from Sutherlandshire on the opposite shore of the firth. They shouted to me in Gaelic. I shook my head. One of them waved a bottle of whisky. "This will be a language that you will be understanding," he said in English. We drifted together. I took the bottle and had a dram. "Another," they said. Once more bottle and head tilted at their different angles and my throat burned. "Ah," said an old Highlandman, "but you Orkneymen are terrible ones for the strong drink. Tell me," he said, "are they still making whisky up among the Orkney hills?" "A few," I said, "but it's dangerous." "Ah, now," said the old man, "that is the real whisky, water of life, and could a man get that stuff to drink every day from the day of his weaning he would live forever." "I drank it once," I said, "and it nearly killed me." "People are made different," said the old man; "to me now it is like mother's milk."

"I wish, however," said a young red-headed man, "that you Orkneymen would stay more to your own side of the firth and not poach in our waters." "The sea is free," I said. "No," said another tall man, "but you take our fish." This last man who had spoken was drunk and I didn't care for the look of him, the black smoulder in his eyes when he spoke to me. "Just as," he went on, "in the old days you Orkneymen came to our place and took our sheep away and were a trouble to our women...." Then he said something in Gaelic which I took to be an insult. Some of the other fishermen laughed. The old man held up his hand and said, "That is an old story that should be forgotten. It is true enough, God made the sea for all men and he created all men to be brothers. There should be no more talk of sheep and women...." He offered the whisky bottle for the third time. "No" I said, "for I must be getting to the lobsters now." "You will drink," said the old man sharply, and I saw at once that I had offended his peace-offering. I drank a third mouthful. My body glowed like a banked-up fire. "You will get no lobsters this day," said the young red-headed fishermen, "for the storm. You will be the lucky one if you manage to save your creels at all." I looked round. The delicate egg-shell blue sky was grey as oysters, purple as mussels, and the sun slid through thickening clouds like a wan pearl. "May God bring us safely through this bad weather and all tempests whatever," said the old one, "each one to the safety of his own home." "Amen," spat out the tall vicious one. And at that moment the wind struck us.

All the boats turned for home.

I steered the *Susanna* through rising seas. I felt very brave on account of the Gaelic whisky. I might have been a bit frightened otherwise, for I had never been out in such seas.

I left the lobster creels under the crag and steered straight home. The lobster creels would have to wait until tomorrow, if there were any of them left at all.

The crags gathered round the *Susanna* like ghosts. She lurched and wallowed through the shallower waters. And there, through veils of rain and spindrift, I saw the beach and a solitary woman standing on it. The other boats were in a while ago. The shawled woman stood with the protective hills all round her. The valley offered her to me, Ingi, a figure still as stone. And the savage glad hand of the sea thrust me towards her.

*

Sheepay oatfield was the first to ripen. We went there with our scythes and we cut the oatfield in a day. The field was too steep for the reaper to operate. The women of Sheepay made a supper for us in the evening, as much ale and cheese and bannocks as we could eat. It was very hot in the valley that day. The men worked bare to the waist.

Then Hawkfall barley took the burnish. The field was steep also and right on the top of high crags. Gannets circled under the circling scythes. It was a rather thin crop but it was dark before the last of it was cut. "The old man of Hawkfall shouldn't have opened that bottle of rum in the middle of the morning," said Jeremiah of Whalerest, "and in the hot sun too. It slowed us up...." We had a sleepy supper of oatcakes and ale at Hawkfall.

The good weather held. The third morning the widow of Girss was at every door before daybreak screeching that her oats were ready. We cut her half-acre with the reaper before dinner-time. There was no drink at Girss, neither whisky nor ale, for she was a very religious woman. But she was generous with her bread and slices of mutton. We must have eaten half a sheep. And in the heat her buttermilk tasted better than any beer.

Still the rain kept off. Two-Waters's oats that had been green the day before echoed the sunlight next morning. Peter of Two-Waters, cap in hand, stood in my door. "We would be pleased," said the old man, "if you would help in our field." "Get the lobsters to help you," said I. "We're sorry for speaking to you as we did that day on the beach," he said, "we realize now that you didn't take our lobsters." "Keep your mouth shut," I said, "and maybe you'll get more harvesters...." I fished all that day alone. The other men turned up at Two-Waters, and after the field was cut they had a great night with fiddles and dancing till after midnight. I couldn't sleep for the noise of them. Ingi said she was sorry I hadn't gone to the Two-Waters oats. "We must repay hatred with kindness," she said. "Anna was very hurt."

I never saw such sorry-looking agriculture as the barley-field of Cleft, where we all gathered next morning—a few droopy golden beards like kings that had been long in exile. The field wasn't worth to cut. But we cut it. And Andrew of Cleft thanked us. He said if we were thirsty he had a barrel of sweet water at the end of his house. That was the meanest most miserable man in the world. He thanked us very much indeed for our trouble. He only wished he could reward us better, he said (and we all knew for a fact he had a thousand pounds, the legacy from his uncle in Australia, in the bank at Hamnavoe). We left his barley lying like a few slaughtered kings in the high field and we went home. His meanness didn't anger me so much as it might have done because I saw that it was my turn next. My oats had heaved at the sun like a great slow green wave all summer. Now the sun had blessed it. The whole field lay brazen and burnished under a blue sweep of sky. And the wind blessed it continually, sending long murmurs of fulfilment, whispers, secrets, through the thickly congregated stalks. "Your field tomorrow, Bill," they all said. I had laid in whisky. Ingi had been brewing and baking for a week (and now her ale for the first time was beginning to taste good). She had boiled eight cock chickens for the harvesters.

The sound of rain and wind woke me after midnight. I could hear the deep gurgle in the throat of the burn. "Just a shower," I said to Ingi who had woken also with the noise of rain on the window and the sough in the chimney.

But next morning when I went to the door at first light my cornfield was all squashed and tangled. And the rain still fell, flattening, rotting, burning, destroying. It would have been foolishness trying to cut such mush that day. All the harvesters went out in the storm to save their lobster creels. And the man of Malthouse said it was his turn next for the reaper, "because Bill," he said, "has missed his turn."

"It will be a fine day tomorrow," said Ingi.

The rain lasted a full week.

"The plain truth is," said Jeremiah of Whalerest, "You're an unlucky crofter. Some crofters are lucky and some are not. You're a good fisherman, Bill. Stick to the sea."

10

I spent the whole morning in the office behind Mr. Sinclair's general merchant shop in Osmundwall. We had been perhaps a little bit more cordial than the last time we met, but still it was the same as always with Mr. Sinclair and me, as if we were closed up together in a hut in the deep Arctic, with no fire in it.

"Well, Bill," he said, "if you just sign this paper I think that will be satisfactory to all concerned. I'm a lonely man since Mrs. Sinclair died and my chiefest worry now is the happiness of Ingi. You understand that."

He had proposed before harvest to lend me and Ingi two hundred and fifty pounds at four per cent interest, so that we could finally establish ourselves. In the first instance the loan was to buy more stock and new fishing gear (I had lost all but five of my creels in the October storm).

"Bill," said Mr. Sinclair, "before you sign that paper I want you to promise me two things. I want you to promise me, for the sake of Ingi, that you won't drink so much. Maybe a small dram on a Saturday night, there's no harm in that, and on a market day, and at New Year of course. And the second thing I want you to promise is this, that you'll go to the services on Sunday. Ingi was brought up in a religious home, and I can tell you this, it hurts her that she has to go to the meeting alone every Sabbath...."

I signed the agreement without bothering to answer him. My two particular saints are Robert Burns and Tom Paine. I was not buying two hundred and fifty pounds worth of hypocrisy.

"William," cried Mr. Sinclair sharply. His assistant hurried in from the shop. "Witness these signatures, William." William scratched with the pen at the foot of the paper, then went drooping back to the shop.

"I will deposit the money in Ingi's name in the bank at Hamnavoe," said Mr. Sinclair coldly. "In Ingi's name. Goodbye."

I cycled back to the valley, fifteen miles.

When I came between the hills I saw a young woman standing in the door of our house, as if she was keeping guard. It was Anna of Two-Waters, a thick strong ugly girl. Jessie of Topmast was at our peatstack, putting peats in her apron.

I leaned the bicycle against the telegraph pole beside the shop. John Wilson the shopkeeper was standing in his door. When he saw me he popped inside like a rabbit. I knew what it was—I was about to become a father, a tainted unlucky outcast until the christening was over.

I leapt across the burn and walked through the wet field towards the house. Across the valley I saw the widow of Girss, a gray shawl on her head. She was moving slowly towards our house.

Anna looked at me with her young freckled wondering face. "It's Ingi," she said. My heart failed and faltered and thudded frighteningly at my ribs. "The house is full of women," said Anna. "Her time has come. It isn't easy for her."

Just then Williamina of Moorfea came to the door, two empty pails in her hand. "Is she coming?" Williamina said impatiently to Anna. "Yes," said Anna, "I see her now." "I'm just going to the burn for water," said Williamina. Then she turned to me. "You go away," she said. "You're not needed here today. I think you've done enough."

The widow of Girss was in the next field now.

Jessie of Topmast came round from my peatstack, her apron full of peats. "Keep away from here," she said to me sharply. "You're not wanted." Her arms were red with attending to my fire.

By now the widow of Girss was at the corner of the house. Two other women came to the door from inside, Elsie of Calvary and Merrag of Sheepay. They received the midwife reverently and speechlessly, as if she was some kind of priestess. "You clear off," Elsie of Calvary whispered harshly at me. "Get down to your boat. Go somewhere out of here."

The widow of Girss gave me one cold look before she turned in at the door, followed by the other women except Williamina, who was hurrying across the field to the burn, her empty pails clattering.

Inside, Ingi cried out.

I turned away in a panic. First I made for the shore, thought better of it, and turned to the school-house and my old rationalist teacher Mr. Simpson. But the gentle murmur of multiplication tables drifted through the tall window and I knew that the school was still in session. I hurried up the hill to my sheep. Andrew of Cleft and John of Sheepay saw me coming and veered away from me, each in a different direction. So did the tinker who had been in the hill all month after rabbits.

I was an outcast in my own valley.

Finally the only man I could find to speak to me was Arthur in the ale-house. I remembered little of what he said—for an hour it seemed he reeled off the names of the women who to his knowledge had died in childbirth. But his whisky was a comfort. I stayed at the bar counter till it began to get dark. "It's a pity," said Arthur, "Ingi is not a strong woman."

The lamp was burning in our window when I crossed the field again. "To hell with them," I said, "It's my own house. I'm going in." I opened the door softly.

Only the high priestess was inside. The servers had all gone home. She turned to me from the bedside, a gentle sorrowful old woman in the lamplight, the widow of Girss. "Look," she said. Ingi lay asleep in the bed. A small slow pulse beat in her temple. Her damp hair sprawled all over the pillow; one thin bright strand clung to the corner of her fluttering mouth.

The old woman pointed to the wooden cradle that I had made in the seven rainy days of harvest.

"There's your son," said the widow of Girss.

11

Gales of lamentation I could have put up with from the women, as the terror went through them, the long ritual keening with which they glutted and purified the world from the stain of death. (My grandmother and her neighbours went on for three nights before a funeral, their cries simple and primitive and beautiful as the sea.) Now minister and elders had told them such exhibitions were unseemly and godless; the keening had gradually become in the past twenty years a kind of sickly unction, a litany of the dead person's virtues and sayings and doings—most of them lies—repeated over and over again, a welter of sentimental mush.

The black keening I could have endured.

Ingi lay in the bad, long and pale as a quenched candle. From time to time the child woke up in his cradle and gave a thin cry. Then Anna of Two-Waters would stir and attend to him, while the flat litany went on and on. As for me, I was more of an outcast than ever. None of them paid the slightest attention to me. Once Anna of Two-Waters said, "Do something. Go and feed the kye. You'll feel better."

On the third day the missionary came. He opened his Bible and the shallow grief of the women became formal, austere, beautiful.

> *Or ever the silver cord be loosed, or the golden bowl be broken, or the pitcher be broken at the fountain, or the wheel broken at the cistern. Then shall the dust return to earth as it was: and the spirit shall return unto God who gave it.*

We buried Ingi that day. Four of us lowered her into her grave—her father, Howie of Two-Waters, Mr. Simpson the teacher, myself.

The missionary stood at the graveside and murmured:

> *All flesh is grass, and the glory of flesh is as the flower thereof. The grass withereth, the flower fadeth, but the word of the Lord shall endure forever.*

Afterwards all the men returned from the kirkyard to the house. The women were still there, silent now. "Give the men whisky," I said to the widow of Girss, "and I'll take a cupful myself." There were two full bottles and a score of cups on the table.

Anna of Two-Waters sat at the fire with the child in her arms. Ever since Ingi's death Anna had fed him and washed him and comforted him. "Do you want to die as well?" she said to me. "You haven't eaten for four days. That whisky will finish you."

"She's in a happier place, poor Ingi," said Mr. Sinclair among the old women. "That's true," they cried in their different voices.

"She's in the earth," I said. "We've just done putting her there. The ground isn't a particularly happy place to be."

"She's by with all her troubles," said Merrag of Sheepay.

The mourners drank the whisky and one by one shook my hand silently and went off home. The missionary stood beside me, dispensing uneasy unction, but I wouldn't speak to him. Mr. Sinclair came over to me and said, "Peter of Two-Waters has spoken to me. As far as I'm concerned it'll be all right. Anna is a hardworking girl. You should think about it...." I didn't know what the man was talking about, "You'll get your money all right," I said. "Go away."

Anna of Two-Waters put a bowl of hot soup on the table in front of me. "Eat that," she said.

The house was getting emptier all the time, as one by one the women made off homeward, their death watch over. At last there were only three of us left, the missionary, Anna of Two-Waters, myself. I heard Mr. Sinclair's car coughing distantly among the Coolags.

"Mr. McVey, the Osmundwall minister, has agreed to christen the child on Wednesday next week," said the missionary.

"He needn't bother," I said. "I'm not having any nonsense of that kind."

Silently the missionary went away.

The child slept, and Anna of Two-Waters rocked the cradle on the stone floor. It was growing dark.

"My father has spoken to me," she said, "and so has Mr. Sinclair. Finish your soup now."

"What were they speaking to you about?" I said.

"Somebody must look after this bairn and this house," said Anna, "when you're fishing and ploughing. I don't like *you* at all, but I love this bairn of Ingi's. And so I'll do it."

"Go away," I said.

"Maybe I'll get used to you after a time," said Anna.

"Get away out of here, you ugly bitch," I shouted at her. I took the sleeping baby from the cradle and carried him outside. The first stars shone on him. I carried him down over the fields to the beach. We stood before a slow darkening heave of sea. A fleck of spindrift drifted on to his cheek. The wind had lain in the south-west since before his birth and Ingi's death. He slept on in my arms, with the bitter blessing of the sea on him.

"Be honest," I said. "Be against all darkness. Fight on the side of life. Be against ministers, lairds, shopkeepers. Be brave always."

When I got home Anna was lighting the lamp.

"Put the bairn back in his cradle," said Anna, "and then get to bed yourself. You haven't slept for nights. You're a fool."

She put on her shawl and moved towards the door.
"I'll be back in the morning," she said.

12

Anna came through the fields from the Christmas service in the school, carrying the shawled child in her arms. I met her at the burn.

"I do believe," said Anna, "you've let the fire go out! There's no smoke from the chimney."

A cold north wind streamed between the Coolags and the Ward over the valley. The stones rang like iron under our feet. Black bags of cloud bursting with snow sat heavily on the hills.

"Everything's settled," I said to Anna. "Peter your father has agreed to take over the croft from me. I'm going to concentrate on the fishing. I'll fish for both families, of course. I'm a lucky fisherman. We're to go on living in the house."

"Yes," said Anna, "I think that's the best plan."

The child was warm enough. His small face lay against Anna's shoulder with the eyes open and a faint flush on the cheeks.

There were times I could scarcely look into the shifting pool of his face; the skull stared back at me through a thousand trembling resemblances. But today he was a baby like any other baby, a small blind sack of hungers. He began to cry.

"He's tired," said Anna.

My twenty sheep moved on the hill above the house. In the new year they would belong to old Peter of Two-Waters.

We looked into the byre as we went past. It was warm with the breath of the five kneeling animals. I would have to feed them more hay and turnips before it got darker. The old cow looked round at us with shifting jaws, grave and wondering.

"God help any poor body," said Anna, "that has no home on a cold night like this. God help tinkers and all poor wandering folk."

"Yes," I said, "and don't forget the drunkard in the ditch."

The fire wasn't out after all. There was a deep glow in the heart of the peats. Anna broke the red core with the poker; flames flowered everywhere in the fireplace, and the room was suddenly alive with the rosy shifting dapple.

"It was a beautiful service," said Anna, "just lovely. All about Mary and Joseph and the baby and the shepherds and the three kings. I wish you had been there. Who would ever think such things could happen in a byre? Merrag of Sheepay had a new hat on her head. And peedie Tom was so good."

Before morning, I knew, the valley would be a white blank. And the sea would be flat with the first frost of winter. And, beyond The Kame, fathoms down, the shoals of cod would be moving, bronze soundless streaming legions.

I went out to the shed where I kept my fishing gear.

HAWKFALL

1

He was dead. The spirit of The Beloved One had gone on alone into the hall of death. His body was left to them for seven days yet so that they might give it a fitting farewell. Now it was time for it too to be sent after. The priests washed his old frail bluish body with water that had been drawn at sunrise. They arrayed him in his ceremonial vestments: the dyed woolen kirtle, the great grey cloak of wolfskin, the sealskin slippers. Across his breast they laid his whalebone bow, and seven arrows of larch. In his right hand they put the long oaken spear. The old mouth began to smile in its scant silken beard, perhaps because everything was being done well and according to the first writings.

Now it was time. All was ready.

A young man blew a horn on the hillside. The six bearers of the dead lifted the body and set out with it from the Temple of the Sun. They crossed between the two lochs, over a stone causeway. They walked solemnly, keeping step, towards the House of the Dead a mile away. Women walked alongside, wailing and lamenting, but in a ritual fashion, not as they would weep over the cruelty of a lover or the loss of a bronze ring. There were six women: a very old woman, a woman with the black mark of widowhood on her brow, a woman with the ripe belly and breasts of pregnancy, a woman with a red bride-mark on her cheek, a tall girl with new untapped breasts, and a small child of five or six years. They flung their arms about in anguish, they beat their heads and covered their faces with their hands, their shoulders convulsed in loud wails as they stumbled blindly behind the corpse. (But from time to time one looked shrewdly to see where she was putting her feet; and sometimes one wailed till she had to stop for breath, and then she would turn her head and smile to one or other of the chorus, before falling once more to her prescribed lamentation. The little girl uttered cries like a bird,

looking round from time to time at the other women and imi-
tating their gestures.)

The procession arrived at the House of the Dead. Boys were
waiting at the lee of the wall with unlit lamps at their feet. The
priests laid down their awesome burden. The women wailed
louder than ever. The old one knelt on the ground and shrieked;
she held her skinny arms out as if all the world's joy and love
had been reft from her.

A priest turned and rebuked these distracted ones. Foolish
women, he said sternly, to weep so, when you should know that
a great chief is going now into his nuptial joys, so that the light
may be reborn, with primrose and tern, seal and cornstalk, and
that you yourselves may be possessed with all abundance.

Meantime the boys kneeling at the lee of the House of the
Dead had been putting flint sparks to their lamps, and guarding
the small flames anxiously from the wind. And sometimes, so
bright the spring sun shone, it seemed their precious flames
were lost. But no: as they stooped in under the low lintel of the
House of the Dead, all five of them, one after the other, the
lamps glowed like opal in the gloom of the long corridor. So
they passed in to the central chamber, uttering an elegy in their
high or newly broken voices.

> *He is gone from us, The Brave Hunter*
> *He is gone from us, The Opener of Wells*
> *He is gone from us, Fosterer of the*
> *Children of the Sun (the kindly*
> *kindled fires, the lamp flames in*
> *winter)*
> *He is gone from us, our Shield*
> *He is gone from us, The Wise Counselor*
> *He is gone from us, The Corn Man....*

After them came the dead chief with one bearer in front and
one behind, for it was impossible for more than one person to
enter at a time. Very low they had to stoop, these grown men,
at the entrance of the House of the Dead. Almost on their knees
they had to proceed along the stone corridor; for death should
make men lowly and humble, and so they groped their way
forward like moles into the flaming heart of the howe.

The central chamber filled silently up with the priests of the sun. The boys stood against the dripping walls, holding their lamps high. The bearers of the dead reassembled. They lifted their king-priest in his litter. A huge square stone block had been levered out of the wall and lay on the floor. Inside the tomb they could see, shadowy and flickering, the bones of former rulers, a knuckle bone, ribs, a skull. Now they prepared this latest traveler for his journey. They laid on him brooches of silver and horn, agates, polished cairngorms, a bronze sword; beside his head a silver cup to refresh him if perhaps he should falter in the arms of his dark bride.

The loaded body passed into the aperture. The stone was lifted and set in the wall once more. One by one the priests of the sun knelt and kissed the stone, and passed out, stooping low for a score of paces, into the spring wind and the sun.

The boys followed with their lamps. Outside they extinguished them; but the sun was so bright that the flames were only small invisible quivers. The boys puffed their cheeks over them. A little smoke rose.

And there on the inside slope of the great fosse that circled the House of the Dead sat the six women, laughing at some lewd story that the old crone was telling. The big-bellied woman seemed to shake the earth with her thunderous mirth. Even the widow smiled. The child was on the far side of the fosse, stooping and rising, daisies spilling out through her fingers.

A priest rebuked them. "Foolish women," he said, "do you still not know that your king and your high priest is dead?..." The women turned away and drew their shawls over their faces, but the shoulders of the child-bearer continued to shake for a long time.

A thin cry shivered across the still waters of the loch. Many voices responded with a shout. In the Temple of the Sun a new priest-king had been chosen. At the very moment of entombment the power had fallen upon a chosen one.

The priests, the women, the boys walked slowly and silently, in procession as they had come, to the Temple beyond the two lochs. Soon they would know who the new father of the people was to be.

He stood in the heather, his upper body naked, alone in the

still center of the huge monoliths: a young man, scarcely more than a boy, a virgin: on him the choice had fallen, his name the voice of the gods had uttered. "This is the man," proclaimed the caucus of ancient priests who alone could interpret the unutterable will of the gods. And, the choice having now been made, these old ones fussed around here and there, issuing orders to priests and acolytes and people, anxious that everything should be done in accordance with the ancient writings.

The young man with his bright body stands in the center of the Temple.

He will never again kiss a country girl in the dark of the moon. He must bear now all his days the burden of perpetual virginity so that all else might be fruitful in field, in loch, in the great sea, in the marriage beds. In him the sorrows and triumphs of the tribe will be enacted ritually, and through his mouth the ancient wisdom interpreted; until at last, after very many years, the sun becomes a burden to him and he fares gladly to the House of the Dead and to the dark bride.

A priest kneels before him, puts into his hand a flint knife.

The ceremonies of initiation and consecration will last for a whole week. These rites are solemn, ancient, intricate, and of an almost impossible delicacy (for let a word be spoken wrong, or a gesture obscure the sun, or a foot step withershin, and much misfortune may stem from the flaw).

A young boar is dragged squealing across the heather to the Father of the People. Four priests manhandle the gnashing squealing slithering outraged beast. They up-end it in front of the Father of the People. Gravely, nervously, compassionately he bends over and pushes the flint knife into the boar's gullet. Blood spurts over his arms and shoulders. The boar twists about, staggers to its feet, looks about it very bewildered, runs a few steps this way and that way, stops, stumbles, slowly keels over on its side, hind legs faintly kicking. The priest-king holds cupped hands under the terrible throat wound. The people crowd about as he stands and scatters the sacrificial blood among them.

Now an ox is sacrificed. It is a quiet patient beast. It thrashes and goes limp under the knife. Blood is showered to the four quarters of the sun, and falls among the people. Happy the man who has a single red spot on his coat.

The arms and shoulders and breast of the Beloved of the Sun are smeared and daubed as if a tattered scarlet shirt had been thrown over him.

A hooded falcon is carried through the heather on a priest's fist; and is unhooded; and glares once, fiercely, at the celebrant; and flares out and flutters under the knife and is still. And again a small scattering of the life-giving essence.

For the animals bless us with their blood: whom the sun and moon and stars love, and who love those brightnesses in return, but who cannot articulate blessing, the innocent ones; they bless the wintry hearts of men with passionless perpetual steams of sacrifice.

That same day, near a village on the west coast of the island, the men prepared for the first fishing of the year. Two by two the fishermen stood beside their boats among the sheltering rocks. Then with a cry and a heave they swung the inverted boat up over their heads, and turned, an immense purposeful four-footed insect, across the broad sand to the edge of the water; and with a cry and a heave were again two fishermen and a floating curragh.

Next they brought down to the sea their stack of crab-pots. With concentration, a dark intentness, they stowed them on board. The stone brine-prisons in the Skara Brae houses were almost empty of limpets and dulse and whelks and mussels, but today they were after more succulent fish, the crab and the haddock. Creel by creel was handed from shore to boat.

In one of the Skara Brae houses an old mouth, so very dry and whiskered and shrunken that the young ones forgot sometimes whether it belonged to a man or a woman, began to mutter over the ashes, "The Beautiful One is dead." It soughed out the same words, over and over again. Once it said, "His mouth was a delight to my mouth." Then, over and over again, like the creaking of ash when a fire is dying, "The Beautiful One, the Beautiful One, he is dead."

A young woman came to the sea-bank and called to the busy fishermen, "The chief has died between the two lochs. Old Mara, she has seen it."

The fishermen paid no attention to her. It was a good day for fishing: a pewter sea and a gray sky. The crabs had put on their new hard coats. They would have issued from their crannies and ledges to see what polyps and algae they could prey upon. And they would certainly not despise the bait that men offered them.

The fishermen worked on.

Three women came and stood on the low sea-bank that protected the village. A fierce elderly woman cried to the fishermen, "Does a man work the day his father dies? The Father of the People is dead. He who feeds us is dead, the Provider. Do you want a darkness to fall on us?"

Two of the curraghs were afloat. The men in them hesitated and were half turning back to the sand. A young man with a curiously flattened nose spoke across the water. "Pay no attention to the women. What if some old man or other is dead? We have been making creels all winter for this day." He handed the oars to his companion in the boat and leapt aboard. Half-a-dozen groups were still stowing creels aboard. The first three curraghs drifted slowly into the west.

2

A boat scraped on the stones of the steep green island. Two young men leapt from the bow and dragged the boat clear of the water. A man with a hawk on his fist stepped from the slippery stones to the sand. He was a tall dark ugly man, with a hook nose and a sharp grey eye. The falconer followed him on to the island. The dark man flung the hawk from him. It would not go; it fluttered and flared and swung on his hand, rooted there, a fierce flaring of wings. The falconer stooped to it, whispered, offered it his hand, sang. The bird hopped gently from one fist to the other. Then the dark man walked up the beach, leapt over the low sea bank, and ran across a field to a carved stone doorway. He entered the Hall boisterously.

In the church a stone-throw away the clergy and the boys were trying out their voices at a new setting of a penitential psalm:

Miserere mei, Deus, secundum
magnam misericordiam tuam

*Et secundum multitudinem
miserationum tuarum dele iniquitatem meam*

A cantor was trying to make a proper contrast of voices, a better interweaving of treble with bass and tenor. "Try once again," said the offended clerical voice. "Once more now."

Miserere mei, Deus,...

The dark man's feet thudded over the wooden floor of the Hall. The fire in the central hearth was almost out, charred logs with one yellow flame gulping among them. The man stopped and clapped his hands. A boy came running from the women's quarters beyond. "Blow up the fire," said the man. "It's February, not June. Bring in more logs. Start a flame with some broken peats."

"Yes, lord," said the boy, and lifted a large straw basket from the hearth.

He was a rather ugly boy; he seemed to have no proper nose-bridge, so that his nostrils flared out over his cheeks; also his face was a constellation of freckles; but in spite of these defects everyone in the Hall found him attractive, and the women especially were inclined to spoil him.

"Lord," he said now, pleadingly, "please give me leave to go to the burn after dinner. There is an otter in the burn. I have sharpened a long stick."

"Tomorrow," said the man. "Today there are more important things to do."

The boy pouted a little. He turned and carried the basket in front of him to the fuel-hoard outside.

At the far end of the long Hall a woman sat at a loom. She was still beautiful though her hair was streaked with gray and there were wrinkles about her eyes and mouth. Around her sat three girls. One was on a low stool. The two on the floor had their feet tucked demurely under their skirts. The three girls were sewing. They drew coloured woolen threads through one long undulation of linen. Truncated pictures appeared on the linen—the wing of a raven, the leg of a soldier, the stern of a ship.

The men who had hauled the boat ashore entered, carrying

93

dead birds and hares, and passed through into the kitchen, a hound flowing and lolloping among their legs.

The dark man approached the women round the loom. He strode across the tapestry. One of the girls cried "O" and put her hands to her mouth as the deerskin shoes, soiled with sand and mud and seaweed, brushed against the linen. The man bent over the woman at the loom. She tilted her face towards him. "Ingibiorg," he said. He kissed her once on the mouth (still red and beautiful, though with wrinkles and unwanted hairs about the corners now). He touched her coiled bronze braided hair gently. Then he passed out of the chamber into the dark corridor beyond.

The boy came staggering back into the Hall with logs and peat in the basket. He dumped it down beside the hearth. The girls called out to him to take care.

The dark man took off his hunting jacket in his room. He took off his hat with the swan's feather in it. He took off his red woolen shirt. He kicked off his shoes. He went to the door and clapped his hands. He loosed the thong at his waist and slid his skin trousers off and threw them on the heap of clothes on the bed. He turned. A silent figure stood in the door with a garment over his arm. The naked man went down on his knees and stretched out his arms for the penitential sackcloth to be put on him.

"Mis-er-er-e," said the ill-natured voice from the choir of the church. "You are not exactly at a feast when you sing that. You are not in a dance-hall or a tavern. Not exactly. You are souls in torment. You are standing in holy fire. Pray that it may be the cleansing fire of Purgatory and not that other unquenchable brimstone. Now once again—and remember your sins and be sorry for them while you sing it—Mis-er-er-e."

The bass voices made utterance, dark with sorrow.

The man in sackcloth followed the summoner across the field to the church. The walls still had skirtings of snow, under the blue cold sweep of sky. Revay Hill had a white worn cap. Bare feet followed bare feet across the grass and into the gloom of the church. The penitent knelt beside a pillar and, shaking with cold, tried to remember his sins. The killing of his nephew Rognvald in the seaweed in Papa Stronsay. The burning of Rognvald's men earlier that same night. The holocaust of the King of Norway's men the next morning, a heap of reeking corpses on the shore of Kirkwall. He tried to imagine these things, the sword in the guts—a lingering bitter death that; the fire climbing from belly to chest to beard, bones crackling and marrow bubbling and the man still not dead, unless he had mercifully choked on a lump of smoke; the axe in the skull between one word and another. He tried to imagine the sins he had committed, and to be sorry for them, but he could think of nothing except the spasms of cold that were going through is body.

Meantime the Mass had begun. *"Introibo ad altare Dei,"* sang the Bishop in his fine Latin that he had learned to pronounce in the colleges of Paris.

"Ad Deum qui laetificat juventutem meam," responded the choristers in the coarser Latin of the north.

Kyrie eleison. Christe eleison. Kyrie eleison. Backward and forward the voices shuttled, weaving the unseen garment of penitence, weaving the sackcloth.

There was silence. The penitent looked up. An acolyte was bringing to the Bishop the bason of ashes. The boy knelt before the altar, delivered the ashes, knelt again, retired. The penitent swung his head round the church slowly. Ingibiorg, his wife, was kneeling behind him, but in the clothes that she had worn at the loom; only her hair was covered with a grey cloth. Three grey-kerchiefed girls knelt beside her. The falconer and the young men were there in their hunting clothes, their feathered caps on the stone floor beside their knees. Erlend his second son knelt over by the statue of Saint Olaf. The cook was there, carrying his ladle as though it would take a blessing from being in church and pour out better broth and stew. He did not see the boy who looked after the fires in the Hall. The stewart was there. The men from the fishing boat had brought their nets. The ploughmen and the cattlemen and the shepherds and the keeper of the pigsty were there, and their women. All those cheeks were gaunt in the taper light, as if sorrow had indeed hollowed out their faces. He alone wore the sackcloth for them all.

De profundis clamavi, Domine. A bass voice rose up, imploring, out of woeful pits of shame. *Domine, exaudi orationem meam,* sang the tenors. The phrases were a little brighter, as if hope were a possibility—it was there, somewhere, surely—it was not entirely extinguished. At least sorrow was something—

the people of Orkney had this day put off the many-coloured coat of vanity.

But had they? Thirfinn Sigurdson, Earl of Orkney, Shetland, Caithness, Sutherland, Ross, the Hebrides, Man, Lord of the Western Sea, could not concentrate on anything because of the great qualms that shook his body. Springs of coldness rose from his knees where they touched the stone floor and passed up through his loins and his belly and his chest and his face. His clasped hands shook. He tried to concentrate on his sins. Unfaithfulness to the Lady Ingibiorg on three occasions this past winter, with one of the handmaidens (the innocent-looking one) and with Sven the ploughman's eldest daughter and with the Gaelic girl in Caithness—O God, he could not even think of the girl's name or her appearance because of the cold gules that were chilling the sinuses of his forehead and obliterating his ears and fingers.

Sacerdotes tui induantur iustitiam: et sancti exultent, sang the farm boys, their pure high blessed notes rising to the roof.

And I did not go to Mass at Christmas midnight, because I had drunk too much honeyed ale. And I accuse myself of the constant sin of pride. And while many of my people eat limpets and roots I never fail to stuff my belly with roasts of pork and trout from the grill and Irish wines. And I... But he existed within the heart of an iceberg.

Benigne fac, Domine, in bona voluntate tua Sion: ut aedificentur muri Jerusalem, sang the redeemed voices, base and treble and tenor part of a single whole, interwoven, reconciled, a fitting Lenten garment to offer to the Lord.

In the following silence the worshippers heard, borne into the church on the uncertain east wind, very faintly, the cry of a transfixed otter.

The Bishop descended from the altar, carrying the bason. He paused before the Earl. The Bishop dipped his thumb in the ashes. He marked a gray cross on the forehead of the Earl. *Memento, homo, quia pulvis es, et in pulverem reverteris....*

All the people bowed their heads, waiting for the ashes of humiliation to be written on their brows.

3

The principal clerk at the Palace of Birsay, Jonathan Fraser, a Scotsman, sat at a table in the library on the morning of June the tenth and wrote, as every morning, the diary of Patrick Stewart his master as far as he had observed the Earl's business, pastimes, conversation, bodily health, etcetera, on the previous day, the ninth of June. The clerk wrote with a quill upon parchment, dipping the point frequently in a stone bowl of ink, elaborating the capital letters with fine intricate flourishes, and cursing sometimes under his breath when the ink failed in the middle of a well-conceited phrase, or if the quill required the penknife.

The 9th day of June in the year of the Lord 1593

His lordship rose too late for divine service. *I am concerned, yet not concerned, touching the state into which religion has fallen,* he said to me breaking his fast with white bread and a capon limb and a small beaker of goat's milk. *They are up and down like a seesaw, Presbyter and Bishop, sermon and sacrament, black gown and white gown. The cursing that they put one on another! (Yet all holds: I observe not one blasted with perdition. I think, Master Fraser, these preaching men are not necessary unto us. What are their prayings but puffs of air? Yet Kirk serveth to hold the people in awe. Therefore I say I am concerned and not concerned. Make an apology to Canon Fulzie that I did not attend his Matins this morning.*

His lordship received at noon Master Simon Buttquoy his factor and they sat an hour and more over the estate books, going as it were with a comb through every farm and cot and the rental each paid. And, *By God,* said his lordship, *this is a mouse's yield that they make. How can they be well governed and protected, yea, and cherished, when this is all that the estate receives from these Orkneymen? It is not before time that we are come hither into the north. There will be here a new ordering of things, Master Buttquoy.*

At half past two in the afternoon, his lordship having sat down to a light repast of hare-broth and crab and barley bread with a bowl of Spanish wine, and last a gobbet of white cheese, ordered the horses saddled and the hounds leashed. There was much merriment round the table. Master Abercrombie described how he had gotten lost in deep snow in the parish of Orphir in the previous winter, going about some business of the estate, so that he saw small prospect of reaching either Birsay or Kirkwall before nightfall. He called therefore at a cottage on the side of a hill. The man of the house gave him buttermilk and oatmeal for refreshment. Alack, said the crofter, there are two beds, I and my old Margit Ann sleep in the one, and the bairn in the other. Would you pass the night with our lass, sir? ...But Master Abercrombie, not choosing (as he said) to have his night broken with a child's bawlings and shittings, assured the man he would be comfortable enough in the deep straw chair before the hearth, with a blanket about his knees. And so the night passed, somewhat sleepless. Then morning came, and the family assembled to break their fast. First came to the table the man of the house, and then Margit Ann his spouse (an ugly enough old beldame) and then "the bairn," who was a lass of sixteen years, with new-formed breasts and hair like a torrent of sunshine, and all the meal-time she looked slyly and shyly and yearningly at Master Abercrombie, the red and the white roses coming and going upon her cheeks....

His lordship had great mirth from that tale.

When the table was a scatter of crusts and cheese parings and empty goblets, they rose and went out to the stable yard where the horses were pawing the cobbles, and the hounds tautening the leashes.

This afternoon was brought under guard to the Palace Adam Thorfinnson, a farmer in the parish of Saint Michael, to be interrogated, and was taken downstairs.

And somewhat later came Monsieur Bouchet, an architect, who was set at a fire in the great hall and given wine to wash away somewhat the stour of travel.

His lordship and retinue of coursers returned in the early evening, Nelly the mare's flanks burgeoning with hares. They passed round a cup of wine in the courtyard. I told his lordship that M. Bouchet the French architect was resting in the Angel Chamber, having ridden from Hamnavoe that morning, whither he had arrived in a ship out of Leith.

Earl and architect sat together in the Angel Chamber for a long time over M. Bouchet's drawings. *Your red sandstone, it is beautiful,* said M. Bouchet. *It is like fire that does not go out. It is like roses that do not fade. It is like blood that does not drain away into the earth. Truly this palace that I will build for you in Kirkwall will be a rose of exquisite beauty. Here, observe it well, is the great hall where the tapestries will flow and tremble in the wind. Here are the windows that look out on the world passing; they will be like the eyes of gods, all-seeing and inscrutable. Now look at this great fireplace. Up above I have made blowers, little circular turrets, where the ladies may sit and sew, and write letters, and read their romances. When I devised these bowers, however, I thought in especial of candle light and secret kisses, and after an hour or thereby, of darkness. Now I call your attention to the doorways....*

So he went on, his mouth oozing with foreign honey, for an hour and more, while his lordship listened and observed with veiled intent eyes.

Finally, said M. Bouchet, *you will observe that I have placed this most gracious and beautiful building, the like of which has never been seen before in Scotland, in close proximity to the cathedral church of Saint Magnus. So men will observe with admiration, how the huge and heavy superstition of the dark centuries gave way at last to such beauty as only the free renascent human spirit can exult in. This opus will be like Venus risen from an April sea.*

In the corridor the bronze boomed for dinner.

His lordship said nothing for full five minutes. Then he searched about in the pouch of his breeches and silently put two gold sovereigns in M. Bouchet's palm. There would be no trouble about labourers, he assured M. Bouchet. He would impress men from fields and ships if necessary. Stone-masons would be brought from Edinburgh and Fife. Could M. Bouchet recommend a good master mason? He trusted that M. Bouchet would return now and then—as often as his many commissions allowed—to see his work in progress. It gave him joy, he assured M. Bouchet, simply to look at the drawings on the parchment. The proportions seemed to him to be good, very fine, exquisite.

I have done worse work, I am content, said M. Bouchet. He was standing over by the window, this little cock-sparrow of a man, looking out into the bright evening courtyard. *This building,* said he, *where we find ourselves now, this Earl's Palace in Birsay, it is the work of a barbarian. I could spew.*

His lordship took M. Bouchet by the arm and led him gently through the door and so on towards the great hall. (If his lordship has reverence for any men, it is for artists and musicians.)

No, cried M. Bouchet at sight of the diners at the long table, *I cannot eat unless I wash first in warm water.* This astonished his lordship, who occasionally dips his fingers in cold water, and splashes his face at most but once a week. Dinner therefore grew cold while water was drawn and heated and carried up to the lavatorium. When at last M. Bouchet came down again, his face shone like a peach.

His arrogance at the table was to me (a close observer of human quirks and foibles) a joy to watch.

He conceded that the fish soup had some flavour. He sipped the claret and spat it out again. *No,* said he, *this roasted pork is too tough, it is like a tight wad of string.* Mistress Coubister, who has charge of the kitchens, stood in the shadows and made strangling motions with her hands.

There were present at the table (besides his lordship and M. Bouchet) Canon Fulzie, Master Malachi Lorimer the sheriff, Simon Buttquoy, Mistress Marjorie Colquhoun, Mistress Jane Wylie, and myself. I think none spoke except this small-faced architect. And his lordship, who would have broken such impudence and arrogance with some salutary obscene barbed witticism on other occasions, listened as meek as a dove to the creature, the only begetter of his future palace in Kirkwall.

Simon Buttquoy begged to be excused; he had to preside over an interrogation in the cellar.

Nor did M. Bouchet care for the lobster and cheese sauce.

He cupped his hand over the buttock of the girl that carried in the cheese.

Over by the fire, when viol and lute began to play, M. Bouchet covered his ears.

Carrying my writing materials, I followed Master Buttquoy down to the cellar.

In the cellar the interrogation of Adam Thorfinnson, farmer in Garth in the parish of Saint Michael, commenced. Two years since, Earl Patrick Stewart was put in possession of ancient deeds and titles in which it was plainly set out that the Earl's predecessors had had sole ownership of the lands of Garth in Saint Michael parish. He had therefore required, in all civility, the said Adam to make due acknowledgement of his (Adam's) ancestors' usurpation of the said lands. This usurpation had occurred in that difficult time when there was no clear distinction between Norse and Scottish in the islands and two diverse laws, languages, codes, contended one with another in extricable confusion; which ravelment was intensified by the Norse use of the patronymic; according to which, for instance, Adam's father was called Throfinn Paulson, his grandfather Paul Swanson, his great-grandfather Sweyn Janson, and so on back to an original called William Otter, or Flatnose, who, vehemently claimed the said Adam, was gifted these lands of Garth in perpetuity by his master, a Norwegian earl called Thorfinn Sigurdson. This claim had no written documentation but was, claimed Earl Patrick, rooted in fable; and it is likely, said his lordship, that this Earl Thorfinn, if he existed at all, fought against dragons and had his helmet hammered by mountain trolls and took an ice maiden to wife.

Now that the dove of peace was fallen and furled in the north, the Earl required Adam to quit the said lands of Garth at the season of Martinmas. Of his charity the

Earl would not press for past payment of rent, an onerous sum indeed if a century's unpaid rent were to be computed, together with interest on the same. And the Earl further offered the said Adam the tenancy of the farm of Lang Klett in the same parish, which farm to some degree had reverted to bog and heather with long unoccupancy, but a young man of Adam Thorfinnson's vigour (argued the factor) could speedily restore these acres to their former yoke and yield.

The Earl had required Adam Thorfinnson, eighteen months since, to put his mark to a document drawn up by Master Lorimer the sheriff and myself, acknowledging the undoubted rights of the Earl in this matter, but Adam Thorfinnson had up to the present steadfastly refused.

The said Adam had therefore been removed under duress from the farm and lands he occupied unlawfully to the Palace of the said Earl Patrick Stewart in Birsay, in order that one only question be put to him, namely, did he propose to yield Garth to its rightful owner Patrick Stewart; the interrogator to be Master Simon Buttquoy, factor to the said Patrick Stewart.

Adam Thorfinnson answered, *No.*

Thereupon Adam Thorfinnson was shown the iron boot, the wedges, the hammer; the Earl's men made a great clattering on the stones with these instruments.

Adam again answered, *No*— he had the lands from his father and his father's father before him.

The iron boot was thereupon put on the right leg of Adam of Garth, and it reached to his knee. A wooden wedge was inserted between bone and metal. A naked-shouldered man stood by with a raised mallet.

Answer, said Simon Buttquoy.

No, said Adam Thorfinnson.

Strike, said Simon Buttquoy.

The wedge took the full weight of the hammer. Adam Thorfinnson's face was silvered with a sweat.

Answer, said Simon Buttquoy.

I call upon God to witness, said Adam Thorfinnson, *that I have worked these acres well and enriched them yearly with manure and seaweed. I have opened two wells about the place, and a quarry. With my own hands last summer I built a barn. I have greatly enriched the place.*

Strike, said Simon Buttquoy.

The hammer fell and the iron rang and a bone cracked.

I have a son that is to come after me, said Adam Thorfinnson. *I would not have him inherit the wilderness and wetness of Lang Klett.*

His head was fallen on his breast.

I had not seen this Adam Thorfinnson previously. He had the usual appearance of the peasantry, thick shoulders and red cheeks, and in addition his nose was squashed somewhat as if he had been kicked by a horse or perhaps had it broken in a tavern brawl—this gave to his face a hard obdurate cast.

Now two guardsmen held him by the shoulders.

You are young, said Simon Buttquoy. *You are strong. It is well known that you are a good and a provident farmer. In six years the Lang Klett will be as rich a place as any to be seen in the west part of Orkney. There is a burn. You could quarry big stones. All that district stands in sore need of a mill.*

No, said Adam Thorfinnson.

Strike, said Simon Buttquoy. The hammer fell. The iron rang. Adam Thorfinnson swooned in his chair. A guardsman wound his hands through Adam Thorfinnson's hair and jerked his head back. Another dashed water into Adam Thorfinnson's face. Adam Thorfinnson looked around as if he had but newly arrived among us. He half smiled. Then his whole body was deluged with pain and he groaned for the first time. Simon Buttquoy went over to the chair where he was held. Simon Buttquoy looked close at him with much seriousness and a shaking of his head. *Adam, Adam,* he said, *what possesses you? What in the name of God ails you? A cripple man will not be able to plough the Lang Klett. A man with one leg shorter by six inches than the other will make poor twisted cuttings with his scythe. The parish children run after men like that and mock them. In the name of God, all Earl Patrick asks*

ding. Not only in the nuptial bed." He winked at the laird. "Fornication rampant under the stars.... Molly, I am coming now."

An upper window flushed with the rousing of a fire in the hearth.

The minister mounted his mare, throwing his leg with a certain formal abandonment. He waved his hat twice towards the door of the Hall, where the laird stood with a hand raised. The mare, urged on, plodded forward through the soft now.

The laird went in and closed the door. He returned thoughtfully to the flickering library. He put the glass stopper in the decanter. He stirred the fire with the brass poker. He wandered over to the book-clad wall. He fingered a volume here and there, pursing his lips, dropping on one knee occasionally to examine a title near the floor. He withdrew a tall calf volume and opened it at random.

Thou hast seen the falcon adrift between two clouds, how it seemeth on a sudden to check and to hang motionless in the pure upper stream, and keepeth a high lonely speculation there awhile; anon it seemeth to stumble on a steep blue step of sky, and falleth free; no, rather it hurleth itself downward, earth-true, and maketh a brief check again above the tranced prey; then its claw reacheth down to make an immaculate consummation; and the earth is hallowed again with red lustral drops.

A gray cat cried thinly at his knee; he rubbed the furry throat with his knuckles till the cat was all one breathing purr. The window darkened. Snowflakes fell on the panes like gray silent moths, and clung there for a moment, and became black quick beads. The laird rose to his feet and closed the heavy curtains. He returned to the bookshelves. He drew out a volume of poems and opened it idly.

> My banks they are furnished with bees
> Whose murmur invites one to sleep;
> My grottos are shaded with trees,
> And my hills are white-over with sheep.
> I seldom have met with a loss,

Such health do my fountains bestow;
My fountains all border'd with moss,
Where the harebells and violets grow.

His lips moved occasionally, relishing the words. He brought the book over to his chair beside the fire. He arranged the candelabrum on the table so that the brightest waverings of light moved over his chair. He sat down and lifted the book and turned a page. The cat crouched in the hearth; its hind leg stuck straight out, and burrowed violently in its belly for a flea. Then it sat up and blinked and leapt on to the laird's knee and sought for first the hard calf edge of the book and then a dreaming knuckle. It purred occasionally. It padded the velvet lap with its velvet feet and found a place at last and curled up and closed its eyes. The long sensitive fingers turned a page.

But where does my Phyllida stray?
And where are her grots and her bowers?
Are the groves and the valleys as gay
And the shepherds as gentle as ours?
The groves may perhaps be as fair,
And the face of the valleys as fine;
The swains may in manners compare,
But their love is not equal to mine.

The fiddler was almost exhausted. Apart from the long bridal procession to the manse and back he had kept the dance going for five hours and more in the barn of Eldquoy. Around ten o'clock the music began to falter. The groomsman brought him a glass of whisky and the ale-keg. The dance stopped. Then the music resumed, with all its old energy but with a mistake here and there—rents in that coarse-spun sark of song.

It was all too energetic for the older guests. They had retired to the benches along the wall.

The night was cold for kissing under the stars, but there was a constant coming and going of the younger guests through the barn door. A girl would come in with snowflakes clinging to her hair. "Where has thu been?" some old man would ask her, then turn and wink at the other old men. Then her cheeks would flush more than ever, and the old men would wheeze and clap their knees with their hands and wipe tears from the corners of their eyes. And a minute later the girl's partner would come in from the chaste kisses of the snow and turn from her as if she was nothing to him; and seek the circling whisky jug.

Another young man would seize a girl by the wrist in the middle of a reel and pull her towards the door. The girl would look anxiously to see if her father was noticing. He was not— he was seated over by the wall, smoking his clay pipe and gossiping behind a whirl and a shriek of dancers—but her sister who carried round a tray of sliced mutton had turned round and was eyeing every move. She plucked her hand from the hand of her partner, very offended, and joined some elderly women at the north end of the barn whose days of dancing and love were over.

The fiddler raised his bow high in the air. He needed more refreshment.

The bride and bridegroom sat in a corner of the barn in some kind of secret painful consultation. The girl was upset. Her mouth trembled. Her new husband bent forward and murmured consolingly to her. She waved away the chicken and the bannock; no, she couldn't eat. She pressed the lace handkerchief to her hot cheeks. The dance had such fury and impetus in it now that only the bridesmaid, who came to tell her she must mix the most important drink of the evening, the Bride Cog, noticed her distress. The bridesmaid hastened to tell the host, who was arranging the whisky, the honey, the ale, the Jamaican sugar, the rum, about the varnished well-turned wooden vessel. Somberly the bride's father eased his way through the dancers till he reached the bride. He bent down and spoke earnestly to the girl, occasionally turning for confirmation to the bridegroom. It was no use; the bride would not be comforted; her eyes were brilliant with new tears. The mother and the youngest sister came, easing their way past the knees of the seated whispering nodding old ones. The mother took the bride's hand and sat down beside her. This made things worse than ever; the bride bent her head into her hands and her fingers were wet with tears; a few drops shone over her knuckles on to the floor.

Nothing of this little drama could be heard for the noise of the dance. Once more the fiddler had faltered, and the whisky bottle had been passed to him. The music resumed, a jig, but

hardly recognizable on account of the waywardness of the performance. "My God, what's he trying to do, strangle a cat?" said the
beadle to the blacksmith. The young ones, men and girls, threw
up their arms and circled each other.

The mute mime in the corner of the barn had been observed
by a very old woman seated near the door, alone. She was so
old and so incapacitated with rheumatism that she had to be
excused every task, such as carrying round portions of chicken
and keeping the mouths of the men wet. Everyone paid her
deference as they passed, half in awe and half in raillery. An old
man, hurrying past her after the circling ale vessel, would stop
and say a few laughing words to her. She would smile and shake
her head and say nothing. Now she noticed the sorrow of the
bride, and the cajolery and threatening and pleading all about
her. She rose. She balanced her twisted body on a long stick.
She shuffled and hobbled along the wall. Half-drunk dancers
dragged their partners out of the way of this painful progress.
The bridegroom made way for her beside the bride; taking the
old one's elbow gently and easing her down on to the bench. At
once she sent them all away: bridegroom, host, hostess, sisters,
aunt. They were raveling up a very simple situation—leave the
girl to her. They went without question; they mingled with
the wedding guests. The bride and the old woman sat alone in
the corner.

Because of the stamping of feet and the laughter and the rant
of the fiddle nobody knew what words passed between the old
woman and the girl. But the girl listened with growing absorp-
tion to what she heard now; as if she tasted, sip by quickening
sip, the mellowness that many winters bestow on the chalice
that must be drunk by all women born. The withered hand
touched, in turn, the young mouth and the breast and the thigh.
Presently the bride smiled. She turned and kissed the grey sag-
ging cheek. The old woman put her hand, last, to the bride's
belly, and nodded decisively. Thus indeed it must be.

The music had stopped once more, finally this time it seemed,
for the fiddle had fallen on the floor with one wild despairing
shriek and the fiddler was making his way unsteadily among the
stone jars of ale. It was midnight. He had saturated the entire
parish with music. He could give them nothing more. He had

emptied himself utterly. The groomsman set him down against the wall and put a mug of ale between his hands.

A couple came out of the night, shyly, lightly clung about with snowflakes.

The bride stood at the main table, smiling, and mixed the Bride Cog. She emptied the whisky bottle and the rum bottle into the vessel, then a reluctant golden flood of honey, then a jar of Jamaican sugar like old soft snow. From the farm kitchen two men carried in a pot of scalding hot ale.

The host tasted the liquor, and nodded.

Bridegroom and bride carried the vessel first to the sibyl in the corner. She frowned into the rich rising fumes.

Then mouth after mouth tasted the blessing as it went round sunwise, until everyone had drunk; they even touched the liquor to the mouth of a child who lay half asleep in his mother's arms.

Three young men urged Walter Flett the weaver into the fiddler's chair. They sat him down and put the fiddle into his hands. A girl urged him with a kiss on the cheek. Walter raised the bow. He could dispense only a thin sour music. But by now they were past caring for excellence. The strings shrieked and keened. The feet beat on the floor once more. A wild cry rose to the roof beams.

In the middle of this dance there came two slow loud knocks at the door. The host crossed over and lifted the sneck. Andrew the servant from the Hall stood there. He had a lantern in his fist. He squeezed the snow out of his beard. "It's time," he said. "The master's waiting."

No, he wouldn't come in. No, he wouldn't take a dram. The master was ready now. They must hurry.

A new cloak was put over the bride's shoulders. Her hair was pushed under a new finely-knitted lace shawl. The two sisters fussed round her. The mother murmured encouragement and consolation into her ear. Nobody moved in the barn; it was as if the appearance of Andrew had turned them all to stone. The bride's eyes sought out the bridegroom, but he had passed from the barn into the house as soon as the summons came. The old woman nodded: a slow resigned sorrowful fall of the head: this must be. The father, muffled hurriedly in a grey cloak and a grey bonnet, touched the bride on the elbow. Andrew and the host and the bride passed out into the snow. The groomsman shut the door. The barn broke out again with its babble of a hundred tongues. Walter Flett put the fiddle under his chin. The true fiddler slept against the wall. The barn swooned and lamented and, slowly but with gathering impetus, began to turn.

The bridegroom stood alone at the cold kitchen window of Eldquoy. He saw the three small dark figures moving up the ridge towards the Hall. They dwindled in the snow. At last all that he could see was the frail flicker of the lantern.

But his mind, as he stands with his face against the pane, is possessed with another image. He sees himself on the moor one day next summer. He has his gun over his shoulder. He is after grouse and hares. A horseman breaks the skyline, urging his horse through the heather, going in the direction of the village. It is the young laird. They are alone, those two, in the world. Horse and horseman come nearer. The hunter waits. The handsome laird is now within the radius of death. The tenant with the flat ugly nose, Thomas Langclett, turns to face him. He raised his gun to his shoulder....

It would never happen that way. If he did find himself in such a situation, alone with the ravisher of his bride, he knew he would never shoot. Instead he would take off his cap and mutter a polite greeting; perhaps, if the laird lingered to speak (for he was otherwise an agreeable gentleman) he would thank him humbly for allowing him to shoot over his lands again that year.

The mind of the bridegroom throbbed with a bitter impotent rage.

No, but what he would truly like to do would be to shoot the minister in his own kirkyard.

An upper window of the Hall flushed with the firelight and the candles inside.

5

Mr. Humphrey Langclett murmured and smiled farewell in the town square to Mr. John F. Norton the draper, Mr. Thord Swann the ironmonger, and Captain Aram. It was a beautiful morning in June. The sun poured up the steep seaward closes of Hamnavoe and barred the main street with alternate brilliance and shadow. Draper and ironmonger and retired skipper smiled and raised their sticks in farewell to Mr. Langclett, and moved on northwards along the street.

Those four walked, every morning whatever the weather, winter and summer, as far as the boatyard and back, discussing national politics and the affairs of the town and sometimes, with smiles and tolerant head-shakings, some intriguing titbit of local gossip.

Mrs. Andrina Holm was standing at the window of the jeweler's shop, gray head under gray shawl humbled to the town fathers going past.

Mr. Langclett, before he inserted the key into the main shop door, saw that the parlour curtains upstairs were drawn against the sun. The breakfast dishes were washed now, obviously, and the cat and the canary fed.

Today, at dinner-time, Harriet would have to be told. He had promised. It would not be an easy announcement to make by any means.

The shop had a glass paneled inner door. When Mr. Langclett depressed the latch and pushed, the little bell on top gave out a bright *ping*. There was a dark fragrant delicious smell inside the shop, compounded of apples, cloves, liquorice, coffee, treacle, tobacco, and the other items of merchandise that Mr. Langclett sold. Mr. Langclett tugged at the blind-cord in the window. The sun came dazzling in. A bluebottle throbbed and bounced in the large pane; another lay inert between the bowl of oranges and the jar of brandy-balls.

The eye of a stuffed hawk glittered from the counter.

Mr. Langclett removed his jacket and hung it on a hook. It was quite warm in the shop. Upstairs now there was a rumble, a small shrieking of castors, a thud, muted measured flutters. Harriet was making the beds. His daughter's domestic routine never varied from day to day.

The shop door pinged.

Mr. Langclett, bent over the open account book on the desk, was aware of a hovering doleful presence. He turned with a sigh; it was of course Mrs. Brewton. She stood at the counter with her shopping bag. He noticed that she had no purse in her hand. Mrs. Brewton said, sadly, that it was a beautiful morning but that she expected they would pay for it with some bad weather later on. Two pounds of sugar, please. A jar of raspberry jam. A tin of salmon (what on earth was a fisherman's family wanting with tinned salmon?) Twenty woodbines. A packet of cream crackers.... She thought that was all. O no, a bar of milk chocolate for Linda. Linda had a bit of a cough. She had kept Linda from school till tomorrow at least. Linda was kind of delicate, the poor bairn.

And she would pay before closing time. Sando would be back from the lobsters by then.

"There's five pounds odds against you in the book, you know," said Mr. Langclett after a pause, glancing towards the ledger on the desk.

"I know, I know," said Mrs. Brewton. She took a woodbine out of its packet. "I told Sando about it." She had matches in her apron; she rattled the box. "Sando says he'll settle as soon as ever he's in from the sea." She scratched the match into flame.

"Well, I hope so," said Mr. Langclett in a tone of mild reproach.

Mrs. Brewton's cheeks hollowed and her bosom heaved. Her mouth emitted a hank of blue-gray smoke. She began to cough. The smoke shredded out. She put her free fist to her mouth. Coughing, Mrs. Brewton sought the door, and coughing still crossed the street towards the steep sunlit close where, in squalor and contentment, the Brewtons lived.

Mr. Langclett had heard more than once about this week-end settling-up, which sometimes took place and sometimes not; it depended on whether and to what extent Brewton was on the booze.

There was a sound of subdued voices upstairs. Harriet was having a morning visitor. That was unusual. Very few visitors came to the Langcletts'; it was a discreet withdrawn household. The muted exchange of voices went on—the quiet murmurs of Harriet mingling with elegiac plaints and queries. Mr. Langclett realized with a start that no other voice in Hamnavoe resembled that voice—the visitor could only be Andrina Holm. What on earth did Harriet and Andrina Holm have to say to one another? Andrina Holm had not been near his premises for a year—in

fact since the day he had rebuked her for slandering Captain
Aram. She had said in his shop before other customers that Captain Aram took his rum bottle into the kirkyard and sat on the
kerb of his young wife's grave and got drunk there—so-and-so
and so-and-so and so-and-so had seen the performance—who
ever heard the like?—what a disgrace.... Mr. Langclett knew
these talebearers to the bone. They hawked slander and gossip
about the doors under the pretext of being the old wise kindly
ones, and that Andrina Holm was the wickedest gossip of all.

Upstairs the dialogue went on.

The thought of what he himself must say to Harriet at din-
nertime brought a dew of sweat to his upper lip. He had promised to do it. This was the day. When he and Martha met at the
cemetery gate for their Thursday afternoon walk along the sea-
banks, he would tell her that he had kept his promise: he had
broken the news to Harriet, everything was now settled. *Ping.*
He paused. He smiled. His breath fluttered with pleasure when
he thought of Martha and himself walking between the cornfields and the sea, under the great blue sweep of sky.

A tall stranger, buoyantly and happily smiling, was offering
him a bill cross the counter. If he would be so kind as to put
this notice in his window. A beautiful Irish brogue. Mr. Langclett
took his reading spectacles out of his waistcoat pocket, shook
out the horn legs, and poised, glintingly, the frame over his
ramshackle nose. The stranger held his head a little to one side,
quizzically. EVANGELICAL MEETING / *There will be an
Evangelical Meeting in the Temperance Hall every night next
week, from Sabbath on, beginning (D.V.) at 8 p.m.* / *Speaker,
Mr. Albert Murphy, the noted Ulster evangelist.* / *All are welcome.*

"I'm sorry, I never put bills in my window," said Mr. Langclett,
handing the sheet back to Mr. Albert Murphy. The evangelist's
face lost its dimples, though it remained serene. He tilted his
head even more, as if estimating Mr. Langclett's worth in the
scale of spirituality.

"Not even for the Lord's sake?" he asked.

Mr. Langclett shook his head. "I've told you," he said.

"I see," said the evangelist. He was smiling again, all forgiveness. "God bless you."

Mr. Langclett watched the tall dark figure, smiling and touching his dark hat to Mrs. Thomasina Smith and Wilma Freyd who were slowly circling about each other on the pavement, clasping their shopping bags, gossiping—one face shocked, the other dimpled with pleasure—and saw him stooping under the lintel of Webster the tailor's shop, smiling, and tightly clasping the notice that Mr. Langclett had rejected, going out of the light into a cave of cloth and shadows.

Don't hold with that sort of thing, extremes, all that sickly smiling too, like a tin of syrup lying with the lid loose, as if they and they alone basked in the divine favour. Such arrogance. "For the Lord's sake." The Lord was well enough served in this town, three kirks—no, four, counting the Piskies—forby the Pentecostals and the Brethren and the Salvation Army.

Upstairs in the parlour the dialogue was still going on, with Harriet's contributions punctuating only briefly the mournful sing-song of Andrina Holm. Mr. Langclett tilted his head. He listened. He could not distinguish one word; he had an uncanny feeling, as if he was a ghost just out of hearing of the chorus of the living. *Ping.* Poor Emily entered the shop, bearing a copy of *The Orcadian.* Harriet would have nothing to complain of. He would see to that. She would have a roof over her head. She would of course never get married now—with men she was either shrill or silent—she was thirty-two—the first fadings and moth-marks of spinsterhood were on her. Emily—pink face and almond-shaped eyes—proferred, wordlessly, the newspaper.

"Well, Emily," said Mr. Langclett, "Thursday again is, it? Is this my *Orcadian?* That's a good girl, Emily. And how is mother, fine, eh?"

Emily, in a light hollow voice, said yes, that her mama was fine, and Silver had had four kittens in the coal-shed last night, and the water-closet was choked and there was a stink but a man was coming to see it.

Mr. Langclett laid a penny and a halfpenny on the counter, in payment of *The Orcadian.* (Emily brought him his copy every Thursday morning from the newsagent's.) He took down a sweet jar from the middle shelf, unscrewed the lid, groped inside with his forefinger to slacken the coagulated mass, and laid three "jelly babies" on the counter.

Emily put a long yellow gum into her mouth, mindlessly. She
was the girl from next door. Mrs. McCorbey had been very hurt
when the medical officer, last month, had described Emily as a
mongol. But a mongol she undoubtedly is, thought Mr. Langclett,
noting again the almond eyes, pink and white skin, bulbous
jowls, broad nose, tongue lolling in the mouth.

"Thank you, Emily," he said kindly.

Emily picked up the remaining two sweets in her chunky
fingers and left the shop. She stood outside in the street for a
moment, slatting her eyes against the sun, and bent to stroke
Spot, the ironmonger's collie pup, dancing and barking happily
round her. Mr. Langclett, once more unfolding his spectacles,
saw that Andrina Holm had left the house and was stationed at
the mouth of the close opposite, looking left and right along the
street.

Mr. Langclett's eye glided over the solid block of advertisements on the front page of *The Orcadian,* then he opened the
paper and spread it flat out on the counter. HARBOUR BOARD
FINANCES. DISASTROUS FARM FIRE IN NORDAY. HAM-
NAVOE COUNCILLOR RESIGNS. He reserved the serious reports for his after-dinner cup of tea. One column in the center
page he always read first: *Births, Marriages, Deaths, In Memoriam.* His eye leapt down the rung of names—Adamson,
Buchan, Dennis, Eason, Farquhar, Isbister, Learmonth, Langclett.
What Langclett would that be? He read.

In loving memory of Cecilia Langclett (née Graham), wife
of Humphrey Langclett, general grocer, Hamnavoe, and
dear mother of Harriet, who passed to her rest 9th June,
1920

A year has passed since the sad day
When that dear one was called away.
Here we can only sit and sigh,
Hoping some day to meet her again on high.

Mr. Langclett stood behind the counter as though he had been
struck on the face. Cissie's death. This was terrible. He had clean
forgotten that today—yes, the ninth—was the first anniversary.
After a long illness borne with Christian patience. He saw again
the waxen face on the pillow. He saw the first strewment of clay

on the coffin. Harriet had never once mentioned the anniversary to him. Harriet had inserted the announcement without consulting him. *Ping.* The newspaper creaked in his hand.

"Well, Humphrey, there must be something very interesting in the paper today."

He had not even heard William Corston come in. His mouth was cold with shock. When he spoke, the words came bleak and wintry.

"Nothing much," he said. "Deaths. I see that Tim Isbister has died in New Zealand. You won't mind him. He was in my brother James's class at school. In Wellington, New Zealand."

"Before my time," said William Corston. There was a pause. "Humphrey, it's more than my tobacco I've come for." He cleared his throat and consulted, briefly, his silver watch. William Corston had a proposal of some delicacy to put to Mr. Langclett— that much was obvious. "I suppose you might just have an idea what I mean." Mr. Langclett began to shake his head slowly. "Humphrey, this town will be none the worse of your services."

William Corston's right hand, shyly seeking Mr. Langclett's on the counter, depressed with the thumb the knuckle of the forefinger. Mr. Langclett's cold mouth relaxed in a small swift private smile. William Corston was a far more earnest freemason than himself: all these signs were a mysterious potent language to him; without that communication, as far as William Corston was concerned, the pillars of the world would collapse—all would revert to superstition and popery and the beasts of the night.

"You're wasting your time," said Mr. Langclett.

"Think about it, man," said William Corston gravely. "You would be a welcome face at the table."

"I'm sorry," said Mr. Langclett.

"You more than anybody," said William Corston. "I said to the Provost after Monday night's meeting, 'Well (said I) there's Coubister resigned, and the only man in Hamnavoe to fill his place is Humphrey Langclett. But (I said) I doubt he'll refuse, as usual.' . . . 'We can but try,' said the Provost. . . . So that, in short, is why I'm here, Humphrey."

"No," said Mr. Langclett.

"A long family tradition of municipal service," said William Corston. "Archibald Langclett, your grandfather, provost of the

town. Your father a bailie. Wasn't there a Langclett in the first
Council of all, in 1817?"

"Thomas Langclett," said Mr. Langclett. "He was the eldest
son of the miller of Lang Klett. He came to Hamnavoe and
founded this business in 1809."

They stood silent for a moment, reverencing the dust of the
generations.

"I'm sorry to disoblige you, William," said Mr. Langclett at
last. "But I don't like that sort of thing. All that wrangling, bitterness. And folk knocking at your door at all hours, wanting you
to do this and that for them. I just have no talent for it." More
solemnly he said, "It's not good for business either, I can tell
you that."

William Corston considered these arguments, then shook his
head at Mr. Langclett in friendly displeasure.

"You know this, Humphrey," he said, "we're going to hound
you. Every election time, every time there's a vacancy, we're
going to be after you. You're going to get no peace at all."

"I have plenty on my plate as it is," said Mr. Langclett. *Ping.*
"Museum Committee, Lifeboat Committee, Liberal Party. The
Lodge. The Bowling Club."

A thick-set man shambled into the shop, bearing between his
fingers a dark disc. He came and stood right between Mr.
Langclett and William Corston; he put a barley breath all over
the shop. "I found this when I was digging the garden," he
muttered. "The boys in the pub, they told me to bring it here.
Sando Brewton said, *Humphrey Langclett is the man to show
it to.*"

(Mr. Langclett was one of the leading antiquarians and nat-
uralists in the town. People brought to him the flint arrowheads,
the fossils, the foreign coins that are hidden in every nook and
corner of Orkney.)

"Now then," said William Corston sharply, "Mr. Langclett
and I happen to be discussing important business."

Mr. Langclett accepted the coin. He breathed on it. He pulled
a handkerchief from his pocket and rubbed the metal vigorously.
He opened the counter drawer and brought out a magnifying
glass. He squinnied through the glittering convex, turning the
coin over and over, this way and that.

"You mustn't come bothering Mr. Langclett with every bit of rubbish you dig up," said William Corston to Robert Jansen.

Robert Jansen shuffled his feet and hung his head.

"A James the Sixth shilling," said Mr. Langclett at last. "That's what it is. *Rex Scotorum*. And the lion on the other side." He offered the lens and the coin to William Corston. "Have a look, William."

William Corston glanced into the curve; a gravured lion was startlingly enlarged.

A reverence for history, for the dead magnificent dust that had lorded it over the humbler dust of their fathers, held them in a deeper silence. The coin passed between them like a sacred object.

"Now Robert," said Mr. Langclett, "that was an interesting thing you found. It isn't *very* valuable. I mean it wouldn't fetch much on the market, maybe a pound or thirty shillings. Now what I'm thinking is this. If you go back to the pub some of them will try and get it off you for a pint. Or you might easily lose it. The best thing, Robert, would be for you to present it to the town museum. The Museum Committee would be very pleased. They would send you a letter of thanks. I'm sure we don't have a James the Sixth shilling in our coin case. Now what about that, eh?"

Robert Jansen's blunt fingers received back the small heraldic round. He muttered that he would have to think about it. Obviously the men in the pub had told the poor simple creature that this find had made him the wealthiest man in Hamnavoe.

"Mr. Langclett will see that it is placed in the town museum for you," said William Corston. "Just leave it with him, man."

But Robert Jansen, still muttering, passed out into the sunlight. He turned this way and that on the cobbles, uncertain now whether to go back to *The Arctic Whaler,* or bear his treasure to the safety of his house, or perhaps indeed after all return it into the wise keeping of Mr. Langclett.

Andrina Holm had crossed the street and was standing now at the very threshold of the shop, shielding her brow against the steady silent torrent of noon light. Once she turned and squinnied in through the glass panel of the door: old-ivory face, soft shadowy whiskered mouth, blue eye-stones in warped leather purses.

"What way can Jansen afford to drink?" said William Corston. "He's on poor relief. I can't think why the health people don't do something about him. They say his room's in a filthy state."

"That was interesting," said Mr. Langclett. "The house Robert lives in, it's one of the oldest houses in the town, you now. A coat-of-arms over the door, a worn inscription on a sandstone shield. You can just make out a date, 1596, I think."

"An ounce of the usual mixture anyhow," said William Corston. "Then I must be getting back."

"Think of it," said Mr. Langclett. "A Stewart walking in his Hamnavoe garden on a summer evening after his dinner. Some illegitimate son of that Earl Patrick Stewart in Birsay, Black Pat. He would have been a near cousin too, of course, of the King of Scotland. Well, then, there he walks, with one of his fancy-women. He takes out his lace handkerchief to wipe the claret and the ox-fat from his mouth. A coin falls out. A small tinkle among the stones—he never hears it. Three hundred and thirty years later his house is a slum. The rose garden is a tattie patch. Robert Jansen turns up the coin with his spade."

"Humphrey," said William Corston, "you should have been a writer of romances."

Mr. Langclett smiled. He loved the relics of history: those small objects that have fallen intact between the great millstones of necessity and chance.

William Corston laid his tobacco pouch on the counter. "They'll be wondering in the office where on earth I've got to," he said.

Mr. Langclett, opening the tobacco jar, glanced through the window. His heart gave two erratic thumps—a lift—a swoon—a lingering delicious flutter. Was it? Yes, it was she. Alone, primly, a woman was descending the steep close opposite. She carried her shopping bag in front of her. She had lifted, becomingly, her skirt above her ankles, the better to negotiate one of the short flights of steps that led down from her house to the street and the shops. Miss Martha Swift was going as always on a Thursday to get her messages before closing time. Mr. Langclett flushed with pleasure. Where would she go first? She reached the street and turned left. Sorenson the butcher's. Old Sorenson—poor blind soul that he was—would serve her in the light of common day. *Obliged, Miss Swift. Your change now. Thank you so much.* That such a one should care for Humphrey Langclett. The woman smiled at some person coming towards her along the street. *Ping.* She lingered, her lips moved. She passed, elegant and perfect, out of the window frame.

Mr. Langclett's hands held, enchanted, the stone tobacco jar.

"And a box of matches," said William Corston. He laid a considered row of coins on the counter.

That such a dear person should ever conceivably care for an aging ugly graceless man like himself. It was as if fragrance and dew should enter into a stone kirkyard rose, and that the wind should shake it, and that it should bleed with overspill of petals.

A faded voice broke the spell: "A quarter pound of tea, if you please." A fumble, a sigh, a shuffle. It was Andrina Holm. "I saw a certain person on the street this minute. I had to laugh. Tip-tipping along. Too grand to speak to the likes of me, of course. The grand-niece of Governor Swift of Hudson's Bay, if you please. That same madame, she had a fine carry-on with the marines in the war-time. Officers only, though. Nothing under a lieutenant ever crossed her threshold. They usually stayed to their breakfast."

"I am serving Bailie Corston at the moment," said Mr. Langclett.

The soft ancient mouth went on. "I've just been speaking to your Harriet, Mr. Langclett. She's a gem of a girl, that. I never saw such a shining well-kept house. You're a lucky man to have a daughter like Harriet. Ceylon tea. One thing Harriet can't abide, in any shape or form, and that's loose behaviour, especially in folk that are of an age to know better."

"I do not stock Ceylon tea," said Mr. Langclett.

"A loyal girl she is too," said Andrina Holm. "Loyal as the day, to her home and her family and to them that are no longer here." Utterance of dark evil wisdom. Crepitation of the dust of gravestones.

"You are not welcome in this shop,' said Mr. Langclett. "I told you that some time ago."

"Harriet will be a lamp to your age," said Andrina Holm, turning away. "When your time comes she will close your eyes. I can buy my tea somewhere else."

The glass panes clashed and rattled upon her departure.

"I swear to God," said William Corston, "I can't bide that old creature. She puts the grues on me."

Mr. Langclett's hand trembled as he emptied rather more than an ounce of Virginia mixture out of the aluminium scoop into William Corston's tobacco pouch.

William Corston drew the silver watch from his waistcoat pocket and looked at it. "Five to one," he said. He laid his hand on Mr. Langclett's and said very earnestly, "Humphrey, do what your best instincts tell you to do."

From above came a rattle of plates, and the smaller music of knives and forks and spoons being laid on the table.

William Corston passed out into the street. There he raised a hand to Thomas Webster the tailor who was putting the wooden shutters on his shop window.

The street was total brightness now. The noontide sun poured northwards through the street, a full silent golden flood. In the afternoon the shadows of tall houses would begin slowly to encroach again from the west, and by evening this heart of Hamnavoe would be a deep cool ravine.

High on the side of the hill the school bell rang.

Mr. Langclett's eye fell bleakly on the *In Memoriam* column in the newspaper. All Hamnavoe would have read that awful piece of piety before nightfall. He could imagine the mockery at the foot of this close, at the head of that pier, in house-doors all along the street: *What an old hypocrite, Humphrey Langclett!* Of course all the town knew, and had known for a long time. Harriet, Andrina Holm, John F. Norton, Thord Swann, Captain Aram, William Corston, Robert Jansen, Mrs. Brewton, even poor Emily: they all knew about him and Martha. It must be all of three months since the first farmer's wife had seen the two of them walking westward above the shore and next morning had told the story at the van door. A strange thing—you always act as if it is a honeyed secret between the two of you. How foolish he had been, to think otherwise.

A desolating image came into his mind: :Martha sitting in her kitchen at Holm View, within the next half-hour, waiting for the potatoes to boil. She opens *The Orcadian*. She reads the *In Memoriam* column, the death warrant of their love.

Harriet had contrived things with admirable skill. To make doubly sure, she had enlisted the services of Andrina Holm.

His community had condemned him through the mouth of that old hag.

It *was* shameful, the more he thought about it. Drinking rum in the kirkyard, kissing in the kirkyard. Death is swallowed up in lust. He understood the impiety of the living and the rebuke of the silent dead. *Dear Cissie, I am truly sorry. The dream will pass. Not a word will I say to my daughter today. I will be what I was meant to be, a sober respectful widowed businessman, a lonely walker in the sun and the snow for a year or two. Then I will come and lie down beside you at last in the faithful dust.*

There came two loud thumps on the ceiling. It was the signal that dinner was ready. On Thurdsay it was always Irish stew, followed by custard and prunes, and finally a cup of tea.

Yelling chattering cooing bands of school children appeared and disappeared across the open door, eddying homeward. One small face drifted and hung in the glass of the shop window, above the apples and the brandy-balls, in a wide-eyed impossible dream of sweetness, then drifted away again.

Shop girls began to flow in both directions along the street. It was early closing day in Hamnavoe. This fine afternoon the beaches and the golf course would be well attended, and every plot of ground would have its elderly gardener. He himself, at a quarter past two, was due to put on his tweed jacket and his dark blue tie, and take his silver-handled walking-stick out of the rack in the lobby, for another meeting among the tombs.

Not today. He could not do it. Perhaps never again. The stones, love and death, that whirl upon one another at the center of every man's life, were slowing down for Mr. Langclett. Soon they would stop. He knew now that there would be no grains of his to nourish the future. No innocent beautiful mouth would eat at the table between Martha and himself. His generation must perish from the land.

Between father and daughter a lasting silence would be kept.

Mr. Langclett stood at the shop door with his key in his hand. The burning flagstones were possessed, extravagantly, by a solitary figure. Sando Brewton had emerged from *The Arctic Whaler*. A bottle was stuck awry in his jacket pocket. He stood for half-a-minute swaying on the cobbles. Then, blind and blundering, he set a course for home.

Mr. Langclett returned into the shop. He drew the blind down the droning window; the shop was all gloom and fragrance once more. The stuffed hawk was lost in the shadows.

The heart is bruised in that thunder and contention of stones. They would stop soon. Then he would have peace.

The door between the house and the shop opened. Harriet, dressed all in black, stood in the glimmering rectangle. She said nothing. She stood and looked at him. She had come to summon him, wordlessly, to his stew and prunes.

Stone upon fruitless stone laid.

"Harriet," said Mr. Langclett, "I have something to say to you."

THE DROWNED ROSE

There was a sudden fragrance, freshness, coldness in the room. I looked up from my book. A young woman in a red dress had come in, breathless, eager, ready for laughter. The summer twilight of the far north was just beginning; it was late in the evening, after ten o'clock. The girl peered at me where I sat in the shadowy window-seat. "You're not Johnny," she said, more than a bit disappointed.

"No," I said, "that isn't my name."

She was certainly a very beautiful girl, with her abundant black hair and hazel eyes and small sweet sensuous mouth. Who was she—the merchant's daughter from across the road, perhaps? A girl from one of the farms? She was a bit too old to be one of my future pupils.

"Has he been here?" she cried. "Has he been and gone again? The villain. He promised to wait for me. We're going up the hill to watch the sunset." Again the flash of laughter in her eyes.

"I'm sorry," I said, "I'm a stranger. I only arrived this afternoon. But I assure you nobody has called here this evening."

"Well now, and just who are you?" she said. "And what are you doing here?"

"My name is William Reynolds," I said. "I'm the new schoolmaster."

She gave me a look of the most utter sweet astonishment. "The new—!" She shook her head. "I'm most terribly confused," she said. "I really am. The queerest things are happening."

"Sit down and tell me about it," I said. For I liked the girl immensely. Blast that Johnny whoever-he-is, I thought; some fellows have all the luck. Here, I knew at once, was one of the few young women it was a joy to be with. I wished she would stay for supper. My mouth began to frame the invitation.

"He'll have gone to the hill without me," she said. "I'll wring his neck. The sun'll be down in ten minutes. I'd better hurry."

She was gone as suddenly as she had come. The fragrance
went with her. I discovered, a bit to my surprise, that I was
shivering, even though it was a mild night and there was a decent
fire burning in the grate.

"Goodnight," I called after her.

No answer came back.

Blast that Johnny. I wouldn't mind stumbling to the top of a
hill, breathless, with a rare creature like her, on such a beautiful
night, I thought. I returned regretfully to my book. It was still
light enough to read when I got to the end of the chapter. I
looked out of the window at the russet-and-primrose sky. Two
figures were silhouetted against the sunset on a rising crest of
the hill. They stood there hand in hand. I was filled with happiness and envy.

I went to bed before midnight, in order to be fresh for my
first morning in the new school.

I had grown utterly sick and tired of teaching mathematics
in the junior secondary school in the city; trying to insert loga-
rithms and trigonometry into the heads of louts whose only wish,
like mine, was to be rid of the institution for ever. I read an
advertisement in the educational journal for a male teacher—
"required urgently"—for a one-teacher island school in the north.
There was only a month of the summer term to go. I sent in my
application at once, and was appointed without even having to
endure an interview. Two days later I was in an aeroplane flying
over the snow-scarred highlands of Scotland. The mountains
gave way to moors and firths. Then I looked down at the sea
stretching away to a huge horizon; a dark swirling tide-race; an
island neatly ruled into tilth and pasture. Other islands tilted
towards us. The plane settled lightly on a runway set in a dark
moor. An hour later I boarded another smaller plane, and after
ten merry minutes flying level with kittiwakes and cormorants
I was shaking hands with the island representative of the education committee. This was the local minister. I liked the Reverend Donald Barr at once. He was, like myself, a young bachelor,
but he gave me a passable tea of ham-and-eggs at the manse
before driving me to the school. We talked easily and well together all the time. "They're like every other community in the

world," he said, "the islanders of Quoylay. They're good and bad
and middling—mostly middling. There's not one really evil person in the whole island. If there's a saint I haven't met him yet.
One and all, they're enormously hospitable in their farms—they'll
share with you everything they have. The kids—they're a delight, shy and gentle and biddable. You've made a good move,
mister, coming here, if the loneliness doesn't kill you. Sometimes
it gets me down, especially on a Sunday morning when I find
myself preaching to half-a-dozen unmoved faces. They were very
religious once, now they're reverting to paganism as fast as they
can. The minister is more or less a nonentity, a useless appen-
dage. Changed days, my boy. We used to wield great power, we
ministers. We were second only to the laird, and the schoolmaster got ten pounds a year. Your remote predecessor ate the
scraps from my predecessor's table. Changed days, right enough.
Enjoy yourself, Bill. I know you will, for a year or two anyway."

By this time the manse car had brought me home with my
luggage, and we were seated at either side of a newly lighted
fire in the school-house parlour. Donald Barr went away to prepare his sermon. I picked a novel at random from the bookcase,
and had read maybe a half-dozen pages when I had my first
visitor, the girl with the abundant black hair and laughter-lighted
face; the loved one; the slightly bewildered one; the looker into
sunsets.

The pupils descended on the playground, and swirled round
like a swarm of birds, just before nine o'clock next morning.
There were twenty children in the island school, ranging in age
from five to twelve. So, they had to be arranged in different
sections in the single large classroom. The four youngest were
learning to read from the new phonetic script. Half-a-dozen or
so of the eldest pupils would be going after the summer holidays
to the senior secondary school in Kirkwall; they were making a
start on French and geometry. In between, and simultaneously,
the others worked away at history, geography, reading, drawing,
sums. I found the variety a bit bewildering, that first day.

Still, I enjoyed it. Everything that the minister had said about
the island children was true. The impudence and indifference
that the city children offered you in exchange for your labours,

the common currency of my previous classrooms, these were absent here. Instead, they looked at me and everything I did with a round-eyed wonderment. I expected that this would not last beyond the first weekend. Only once, in the middle of the afternoon, was there any kind of ruffling of the bright surface. With the six oldest ones I was going through a geometry theorem on the blackboard. A tall boy stood up. "Please, sir," he said, "that's not the way Miss McKillop taught us to do it."

The classroom had been murmurous as a beehive. Now there was silence, as if a spell had been laid on the school.

"Please sir, on Thursday afternoons Miss McKillop gave us nature study." This from a ten-year-old girl with hair like a bronze bell. She stood up and blurted it out, bravely and a little resentfully.

"And what exactly did this nature study consist of?" I said.

"Please, sir," said a boy whose head was like a hayrick and whose face was a galaxy of freckles, "we would go to the beach for shells, and sometimes, please, sir, to the marsh for wild flowers."

"Miss McKillop took us all," said another boy. "Please sir."

Miss McKillop...Miss McKillop...Miss McKillop...The name scattered softly through the school as if a rose had shed its petals. Indeed last night's fragrance seemed to be everywhere in the classroom. A dozen mouths uttered the name. They looked at me, but they looked at me as if somebody else was sitting at the high desk beside the blackboard.

"I see," I said. "Nature study on Thursday afternoons. I don't see anything against it, except that I'm a great duffer when it comes to flowers and birds and such-like. Still, I'm sure none of us will be any the worse of a stroll through the fields on a Thursday afternoon. But this Thursday, you see, I'm new here, I'm feeling my way, and I'm pretty ignorant of what should be, so I think for today we'd just better carry on the way we're doing."

The spell was broken. The fragrance was withdrawn.

They returned to their phonetics and history and geometry. Their heads bent obediently once more over books and jotters. I lifted the pointer, and noticed that my fist was blue with cold.

And the mouth of the boy who had first mentioned the name of Miss McKillop trembled, in the heart of that warm summer afternoon, as he gave me the proof of the theorem.

"Thank God for that," said Donald Barr. He brought a chessboard and a box of chessmen from the cupboard. He blew a spurt of dust from them. "We'd have grown to hate each other after a fortnight, trying to warm each other up with politics and island gossip." He arranged the pieces on the board. "I'm very glad also that you're only a middling player, same as me. We can spend our evenings in an amiable silence."

We were very indifferent players indeed. None of our games took longer than an hour to play. No victory came about through strategy, skill, or foresight. All without exception that first evening were lost by some incredible blunder (followed by muted cursings and the despairing fall of a fist on the table).

"You're right," I said after the fourth game, "silence is the true test of friendship."

We had won two games each. We decided to drink a jar of ale and smoke our pipes before playing the decider. Donald Barr made his own beer, a nutty potent brew that crept through your veins and overcame you after ten minutes or so with a drowsy contentment. We smoked and supped mostly in silence; yet fine companionable thoughts moved through our minds and were occasionally uttered.

"I am very pleased so far," I said after a time, "with this island and the people in it. The children are truly a delight. Mrs. Sinclair who makes the school dinner has a nice touch with stew. There is also the young woman who visited me briefly last night. She was looking for somebody else, unfortunately. I hope *she* comes often."

"What young woman?" said the minister drowsily.

"She didn't say her name," I said. "She's uncommonly good-looking, what the teenagers in my last school would call a rare chick."

"Describe this paragon," said Donald Barr.

I am no great shakes at describing things, especially beautiful young women. But I did my best, between puffs at my pipe. The mass of black hair. The wide hazel eyes. The red restless laughing mouth. "It was," I said, "as if she had come straight into the house out of a rose garden. She asked for Johnny."

Something had happened to the Rev. Donald Barr. My words seemed to wash the drowsiness from his face; he was like a sleeper on summer hills overcome with rain. He sat up in his chair and looked at me. He was really agitated. He knocked the ember of tobacco out of his pipe. He took a deep gulp of ale from his mug. Then he walked to the window and looked out at the thickening light. The clock on the mantelshelf ticked on beyond eleven o'clock.

"And so," I said, "may she come back often to the schoolhouse, if it's only to look for this Johnny."

From Donald Barr, no answer. Silence is a test of friendship but I wanted very much to learn the name of my visitor; or rather I was seeking for a confirmation.

Donald Barr said, "A ghost is the soul of a dead person who is earth-bound. That is, it is so much attached to the things of this world that it is unwilling to let go of them. It cannot believe it is dead. It cannot accept for one moment that its body has been gathered back into the four elements. It refuses to set out on the only road it can take now, into the kingdom of the dead. No, it is in love too much with what it has been and known. It will not leave its money and possessions. It will not forgive the wrongs that were done to it while it was alive. It clings on desperately to love."

"I was not speaking about any ghost," I said. "I was trying to tell you about this very delightful lovely girl."

"If I was a priest," said Donald Barr, "instead of a minister, I might tell you that a ghost is a spirit lost between this world and purgatory. It refuses to shed its earthly appetites. It will not enter the dark gate of suffering."

The northern twilight thickened in the room while we spoke. Our conversation was another kind of chess. Yet each knew what the other was about.

"I hope she's there tonight," I said. "I might even prevail on her to make me some toast and hot chocolate. For it seems I'm going to get no supper in the manse."

"You're not scared?" said Donald Barr from the window.

"No," I said. "I'm not frightened of that kind of ghost. It seemed to me, when we were speaking together in the school-house last night, this girl and I, that I was the wan lost one, the squeaker and gibberer, and she was a part of the ever-springing fountain."

"Go home then to your ghost," said Donald Barr. "We won't play any more chess tonight. She won't harm you, you're quite right there."

We stood together at the end of his garden path.

"Miss McKillop," I murmured to the dark shape that was fumbling for the latch of the gate.

"Sandra McKillop," said Donald, "died the twenty-third of May this year. I buried her on the third of June, herself and John Germiston, in separate graves."

"Tell me," I said.

"No," said Donald, "for I do not know the facts. Never ask me for a partial account. It seemed to me they were happy. I refuse to wrong the dead. Go in peace."

There was no apparition in the school-house that night. I went to bed and slept soundly, drugged with fresh air, ale, fellowship and a growing wonderment.

The days passed, and I did not see the ghost again. Occasionally I caught the fragrance, a drift of sudden sweetness in the long corridor between kitchen and parlour, or in the garden or on the pebbled path between the house and the school. Occasionally a stir of cold went through the parlour late at night as I sat reading, and no heaping of peats would warm the air again for a half-hour or so. I would look up, eagerly I must confess, but nothing trembled into form and breathing out of the expectant air. It was as if the ghost had grown shy and uncertain, indicated her presence only by hints and suggestions. And in the classroom too things quietened down, and the island pupils and I worked out our regime together as the summer days passed. Only occasionally a five-year-old would whisper something about Miss McKillop, and smile, and then look sad; and it was like a small scattering of rose-petals. Apart from that everything proceeded smoothly to the final closing of books at the end of the school year.

One man in the island I did not like, and that was Henrikson
who kept the island store and garage, my neighbour. A low wall
separated the school garden from Henrikson's land, which was
usually untidy with empty lemonade cases, oil rums, sodden
cardboard boxes. Apart from the man's simple presence, which
he insisted on inflicting on me, I was put out by things in his
character. For example, he showed an admiration for learning
and university degrees that amounted to sycophancy; and this I
could not abide, having sprung myself from a race of labourers
and miners and railwaymen, good people all, more solid and
sound and kindly than most university people, in my experience.
But the drift of Henrikson's talk was that farmers and such like,
including himself, were poor creatures indeed compared to their
peers who had educated themselves and got into the professions
and so risen in the world. This was bad enough; but soon he
began to direct arrows of slander at this person and that in the
island. "Arrows" is too open and forthright a word for it; it was
more the work of "the smiler with the knife." Such-and-such a
farmer, he told me, was in financial difficulties, we wouldn't be
seeing him in Quoylay much longer. This other young fellow
had run his motorcycle for two years now without a license;
maybe somebody should do something about it; he himself had
no objection to sending anonymous letters to the authorities in
such a case. Did I see that half-ruined croft down at the shore?
Two so-called respectable people in this island—he would mention no names—had spent a whole week-end together there at
show time last summer, a married man and a farmer's daughter.
The straw they had lain on hadn't even been cleaned out....
This was the kind of talk that went on over the low wall between
school and store on the late summer evenings. It was difficult
to avoid the man; as soon as he saw me weeding the potato
patch, or watering the pinks, out he came with his smirkings and
cap-touchings, and leaned confidentially over the wall. It is easy
to say I could simply have turned my back on him; but in many
ways I am a coward; and even the basest of the living can coerce
me to some extent. One evening his theme was the kirk and the
minister. "I'm not wanting to criticize any friend of yours," he
said. "I've seen him more than once in the school-house and

I've heard that you visit him in the manse, and it's no business of mine, but that man is not a *real* minister, if you ask me. We're used with a different kind of preaching in this island, and a different kind of pastoral behaviour too, I assure you of that. I know for a fact that he brews—he bought two tins of malt, and hops, from the store last month. The old ministers were one and all very much against drink. What's a minister for if he doesn't keep people's feet on the true path, yes, if he doesn't warn them and counsel them in season and out of season, you know, in regard to their conduct? The old ministers that were here formerly had a proper understanding of their office. But this Mr. Barr, he closes his eyes to things that are a crying scandal to the whole island. For example—"

"Mr. Barr is a very good friend of mine," I said.

"O, to be sure," he cried. "I know. He's an educated man and so are you too, Mr. Reynolds. I spoke out of place, I'm sorry. I'm just a simple countryman, brought up on the shorter catechism and the good book. Times are changing fast. I'm sure people who have been to the university have a different way of looking at things from an old country chap. No offense, Mr. Reynolds, I hope."

A few moths were out, clinging to the stones, fluttering and birring softly on the kitchen window. I turned and went in without saying goodnight to Mr. Henrikson.

And as I went along the corridor, with a bad taste in my mouth from that holy old creep across the road, I heard it, a low reluctant weeping from above, from the bedroom. I ran upstairs and threw open the door. The room was empty, but it was as cold as the heart of an iceberg, and the unmistakable fragrance clung about the window curtains and the counterpane. There was the impression of a head on the pillow, as if someone had knelt beside the bed for a half-hour to sort out her troubles in silence.

My ghost was being pierced by a slow wondering sadness.

Henrikson my neighbour was not a man to be put off by slights and reprovings. The very next evening I was fixing lures to my sillock rod in the garden, and there he was humped over the wall, obsequious and smiling.

It had been a fine day, hadn't it? And now that the school

was closed for the summer, would I not be thinking of going off
to Edinburgh or Brighton or Majorca for a bit of a holiday? Well,
that was fine, that I liked the island so much. To tell the truth
most of the folk in Quoylay were very glad to have a quiet respectable man like me in the school, after the wild goings-on
that had been just before I arrived....

I was sick and tired of this man, and yet I knew that now I
was to hear, in a very poisoned and biased version, the story of
Sandra McKillop the school-mistress and Johnny. Donald Barr,
out of compassion for the dead, would never have told me. So
I threw my arms companionably over the wall and I offered
Henrikson my tobacco pouch and I said, "What kind of goings-
on would that be now, Mr. Henrikson?"

Miss Sandra McKillop had come to the island school straight
from the teachers' training college in Scotland two years before.
(I am paraphrasing Henrikson's account, removing most of the
barbs, trying to imagine a rose here and there.) She was a great
change from the previous teacher, a finicky perjink old maid,
and that for a start warmed the hearts of the islanders to her. But
it was in the school itself that she scored her great success; the
children of all ages took to her at once. She was a born teacher.
Every day she held them in thrall from the first bell to the last.
And even after school there was a dancing cluster of them round
her all the way to her front door. The stupid ones and the ugly
ones adored her especially, because she made them feel accepted. She enriched their days.

She was a good-looking girl. ("I won't deny that," said Henrikson, "as bonny a young woman as ever I saw.") More than
one of the island bachelors hung about the school gate from time
to time, hoping for a word with her. Nothing doing; she was
pleasant and open with them and with everybody, but love did
not enter her scheme of things; at least, not yet. She was a so-
ciable girl, and was invited here and there among the farms for
supper. She gave one or two talks to the Rural Institute, about
her holidays abroad and life in her training college. She went
to church every Sunday morning and sang in the choir, and
afterwards taught in the Sunday School. But mostly she stayed
at home. New bright curtains appeared in all the windows. She

was especially fond of flowers; the little glass porch at the front of the house was full all the year round with flowering plants; the school garden, that first summer after she came, was a delight. All the bees in the island seemed to forage in those flowers.

How she first met John Germiston, nobody knows. It was almost certainly during one of those long walks she took in the summer evenings of her second year. John Germiston kept a croft on the side of the Ward Hill, a poor enough place with a couple of cows and a scatter of hens. Three years before he had courted a girl from the neighbouring island of Hellya. He had sailed across and got married in the kirk there and brought his bride home, a shy creature whose looks changed as swiftly as the summer loch. And there in his croft he installed her. And she would be seen from time to time feeding the hens at the end of the house, or hanging out washing, or standing at the road-end with her basket waiting for the grocery van. But she never became part of the community. With the coming of winter she was seen less and less—a wide-eyed face in the window, a figure against the skyline looking over the sound towards Hellya. The doctor began to call regularly once a week at the croft. John Germiston let it be known in the smithy that his wife was not keeping well.

There is a trouble in the islands that is called *morbus orcadensis*. It is a darkening of the mind, a progressive flawing and thickening of the clear lens of the spirit. It is said to be induced in sensitive people by the long black overhang of winter; the howl and sob of the wind over the moors that goes on sometimes for days on end; the perpetual rain that makes of tilth and pasture one indiscriminate bog; the unending gnaw of the sea at the crags.

Soon after the new year they took the stricken girl to a hospital in the south.

Of course everyone in Quoylay was sorry for John Germiston. It is a hard thing for a young handsome man to work a croft by himself. And yet these things happen from time to time. There are a few cheerful old men in the folds of the hills, or down by the shore, who have been widowers since their twenties.

Somewhere on the hill, one evening in spring, John Germiston met Sandra McKillop. They spoke together. He brought her to his house. She stood in the door and saw the desolation inside; the rusted pot, the torn curtains, the filthy hearth. The worm had bored deep into that rose.

From that first meeting everything proceeded swiftly and inevitably. No sooner was school over for the day than Miss McKillop shook the adoring children off and was away to the croft of Stanebreck on the hill with a basket of bannocks or a bundle of clean washing. She stayed late into the evening. Sometimes they would be seen wandering together along the edge of the crags, while far below the Atlantic fell unquietly among shelving rocks and hollow caves; on and on they walked into the sunset, while near and far the crofts watched and speculated.

Night after night, late, as April brightened into May, she would come home alone. A light would go on in the school-house kitchen. She would stand in the garden for a while among her hosts of blossoms. Then she would go in and lock the door. Her bedroom window was briefly illuminated. Then the whole house was dark.

"I suppose," said Henrikson, "nobody could have said a thing if it had stopped there. There was suspicion—well, what do you expect, a young woman visiting a married man night after night, and her a school-teacher with a position to keep up—but I don't suppose anybody could have done a thing about it.

"But in the end the two of them got bold. They got careless. It wasn't enough for this hussy to visit her fancy-man in his croft—O no, the bold boy takes to sallying down two or three times a week to the school-house for his supper, if you please.

"Still nobody could make a move. A person is entitled to invite another person to the house for supper, even though on one occasion at least they don't draw the curtain and I can see from my kitchen their hands folded together in the middle of the table and all that laughter going on between them.

"Mr. Reynolds, I considered it my duty to watch, yes, and to report to the proper quarters if necessary.

"One Friday evening Germiston arrives at the school-house at nine o'clock. A fine evening at the beginning of May it was. The light went on in the parlour. The curtain was drawn. After an hour or so the light goes on in her bedroom. 'Ah ha,' says I to myself, 'I've missed their farewells tonight, I've missed all the kissing in the door.'...But I was wrong, Mr. Reynolds. Something far worse was happening. At half past five in the morning I got up to stock the van, and I saw him going home over the hill, black against the rising sun. At *half past five* in the morning.

"That same day, being an elder, I went to the manse. Mr. Barr refused to do a thing about it. 'Miss McKillop is a member of my church. If she's in trouble of any sort she'll come to me,' he said. 'I will not act on slanderous rumours. There's more than one crofter on the hill at half past five in the morning.'...There's your modern ministers for you. And I don't care if he is your friend, Mr. Reynolds, I must speak my mind about this business.

"By now the whole island was a hive of rumour.

"Neither John Germiston nor Miss McKillop could stir without some eye being on them and some tongue speculating. And yet they went on meeting one another, quite open and shameless, as if they were the only living people in an island of ghosts. They would wander along the loch shore together, hand in hand, sometimes stopping to watch the swans or the eiders, not caring at all that a dozen croft windows were watching their lingerings and kissings. Then, arms about one another, they would turn across the fields in the direction of the school-house.

"Ay, but the dog of Stanebreck was a lonely dog till the sun got up, all that month of May.

"One Tuesday morning she arrived late for school, at a quarter past nine. She arrived with the mud of the hill plastered over her stockings, and half-dead with sleep. 'Hurrah,' cried the bairns congregated round the locked door of the school. They knew no better, the poor innocent things. They shouted half with delight and half with disappointment when she gave them the morning off, told them to come back in the afternoon. They were not to know what manner of thing had made their teacher so exhausted.

"Of course it was no longer possible to have a woman like her for the island teacher.

"I had written to this person and that. Enquiries were under way, discreetly, you know, so as not to cause any undue sensation. I think in the end pressure would have been put on her to resign. But as things turned out it wasn't necessary.

"One night they both disappeared. They vanished as if they had been swept clean off the face of the island. The school door remained locked all the next week. John Germiston's unmilked cow bellowed in its steep field. 'Ah ha,' said the men in the smithy, 'so it's come to this, they've run away together....'

"Ten days later a fishing boat drew up the two bodies a mile west of Hellya. Their arms were round each other. The fishermen had trouble separating the yellow hair from the black hair."

Henrikson was having difficulty with his breathing; his voice dropped and quavered and choked so that I could hardly hear his last three words. "They were naked," he mouthed venomously.

Moths flickered between us. The sea boomed and hushed from the far side of the hill. In a nearby croft a light came on.

"And so," said Henrikson, "we decided that we didn't want a woman teacher after that. That's why you're here, Mr. Reynolds."

We drifted apart, Henrikson and I, to our separate doors. Eagerly that night I wished for the vanished passion to fill my rooms: the ghost, the chill, the scent of roses. But in the schoolhouse was only a most terrible desolation.

On fine evenings that summer, when tide and light were suitable, Donald Barr and I would fish for sillocks and cuithes from the long sloping skerry under the crag. Or we would ask the loan of a crofter's boat, if the fish were scanty there, and row out with our lines into the bay.

The evening before the agricultural show was bright and calm. We waited in the bay with dripping oars for the sun to set behind the hill. We put our rods deep into the dazzle but not one cuithe responded. Presently the sun furled itself in a cloud, and it was as if a rose had burst open over the sea's unflawed mirror. Cuithe fishing is a sport that requires little skill. Time after time we hauled our rods in burgeoning with strenuous sea fruit, until the bottom of the dinghy was a floor of unquiet gulping silver. Then the dense undersea hordes moved away, and for twenty minutes, while the rose of sunset faded and the long bay gloomed, we caught nothing.

"It must have been about here," I said to Donald Barr, "that they were drowned."

He said nothing. He had never discussed the affair with me, beyond that one mention of the girl's name at the manse gate.

A chill moved in from the west; breaths of night air flawed the dark sea mirror.

"The earth-bound soul refuses to acknowledge its death," said Donald. "It is desperately in love with the things of this world—possessions, fame, lust. How, once it has tasted them, can it ever exist without them? Death is a negation of all that wonder and delight. It will not enter the dark door of the grave. It lurks, a ghost, round the places where it fed on earthly joys. It spreads a coldness about the abodes of the living. The five senses pulse through it, but fadingly, because there is nothing for the appetite to feed on, only memories and shadows. Sooner or later the soul must enter the dark door. But no—it will not— for a year or for a decade or for a century it lingers about the place of its passion, a rose garden or a turret or a cross-roads. It will not acknowledge that all this loveliness of sea and sky and islands, and all the rare things that happen among them, are merely shadows of a greater reality. At last the starved soul is forced to accept it, for it finds itself utterly alone, surrounded as time goes by with strange new unloved objects and withered faces and skulls. Reluctantly it stoops under the dark lintel. All loves are forgotten then. It sets out on the quest for Love itself. For this it was created in the beginning."

We hauled the dinghy high up the beach and secured her to a rock. A few mild summer stars glimmered. The sea was dark in the bay, under the shadow of the cliff, but the Atlantic horizon was still flushed a little with reluctant sunset, and all between was a vast slow heave of gray.

"I have a bottle of very good malt whisky in the school-house," I said. "I think a man could taste worse things after a long evening on the sea."

It was then that I heard the harp-like shivering cries far out in the bay. The sea thins out the human voice, purges it of its earthiness, lends it a purity and poignancy.

"Wait for me," cried the girl's voice. "Where are you? You're swimming too fast."

Donald Barr had heard the voices also. Night folded us increasingly in gloom and cold as we stood motionless under the sea-bank. He passed me his tobacco pouch. I struck a match. The flame trembled between us.

"This way," shouted a firm strong happy voice (but attenuated on the harpstrings of the sea). "I'm over here."

The still bay shivered from end to end with a single glad cry. Then there was silence.

The minister and I turned. We climbed over loose stones and sandy hillocks to the road. We lashed our heavy basket of cuithes into the boot of Donald Barr's old Ford. Then we got in, one on each side, and he pressed the starter.

"Earth-bound souls enact their little dramas over and over again, but each time a little more weakly," he said. "The reality of death covers them increasingly with its good oblivion. You will be haunted for a month or two yet. But at last the roses will lose their scent."

The car stopped in front of the dark school-house.

THE CINQUEFOIL

UNPOPULAR FISHERMAN

There are a few men in the island I don't speak to, one especially: Fred Houton that I used to fish with in our boat the *Thistle* until the day two or three years ago when he struck a savage unexpected blow at my pride.

If he had taken a five-pound note out of my wallet I would have forgiven him, or whisky from my cupboard; or even if he had not turned up for the fishing one morning. For Fred Houton and I understood each other, there was a grudging muted friendship.

He lived with his mother in a croft in the hills, a poor place called Ingarth.

I was pleased enough to see him most evenings. He would throw open the door of my hut without knocking and say, "Come on, then, boy, we're going for a pint." Or, if we had no money, we would sit silent and play draughts and smoke till after midnight.

After I got to know Rosie, all that changed. It's true, I had known Rosie all my life—all the islanders are acquainted with one another. And a plain little thing I thought her. She stood all day at the counter of her father's shop above the pier and served the island with groceries, bread, knit-wear, confectionary, tobacco. She was just one among the hundred faces, old and young and aging, that drifted about the island.

She came to the hut one day with a copy of the *Fishing News* that I hadn't collected for a week. She came dripping with rain; my window was a grey throbbing blur. I asked her in while I rummaged in the cupboard for coppers. She said, "Your floor could do with a wash." She said, trembling—the four pennies in her fist—"That's a poor fire you have...." She stayed for a bite of supper. She was pretty enough with the rain-washed apples in her cheeks. She promised, at the end of the house under the stars, to come back the next night.

Soon it was a strange night that didn't bring Rosie to my hut, with a few fresh-baked scones, or a pot of jam, or a book.

I never really got to like her. I never thought her long freckled face beautiful. She brought a disturbance into my days. I enjoyed fishing more, and breathing, and drinking, because of Rosie.

"If you think I'm going to marry you," I said, "you're mistaken. I don't believe in that nonsense. I won't go to the kirk with you on Sunday mornings either." (I knew she sang in the church choir.)

She said that that was all right as far as she was concerned. But maybe I would change my mind after a time.

There was a certain amount of difficulty with Fred Houton. He would come crashing through the door—as he always did—upon our silence. "Are you here again?" he would say to Rosie. And to me: "Come on, come on. They're wanting us to play darts in the pub."

I told him in the boat one morning when we were setting creels that I would appreciate it if he didn't come so much about my place in future. I let him know—surely the man must have guessed—that there was an understanding between Rosie and me. Then, seeing the hurt look on his face, I said, "Well, say one night a week. Friday—that's always a good night in the pub. We'll have a drink every Friday. Rosie can bide home on Friday and do her knitting. But mind you knock at the door in future."

One day that winter Fred Houton said to me, "Look, Gurness, I won't be able to fish with you after Christmas. We'd better come to some arrangement about the boat."

It turned out that his mother had had a bad twelvemonth of it with rheumatism, and the work of the croft, though it was small, was too much for her now. So, Fred had to give up the fishing and resume the work of barn and byre and peat-hill.

I was vexed at the prospect of losing him. He was a good worker (and a luckier fisherman than me, I admit that). But we do not show our feelings in the island. I said, "That's all right."

At the new year, I gave him a hundred pounds for his share in the *Thistle*.

junction is plain—'Love your neighbour'—we are bound as Christians. What does it mean? It does not mean, I think, that we should go about the world with holy long-suffering smiles on our faces for this one and that, high and low, good and bad. By no means; one of the qualities of love is honesty, sincerity. I think it may mean this—we are bound to enter upon any relationship, however fleeting, with a deep respect for the other person. You may say, 'Instinctively I do not like this person!' and closer acquaintance may not by any means sweeten your opinion of him. Yet we must think of ourselves as limited people—even the saints are limited—and we simply do not understand. The distasteful person was created by God, he is one of God's children, when we are introduced to him we are in the presence of a marvelous mystery. Before that mystery we must school ourselves to be patient, long-suffering, modest, understanding. This may not be 'love' as St. Paul meant it in his great meditation on love in the Epistle to the Corinthians, but it is to stand perhaps on the threshold of love, hoping—if we stay there long enough— that the door may be opened to us.

"Thus it is possible to feel dislike for a person, and yet to be in a state of charity towards him...."

The minister of Selskay was interrupted at this point in the writing of his sermon. There was a knock at the door. He put down his pen and called, "Come in." No one answered. Finally he went to the door and opened it. Tilly Scabra stood there. She muttered something that John Gillespie could not quite catch, but he did hear the words "trouble" and "help."

The Scabras were a family that lived at the other end of the island. Even among the crofters and fishermen, who are never snobs, they were poorly regarded. Arthur Scabra, the minister had heard, was not really a bad man, and in fact he had liked him the once or twice they had met and chatted on the road. But this Arthur had come home from doing his National Service taking with him a trollop of a girl from Leith or Granton, and whether they were married or not nobody knew, but anyway they took up residence with Arthur's old mother. Old Mrs. Scabra did not live to see her grandchildren, but she can't have ended her days in tranquility; for Angela, Arthur's woman, was not long in showing her mettle. Debts and drink and quarreling—among such squalid unknown things the old woman took ill, and turned her face to the wall, and breathed her last. Arthur and Angela, after the funeral, found the "kist" under the bed with the mother's savings in it: a bundle of notes, a few sovereigns, a gold brooch. Then for a month or so Anscarth was the gayest house in the island, with parties two or three nights a week (to which all the young men went, of course); and Angela had new flashy clothes, and new ornaments of appalling ugliness littered the mantelpiece and sideboard. Of course the money gave out, and then the parties stopped, except for the weekend half-bottle and the home-brew; and at Anscarth it was back to the old cycle of debts, drink and quarreling.

The good folk of Selskay held up their hands at the stories of the on-goings at Anscarth, which up to then had been an austere respectable place. Between one lurid story and another, Angela gave birth to her first-born, a boy.

The sad thing was, she had dragged Arthur down with her. Before going away to his calling-up, Arthur Scabra had been a quiet hardworking boy. He came back after three years utterly changed, and this Jezebel from the street-corners with him. From that day on Arthur had never put a hand to plough or oar. The creature wasn't ill, that was obvious—he could forage all day among the seaweed for whelks or driftwood, in rain or sun—it was just that he had lost the taste for work. "Arthur Scabra doesn't incline work," said an old crofter to the minister, and spat, and laughed.

They managed to live, all the same. Hardly a winter passed without another little Scabra filling the cradle in the corner of the house. The dreariness, the drink, the fighting went on monotonously, among periods of tranquility. If things got too oppressive indoors, Arthur would wander along the shore for an hour or two, probing in this pool and that swathe of seaweed. Then after a time one of the little ones would appear on the banks above and shout across the sand, "Dad, come on, your dinner's ready...." Then Arthur would come slowly back, and gather the bairn into his arms, and kiss it. And together they would stoop under the chattering wailing laughing soup-smelling lintel of Anscarth.

One winter little Tilly appeared on earth, and opened her

eyes, and wailed. It was the minister's predecessor who had, out of charity, gone to the croft and baptized her; for the Scabras never went to the kirk.

Now here she stood, some sixteen years later, on the doorstep of the manse, muttering something about "fighting" and "blood."

"You'd better come in," said Rev. John Gillespie.

Extracts from the Diary of a Minister

I knew it would come, sooner or later. They are trying to marry me off. It is the youngest daughter of Fiord who has been chosen. At least, her old madam of a mother has chosen her to be the lady of the manse. Three times this month a note has come from Fiord—through the post, if you please: "We would be very happy," said the first note, "if you could find time to come to tea on Friday afternoon. There will be no other guests. Bet has been baking a cake with cherries in it. We know you like that...." I couldn't go—I had this presbytery meeting in the town. The second invitation, a week later, I accepted. A drearier afternoon I have rarely put in. There we sat round the table in the parlour, eating the cherry-cake and sipping the tea: Mrs. Dale the hostess, and Mrs. Hunda the doctor's wife, and Bet. Pressed, I said the cake was very good (so it was). The conversation was mostly about the wickedness of strikers, the scandalous things that were shown on TV, Arthur Scabra's laziness.... Almost before I knew it the ladies had withdrawn and I found myself alone with Bet Dale. The poor girl had been instructed to put on an impressive show—it was all chatter, giggles, blushes, long silences. I couldn't stand much of that. "My respects to your mother," I said. "The cake was marvelous. Thank you...." She gave me a last hurt look. Then I went.

What she told old madam I do not know. All was not yet lost. Another billet-doux a few days later through the letter-box: "We *did* enjoy your company that afternoon last week, especially Bet. She hasn't stopped talking about it since. Bet, I know, is intelligent and she is starved of serious conversation in this island. So *please* come to tea on Friday afternoon, 4 p.m...." Starved of conversation! Bet's destiny, I'm sure, lies in a farmhouse, with children and cheese-making and the growing of roses. She would be deadly miserable in a house like this. I wrote this morning:

"Dear Mrs. Dale, Thank you for your invitation. Unfortunately I am not able to accept. I find that afternoon tea is bad for my digestion...."

I think I have made at least two more enemies in Selskay; and one of them quite powerful.

Now it is Mr. James Wasdale the merchant having a go, on behalf of his daughter Rosemary who sings in the choir.

Rosie is a more interesting girl than Bet Dale, though much plainer. I sense depths in her. She might suddenly do something unexpected—goodness knows what. She has a high true sweet soprano.

What did I find on my doorstep a few weeks ago but a bottle of Beaujolais, well wrapped against the eyes of passers-by. No note to say who the donor was. The mystery was explained that same evening when I went to the shop for my tobacco: "O, Mr. Gillespie, and did you get the wine all right?... Well, I thought you might like it. Rosie called with it, but you were out. No, no, of course not, you mustn't pay—it's a gift. A pleasure, Mr. Gillespie...."A few days more, and the second cannon in the campaign was fired—Rosie is at the door with a parcel: beautiful crisp brown paper, virgin string. She held it out to me. "For you, Mr. Gillespie," she said...."But what is it? Who is it from?"..."It's a fair-isle jersey. I knitted it. I'm a good knitter. I didn't knit it for you. My father said I was to take it here, to you, as a present. So here it is...." I said I had plenty of jerseys. I thanked her. But really, if it was for giving away, somebody else who needed it should have it—Jake Sandside, for example, or Arthur Scabra. "I think so too," she said. "But please, you take it, and give it to one of them. Then I can tell my father I handed it over at the manse door." She is a strange honest girl. I like her, and I think she respects me, but her affections are elsewhere.... I gave the jersey to Jake Sandside who has no shirt under his jacket.

The last dying shot in the campaign was fired today. Mr. Wasdale the merchant comes to me, very troubled, after closing-time. "It's about Rosie, you see, Mr. Gillespie. I'm worried about her. Perhaps if you spoke to her. I'll tell you what the position is, as far as I can make it out...." Rosie, it seems, has fallen for somebody quite unsatisfactory—none other than that great growling bear of a fisherman called Gurness who lives alone in a hut on the point. Sometimes, it seems, she isn't home all night. Mr. Wasdale is very very worried—Gurness is a mean violent man. It is terrible, terrible. He never thought his Rosie, etc.

I promised to speak to Rosie about it. But what right have I to put my blundering hands upon that most delicate and subtle web, the heart's affections?

This is the saddest of all—old sweet balmy Miss Fidge, the sea-captain's daughter, who lives in the big granite house on the side of the hill, has taken a fancy to me! That it should come to this! I noticed the first onset of affection about a month ago, as she was leaving the church after the morning service. (She has been a devoted church-woman all her life.) Instead of the slight formal bow to me, as she passed, she lingered, she was all smiles and crinkles, she got in the way of other worshippers who were following her. "A dear beautiful sermon," she said. "O how it touched my heart!" And I trying to nod and smile goodbye to this one and that one and the other one. "You are a gifted young preacher—greatly gifted—the hearts of everyone were so touched—I could tell—O yes, indeed." In fact it had been a rather poor sermon, not in my usual earthy-subtle style at all; a disappointment to me at the time of writing and at the time of delivery; not one for my book of collected sermons, to be published when I am ninety years old and past caring what anybody thinks. "A little spiritual gem!"..."Well, thank you, Miss Fidge, God bless you" (eager to get back into the church and have a word with the beadle about the faulty heating). "You are a dear good young man. I bless the day you came to Selskay. I feel that in some way you are a son to me, a spiritual offspring...."It was time to bolt after that. Old Flaws the beadle must have noticed my blushes....And so it has gone on even unto this present: that grey austere old lady dotes on me. What she has left of tenderness is spent on me. She monopolizes me after the morning service every Sunday now—the other parishioners never get a chance at all with her. It is touching—sometimes when she beams at me a vanished ghost of beauty—that must have been fifty years ago—flits across her tired face. It suddenly occurred to me yesterday that, in her present frame of mind, she might easily leave me everything in her will. That would be terrible!—she has poor cousins, I hear, in Gateshead and South Shields. God bless you, Miss Fidge. This little last blossoming of earthly affection is touched somehow, I think, by "caritas," the divine love; which should however be centered on no single individual but should hold out arms to the whole universe: in the manner of the heroes of God.

Last night after tea one of the Scabra girls came to the manse. Her mother and father had been fighting over at Anscarth—an old story, but Tilly seemed to be frightened. I took her hand to comfort her. My heart trembled for the trembling child, with pity, yes, but—I recognize it now—with something different and new and utterly unexpected.

She sat beside me in the car.

When we got to Anscarth all was sweetness and light again. But Arthur's smiling face had a long scratch down it.

The younger children were asleep all about the slatterny place: rosy tranquil tear-stained faces.

Angela made me a cup of coffee. "That Tilly!" she said. "Fancy disturbing you like that, Mr. Gillespie! I'll talk to her, the little bissom...."

For Tilly was no longer there. She was ashamed, obviously, of raising that false alarm; she had made herself scarce.

That white face kept me from sleep all last night.

A FRIDAY OF RAIN

I might have known. I might truly have known. What a fool. I might as well have sat on my arse. I might.

She must have crossed over last night or early this morning. That's it. She must have been in Quoylay all last week, taking her stink and her whine with her from door to door.

Friday is my day. Friday's the day I do my rounds. The whole wide world knows that, including Annie. Friday, Jake Sandside's day. She, and anybody else, can have the rest of the week.

Selskay, on a Friday, belongs to me.

It is not grudged, the bite I get here, the sup I get there. It is well recognized what I did in my youth, for my country, in His Majesty's navy, twenty-one years, man and boy, four war years and more, among burnings and drownings. They know, all right. People don't forget. (Well, some do.) There's always a copper for an old sailor, a pair of boots, a plate of broth. Friday, Sailor Jake's day. Now this old bag has come poaching.

I'll speak to the laird, I will.

I'll speak to Mr. Gillespie up at the manse, though he has troubles of his own. Still, a word.

What's she ever done, except frighten children, and steal eggs, and pretend she had the evil eye when a fist or a face in a doorway was hard? An old bag. A boil on a decent community.

I served my country. There's the discharge papers and the fifteen bob a week pension (that wouldn't keep a libbed cat of course, but still).

In the shop, early on, I got the first hint of something wrong. "Nothing today," he says, his mouth like a trap. "Sorry. No broken biscuits. The end of ham has been taken." So, there was an intruder.

"Good day to you," I said with straight sailor shoulders and a salute. I keep my courtesy in every trying circumstance.

He turned away to his desk and cash-book.

It began to look then as if the wolf in the fold was Annie. But she had never been known to come on a Friday before....

I stood on the road outside. It had begun to rain. Where now? If I could track the old bag down, I could—not for the first time—put the weight of my tongue on her. My English words, that I learned in the navy, always make her uncomfortable.

I did not see Orphan Annie anywhere in the village. She must be calling, I concluded, at farms in the hinterland. She would be leaving the village till evening. Good thinking—then the roadmen would be home with their wages. The baskets of fish would be on the pier.

A raindrop hit the back of my hand.

The morning village was mine, at least.

Jake, old friend, your wits are losing their edge. Mr. Sandside, you are drinking too much of that wine and meth. The village had been broached before breakfast time. The great queen Annie had hardly waited for the women to get their knickers on. She was out of the village, loaded, and up among the hill farms.

It was "Nothing today, sorry," all along the village street, like an echo. "Nothing. Call next week." I am always polite. Perhaps they are tired of me, after thirty years at the game. I touch my cap. "Is there any firewood to break? Kittens to be drowned?" There was nothing."

Sure enough, there was the imprint of an ancient boot in the mud, beside the pump. Her Majesty had stopped for a drink.

Outside the doctor's that big black-and-white dog took me by the sleeve. I put a stone in his mouth.

Despised and rejected.

I had been confined to the house Monday and Tuesday with rheumatism in my leg. It wasn't better still.

Up among the crofts the evil old mouth would be whining for eggs, and a bit of butter—and saying, "Oh, that's the sweetest ale, now, I swear to God I ever put in my mouth." The locust is in my field. While I slept it came.

In that village, only at the hardest door did I get charity. Gurness the fisherman, he gave me a fill of my pipe and a clutch of matches.

It is very strange, Friday and fishermen. They are always kinder and gentler on a Friday. How is that? Do they still remember their patron, Peter, cursing and swearing and denying that Friday morning in the courtyard of the high priest, while inside the Man of Sorrows began to enter upon his agony? All the generations of fishermen have been sorry ever since. The Catholics have their fish on a Friday. There might be something in it. I don't know.

"Don't stuff in any more shag," said Gurness. "That's half an ounce you've taken. Your pipe'll break."

"Much obliged," I said, and touched my cap-brim. "It's Friday."

"What is there about me?" said Gurness. "You're not the first this morning. That old hag—what's her name, Annie—she was here when I was having my breakfast. I gave her a piece of salt fish to get rid of her."

I saluted again, and left Gurness pulling his sea-boots on, with a spatter of rain on his window.

It amounted to this: I might not starve at the weekend, but I would be on iron rations: a turnip, limpets, tap water.

Which road had the old trash taken? She was quick as an otter, but she couldn't cover the whole island in one morning. If I took the opposite way, there might still be a picking or two. Also, there was the chance I might meet her half-way, near the crossroads. Then I would have something to say to her ladyship.

I reckoned, in this rain, she would take the fertile end of the island first, the region of the big farms. Towards nightfall she might drop among the hill crofts, for a last over-brimming to her bag. It was the poverty-road for me, then.

I was right. I got a sup of oatmeal and butter-milk here, and a dried cuithe there, and an end of cheese in the other place. Near Anscarth the kids threw clods at me. It was worth enduring that black earth-storm to discover that the ale they had put on last weekend was ready and was being broached by Arthur and Angela; and in the middle of the day too, with a teething infant yelling from a crib in the corner. They are kind and reckless, as far as their means go, at the croft of Anscarth at ale-time. So, I got my cup filled maybe half-a-dozen times.... The climate suddenly changes, for no reason, at an ale-session. Arthur and Angela turned from singing and laughing to say, had I heard about their lass Tilly and the minister, and what folk were saying, but they didn't care, Mr. Gillespie was a fine man. Arthur said that was right. His daughter too, Tilly, she was a gem of a lass. Tilly and John (fancy, to call the minister by his Christian name!) were very fond of each other. But Angela said that Tilly was a little tart.... At that Arthur and Angela glared above their ale-mugs at each other: but only for five seething seconds. Then it was time to dip in the mugs again.

Rain drops shone and tinkled from the lintel. Outside the Anscarth children played in the downpour.

I told Arthur and Angela some of my war-time adventures in the Med and the North Atlantic and the Arctic. My only ambition, in those terrible times, had been to come home to my own folk, with my wound, and throw myself on their care, and so end my

days in peace. But even that—I said—was not to be. A thief
from another island, that very day, was taking the bite out of my
mouth. "O never never," I said, and I cherished the gathering
glitters in my eye, "give old Annie Ross, that bitch of hell, a
bite."

Angela, to comfort me, filled up my mug again.

The truth is this—I hardly remember leaving Anscarth. I
didn't mind the rain on the road at all—it fell on me like wild
sweet dew. They make their ale strong at Anscarth. (It's a good
job old Mrs. Scabra, who was president of the temperance guild
in her day, isn't there to see their kirn and their mugs.) The sole
of one of my boots was going flip-flap, splash-splurge, along the
road and through puddles. For half-an-hour I didn't mind Annie
Ross at all. Let her get what she could. We have a short time
only.

I lost my joy in the doorway of Fiord. A face looked at me as
if it had lain for a month in a deep-freeze. *Off with you.* And a
dog growling inside. Rain bounced off the flagstones. The door
quivered in its frame. A virtue went out of me.

I gave myself once more to the road and the weather. The
rain had begun to search to the roots. My sinus throbbed, my
left lung whistled. Drink should never be taken before the sun
is under the yard-arm. Mr. Sandside, when will you ever learn?

Now the weather began to concentrate on my rheumatism.
It plucked at my thigh-bone till the whole left leg, from haunch
to knee, made mad music. On I went, hirpling and hobbling.
Bubbles gathered and burst at the lace-holes of my boots. I stood
against a wall to add my dribble to the sky-tumults.

I edged, after a time, into the barn of Ingarth.

I took off my jacket and trousers and drawers and boots, and
crept under the straw. I hung inside a yellow shaking wave. After
a time I must have drowsed....

Words dragged me back out of a good sea-dream. *Where are
you? Come on, Sailor Jake. I saw you going into the barn. No
use hiding in the straw. I've got something here to warm you.*

When a man is old and wretched, and near death, shame
leaves him. I raised naked shoulders through the straw. Rosie
Houton stood there with a steaming bowl between her hands.

I put my face among the fumes. That broth was well worth

the lecture I got. *Been at the meth again. No use denying it. Folk are getting tired of you. Very very tired. That's a fact. Do you realize what you're doing to yourself?*

Spoonful after spoonful after spoonful of the thick golden-grey stuff I put in my mouth. I burned my tongue. Bits of crust stuck in my beard. I rose and fell in the wave of straw.

Killing yourself, that's what you're doing. Your pension— spending it all on meth and cheap wine. And wandering about in all weathers.

The spoon rasped the bottom of the bowl.

"I have not drunk any meth," I said. "And it's Friday. I always go out on a Friday."

Listen to that chest of yours!—You've got severe bronchitis. It might turn into pneumonia. Half-starved you are too. How much of your pension have you got left? For goodness sake buy some bread and cheese and margarine. Let me hear of you drinking meth again, I'll report you to the authorities. They'll sort you out. They'll put you in their home.

I thanked Mrs. Houton for her wonderful soup.

The good woman; while I slept she had taken my clothes indoors and dried them at her fire. They steamed gently on her arm.

"You better go home soon," said Rosie. "The rain's stopped. Fred's in the village. Fred doesn't like tramps in his barn."

"I am *not* a tramp. I am a pensioned sailor of the Royal Navy," I said with as much dignity as a naked man in straw can summon.

You would never think Rosie Houton was the daughter of that misery down at the shop. She turned round while I put my clothes on. She knelt and tied the string on my boots in the barn door. *Now remember, straight home with you. No more drink.*

"Don't give anything to Annie Ross," I said from the end of the farm road. The sun had come out. The pools on the road were burning mirrors. The rain had crossed the Sound to Torsay. The hills of Torsay were hung with sackcloth—the Selskay air was purest crystal.

I met Fred Houton near the smithy. He stopped for a word. I didn't tell him about the barn and broth. No sense in taking the edge off their charity. (He gave me a shilling.)

I called at the big house where Miss Fidge lives alone. Miss

Fidge likes sailors. Her father was skipper of a coaster. Miss Fidge gave me two slices of ginger cake in a paper poke. I enjoy Miss Fidge's ginger cake with a cup of tea.

I was done in. I was completely buggered. The Anscarth ale slumbered still in the marrow of my bones. The weight of old rain was on me. Bad thoughts too wear out the spirit.

My feet dragged homewards. The rat began to gnaw again at my haunch-bone.

I wondered whether I should call at the manse. Tilly Scabra stood outside, on tiptoe, scouring the study window. Her little fist went round and round and then another pane glittered among the salted panes. Officially she's the manse housekeeper. Things are building up to a crisis there. There's to be a meeting of the kirk session on Tuesday evening next, I hear. I decided not to intrude upon Mr. Gillespie and his troubles.

I turned the corner and there was my cottage down beside the loch.

I took the silver whistle out of my trouser pocket and blew two blasts—a signal to the whole of Selskay isle that Sailor Jake was nearing port.

The dog of Skaill barked in the distance.

I *was* tired. I fell asleep in the rocking-chair beside the dead fire, a thing I hardly ever do so early in the evening.

When I woke up it was night. My paraffin lamp was lit. A few flames tumbled in the hearth.

There had been an intruder.

The room was different. Someone had shifted a chair. The water bucket was filled to brimming. There were strange shapes on the bed.

I hirpled over to investigate. A turnip—potatoes—eggs in a stone jar—butter in a saucer—a pot of rhubarb jam—bannocks and oatcakes—a poke of tea—a poke of sugar—brown serviceable boots—a jersey with darnings at elbow and neck.

What good ghost had come through the night to visit me?

I handled each item with lust and gratitude. All was well. The week-end was saved. My pipe with its tight knot of tobacco was on the mantelpiece. If only I had a sup of wine, I wouldn't have called the queen my cousin. (My tongue, after that Anscarth ale—need I say it—was like a flap of old leather.)

A presence was standing in the door with a bottle.

"I thought you were never going to waken," said Annie Ross, and set the wine on the table. "I had a job getting drink out of old Wasdale at this time of night."

I couldn't say a thing.

"I heard," said Annie Ross, "that you were bad with rheumatics. A man told me that on the pier at Kirkwall yesterday. *Laid up*, he said— *the sailor's in his bed not able to stir. Looks as if this might be the end of him....* So I thought, *Tomorrow's his day. Friday. And what'll Jake do if he can't get round the houses?* I thought, *I better see what's what.* So I got a lift in Tomison's lobster boat this morning early."

John Sandside, you are a fool.

"There's your takings," said Annie, "over there, on the bed. It's a fair haul. Them boots should see you through till the spring. I got enough money for a bottle of wine. There's your change...." She put a couple of coins on the dresser.

You are a slanderer, John Sandside. You have taken away the character of an angel of light.

"It's started to rain again," said Annie. "Can I bide to my supper?"

"Yes," I said. "Thank you, Annie."

"I did it for the sake of the old times," said Annie. "Though you haven't got a good word to say for me a many a time, and you blacked my eye the last Hamnavoe market. I did it because we were sweethearts once."

"Forgive me, dear," I said.

We had a good supper of bannocks and cheese and jam, and we finished the wine.

Annie stayed the night. She got a passage across the Sound in Gurness's boat on the Saturday morning.

My rheumatics, I'm sorry to say, are none better.

SEED, DUST, STAR

A community maintains itself, ensures a continuance and an identity, through such things as the shop, the kirk, the stories told in smithy and tailor-shop, the ploughing match, agricultural show, harvest home, the graveyard where all its dead are gathered. (It is the same with all communities—city or island—but the working-out of the ethos of a community is best seen in microcosm, as in the island of Selskay.) Most of all the community ensures its continuance by the coming together of man and woman. There will be a new generation to plough and fish, with the same names, the same legends, the same faces (though subtly shifted, and touched with the almost-forgotten, the hardly-realized), the same kirkyard.

The place where the community lives is important, of course, in perpetuating its identity. There is that cave under the crag with a constant drip of fresh water from its ceiling; a seaman called Charlie was thrown into the cave by a surge, miraculously, when his ship foundered one day in the year 1824, and Charlie lived for a week on the sweet cave-drops before he found courage to climb up to the crofts above. So any place is enriched with quirks of nature and of chance, that make it unique.... That the same hill was there ten thousand years ago, and will still stand solid under the blue-and-white surge of sky in ten thousand years' time, moves even the coldest islanders to wonderment with mysteries of permanence and renewal (though the hills are shadows too.) And at night, in the north-east, the same star shines here as everywhere else in the northern hemisphere; but here alone it smoulders on the shoulder of the hill Foldfea and sparkles in Susill burn, and puts a glim on the hall of the laird with its brief heraldry.

The people themselves are moulded by the earth contours and the shifting waters they live among. They are made of the same dust as the hills they cultivate. It would be sentimental to say the islanders love the island they live in. Nowadays many of them say they do, and genuinely in some cases; but their great-grandfathers had an altogether different relationship with the land and the sea. They saw no "beauty" at all; at least, if they did, no record of it has come down to us. Men and the elements had a fierce dependence on each other, a savage thrust and grappling, that was altogether different from what we commonly think of as "love" in these gentler times. Perhaps their attitude to their women was not so very different. They would grow old; there must be a new strong generation to bring in harvest and consider the drift of haddocks; so a wife was taken as a promising seed-vessel, not a creature of transient scents and gleamings and softnesses.

The croft children came weeping into time, one after another. So the ancestral acres remained "real," and might not still— through barrenness or bad luck or improvidence—crumble into shadow. The love that croft parents two hundred years ago put on their children had a desperateness and depth in it that modern islanders hedged with security can hardly conceive of.

Yet who could bear to root a child in the womb, and have it cherished there and brought out into time, who stopped to consider for a moment what grief, pain, disgrace, violence, destitution, madness he was releasing into the world; if not for this immediate one, then inevitably, by natural shifts and permutations, for some or other of his descendants, even in the course of a century or two? No family tree from the beginning but has had put upon it, this generation or that, every variety of suffering. These outweigh the little compensatory joys—the boy with his lure and line, the linking of lovers, the old man's pipe and ale.

There must be a starker more compelling summons into life than anything imagined by either the "realists" of art and fiction or the "romantics."

For the Greeks, the actions of men were shadows projected by archetypes. The bread that we sow and reap is a tastelessness in comparison to that "orient and immortal wheat." The weave we put on our bodies, however comfortable and beautiful and well-cut—what are they to "the heaven's embroidered cloths?" All the elements we handle fleetingly "is diamond, is immortal diamond." And all loves and affections become meaningful only in relation to Love itself. The love of a young man and a girl in a small island is cluttered always with jealousy, lewdness, gossipings in the village store. But the mystics insist that Love itself "moves the stars." They say that, in spite of the terror and pain inseparable from it, "all shall be well"—in the isolate soul, and in the island, and in the universe.

The meanest one in the community feels this occasionally; he could not suffer the awful weight of time and chance the mortality if he didn't; a sweetness and a longing are infused into him, a caring for something or someone outside his shuttered self.

Mr. James Wasdale the merchant locked up his shop and rattled the door twice, to make quite sure.

On a Tuesday, twenty years previously, Paula had died. Every Tuesday therefore, when it was weather, Mr. Wasdale visited the kirkyard and stood beside Paula's tombstone for a decent time. Then he touched the stone and came away.

The sun was almost down. The chiseled gilt letters filled with shadow. Mr. Wasdale turned from the dust of his wife with one cold finger.

He walked for almost a mile into a magnificent sunset. He passed Sailor Jake's hovel. He passed the empty manse whose windows brimmed with cold fire. (The new minister and his family had not yet moved in.) Down below, at the shore, the croft of Anscarth was sunk in shadow: a hand put a lamp in the window.

Mr. Wasdale walked on.

Before him one gable and chimney of a croft house detached itself from a cluster of smouldering green hillocks. Rosie was there, inside, hidden—his daughter who had left him for an ignorant poor crofter. There was a child in the cradle, and another—so he had heard—in her body. He held no communication whatsoever with the people of Ingarth. They got their provisions from the Tennants' traveling shop every Monday.

Mr. Wasdale took a walk most evenings, before his supper; always in the other direction though, towards the crags and the sea. Why had he come this way tonight? He hesitated. He would not go a step further. He imagined for a moment what it would be to knock at the door of Ingarth. He smiled. He would rather lose a hundred pounds than do that. But, standing between the dead and the unborn, he was moved a little; as if, after long drought, a crofter had come out of the rust of his stable and smelt rain in the wind.

Mr. Wasdale turned. He walked back through the darkening island. Jake Sandside leaned, puffing a pipe, against the doorpost of his hut. Mr. Wasdale raised his hand. Sailor Jake looked the other way.

The kindness that he felt every Tuesday for his dead wife (in spite of repeated meannesses dealt out to her while she was alive, in the name of thrift), his possessiveness and ambition for his daughter Rosie—and they were the only people, apart from his mother, that he had ever cared for in any way—that "love" still existed. He would not deny it. But it was different now. It had nothing whatever to do with money or prestige. Age and estrangement and death had removed the seed from his keeping; it was part now of the precarious continuing life of the island.

A star shone out at the shoulder of Foldfea. His feet stirred the dark dust.

The village was all lighted squares and darkness and sea-sounds when he came back once more among the houses.

Mr. Wasdale fitted his key carefully into the lock.

WRITINGS

Anscarth, Selskay,
12 August

Dear Tony, You have read about it in all the papers, of course, so there's no point in repeating the stark fact that I am out of the kirk. A month ago I resigned—it might have been braver if I had hung on until they sacked me. But I have caused enough distress to everyone. Let's hope there'll be no more fireworks display from the newspapers. (I nearly throttled the last two reporters who called at the manse.) I'm living with Tilly's folk at a croft called Anscarth, just above the beach; but not permanently; I hope to get a place of our own soon, preferably before the baby comes. The Scabras—that's Tilly's folk—are a broody family: the house is in tumult from morning to night. It's small too—Tilly and I have to share a back room with two other infants. It's as different as can be from the silence of the manse: the situation calls for more sweetness of soul than I possess. "Dear God," I pray a dozen times a day—seething inwardly—"give me patience."...Besides which Angela (the mother—she hails from Edinburgh) is forever brewing and sampling the fruits of

Tuesday. I booked on the little nine-seater plane and on Tuesday morning was set down in a field half-a-mile from where the show was.

It proved to be one of the most hectic days in my life. (I had come to Orkney expecting peace, silence, solitude.) I made a tour of the animal pens, and viewed superb bulls, handsome orange-tinted sheep, cockerels in cages giving the sun a ringing salute every minute, well-groomed ponies, new gleaming farm machinery.... All the islanders were there in their Sunday best—and they know how to dress, believe me—and the girl's complexions and skins would break the hearts of the world's leading cosmeticians.

In an adjacent field, like old mushrooms, were the booths of itinerant showmen from the south.

I had a snack in the tea tent, presided over by a gracious lady, Mrs. Dale from the farm of Fiord. A snack, did I say? In London a meal like it would have cost three pounds. There were Orkney cheese, Orkney oatcakes, Orkney crab, Orkney ham, Orkney chicken. At the end of the gastronomic treat the bill came to about fifty pence!

Later I was glad of that lining on my stomach.

How delightful to move about in a crowd and know that not a soul is there with the intention of "doing" you or conning you in any way. There was one exception, an old ex-navy man, but he was such a delightful yarn-loaded character that I didn't mind passing a few minutes with him and parting with five bob—it was worth it. (By the way, why don't some of our writers hard up for a theme get in touch with such folk as Jack Sandside, or "Sailor Jack", as he is affectionately known in Selskay?)

Drawn by a crowd of merry youths in the entrance flap, drinking beer out of cans, I entered the whisky tent.

Because of the press of farmers in good thick tweeds, it was quite a feat to struggle through the marquee to the counter. I was greeted from far and near as if I had lived all my life in the island. Whiskies were set before me by men I had never seen before—not your English tot either, but a brimming noggin of Orkney malt whisky. It was as if I was tasting the essence of all I had seen and experienced that day. It takes a long time to learn how to handle the elixir.

Merriment, song, reminiscence all round me; and I was made to feel at home in the midst of it all.

Only one incident marred a perfect day. Two of the locals, a fisherman and a farmer, had a fight. In the midst of the revelry they suddenly fell on each other, and began to beat the daylights out. The crowd in the marquee seemed to expect this, and even to enjoy it. The tall strong fisherman seemed to be no favourite. Shouts went up for "Fred" to finish the b— off. It was quite violent while it lasted; but eventually the police arrived; and the two pugilists were handcuffed, still struggling and swearing, and frogmarched away.... I feel that one might have to live in a place like this for a decade at least before understanding of the folk begins to dawn—as the doors of the Black Maria opened to receive them, Fred and the fisherman were smiling at each other, and they seemed to be trying to do a difficult thing— embrace with shackled hands....

I was assured that the two were old enemies. They used to fish together in the same boat, but had quarreled two years previously, and since then were at daggers drawn. The Selskay men, smiling, pushed more nips of the island whisky in front of me....

When I went out into the fresh air later, the whole bucolic festival began to waver about me like a merry-go-round. It's like I said—it might take ten years to understand these folk, but it takes a whole lifetime to learn how to hold their heroic whisky.

Two Selskay men, Frederick John Houton (27), crofter, Ingarth, Selskay, and Albert Sigurd Gurness (31), fisherman, Ness Cottage, Selskay, appeared in court last Tuesday charged with committing a breach of the peace at the Selskay Agricultural Show on 12th of August.

Both pleaded not guilty.

The Procurator Fiscal stated that the alleged offense took place in the beer tent in the course of the afternoon. The two accused assaulted each other with such violence that Gurness's nose was subsequently found to be broken and the lobe of Houton's ear was almost bitten through. There had, it seemed, been bad blood between Houton and Gurness since they had sundered their lobster-fishing partnership two years previously. They were apprehended with some difficulty by the police in the beer tent, and after being handcuffed were taken to the police station in the police van. On the way there they continued to struggle with one another. A blood test showed that both had consumed a considerable quantity of alcohol. They made no comment when charged. Their attitude continued to be so truculent that they were detained at the station overnight. Gurness asked that they be lodged in the same cell, so that "they could have it out"—a request that had not been complied with.

Both the accused were unrepresented.

Jerome Scabra (19), fisherman, Anscarth, Selskay, stated that he had gone to the show-park about 1 o'clock on the afternoon of the 12th. He always went to the Show but on this occasion he had a particular errand: to tell the accused Gurness that he would no longer be able to help him in his lobster boat after Saturday, as he was intending to go to the fishing with his brother-in-law. He had seen Gurness at the bingo tent, and told him.

Fiscal—Was Gurness drunk at that time?

Scabra—No, sir. At least, he didn't appear to be.

Fiscal—How did Gurness take the news?

Scabra—I'm sorry, I don't follow....

Fiscal—I mean, that you would no longer be going lobster-fishing with him after the Saturday.

Scabra—He said there was no need to wait till Saturday. He was giving me the sack, he said, there and then. Then he told me to clear off, he couldn't hear the man shouting the bingo numbers. I asked him for my wages, seven pounds. He said as I had only worked four days that week he was only owing me four pounds. If I came to his hut that night, he said, he would pay me....

The witness went on to say that the next time he saw Gurness that day was in the whisky tent. Gurness was standing beside the tent pole drinking with another man. Witness approached Gurness with the intention of placating him—he did not wish them to part on bad terms, as he had a high regard for Gurness as a fisherman and as a person. But before he could reach Gurness through the crowd there was a disturbance at the counter— Fred Houton and a stranger he had never seen before were having a loud disagreement. The next he saw, Gurness had come between them and separated them. But immediately afterwards

Houton and Gurness began fighting with each other. He had seen some fights in Selskay, but never any like that. They resisted all attempts on the part of the public to tear them apart. At last the police arrived, and took them both in charge.

Fiscal—Do you think now, that what you had told Gurness earlier, I mean, that you wouldn't be fishing with him any more, had perhaps upset him?

Scabra—It might have. We had both got on well together. He would have difficulty in getting somebody else to fish with him. He is not the most popular man in Selskay. It wouldn't be easy for him to fish in a boat like the *Thistle* alone—dangerous, I should say.

Houton had nothing to say in his own defense.

Gurness stated that it had been a most enjoyable fight. He did not know when he had enjoyed a fight more. Everybody should have a fight like that occasionally. It would make for a better island.

The Sheriff said it was disgraceful, when people were gathered together on a festive occasion like an agricultural show, that their pleasure should be spoiled by two drunken brawlers. If they couldn't hold their drink they should leave the stuff alone. He fined them each five pounds.

"After I'm dead, everything mine goes to Fred Houton of Ingarth, Selskay. The hut, the boat *Thistle* and all gear, the money in the post-office, the furniture such as it is, and all else whatsoever—A. S. Gurness."

The above document was found in the table drawer of Ness Cottage, Selskay, after the death of Albert Sigurd Gurness in a storm off Borough Ness on the afternoon of 6th November that same year. The deceased was fishing alone at the time. His lobster boat *Thistle* was completely broken up. The body was taken from the sea a week later by two other Selskay fishermen, John Gillespie and Jerome Scabra.

SEALSKIN

1

A sealskin, lying on the rocks—well, he could make use of that all right. Somebody must have dropped it. Simon didn't intend to ask too particularly: put a notice in the window of the general store, for example, or hire the beadle to ring his bell round the parish. Simon rubbed the pelt with his finger. It was a good skin. It might make a waistcoat for his father, he thought, walking back to the croft. His mother might want it for a rug for the best room. He rolled up the skin. He opened the door of the barn. He threw the skin among the low dark rafters.

His mother had the broth poured out. Three of them sat at the table—his father, his mother, himself. His father could work no more because of rheumatism; the trouble had grown much worse this past winter; it was as if his body was newly released from a rack. His mother's only concern was Simon, to see that he was kept warm and well-fed, so that he wouldn't think of taking another woman into the house—at least, not until she herself was dead and in the kirkyard. If ever Simon looked at a woman—on the road to the kirk on Sabbath, for example, or when the tinker lasses came to the door with laces and mirrors— a great silent anger came on her. For the rest of that day the old woman spoke to no one, not even to the dog or the cow. No other woman would share her spinning-wheel and her ale-kirn.

Thank the Lord, she thought, Simon is an ugly boy. That kept some of the parish Jezebels away. Even more important, Simon seemed not to be interested in the lasses at all. That was a great comfort to her.

There had been another son, Matthew, much older than Simon. One spring he had gone to the whaling in the north-west and never returned. That was ten years ago.

Eventually, she supposed, Simon would have to marry. Well, let him, but only after she was dead.

The old man raised his twisted hand and blessed the meal. They lifted their horn spoons and silently dipped them in the soup bowls.

2

In the afternoon Simon went down to the rocks for limpet bait. He did a little fishing now and then. He struck the limpets from the face of the rock into his wooden bucket with a long blue stone. The bucket was half full when he heard the first delicate mournful cry, a weeping from the waters. He looked across the bay. A girl was kneeling among the waves. She was naked.

Simon left the limpets. He stumbled up the rocks and loose clashing stones. He ran across the links to the croft. The old ones on either side of the fire gaped at him. He took his mother's coat from the nail in the lobby, and ran and slithered down the foreshore to where he had seen the girl. The sea was rising about her. She seemed to be quite exhausted. She didn't even cry out when Simon dragged her by the hair on to a rock. He threw the coat over her. Then he carried her in his arms up to the croft and the fire and the pot of broth.

"What's this?" cried the old woman. "Where does she come from? Not a stitch on her! A strange naked woman. She doesn't bide here. Out she goes, once she'd had a bite to eat."

The old man nodded, half asleep over the embers.

Once the girl was fed a shiver and flush went over the cold marble of her flesh. She slept for a while in Simon's bed. The old woman, grumbling, looked for woolen garments in her clothes chest. "That's my Sabbath coat you put about her," she said. In the late evening the girl awoke and sat beside the fire. She was not a girl from any farm in the island. Simon had never clapped eyes on her at the Hamnavoe market. They spoke to her. They asked her questions. She looked at them and shook her head. She uttered one or two sounds. She pointed through the window at the sea.

She is a very bonny lass, thought the woman bitterly. She doesn't look at Simon with any kindness at all, so far. But there would be days and nights to come.

"Well," said the old man, "I think she's a foreign lass. She

doesn't make anything of the English I speak, anyway. I haven't
heard of any wrecks from Hoy to Westray this past week, though."

"She can't bide here," said the old woman, swilling out the
pots with cold water near the open door.

"We're supposed to be Christians," said the old man, and
began to fill his pipe beside the fire.

Simon said he thought they would have to keep the girl for
a night or two at least. She could sleep in his bed. There was
plenty of warm straw in the barn where he could lie down.

The girl looked timorously at the faces in the firelight—the
hostile face of the old woman, the blank face of Simon, the kind
suffering face of the old man.

"You'll stay, my dear," said the old man.

The girl smiled.

The old woman set the iron pot down on the flagstone. It
clanged like a passionate bell.

3

The old woman was dead. Her life had dwindled away all
summer and autumn like a candle-end. She lay now in her plain
cloth-covered coffin with her hands folded over her breast. The
old man sat in his chair at the fire. His withered eyes grew
brilliant and brimming from time to time; then he would dab at
them with a huge red handkerchief. Simon arranged plates of
bread and cheese and fowl round the whisky flagon that stood
in the center of the table.

A face looked in at the window and presently James Scott
their neighbour from Voe came in. There was a shy knock at the
door—more a kind of powerful hand-flutter—and Walter Anderson the blacksmith came in. Presently there was the sound
of many random feet on the cobble stones outside—one by one
men from every croft in the parish entered the house.

Simon poured whisky into a small pewter goblet for each
mourner as he entered.

Everybody spoke in praise of the dead woman: her thrift, her
cleanliness, her decency, the golden butter and the black ale
she had made.

A horse's hooves clattered outside. A tall man in blackcloth entered, carrying a black book. The room went silent as he entered.

Simon poured whisky for the minister.

"Later," said the Rev. Jabez Grant. He opened his Bible and cleared his throat.

The old man, after two attempts, heaved himself up from his chair to hear the holy words. He hung awkwardly over two sticks.

The minister began to read above the shut waxen face in the coffin.

Through the window Simon could see Mara down at the beach, turning over swathe after swathe of seaweed, probing behind every rock. What was she looking for? Some days she came up with a lobster in her fingers, and once a trout flashed in her hands like living bronze.

"Amen," said the minister.

4

"I delivered the bairn," said Martha Gross, "one night in March. It was a very hard birth. Simon came for me near midnight."

"Just answer the questions," said the session clerk, Mr. Finlay Groat (who was the general merchant down in the village).

"So back I goes with Simon," said Martha Gross. "When we got to the gap in the hills, I could hear the screaming of her. It was such a cold high frightening sound. 'Hurry up for God's sake,' says Simon."

"Thank you," said Rev. Jabez Grant. "That's all, Martha."

"It was the hardest birth I was ever at," said Martha Gross. "A right bonny bairn when he did come, all the same. Lawful or lawless, that's not for me to say. I do declare he was as bonny a boy as ever I saw."

The beadle plucked Martha Gross by the sleeve.

"Call Simon Olafson," said Mr. Finlay Groat.

Simon entered the vestry as nervous as a colt in a market ring. He agreed with every proposition they put to him, almost before the words were out, so eager he was to be out of this place of high authority.

Yes, his father Ezekiel Olafson of Corse employed the woman Mara Smith as a servant-lass. Yes, he had carnal knowledge of

the said Mara in the barn of Corse, also in the seaward room of
Corse, on sundry occasions; once in a cave under the crags. No,
he was not married. The said Mara was not married either, to
the best of his knowledge. Yes, he was aware that he had offended seriously against God and the kirk. Yes, he was willing
to thole any public penance the kirk session might see fit to lay
on him.

Simon left the table, dabbing his quicksilver face with the
sleeve of his best Sabbath suit.

The girl entered, led by William Taylor the beadle. She put
a cold shy look on one after the other of the session. She seemed
to have no awareness of the purport of the proceedings at all.
She answered the opening questions with a startled askance
look, like a seabird on a cliff ledge when men with guns are on
the rocks below.

"Look here, woman," said Mr. Finlay Groat at last, "do you
know why you're here?"

She frowned at him.

Their hard questions hung in the air unanswered. Incompre-
hension grew. The men turned in their chairs, they frowned at
each other, they tapped their teeth. A great gulf was fixed between this girl and the kirk session of the parish of Norday in
conclave gathered.

They turned away from the girl. They discussed the matter
among themselves, in veiled voices. Her origins. Found on the
shore. Possibly from a shipwreck. What shipwreck? No shipwreck that winter. Or forcibly got rid of out of some Baltic ship,
put ashore in a small boat. Ignorant of the language. Ay, but the
holy signs and symbols—the Bible, the christening stone, the
black ministerial bands—all Christendom should recognize them.
She didn't seem to. A heavy mystery indeed. What then?...

"She is said to be a seal woman," said Walter Anderson (who
was the blacksmith and rather fond of the bottle when he was
not a member of this holy court).

"Mr. Anderson," said the minister coldly, "I think we will not
adulterate our proceedings with pagan lore."

Walter Anderson, chidden, muttered into his beard.

"A thing should be said in favour of Simon Olafson," said
Saul Renton the joiner. "It was a hard thing for Simon to stand

here this day. Simon is a good lad. Simon of his charity took this woman, whatever she is, into Corse, and fed her and warmed her. It is more than likely that Simon saved her life. I think— apart from the fornication—it was a good and godly thing that Simon did."

"Let her step down, I think," said Mr. Finlay Groat. "We can make nothing of her."

"Yes," said the minister. "I agree."

There was a concurrence of heads round the table.

The beadle tapped Mara on the shoulder.

Mr. Finlay Groat stated that he had a letter from Ezekiel Olafson of Corse. *Reverend elders,* the session clerk read, *I am sore afflicted with rheumatics in haunch and knee, and so unable to obey your summons this day. Simon must thole his punishment. He is in general a dutiful son. He labours hard on the land. There are worse fishermen. His lechery has been towards this one woman alone who has no speech or name. The bairn Magnus is a joy, he greets but seldom and that for a gripe or for a soreness in his gums, like all bairns. Simon has offended and so must be punished. They wish before harvest to be married in the manse if it so be the minister's good will.*

"A righteous letter," said Walter Anderson.

"The usual thing, I think," said Mr. Finlay Groat. "Three Sabbaths on the stool of penitence, before all the congregation, to suffer rebuke."

Another sagacity of heads round the table.

The beadle was sent to bid Simon Olafson and Mara Smith return in to the court, to hear judgement.

5

Simon and Mara were married in the manse of Norday at Michaelmas that year. The wedding feast was held in the barn of Corse. Guests came from all over the island to it.

The girl refused to sit at the supper board. She stayed in the house beside the child, though other women had offered to feed him and rock him to sleep. But when the fiddles struck up and the feet began to beat round in ordered violent circles Mara put on her shawl and crossed the barn yard. The dancers saw the white figure standing in the door, half in shadow. The fiddle sang like some wild bird from the world's farthest shore. Mara lingered in the door. Simon caught a glimpse of her through the whirling circles of the dance. He refused the whisky that was going round just then. He was vexed that he had had to sit alone at the bridal table. The hot whisky had made him arrogant and masterful. At least Mara must walk with him in the bridal march. No wedding was complete without the grand bridal march, led by the bridegroom and bride. He would compel her.

But when Simon reached the barn door, through all those stampings and yells, his wife was not there.

He crossed the yard to the house. The old man was in bed already. He did not hold with whisky and fiddles. For him the wedding was over with the giving of the ring and the minister's sacred pronouncement. He moaned softly in the darkness. He was having bad pain that winter in both his legs.

Simon opened the door of the seaward room. The lamp burned on top of the clothes chest, and flung a little wayward light on the darkness. Mara was bent over the cradle, singing in a low voice to the child.

I am a man upon the land,
I am a selkie in the sea,
And when I'm far from any strand
My home it is in Suleskerry.

The child lay asleep in his crib, quiet as an apple.

From another world came broken fragments of laughter, voices, clattering plates. The fiddle screamed suddenly, once. The barn fell silent again. A voice commanded. The fiddle moved into a sequence of urgent cadences, and the feet of the men moved over the barn floor to where the line of women sat at the wall with veiled expectant eyes.

"Mara," said Simon, "they want us in the barn. It'll soon be time for the bridal march. You must come."

She knelt over the crib, her head enfolded in the soft sweet breathings of her child.

The old man sighed in the darkness next door.

A slow anger kindled in Simon's belly. It would be a disgrace to Corse for generations if the things that must be done at every wedding were not done.

"I am your man," Simon said. "You will come now."

In the barn the dance whirled in ever-quicker circles to the last frenzied circle when the fiddler's elbow twitches like ague and the girls are almost thrown off their feet.

Mara took off her brides-gown and hung it at the hook in the wall. From her nakedness, gently laved by the flame of the lamp, came an intense white bitter coldness: the moon in the heart of an iceberg. Simon in his thick Sabbath suit trembled. His wife climbed into the bed and covered herself with the patchwork quilt.

The taking of the maidenhead had been accomplished twenty months previously. There would be no need for that ceremony again. She breathed softly and regularly on her pillow.

The light and the darkness wavered and interfolded and gestured on the walls of the bedroom like two ancient creatures in a silent dialogue.

Simon took his uncertain shadow away. He went on tiptoe through his father's room. The old man was muttering what seemed to be a fragment of Scripture.

Sick at heart, Simon returned to the barn. The reel was over. The barn was full of smoke and sweat and red faces. It was time for more refreshment. A brimming whisky-vessel was thrust into Simon's hands.

"Where's your wife, man?" said Frank the boatman, mockingly.

6

It was strange how the soul of old Ezekiel clung to his ruined body. He had always been a truly religious man. He loved his nightly readings of the Bible. Even in the days of his strength the words of Ecclesiastes had comforted him:

> I returned, and saw under the sun, that the race is not to the swift, nor the battle to the strong, neither yet bread to the wise, nor yet riches to men of understanding, nor yet favour to men of skill; but time and chance happeneth to

them all. For man also knoweth not his time: as the fishes
that are taken in an evil net, and as the birds that are caught
in the snare; so are the sons of men snared in an evil time,
when it falleth suddenly upon them.

It was good that a young man should know how in the end
all was bitterness and emptiness. He had never had any fear of
death—indeed for the last six or seven winters he would have
welcomed death heartily, like a friend. But death was still reluctant to knock on his door.

He waited upon the Lord, he said.

An unexpected sweetness had fallen upon his latter days: this
grandson. Surely the goodness of the Lord was never-ending.
The delight was perhaps all the greater because the marriage of
Simon and Mara had quickly gone sour. They moved about the
croft and did their appointed tasks in the due season, but they
no longer took any comfort from one another. They broke the
family bread with cold hands. They listened to the Scripture
reading with cold faces.

His own marriage had gone cold like this in the end; but first
he had had a dozen joyous lusty years with old Annie who was
lying now in the kirkyard at the shore. A year, and Simon and
Mara spoke only when it was needful.

It was a great sadness to him. He thought about it one summer
morning. The sun shone. He was sitting in front of the cottage
in the deep straw chair.

Mara was baking bread inside.

Simon was bringing a cow out of the quarry field. He had to
take that one, and Bluebell, to the pier in the village before the
boat sailed. They were to be sold at the mart in Kirkwall.

Old Ezekiel heard distant shouts from the hill. It was Mansie
and the neighbouring boy from Voe. The shouts dwindled. When
they came again they had a new thinness and clarity. The boys
were playing along the shore, where sea and sky are the twin
valves of one cosmic echoing shell.

The sun went behind a cloud.

And yet he should not complain. Simon was a respectful son
to him. And the girl, the stranger, did everything for him that

was necessary. It was not the loving ways of a daughter, of course. Still, he should not complain. He knew he must be a great nuisance to them both.

If only the dark courteous guest would knock soon on his door.

The shouts came from the end of the house. A solitary small boy danced round the corner. The lap of his gray jersey was full of shells and buttercups and stones from the beach. Mansie showered this treasure over his grandfather. Then he leapt into the old man's lap and flung his arms about his neck.

"Ah!" cried the old man in agony, for now the rheumatism was in his shoulders too.

"Get down!" cried Simon, leading the black cow in. "Go back to the shore!" Young flesh disentangled from writhen flesh. The boy ran behind the peat-stack. They heard soon the flutter of his bare feet on the grass of the links.

The old man's face was still twisted with agony.

"You should be inside," said Simon. "The wind's freshening. You should be sitting inby at the ingle."

"Mara is baking," said the old man. "I would only be in her way."

"You should have on your coat then," said Simon. "It'll get colder."

"My coat's on the scarecrow," said the old man, and smiled a little to think that his next coat would be a coat of heavenly yarn.

Simon fingered his chin, considering.

A freshet of wind blew in from the sea and brought with it a little shrill fragment of song. The boy was communing with the seals on the rock. Another sleek head broke the water, and another. The seals were coming close in to listen.

Mansie, thought the old man, always liked best to play by himself. He never played for long at a time with the other boys of the district. He was lonely as a gull.

"Wait a minute," said Simon. He went into the barn.

The blue hot reek of baking drifted from the open door.

Verily I should be very thankful, thought the old man drowsily. The wind on my face. Mansie down at the shore. Seals, sunbursts, singing. The hillside tossing with green oats. The good smell of bread from the hearth inside. . . . His head nodded on his chest.

Simon came out of the barn carrying the sealskin that he had found on the beach seven years before and had almost forgotten. He shook husks and stour out of it; the wind was grey for a moment. His father was asleep in the chair now. Simon draped the skin gently over the man's shoulders.

Mansie, having lured the seals with his singing, began to throw stones at them. Stones splashed in the sea. There was the gentler splash of departing seals.

Simon lifted the rope from the dyke and led the black cow across the field to the road. "Bluebell," he called, "Bluebell!" A red-and-white heifer that had been munching grass in the ditch ambled towards him. The two cows were seeing their last of Corse.

The old man slept peacefully in his chair.

The boy was running on the hill now, and creating panic among the sheep. He barked like a dog among them.

The wind blew colder from the sea. The sun was lost behind a huge cloud mass.

After a time Mara came and stood in the doorway. She was white to the elbows with meal.

"Leave them alone, the sheep!" she called in her strange bell-like voice. "Come back. Come here."

The boy stopped. The sheep were huddled in a gray agitated mass in one corner of the field. He turned. He ran across the shoulder of the hill toward the peat-cuttings.

He would only come home now when he was hungry.

The old man slept in his chair. Mara looked at him. Salt still encrusted the veins that had been nourished too long with corn and milk. She touched the sealskin that covered the shoulders of the old man.

7

"So," said the stone-mason, "what you want is one gravestone of Aberdeen granite to be erected in the churchyard of Norday."

"That's right," said Simon.

They were standing in the stone-mason's yard in Kirkwall, among hewn polished half-inscribed stones. Simon and Mansie, his son, had come in that morning from the island on the weekly boat. It was no idle excursion. Simon had business to do, at the auction mart, in the lawyer's office, with the seed merchant and the ironmonger, and now last with the maker of gravestones.

Mansie was not there. He had gone off to buy something with the few pounds his grandfather had left him—he refused to say what, until the thing was actually in his possession.

"The stone is for my father and mother," said Simon.

The stone-mason wrote the names down in his notebook: EZEKIEL OLAFSON and ANNIE OLAFSON. The chiseling of the names would cost sixpence a letter, he told Simon.

Simon had been meaning all winter, since the old man died, to erect a memorial over his parents. It looked so mean, them lying in a nameless piece of earth in the midst of the blazoned dead of Norday. Forgetfulness had caused the delay—a willed forgetfulness, in a way, for to tell the truth Simon found it unwholesome, all this tearful lauding of the dead that had lately become the fashion; and the stark bones hidden under a heap of wax flowers. The laird's wife even had a stone angel weeping over her.

"It is usual nowadays," said the stone-mason, "to have something like this, *In Loving Memory*. And then, at the base of the stone, some text from scripture, such as *Not Lost But Gone Before* or *Asleep in Jesus*."

"Nothing like that," said Simon. "Just the names and the dates of birth and death."

The stone-mason licked his blunt stub of pencil and wrote the dates in his notebook under the names, 1793–1896 and 1797–1860.

A thick-set fair boy entered the yard from the street, bearing a shape wrapped in sheets of newspaper.

The stone-mason looked up from his notebook. "I think you are a widower, Mr. Olafson?" he said.

"Yes," said Simon, "I am."

"Then," said the stone-mason, lowering his voice a little,

"should there not be another name on the stone?"

Mansie began to tear the paper from the parcel.

"No," said Simon. He shook his head. "She came out of silence and she went back into silence. I don't even know her right name. Whatever it was, it shouldn't be on a Christian stone."

"I see," said the stone-mason.

It was a fiddle that Mansie held up. The strange exotic shape shone among the blank and the half-inscribed tombstones that were strewn about the yard.

"I saw it advertised for sale in *The Orkney Herald*," said Mansie to his father. "It was made in 1695 in Gothenburg by Rolf Gruning. He was a very good fiddle maker."

"A waste of money," said Simon.

Mansie plucked a string. The fiddle shivered and cried.

8

This story is really about a man and his music.

At the turn of the century there was a stirring in the two Orkney grammar schools of Kirkwall and Hamnavoe. Suddenly, within a few years—as if in complete vindication of the Education Act of 1872—they produced a crop of boys of outstanding intellect. These young men went to one or other of the universities of Scotland, afterwards perhaps to Oxford or Cambridge. Most of them made brilliant careers for themselves, mainly in the Dominions (for they still kept some drops of viking blood; their bodies too were restless). All these clever Orcadians were men of science—medicine, botany, theology—and this practicality too was a viking inheritance: even the old sagamen kept to the factual truth in their marvelous stories, and were suspicious of the imagination and all its works.

The sole exception in this feast of scientific intellect was a young man from the island of Norday called Magnus John Olafson.

After tasting the disciplines and delights of two universities, and being uncertain for a while about his ultimate career—for he showed, in common with his peers, considerable aptitude in mathematics and physics—he turned finally to music.

He achieved a certain measure of fame while he was still in

his twenties. Edinburgh, London, Prague heard his music, and approved.

His compositions are out of favour, with most things Victorian and Edwardian, nowadays; one occasionally hears on the Third Programme his Symphony, his tone poem *Eynhallow*, his elegy for piano *The Blue Boat*, his settings of the twelfth century lyrics of Earl Rognvald Kolson, his ballet *The Seal Women*, and most of all perhaps his Violin Concerto with its few spare lovely melodies among all that austerity, like flowers in an Arctic field.

Magnus enjoyed his fame as composer and conductor for a decade and more; then gradually it lost its savour. With fame had come a modest amount of wealth. He did not know what to do with it. One summer he went back to the islands; first to the little town with the red cathedral at the heart of it; then, the following day, on the weekly steamer to Norday.

He did not want acknowledgement of his gifts here, and he did not get it. On the steamer he was the sole passenger, except for a boxed-in horse and a few cows complaining in the hold. He signed in at the hotel at the pier. The bar fell silent when he walked casually in. (They had spoken familiarly enough with him there ten years previously.) One by one the farmers slipped away. He was left with his lonely dram in his hand.

This was their way. They were shy and independent.

All these years he had carried Norday with him wherever he went, but his memory had made it a transfigured place, more like a piece of tapestry than an album of photographs. The great farmhouses and the small crofts had appeared, in retrospect, "sunk in time". The people, viewed from Paris, moved like figures in an ancient fable, simple and secure and predestined, and death rounded all. He knew of course that there was poverty, and such sins as lust and avarice and pride. He had smiled often, for example, to think of the devious lecheries of Walter the blacksmith; and how Willie Taylor, up in the hill in the springtime to cut peats, took his bowel-fruit home in the cart to enrich no land but his own; and how the mouth of Finlay Groat the merchant shone with unction even when it totted up the prices of sugar and tea and tobacco in his shop at the pier.

It was in a fable that these people seemed to move; and Magnus thought that if each man's seventy years could be compressed into a short time, his laborious feet, however plastered with dung and clay, would move in a joyous reel of fruition.

He was to be bitterly hurt and disillusioned as his holiday went on; for the people were changed indeed, but in an altogether different way.

They avoided him as if he was the factor or the exciseman. When the farm women saw him coming on the road they moved shyly out of the fields into barn or byre.

Even the boys who had sat beside him at the school desk, Willie Scott of Voe and Tom Anderson who had followed his father at the forge, spoke only when he spoke to them, and then in a painfully shy embarrassed way; and they were obviously glad when there was nothing more to say and the stranger had passed on.

A coldness gathered about his heart.

A revealing incident happened during his two-week stay in the island. A boy was drowned off the East Head—his fishing boat had been swamped in a sudden squall. Magnus was there with the other islanders at the village pier when the body was taken ashore. It was what the local newspapers called "a tragedy," and the reporters went on to describe the "affecting scenes" and "the stricken island.".... Magnus saw the women standing along the pier with their dabbling handkerchiefs, and the men gulping and turning their faces away as the shrouded stretcher was borne slowly up the road to the church hall.

He himself felt nothing—only a little irritation at the sloppiness of their mourning.

He stood utterly outside this festival of grief. He shook hands with the boy's father (with whom he had been at school) and murmured words of sympathy; but he was quite cold and unmoved.

Standing on that pier, the scales fell from his eyes—the change was not in the islanders but in himself. An artist must pay dearly, in terms of human tenderness, for the fragments of beauty that lie about his workshop. (Later that year, in London, he wrote *The Blue Boat,* an impressionistic piece for piano. It was a time of much give-and-take in the arts—poets had their preludes, composers their ballades and landscapes, painters their nocturnes and symphonies.... Olafson's *The Blue Boat* is what music perhaps should never aim at—it is a description of a passing storm at sea. When at last the wind has swept away the thunder and the rain-clouds there is a brief silence, the dove broods upon the water; and then the piece is brought to a close with a last brief phrase. This is indeed a mystery of art, that a few musical notes, in a certain pattern and tempo, should suggest the fall of a wave on an Atlantic shore; since even in impressionistic music there is no similarity in the sound the piano makes to the actual sound made by salt water spending inself on pebbles, sand, rocks, seaweed. The music nevertheless subtly suggests the phenomenon. And why, more mysteriously still, should the same pattern of notes impress the listener with sorrow, with a grief that belongs to the sea alone, with youth gathered untimely into the salt and the silence? The end of *The Blue Boat* is all heartbreak; as if the tears shed at Norday pier that summer day had been gathered and given over to the limbecks of art for an irreducible quintessence.)

The day before he left Norday that summer he visited the kirkyard at the shore. Fifty years before a new ugly kirk had been built near the center of the island, but the islanders still laid their dead in the earth about an ancient roofless (probably Catholic) chapel. Magnus remembered well where the family grave was. A new name had been cut in the stone.

SIMON OLAFSON
(1837–1884)

He remembered his father and grandfather with sudden deep affection. He wandered from tombstone to tombstone, pausing to read familiar names: Walter Anderson, Martha Gross, Rev. Jabez Grant.

Surrounded by these dead, he felt human and accepted for the first time since he had returned to Norday. He murmured the names on the stones with gratitude.

A dark comforting power rose from the vanished generations.

His wanderings had brought him back to the place where he had started. There was room at the foot of the Olafson stone for another name to be carved. It struck Magnus with a sudden chill that the islanders he loved might not want his dust to be mingled with theirs.

Next day he left Norday. Nobody said farewell to him at the pier. The old ferryman—a friend of his father's—accepted his generous tip and covered up his embarrassment with dense drifts of smoke from his clay pipe. Magnus wandered for an hour in a stone web, the piers and closes of Hamnavoe. A steamer received him; he was borne across the disordered surges of the Pentland Firth. The islands dwindled. At Turso the train bore him south to new orchestras, to brilliant friends, to the new compositions that were already shaping themselves in his imagination.

These were not paltry delights that Magnus Olafson went back to.

He had many good friends in the cities of Europe: musicians, dancers, students, writers, art lovers. They received him back into their circles with pleasure. He went with them on their summer picnics in the forests and mountains. They experienced together the new poetry of Rilke and Blok, and discussed it late into the night; and experienced the new music of Mahler, and analyzed it till the rising sun quenched their lamps. Magnus Olafson was well enough liked by his cultured friends; his clumsiness with their languages endeared him; and how he whose early life had been shaped by the starkness of sea and earth was at a loss with railway timetables, cheque books, wine lists.

He often felt, in moods of depression, that he was caught up in some meaningless charade in which everyone, himself included, was compelled to wear a mask. He would take part in their passionate midnight arguments about socialism, the ballet, anthropology, psychology, and he would put forward—as well as his clumsiness with German or French allowed him—a well-ordered logical argument. But deep down he was untouched. It didn't seem to matter in the slightest. It was all a game, to keep sharp the wits of people who had not to contend with the primitive terrors of sea and land. So he thought, while the eyes flashed and the tongues sought for felicitousness and clarity all around him. He was glad when the maskers had departed and he was alone again, among the cigarette ends and the apple cores. Occasionally, out of the staleness, would emerge a thread of melody; he would note it down on the back of an envelope and, too tired to work that night, begin to loose his boot straps. (In the morning, after breakfast, he would fall on the music paper with controlled lust.)

And his guests would say, going home in a late-night tramcar, "Is he not charming, this Magnus? And how shy! And underneath, such talent!" What they were describing was the mask; few of them had seen the cold dangerous Orphean face underneath.

And they would say, lingering on pavements in the lamplight, "He is so gentle and sensitive, this man from the north...." But Magnus Olafson had long given up the idea that artists are the sensitive antennae of society—art is, rather, the ruthless cutting edge that records and celebrates and prophesies on the stone tablets of time. A too-refined sensibility could not do that stern work.

He had a friend, a painter, who used to argue that art was no separate sovereign mystery, with its own laws and modes and manners, answerable only to itself: "art for art's sake." "No," said this friend, "in this way art will wither from the earth...." Art, he argued, must become once more the handmaid of religion, as it had been in Greece and in the Europe of the Middle Ages. Magnus remembered the harshness of the Presbyterian services in Norday, when he was a boy, and shook his head. He went with this friend one Christmas eve to a midnight Mass in Notre Dame. The endless liturgy bored him, but he was moved a little by the homeliest thing in the huge church—the crib with the Infant in the straw, the Man and the Woman, the Beasts and the Star and the Angels. It reminded him of the byre at Corse, and how there had seemed to be always a kind of sacred bond between the animals and the farm-folk who were born and died under the same thatched roof.... He left the church before the Elevation.

So Magnus Olafson had many pleasant friends, but found himself lonely among the rugs and poems and wine-cups. There is a deeper intensity, love—surely he found release there.... He had the thick peasant body that rises in a slow fruitful surge of earth to the sun, and falls away again. It cannot be denied that this woman and that came to Magnus Olafson's bed—modern memoirs are frank and explicit—but none of these intelligent and attractive girls remained his mistress for long. The spring was choked, and in what loins did the stone of impotence lie, when most of these women afterwards became adequate wives and mothers? His seed, it seemed, had the coldness and barrenness of salt.

So he wandered among the cities of Europe, increasingly celebrated and lonely, and found no place (the gates of his Eden being shut against him) to establish his house.

Lately a new problem had begun to nag at him a good deal—the use of art. In this too he had a peasant's practical outlook. Everything about a croft is there for some specific purpose: the plough, the oar, the quernstones, the horse-shoe, the flail. Each implement symbolized a whole segment of labour in the strict cycle of the year, so that the end might be fruition, and bread and fish lie at last on a poor table. But this fiddle, the symbol of his art—he had squandered all his skill on it, and in return it had drained him of much human warmth and kindliness—what was the use of it after all but to titilate a few rows and boxes of cultured people on a winter evening?

If he allowed himself to brood too much on this, a desolation would come over his mind.

One autumn, after a year in which he had done little work, he thought of writing music—a tone poem, perhaps, or even an opera—with Celtic themes. In the library of Trinity College, Dublin, he was shown an ancient Gaelic manuscript. In the margin, in faded exquisite script, some student had scratched out a translation.

> Thou hast heard how Jupiter changed himself into the likeness of a Swan or a Bull. Many a country spell hath turned a Princesse into a Paddock. Girls have put on leaves and branches and become very Trees. Such Metamorphoses happen now never, or seldom, for it was the curse of the Angel in the Garden, that each creature should seek out its own isolation and build a wall about itself. Then Man (the prime sinner) took after a season a foolish pride in his separateness, for, said Adam with the Apple seed yet between his teeth, We have graces not given unto Plants and Stones and Beasts. Cannot I measure Stars and

atoms of Dust with the span of my fingers, and utter sub-
tleties with my Tongue, and lord it over the Ox and the
fish? This was a false and a foolish thought, that came nigh
to tear asunder that most intricate Web of Nature that God
Himself spun on the Six Dayes of Creation. If Chaos be
not come in againe, the reason is, that the delicate thin
spunne Web I have spoken of still holds, though grievously
riven in sundry partes. There be rocky places yet in the
West and North where young men, finding shy cold creatures of no tongue or lineage, have led the same home to
their mothers' Doors, and begotten Children on them; they
have laboured and grown bent and grey together, and at
last lain twined in the one Grave. This is to say, Man hath
taken a deep primitive draught, and gotten drunk, and so
pledged himself anew to the Elements. Likewise this is
said, that many a country Maid, taking the shore road home
from Mass or Market, hath vanished out of mortal ken, but
she hath been fleetingly glimpsed thereafter lying upon
a Rock in a great company of seales, or (it may be) lingering
alone in a little bay and looking with large sorrowful eyes
upon the Bell and Arch at the shore where she hath learned
in her childhood to say her *Credo* and her *Ave Marias.*

Magnus Olafson was entranced, in a complex way, by the
crude paragraph. He who had never shed a tear for the vanishing
of his mother or the death of his father felt a swelling in his
throat as he read. At the same time his eyes and lips smiled at
the quaintness and innocence of it all. The homily—it was from
an old Irish sermon—seemed to treat of the question that had
troubled him all that winter.

He thought of the men who had thrown off all restraint and
were beginning now to raven in the most secret and delicate
and precious places of nature. They were the new priesthood;
the world went down on its knees before every tawdry miracle—
the phonograph, the motor car, the machine-gun, the wireless—
that they held up in triumph. And the spoliation had hardly
begun.

Was this then the task of the artist: to keep in repair the sacred
web of creation—that cosmic harmony of god and beast and man

and star and plant—in the name of humanity, against those who in the name of humanity are mindlessly and systematically destroying it?

If so, what had been taken from him was a necessary sacrifice.

rid of my book, let him do so by all means, but only in the way of vending, or selling, and only for a lesser sum than the sum that he purchased it with. He that buyeth the book for a farthing, I will have that creature for my squire and servitor in the eternal errantries of hell....'"

"What a strange document!" said the landlord to the minister at the manse gate.

"If such a volume exists," said the minister, "and I pray that is is only the work of some human imagination, but if this writing that you have is the copy of an actual book, I would rather be that dead rat in the ditch there than the man whose library it is in now."

The tavern in Hamnavoe was the scene of some extraordinary incidents in the weeks and months that followed the visit of the landlord to the minister.

For example, Jock Friskin the ploughman ordered a glass of rum at the counter late one winter afternoon. He had been ploughing all day in the rain and he needed some fire put back in his bones. There were a few fishermen and sailors in the tavern. Jock paid his twopence and the rum was set in front of him. He raised the glass to mouth-level and saw that he was about to swallow a glass of clear liquid, like water. He smelt it— it had the smell of water. The tip of his tongue too told him that it was water.

"Landlord," he shouted, "I ordered rum, not water!"

The landlord came scurrying from the opposite end of the counter. "Something wrong?" he said. "What's the trouble? Water, did you say? It looks like rum to me."

And like rum it looked to all the other customers, and now also to Jock himself: a glass of dark smouldering Jamaican fire. He gaped at it. "I'm sorry," he said. "I must have made some kind of a mistake."

"That's all right," said the landlord courteously. The customers returned to their card-playing at the tables.

Jock raised his "rum" again, and again all his senses told him it was "water."

He had a temper like a bull. Besides, he was cold and tired. "Look," he roared, "water!"

The tavern looked round, startled, at the red-faced man and the glass of dark spice-fuming liquor he was holding up.

"It is my best rum," said the landlord in a quiet voice, "out of this barrel of Jamaican." He turned to some of the sailors, who were experts in rum in all its variety. "Go and have a look at the gentleman's glass. See what you make of it, please."

Half a dozen rough characters crowded about the bewildered man from the fields. They smelt, they sipped, they held it up to the lamp.

Finally Amund the Faroese whaler returned their verdict. "Is very goot rum."

The sailors all glared at Jock, for wasting their time, and went back to their "vingt-et-un" and aquavit.

Jock made an act of blind faith and threw the liquor against his throat. A lump of cold water settled on his cold stomach.

He left the tavern like a haunted man.

The landlord began to laugh. He laughed till he cried. He laughed till he was so weak that he had to lay his head down on the counter. His fists trembled on each side of his head. He was beside himself with merriment. For five full minutes he could do nothing in the way of serving his astonished customers. "It worked," he said at last in a weak voice. "Jock and rum and water. Water and Jock and rum. Rum and—" His face crinkled and his eyes grew narrow and he began to sputter again with uncontrollable mirth.

"Is not funny," said Amund. "Zat poor man, he works hard all day, he need drink. He pay goot money. He zink he drink vodda. Is very sad."

He shook his head in a puzzled way.

As for Jock the ploughman, I'm glad to report that he went into the tavern on the opposite side of the street, and ordered a glass of rum, and there the rum remained good rum all the way down to his wintry stomach....

That is only one of the hundred astonishing things that happened in that particular tavern within the space of a few months.

The Leaping Dolphin acquired a reputation for weird and zany events. Folk came from other islands and parishes to see the gantry where one night in front of a score of drinkers the stone jar of brandy turned into a dog that barked thrice and then flowed back into its original ceramic form. (The landlord maintained that they were all drunk—he hadn't seen any such thing—it was some kind of collective hallucination.) Men from the English ships and the American ships came to see the stool where the mermaid had sat: a town bailie and two respectable merchants, having their morning dram, had actually seen a mermaid sitting at the bar. The landlord said no—how could such august townsmen, members of the kirk too, have imagined such a nonsense?—he himself had been in the premises all that day. He was of opinion that their honours had shared a generous jar before ever they entered The Leaping Dolphin. . . . He scratched his head for a long time, furrowed his brow, tried to imagine the exact circumstances of that morning. Well yes (he admitted) there had been someone, and a female too, in the tavern that morning—little Wilma the seamstress with her grannie's pewter flask to be filled with gin (for the sake of her poor grannie's bladder, which was frequently upset and could only be cured by Hollands). Wilma had sat down on a stool at the counter. She had been carrying a cod that one of the Rockall fishermen had given her, a huge fish with its tail swishing the floor. . . . While he was filling Wilma's grannie's flask with gin, the three important townsmen had come in. . . .

The landlord, remembering the scene, began to laugh. He laughed and laughed till he lost his breath and almost choked. One of his customers had to thump him on the back.

From all the islands folk came to have a drink in "the enchanted tavern."

In other ways the landlord prospered. A cousin of his in Virginia that he had never seen, died and left him a thousand dollars.

A deputation of townsfolk waited on him one day and asked him to become a magistrate in place of the mermaid-entranced bailie who was now discredited. He bought a silver-mounted stick and a three-cornered hat and began to walk down the street with a strut and a swagger.

A certain widow, a lady of property, whom he had admired for some time but who had hitherto given him nothing but cold looks, actually smiled at him one morning outside the customhouse. . . .

It disappeared overnight, all that sudden wealth and promise and fantasy. It was destroyed at a stroke, literally.

A black cloud tumbled over Hamnavoe one summer evening. Out of its heart came such drenchings of rain that all the towns-folk ran indoors. The cloud grumbled and belched. It sent out a single stroke of lightning. It tumbled on, diminished, over Graemsay and Hoy.

When the sun came out again, the little town beside the sea glittered and gleamed—all but one building in the center, which stood there, a shattered smoking cavity. The Leaping Dolphin had been struck by the thunderbolt.

The landlord lost everything. The lightning had smashed from roof to cellar, hurtling crazily all the way down among mirrors and panes and pieces of polished brass. Alcohol and ashes seethed and reeked in the foundations. The tin box where all his wealth was—his bonds and notes and securities—was ruptured: a few flakes of ash remained. His newly tailored magistrate's robe—even that was fit only for a scarecrow.

But one thing had not been destroyed, *The Book of Black Arts*. Every drawer in The Leaping Dolphin was charred and shattered, except for the drawer where the book lay.

Next morning, when he came to himself, the landlord gaped at it in terror.

He managed to start up in business again before winter and the return of the whalers from the Arctic, but not in the old spacious Leaping Dolphin. It was a little black hut at the end of a pier that he kept now, with three bottles on the shelf and an ale-barrel for a counter. A few old poor folk with small thirsts drifted in and out. The landlord made a miserable profit—that is, compared to the profits he had once made.

And all the fun was out of him.

Nobody heard any more that dark uncontrollable laughter.

One Wednesday afternoon a farmer who had been at the cattle mart in Hamnavoe visited the drink-hut. He had sold two heifers and his circuit of celebratory drinks brought him at last to the hut on the pier.

He bought more than whisky and ale before night-fall. He

rode home under the stars with a little black book that the land-lord had sold to him for sixpence.

2

The new owner of *The Book of Black Arts* was a surly lazy unpopular man. His name was Rob Skelding. He was resentful of every farmer in the parish, but he kept his worst venom for the neighbour who shared the hill Inglefea with him, a decent hard-working pious farmer whose name was Tammo Groat. Both men were bachelors.

Rob thumbed through the pages of the book he had bought, in the lamplight; his clumsy lips moved; as he read he looked from time to time through the small webbed window to where the lamp of Upgyre (Tammo Groat's farm) sent a glim through the night.

The two farms on Inglefea could not have been more differ-ent. On one side lay a fertile burnished slope, with silken-flanked cows and thick-fleeced sheep on the pastures beyond. On the other side of the boundary-stone were lank thin-eared fields, and indifferent stock, and a steading dappled with rot and rust.

Rob studied his sixpenny book every night that autumn....

Next year an astonishing thing happened, as between those two farms on Inglefea Hill. It was as if a great wheel had turned, against the sun.

The good farm of Upgyre withered and sickened. The seed died in the furrows, though Tammo dowered it with dung and seaweed. A few gray shoots broke the earth in June. A few gray ears smouldered like ash.

And the lithe animals dwined among the thin grass. The bull crouched in his field like a broken king. The gander and the ram mourned their lost potencies.

"It is a thing that happens," said Tammo. "I must have bought good seed. It is a cross that every farmer must bear now and then...."

But what struck the whole parish as extraordinary, and un-canny, was that the poorly tilled farm of Stark, across the burn from Upgyre, began that same summer to burgeon mightily.

It seemed that the surly one had sowed the sun in his furrows.

And his cows wore the sun between their horns. Their mouths uttered brightness on the morning. Their udders yielded continual brightness of milk. Rob had to employ a girl to make butter and cheese. And Rob's hundred hens bickered and ran and laid eggs like little moons under every tuft of grass and heather.

His cock announced royally the beginning of each day.

And his dog barked louder that August than all the dogs of the parish.

In the old days, when such a perversity in nature was observed, "witchcraft" would have been whispered fearfully at every hearth and threshold.

But some of this generation of farm-folk had learned to read and count. They had sat at the feet of a dominie, and had received a small measure of enlightenment. They had left forever the dark region of ignorance where witches and fairies breed.

That perverse turn of the wheel, as between Tammo's farm and Rob's, that was—must be—a sheer stroke of chance.

Rob reaped an abundant golden harvest. Tammo helped him to bind the sheaves. His own field was hardly worth putting a scythe to.

And Rob treated his harvesters, once the last scythe was hung up in the barn, with a kind of coarse joviality. There was a mighty supper of beef and bannocks and cheese and whisky. After the women had gone home to see to their fires and cradles a few crude ploughmen's choruses were sung. Rob gave his helpers a half-sovereign each to take home with them; like splinters of the fruitful sun the coins lay in those dark country hands. To his neighbour Tammo he gave as much butter and eggs as he could carry. "Look, man, my barn will be full to the rafters with oats and barley. There's enough beef and mutton and pork out there to fill the hold of a Balticman. That stone jar on the sideboard, it never lacks for whisky. Your land, Tammo, it's had too much of the sun in its time. Now it's all ashes—burnt-out cinders and dust...."

But Tammo shook his head and returned to his unlucky acres. He had faith that upon cinders a new breath falls—no man knows how—and dead flames rekindle themselves. That is to say,

Tammo was a good kirk-going man, and "resurrection" was no empty theological concept to him.

Winter whitened Inglefea. Then spring came back to the hill with birds and ploughs and oxen. Tammo ploughed his field with stubborn patience. Rob ploughed his field carelessly and brutishly. He shouted across the burn to his neighbour, "It's no use ploughing ashes, man!"

After seedtime a first shadow came about Rob's face.

What he had boasted about was true. In his cupboard beef, pork, ale, eggs, cheese never failed, and his whisky-jar was a well that perpetually renewed itself. But the good things of the earth mean little once the hungering mouth is a shadow.

The crofters waited for the green shoots to break sunward through the furrows.

Tammo's barley came up strong and green. Rob's came up as it always had until last year, sparse and wretched. (Not that the sick man, moving painfully between bed and fire, cared how his fields did.)

Neighbours came and did odd bits of farm work for Rob. Tammo milked his cows and set traps for the rats in the barn of Stark. Tammo had never seen such a plague of rats on a farm. They tarnished, they gnawed at, the hoarded treasures of last summer.

The servant girl of Stark went home to her mother, frightened by the skull that began to stare through the skin of her master's face.

The kindest man in the parish to the sick farmer was Swart the blacksmith. Swart sat beside his bed all night when he had his fever and bad dreams. Swart kept the fire and the lamp burning for him, and wet his gray mouth with water.

Swart spelled through the few books (mainly theological) in the kitchen of Stark, to keep himself awake in his long vigils. One book that he tried to read was a small black-bound volume with white print on jet pages.

"Take it away," said Rob when he woke up. "Take it away, man. Take it to hell out of here. That book will give you your heart's desire."

Swart thought that was a strange way for Rob to speak. But

They asked themselves that question more and more as the weeks and months went by. What ailed Swart? What had gone wrong with their good blacksmith?

His defeat in the wrestling match seemed to have changed him utterly.

The smithy was different too. The old happy winter evenings were no more, with the story-telling and the fiddles and the long patient analysis of the minister's sermon the previous Sabbath. It had suddenly become a stage for the performance of all sorts of weird and silly acts, and the only performer on the bill was the young blacksmith himself, Swart.

A pleasant man had suddenly become a braggard and a show-off.

One evening, when the smithy was full, he took a red-hot bar out of the forge and licked it. His tongue sizzled. Swart smiled and went on licking. The bar turned gray. He thrust it back into the white heart of the furnace, and drew it out, and folded his tongue languorously about the glowing iron.

Once or twice would have been enough. People get tired of tricks, however clever. But Swart kept re-kindling and kissing the bar for an hour and more. He was very pleased with his performance, and he showed it. Some of the older men went home before the smithy closed.

"I'll tell you what, men," said Swart to those who remained. "You remember that stallion-master who cheated at the wrestling? I'm longing for that man to come back again. Next time I'll kill him."

He spoke with such venom that the crofters looked at each other and slowly shook their heads.

"He was a fine man," said the miller.

"I'll break him in two," said Swart darkly. "You wait and see."

Perhaps, the crofters all reasoned with themselves in the following days and weeks, as they worked in their barns and byres and kilns, perhaps all will be well again soon with Swart the blacksmith. Sometimes a cloud passes through the clear spirit and darkens the words and actions of a man. "That happens to the best of men. The cloud passes. Then we will have our old happy evenings again in the smithy."

But, if anything, things got more disagreeable in the smithy.

Swart's perpetual obsession was the stranger who had thrown him twice at wrestling. "That man," he said, "God help him when next he comes to this parish! I hate a cheat. You saw how he tripped me. You all saw that with your own eyes. You saw the way he butted me with his head. He will be made to suffer for it. He'll never lead a stallion through the hills again, not after I've seen to him. I hope he comes, and that very soon."

Tammo of Upgyre said he had heard that The King of the Glens and his master were in Caithness.

"Good, good," shouted Swart. "Thank you, Tammo. Thank you for your good news. What chance, I ask you, has the man against strength like this?...." He took a horse-shoe from the wall and snapped it like a barley-stalk. It was truly an impressive performance. Swart had never managed to do *that* before. The previous winter the younger men had all tried their strength on a horse-shoe, without success. At the end of an hour's grunting and sweating Swart had said, "It's too much for us. We'll have to eat more porridge." And the inviolate horse-shoe had been hung once more from its nail in the wall.

And now Swart had broken the same horse-shoe with one twist.

A few of the crofters clapped their hands. The oldest one said, "That was right well done, Swart."

Their praise went to his head at once. (This had never happened in the old days either—Swart had been all modesty and gentleness.) Horse-shoe after horse-shoe that night he plucked from the wall and snapped as easily as icicles.

"Careful," said the oldest crofter. "Careful, man." It was not so much the waste that he was worried about as the unseemly twist and glint in the blacksmith's face—a kind of diabolical mask. It was Swart's face all right, but darkened and coarsened and rendered grotesque.

The blacksmith snapped the last horse-shoe in the smithy and threw the fragments on the ringing floor.

"That's what I'll do to him," he said. "When will he come, tomorrow? I hope so."

They called it The Night of the Horse-Shoes in the parish for many a year to come. At midnight Swart said to the three crofters who were still there, "Listen, boys, have you ever seen anything like this?"

The lamp had burned to a low glim.

Swart felt among the sooty rafters, and brought down what looked to them to be a small Bible. But when Swart opened it the white words on the black pages came at them like a scream.

They looked at Swart and shook their heads.

"I tell you what it is, boys," said Swart. "So long as I have this book, I can do whatever I like. Nothing and nobody can stand against me. I hope with all my heart that man and his stallion get a good crossing over the Pentland Firth."

The three crofters walked home on the midnight road without speaking.

The stranger and The King of the Glens arrived in Hamnavoe next day. The man was busy at the farms for a full week. On the Saturday evening he presented himself at the door of the smithy.

The smithy was crowded. Word had got around that there was likely to be a meeting between Swart and his enemy.

"Well, blacksmith," said the stranger pleasantly, "I hear you're eager to meet me. I hear the words 'Swart' and 'wrestling' wherever I go in this parish. We must have another bout, you and I, by all accounts. Well, I'm ready."

He began to take off his jacket.

"That's true," said Swart. "But you see, mister, it isn't every day I have the honour of meeting a famous champion. A smithy is a poor place to wrestle in. We should fight in the fields. Hundreds of people should be there to see. And money should be wagered...." He felt along the rafters and brought down a little bundle of notes tied with tape. "I, Swart the blacksmith, am willing to bet ten pounds."

"Ten pounds is a lot of money," said the stranger. "Ten pounds is as much as I earn in a whole season with The King of the Glens. I wrestle for fun and good fellowship."

"So," said Swart, "you are afraid of me."

"No," said the stranger. "But I do not have ten pounds to wager."

The stranger was not smiling any more. He was plainly put out by the open malice of the blacksmith.

"I will fight you in a field on Monday morning," he said. "I will fight you under the sun. Then I'll take my horse to the next parish. I see I'm not so welcome here as I was last spring."

But the men in the smithy crowded round him and shook him by the hand and clapped him on his powerful shoulder. Before the smithy was closed ten pounds had been collected among them to be the stranger's stake money. The twenty pounds were mingled together in a leather purse, and the grieve undertook to keep it and to hand it over to the winner. (More than one of the parish men hoped that their old friend, the braggart at the anvil, would be humiliated.)

The stranger bade them all goodnight. But when, last of all, he turned to Swart, his eyes fell away from a dark devilish smoulder.

The fight on Monday morning, in the field beside the mill, was the greatest that had ever been seen in Orkney.

Hundreds of folk were there, from six or seven parishes, and whalers and fishermen and shopkeepers. The news had gone round like fire on the wind.

Even the laird and his lady watched from the high window of the hall.

Whoever won the best of three rounds would be the winner. The grieve made that announcement, holding high the heavy prize purse.

Swart won the first round. The stranger was plainly nervous. Not one friend was there to hearten him (though he got plenty of cheers when he appeared out of the crowd.) But the hatred in the face of his opponent put him out more than anything. He went like a man in a dream at Swart. Swart's right arm coiled about his throat, and pressed, and wound. He must choke, or fall. Swart flung him on to the grass. It was all over in two minutes.

A cheer went up from the crowd.

The stranger was more composed at the start of the second bout. He knew now that many of the spectators were on his side.

Swart leapt at him the way a cat goes for a mouse. The stranger side-stepped. Swart blundered on, and was trapped from behind in thew and muscle and sinew. A distracted four-legged beast, the battle staggered here and there. "Face to face!" cried Swart. "Face to face! Fight fair." Then he found his face among the grass and daisies and churned-up mud.

The crowd roared, even louder.

The third bout lasted for half-an-hour. Such rage and cunning and strength had never been seen in the islands. They struck at each other; they kicked; they circled; they enfolded, enwound, threw each other off and away, up and down, right and left. Swart's chest heaved like his bellows—an invisible flame seemed to come from the gape of his mouth. The stranger fought coolly, calmly, as if he trusted that the torrential energy of his opponent must give out soon; and then the exhausted man would be his. Sometimes it seemed that Swart's strength was guttering out indeed. His clinching arms would drop, his legs would tremble. But always new energy came to him, from the sun or the dark earth; and again he turned his baleful power on the stranger. . . . This perpetual renewal of strength seemed unnatural to the stranger—it disconcerted him and discouraged him—the blacksmith should have been his twenty minutes ago. He reasoned with himself that next time Swart showed signs of faltering he would go for him before the devil poured new fire into him. The moment came when the sun stood right over the mill. The stranger thrust Swart from him. Swart groaned and staggered and shook his head. Then the stranger struck him like a thunderbolt, broke through Swart's arms, took him by the shoulders for a final throw. It was a trap he had rushed into. Swart's yielding body grew solid as rock. The stranger was wrapped in ponderous arms. The life-and-death wrestle began and lasted for five tortured minutes. The fighters seemed rooted to the one spot, they swayed as the gale of strength blew itself out. And when it was over the stranger lay on his back. Pale and smiling, he acknowledged defeat. Swart stood astride him, and groaned.

It was then that the crowd saw the blood at his mouth.

Swart turned away from the twenty-pound prize. He went blindly through the cheers and the offered hands. He staggered across the field and in through the door of his cold smithy.

There they found him, an hour later, with his head against the anvil and his beard red-clotted.

They carried him into his bed. And the grieve sent for Teenie Twill, who was the kindest and best nurse in the district.

Swart was grievously injured. Several of his ribs had been cracked in the fight, and he was in continual pain. But that didn't seem to worry him, Teenie Twill reported, so much as something else—a deep wound in the spirit. "I have been in the flames of hell," he said to Teenie one morning. "That man with the stallion," he said after a time, "is he still in Orkney?" Teenie said, yes, the man had gone on into Birsay and Evie, and he seemed none the worse of the fight. In fact, he was continually asking after Swart, and sending him good wishes. Everybody liked him. "Well," said Swart, "I hope I'll get to like him too. For my soul's sake. Meantime, Teenie lass, you see that purse with the twenty pounds in it—that's to be given to him next time he's in the parish. He won, after all. *He* won. He didn't have to fight me *and* the black creature that was inside me that day."

Teenie didn't know what to make of that kind of talk. Swart still wandered a bit at times. Otherwise he was getting better— his ribs were slowly mending. But it was doubtful if he would ever be able to work in the smithy again. The wrestling match had taken too much out of him. He was a broken man.

One day he wanted Teenie to read the Bible to him.

Teenie didn't know whether that was a good sign or not.

She searched the house for a Bible. Finally, beside the forge, she found a little black book, and took it in to Swart.

He screamed and covered his eyes when he saw it.

"Take that out from here," he cried. "Out and away!"

Teenie, who was a curious little soul, opened the book and saw a picture of a man with a forked tail. Strange exciting white words starred the midnight pages.

"Teenie," said Swart in a low voice. "Would you like to have that book?"

"Why, yes," said Teenie, "if you don't want it."

"It will give you anything you want," said Swart. "It will give you what you most desire in the world."

Teenie had a certain heart-hunger; she knew, the poor soul, what most she wanted. But she did not think this weird book would give it to her.

"Well, thank you," she said.

"You must pay for it," said Swart. "It will cost you a farthing."

Teenie smiled at Swart's wayward words. He was not quite better yet, the poor man. He had just given away twenty pounds and here he was demanding a farthing. "Well," she said, "I think I can manage a farthing." And there and then she opened her little purse.

4

Teenie Twill lived by herself in a small cottage at the roadside. How did Teenie Twill live?

In the laird's big house, three mornings a week, she polished oak and silver and mirrors and twenty tall windows.

When there was sickness in any house, Teenie Twill was sent for at once. She had kind healing hands.

Teenie Twill stitched pretty designs, with coloured threads, on linen. The Hamnavoe merchants bought these samplers from her, and sold them to foreign skippers.

She was poor, Teenie Twill. But her hearth-stone shone and her doorstep gleamed and the little panes in her window glittered.

Teenie Twill's cat Twork purred and blinked and washed his face beside the fire, or on the doorstep on a summer day.

She had a certain heart-hunger, Teenie Twill.

Often the fishermen, going home with their baskets of fish, left a haddock or a little skate at Teenie's door.

But Sam the ferryman, he left nothing at Teenie's door. He went past her door without one glance. He did not seem to be aware of the little plain hungry face that watched from the end window of the cottage till he was out of sight.

Sam the ferryman was not interested in a plain creature like Teenie. Four or five bonny girls were after Sam, from the hill crofts and the loch-side crofts and the farms down at the shore.

Nobody knew about Teenie's heart-hunger but herself. If they had known they would have laughed.

One day in August Teenie, and a hundred others, went to the agricultural show in Hoy. Five boats ferried the people across Hoy Sound. Teenie enjoyed the show, with its prize rams and cockerels, and the ginger cake and the ginger ale, and all the crowds of folk. Soon it was time to go home. The sun was down. The ferry boats left, one by one. Sam's boat was the last to leave. Teenie waited on the Hoy shore till the very end. Sam the ferryman carried the other girls on his thick shoulder out to his boat. The girls screamed and chortled and kicked. Sam did not come back for the last passenger. Teenie Twill had to wade through cold sea to the boat. She was wet to the knees. Coarse arms hauled her in.

And at the pier of Hamnavoe Sam took sixpence each from the farmers and the grocers and the town wives. From the giggle of girls he took a kiss each. From the one who lingered last on the boat, Teenie Twill, Sam took sixpence.

That night Teenie Twill cried a little beside the fire.

Arabella her neighbour came in for the loan of an egg for her man's supper. "Mercy." she cried, seeing Teenie's tear-studded face, "have you not enjoyed yourself at the show?"

Teenie nodded, but went on crying, and put a couple of eggs, blindly, in Arabella's hands. (She would of course never see the eggs again—Arabella forgot about loans at once.)

Arabella reported to her man that Teenie Twill was going a bit queer in the head—first signs of spinsterhood—a pity for the creature.

That same night Teenie opened, idly, the farthing book she had got from Swart the blacksmith. She could make neither head nor tail of it. But there were a few loose pages with elegant writing on them tucked into the back cover. This, Teenie thought, must be the English version of the text. The translation was difficult enough, in all conscience. Teenie sighed. Then she came to a section with this heading—"Concerning the Heart, and the Cold Alien Heart of Another, and How that Heart Is to Be Aroused, and Hunted Down, and so Won." ... What on earth did *that* mean? Teenie read on. She read beyond midnight. Her eyes were bright and her cheeks burned. Still she read. Her lamp flared and gulped and went out. Teenie gave a little cry of terror. She left the book on a chair and groped her way to bed. But she did not sleep. Her eyes shone with excitement on the pillow till the sun got up.

The very next morning Teenie was sweeping the ashes from

her hearth. The cat licked daintily from his plate of milk. There came a loud thundering at the door that made Teenie and the cat jump on the flagstones.

"Come in," said Teenie in her small voice.

Sam the ferryman entered. He was in pain. He pointed to his right hand. A splinter from the oar had gone into the palm: not just a little needle of wood either, but a ragged sizeable fragment. He winced with pain. The fishermen had told him to go to Teenie. They said she would get the splinter out and bind up his wound. If anybody could cure it, it was Teenie.

Quietly, without any fuss, Teenie performed the ritual of healing.

Sam the ferryman stayed on for his dinner. He ate the herring and potatoes and butter with his left hand. With his bandaged right hand he stroked the cat.

He said he was in no hurry to get back to the *Swift* (that was the name of his boat.) It was a slack time of year with him.

Teenie brought him a mug of ale. He said it was very good ale. The cat leapt up on his lap. Teenie put more peats on the fire. Then she brought him the full jug of ale and set it on the table before him, so that he could help himself.

Sam the ferryman smiled at Teenie.

Sam stayed all afternoon. He said what a neat clean bit of a place Teenie had. Arabella from next door came in for a loan of a lump of butter. Teenie said, quite sharply, that she had no butter to spare. Arabella had never been sent away empty-handed before. She told Andrew—that was the name of her husband—that Teenie was entertaining a man, none other than Sam the ferryman, in whose company no lass was safe.

The autumn shadows began to cluster in the corners of Teenie's house.

Sam said she must be very comfortable in such a trim bright cosy little place.

Teenie said yes, but for loneliness now and then.

Teenie brought him bannocks with butter and rhubarb jam thick on them; and, of course, more ale. Twork slept on Sam's lap. Sam said he didn't know the time he had enjoyed a day as much; and that in spite of the trouble in his hand.

It grew darker. They crouched, two shadows, at each side of the fire.

Sam said it was a hard and a tiresome life, the life he led: eating coarse ill-cooked food day after day, putting to sea with strangers in all weathers, sleeping under the stars with no cover but a tattered sheepskin. It was not much of a life, when you thought about it.

Teenie went to light the lamp. Sam said there was no need for that. It was cheerier in the firelight. That was another thing he missed in his trade, a good fire to come home to.

Once Teenie thought she saw a face pressed to the window: Arabella's.

Sam said he supposed he would have to be getting back to the boat. He emptied Twork from his lap on to the floor.

Teenie said Sam would be the better of biding for a bite of supper. It was very cold outside. He shouldn't trust his hand to the night frost. It might fester and grow rotten. He wouldn't want to lose his hand! He wouldn't want to end his days with a hook at the end of his arm!

Teenie and Sam laughed, one on each side of the fire.

Sam held out his bandaged hand in the firelight. Teenie took it gently in both her hands. Then she kissed it.

The two shadows leaned towards each other until they made a kind of arch in the firelight, the keystone of which was a red tremulous kiss.

The cat leapt softly on to the bed.

The flames lessened in the hearth. The peats sank through red into gray, with innumerable whisperings. Teenie shivered in the sudden chill. Sam's hand began to hurt. It was time for both to seek another warmth....

Arabella saw Sam going down to the shore before the sun got up, in the twilight before dawn. "That little hypocrite!" she said to Andrew her man. "So prim and proper and respectable! I would never have believed it. But I saw it with my own two eyes. I did. It's as sure as I stand here. Same the ferryman, of all men—a cruel heartless brute if ever there was one. I need the loan of a bottle of ale from her, for your breakfast, but I've a good mind not to go!"

The story of poor Teenie Twill is so painful from here on that I will try to make an end with as few words as possible.

She got her heart's desire. But bitterly she had to pay for it, with sorrow upon sorrow.

Her first sorrow was that Sam the ferryman never visited her again. After a few nights she went down to his hut on the shore. He closed the door in her face. Arabella's estimate of his character was not far wrong—"a cruel heartless brute."

His hand, I'm sorry to say, soon healed.

The second grief that afflicted Teenie was that, after five months or so, once the evidence was plain to be seen, she was haled before the kirk session, and sternly reprimanded for her sin, and ordered to stand for three Sundays in succession, in sackcloth, before the congregation in the parish kirk. And there the minister lashed her with his tongue. And Arabella nodded her entire approval, sitting in the front seat of the gallery. Teenie stood there as cold and still as a statue.

The third grief that fell on Teenie was that the respectable folk of the parish no longer recognized her. The laird's lady dismissed her from her service. Teenie was very poor after that, and very lonely. But still a fisherman here and there left a fish on her doorstep. And such good folks as Tammo of Upgyre saw that she didn't lack for meal and butter and an egg or two. And Swart the blacksmith told her to take as many peats from his stack as she needed.

Arabella never came again to borrow a single thing, for a whole year and more.

Teenie's fourth grief was the birth of a little boy, in that cold house, with much pain, one summer evening. It was a beautiful child. But it drew only a few breaths in this world, and then the surly midwife covered its face, and the sexton carried it to the kirkyard.

After a few blanched days, Teenie was able to rise from her bed. The first thing she did was to take the black book from the drawer where she kept it hidden. "Sorrow on me," she said, "that ever I read in your pages."

She stoked up the fire and threw the book in. Nothing happened. The flames enwrapped it. Teenie thrust it into a red chasm, the very heart of the fire. It lay there, unconsumed. (It had begun in more terrible fires by far.) Teenie piled on peats and bits of driftwood all day. Next morning the book was there, black and baleful, among the ashes.

Teenie took the book to the top of the hill one very windy morning. She ripped the pages from the binding; she tore the pages across and across. She threw the fragments into the wind. They went whirling away in all directions, a small black blizzard.

When Teenie got home the book was lying intact on the table.

That afternoon Teenie wandered along the edge of the crags. She had weighted the book with the heaviest stone she could carry. She dropped stone and book over the edge. She heard the little plop and splash of the drowning.

When Teenie got home she saw a fish lying on her doorstep, and the black book beside it.

That was the fifth and greatest grief that Teenie had to endure—knowledge of the book's indestructibility. Grief is too mild a word for it. It was more like despair, madness, terror, soul's eclipse. For what had the begetter of the book said: "... if he should wish it in his heart to be rid of my book, let him do so by all means, but only in the way of vending, or selling, and only for a lesser sum than the sum that purchased it with. He that buyeth the book for a farthing, I will have the creature for my squire and servitor in the eternal errantries of hell."

Teenie decided to make away with herself, and end her life. No one would miss her except Twork the cat, and a few old folk and bairns and invalids. The parish would not be surprised to learn that her hat had been seen floating in the sea one morning early. Then the tongues would go round the parish like a bell: "Teenie Twill has made away with herself.... Poor Teenie Twill! ...The slut, it was the only thing she *could* do!..."

Teenie decided to walk out into the sea one evening after sunset. She wouldn't stop till the waters covered her mouth.

What was she doing then, lingering outside the manse door with a little hard square shape under her shawl? Not much comfort for her there, surely—the minister had lashed her with his tongue in public for her lust and shamelessness; what would he say to her, what *could* he say to her, who had studied wickedness in this tract and manual of hell?

217

Teenie Twill went up the long path to the manse door, drifting, wavering, once or twice half turning back. Her little fist
seized the brass knocker and let it fall. Then the huge house
was full of clangings and echoes.

A snippety servant girl opened the door and looked at Teenie
Twill like the far end of a fiddle; told her to wait; vanished,
came back again, and ushered her into a book-lined room.

The awful man looked at Teenie over his spectacles.

Teenie told her story in a low toneless voice. Then she laid
the book on the minister's desk.

The minister flicked through the pages. His eyes widened.
He gave a low whistle.

"So," he said, "the book existed after all. The devilish thing
has actually been read by mortal eyes, and here, within my
pastoral bounds! That drink-pedlar, he was the first Orkneyman
to have it. He came here to visit me, with his lies and his unction.
He made a poor end, that one—died of his own bad drink....
Then, let me see, who had it after him? There were plenty of
rumours. I only half believed them.... Stop crying, girl, you came
to the right place.... It was that coarse farmer at Stark. He was
supposed to have it for a time. Much good it did him. He wore
away to a shadow in a month or two. Robert Skelding of Stark.
A great beast of a man—nothing of him but skin and bone in
the end. His coffin was as light as an infant's.... That ever I
should hold in my hands a book hot from the presses of hell!...
They will not believe it in the Presbytery when I tell them, a
week come Tuesday.... Who had it after Rob Skelding? Let me
think."

"It was Swart the blacksmith."

"Speak up, girl. Don't whisper. I'm an old man, I have wax
in my lugs. Swart the blacksmith. I always thought Swart was a
decent young fellow. Very generous, very charitable. It only goes
to show. There's not one of us but has a chink somewhere in his
armour. Not one. And there the great Adversary inserts the point
of his sword. A little bit of vanity—that was Swart's trouble—
his only weakness, as far as I could see. He couldn't suffer to
be beaten, especially when it came to wrestling and lifting gates
from hinges and such-like nonsense. Well, well—so he gets a

good and a fair promise out of this abomination of a book, and he nearly kills himself (poor Swart!) fulfilling the promise. They say he hobbles about on a stick now, like a man of eighty. A stranger labours at his forge."

The minister shuffled through the black pages.

"It must have come here on a ship. I suppose that vagabond in The Leaping Dolphin was telling the truth, for once, when he said that.... Well now, girl, what do you want with me? If you think I'm going to buy this filth from you, you're very much mistaken. How does it come to be in your hands anyway, a little creature like you, eh? Haven't I seen your face before? Yes, I have. You're the lass I censured in the kirk in April...."

Teenie bowed her head.

"You're in far greater trouble now. I hope you realize that. I don't know if I can help you at all."

"God have mercy on me then," whispered Teenie.

"Just go on saying that, *God have mercy,* every morning and every night for a while. Maybe a stray angel will hear you.... Old Professor Macdonald in Edinburgh, I mind, gave us three lectures on exorcism and the outwitting of the Devil. But that was a long time ago, and I might have forgot."

Teenie told how she had thrice tried to destroy the book, in vain.

"So," said the minister. "You're the one who bought it for a farthing. You goose. Follow me, girl. We're going for a walk."

The minister put on a black overcoat and a black hat as big and round as a cartwheel. Together he and Teenie Twill left the manse and walked a mile through the fields to the kirkyard at the shore. The minister hummed fragments of the psalm tune "Kilmarnock" as they went.

The old gravedigger was busy with his spade. "Another funeral, is it?" said the minister. "Who is it this time? Always somebody. Into your shed with you. I have something to do here that isn't for curious eyes. It'll only take two minutes...."

The old gravedigger chuckled and lit his pipe and climbed out of the half-dug grave.

"Leave us your spade," said the minister. "I need it."

The gravedigger wandered away among the tombs.

Spade-flashings, smell of new-delved earth in the late after-noon light. Then the minister threw the spade with a clang against an old tombstone.

Teenie watched with a throbbing heart.

"Creation of evil," intoned the minister above the thing he held in both his hands, "put upon this good and godly earth (we know not how) for the destruction of men's bodies and souls, and for the enlargement of the kingdom of hell, know that a limit has been set to thy workings, and that this very hour and day thou shalt melt like a black flake in the holy fires of God, and never be seen more by mortal eyes. And as for the chaste and gentle person that thou thoughtest to bring down into despair and the pit of hell—for that there is no coin of less value in this realm of Britain than a farthing, or fourth part of a penny, and that farthing she paid for thee (and also for a farthing, Scripture saith, two sparrows are bought, creatures from the hand of God, throbbing jewels compared to thee, thou trash of hell)—as for this girl, I say, she hath fully and frankly confessed, and hath repented her of her folly, and now her face is Godward set as ever it was in the time of her innocency. Begone now, and for ever, out of time and beyond the forbidden yearnings of the children of time."

The minister threw the book into the earth. The swart pages fluttered.

The minister wielded the spade again. He scattered earth over the book. As soon as the first clod hit it *The Book of Black Arts* flared, shriveled, curled, and was a cluster of ashes in the rich last light flooding in from the west.

"Begone, like a dream, into nothingness," said the minister. "Amen."

Teenie sighed deeply. At that moment two birds chirped at her from a bush in the kirkyard. Teenie Twill had never heard such beautiful sounds.

"Bless you," said the minister. "That's it. Nothing more to worry about. We'd better be getting back now. I have a sermon to write."

Together they moved among the tombstones to the gate. Behind one stone the gravedigger was smoking, his pipe upside down in his mouth.

BRIG·O·DREAD

When thou from hence away art past
Every nighte and alle
To Whinny-muir thou com'st at last
And Christe receive thy saule

From Whinny-muir when thou may'st pass
Every nighte and all
To Brig-o-Dread thou com'st at last
And Christe receive thy saule

From Brig-o-Dread when thou may'st pass
Every night and all
To Purgatory fire thou com'st at last
And Christe receive thy saule

"I should say at once who I am, in case it is necessary for me to make a statement soon. My name is Arkol Andersvik. I have been married for twelve years to my dear good wife Freya. We have a son, aged 11, called Thord, a clever fair-haired boy whose craze, at the moment, is science fiction. His school reports are promising—I will say no more. We live in a fine old house in Hamnavoe, and I have a garden that slopes down from the hill to the street. My shop is in the town center. Out of whalebone we—my brother and I—carve souvenirs and mementos and I deal in a variety of sealskin articles. We do a fair business in summer, when the islands are filled with tourists. I am a councillor. I am fifty years old.

"I try not to neglect the cultural side. For the past ten years I have imposed a discipline on myself. I have striven to acquaint myself with the best that has been sung and thought and written. You might call it a quest for truth and beauty. At the moment I am engaged on reading *Hamlet* for the third time. A poem that I chanced on last week really delighted me—the "Ode on a

Grecian Urn" by Keats. It gave me a feeling of great purity and peace.

"My brother says this pursuit of culture is a substitute for the kirk pew. He may be right. I am not a religious man.

"Something strange has happened to me. That is why I am preparing this statement. I am not at home, not in the shop. I don't know where I am, that's the truth. I am sitting on a bench in a bare room, like a prison cell. (But that's impossible.) Or it could be like a room where witnesses wait until they are called to give their evidence. It is worrying. I have never been involved in any kind of legal process. I intend to get to the bottom of it. It is a waste of my time, to put it mildly. I have a business to attend to. I have council work to see to this very evening. Freya will be very worried indeed.

"I have just discovered, with a certain relief, that I am not in prison; they have not removed my tie and bootlaces. I will go on writing in my notebook. That might help to clarify the situation in my mind.

"Wistan and I went seal-shooting yesterday afternoon, it being early closing day in the town. (Wistan is my youngest brother.) We took our guns and motored four miles along the coast to a certain skerry where the seals come and go all summer. Some people wax sentimental over these animals. They invoke all the old legends about the selkie folk, half man and half seal, and their fondness for music. They denounce those who slaughter them, forgetting that they are voracious beasts that eat half the fish in the sea. The legends are charming, but most of that kind of talk is slush. Every man has his living to make. (What about the beasts that are slaughtered for our Sunday joints?)

"Wistan and I got out of the van at the cliff top and, carrying our guns, made our way carefully down salt broken ledges to the sea, only to find that the skerry was bare. The seals were away at their fishing. That was disappointing. We decided to wait for an hour or so, seeing that it was a fine afternoon and still early. I laid my gun along a ledge of rock. Wistan said he would take a walk round the coast, to see if he could find some shells or stones that—properly decorated—might tempt the tourists in search of souvenirs. He offered me his whisky flask. I declined, of course.

"A word or two about Wistan. He helps me in the business. I might have made him a partner but the truth is that there is a certain waywardness about him, an unreliability. He went to sea as a lad—came home after two years. My father used his influence to get Wistan work in a lawyer's office in Kirkwall, but he left, saying he couldn't bear the thought of scribbling and copying all day and every day, maybe for the rest of his life. For the next year or two he was a ne'er-do-well, spending his mornings in the pub, his afternoons in the billiard hall. Most evenings he would take his flute to dances in the parish and that. Wistan's conduct clouded our father's last years—I am certain of that.

"In the end I employed him in the shop. What else could I do? He is my brother. I did not want to see him wasting his life entirely. Wistan has talents. No one can make more handsome sealskin bags and slippers than him, and the way he paints birds and flowers on stone is masterly. He, not I, is the whalebone carver. I pay him twelve pounds a week. He has a small house on a pier and lives there alone. (In case somebody should say, 'That is a poor wage to give a man,' I reply, 'That is all the business will stand. Give him more, he would simply squander it...'Besides, who but myself would employ him?)

"Poor Wistan! He is not highly regarded in the community. He was a delightful child, but some kind of raffishness entered into him at adolescence. It has never left him—the dreams, the deviousness. He drinks too much. Freya does not like him. I inflict him on her all the same—I insist that he comes to dinner every Sunday. In that way I can be sure that he gets at least one good meal in the week. He lounges about in the house all Sunday afternoon while I retire upstairs to my books and gramophone records.

"I thought to myself, between the crag and the skerry, 'How on earth can Wistan afford whisky, on his wage?' I am not a skinflint, I hope, and I have nothing against a dram in the evening—but to booze in the middle of a summer afternoon! So I shook my head at the offered whisky flask. Still holding his gun in the crook of his arm, Wistan took a sip or two.

"A sleek head broke the surface fifty yards out. Large liquid eyes looked at the hunters. I whistled. Wistan whistled, farther off. The creature stirred and eddied towards us. 'Come on, my beauty,' I remember saying. The water was suddenly alive with seals. And this is all I remember, until I found myself an hour ago in this cell-like room.

"It is very strange. Where am I? Where is Wistan? Where is the seal, the shore, the gun?"

*

Mr. Andersvik had no sooner closed his notebook than he saw that the door of the mysterious room now stood open. It was a summer day: there was blue sky and white clouds. He was free to go, it seemed.

Outside a signpost pointed: TO THE MOOR.

The landscape was strange to Mr. Andersvik. The moor stretched, a wine-red emptiness, from horizon to horizon. It was eerie, to say the least. "Well," he thought, "I'm bound to meet somebody who can tell me the way to Hamnavoe." Indeed, when he took the track that wound into the moor, he saw a few people and they too, like the landscape, had a remote dreamlike quality. They moved like somnambulists. Every heath-farer was solitary and did not appear to be going anywhere. The moor was a slow soundless dance of intersections and turnings. The faces were down-tilted and preoccupied. It was soon obvious that the moor-dwellers wanted nothing to do with Mr. Andersvik. As soon as he tried to approach one or other of these lovely ones, to ask the direction, they held out preventive hands—they had nothing to say to him, they did not want to hear anything that he had to say to them. Mr. Andersvik was a bit hurt to begin with at these rebuffs. But after he had walked a mile or two a kind of contentment crept through him. It was quite pleasant out here on the moor. What contented Mr. Andersvik particularly was the account he had written in his notebook in "the court-room"— he had set it down defensively (as if he was actually going to be charged with some offense) in order to put a good face on things, to cover up certain shames and deficiencies in his life that were, after all, his own concern. But here, on this moor, the images and rhythms of his prose pleased him very much indeed; he could savour them with extraordinary vividness in the solitude and silence. The remembrance was all pleasant, a flattering unction. He began the cycle of his life again—Freya and love and the garden, Thord and promise, Wistan and irresponsibility, the shop and sealskins and money, the council and honour, the temple of culture where he was a regular devoted worshipper.... The second round of meditation was if anything sweeter than the first.... This delight, he thought, might go on for a long time. He very much hoped that it would.

Mr. Andersvik discovered, by certain rocks and a certain gorse bush in the moor, that he had drifted round in two wide circles. He was learning to behave in the manner of the moor-dwellers. He halted.

"This will never do," said Mr. Andersvik to himself, breaking the lovely idyll. "I must get back. These memories are not entirely true, I'm afraid. I must open the shop. There is this council meeting tonight."

He turned. He strode on across the moor, frowning and purposeful. He was aware that his ankles had been rather badly scratched with gorse-thorns—he had not noticed the pain till now.

One of the moor people loomed close, with a tranced preoccupied face, drifting on, smiling, in a wide arc across the path of Mr. Andersvik.

"Please," said Mr. Andersvik. "One moment. I'm wanting to get to Hamnovoe. Could you tell me if I'm going in the right direction?"

"What's wrong with this place?" said the dancer on the moor. "What greater happiness could there be than this solitude? If you leave the moor you'll never get back. Beware, man. Your journey will end in ashes and smoke." The man drifted on, smiling, feeding deep on the honey of his past.

A finger of fear touched Mr. Andersvik. To go on like that forever, nourished on delusions! He was sure of one thing now, he wanted to break out of these endless self-flattering circles. He hurried on. Gorse tore at his ankles. Once he fell in a blazing bush—his hands bled and burned. He picked himself up and went on. Clumps of gorse blossomed here and there on the moor—it was impossible to avoid them entirely. Freya would have to put some disinfectant on a multitude of scratches.

He came over a ridge and saw with relief that the track gave on to a road.

It was strange. Mr. Andersvik thought he knew every road in

the island, but he had never been on this particular one. He came after a mile or so to a crossroads. The signpost said: TO THE BRIDGE. He walked on. Soon familiar hills and waters came about him. He recognized Kringlafiold and the twin lochs with the prehistoric stone circle. And over there was the farm where his sister Anne had gone to live and toil when she married Jock Onness thirty years before. Alas, Anne had been dead for four years. That death had been a blow to Mr. Andersvik; Anne was one of the few folk he had ever had affection for. He felt a pang as he looked at the widowed farm. Should he call in and have a word with old Jock? He thought, not today. The shop—souvenirs, sealskin—he was losing pounds. Besides, he did not feel in a mood to explain to the old man all the strange things that had happened to him. Jock was very deaf, and not too bright.

He walked on. Ahead was the little stone bridge that divides sea from loch, parish from parish. Under the triple arch salt water mingles with sweet water twice a day. A woman was standing at the hither end of the bridge. She beckoned to Mr. Andersvik. Her face was tranquil, as if a quiet flame had passed through it.

It was his sister Anne.

He tried to speak, but his mouth locked on the words.

"Arkol," she said. "I've been expecting you. You're been on the moor a long time."

"An hour or two," he whispered.

"Longer than that," said the dead woman. "Oh, much longer. Well done, Arkol, all the same. Only a few folk have the strength to tear themselves away from that moor."

Mr. Andersvik took his first dark taste of death.

"I had to come and meet you," said Anne, "before you cross the bridge. Otherwise the pain would be too sudden and terrible."

The half-ghost understood nothing of this. Death, in his understanding, was a three-day feast of grief, a slow graining and seepage among roots, the last lonely splendour of the skeleton—but all enacted within a realm of oblivion (except for a few fading fragrances in the memory of friends). An eternity of harps, or flames, had always seemed to Mr. Andersvik an insult to the human intelligence.

He could not by any means accept his present situation. Yet here he was, in dialogue with a solicitous riddling ghost.

"Arkol, you've chosen the truth," said Anne. "That's splendid. But the truth is cruel, Arkol. A poor naked truth-bound ghost has a terrible journey to go."

"What happened to me?" said Mr. Andersvik after a time.

"A gun-shot wound. In the head. The court said 'Death by misadventure.' Poor Arkol."

"My gun was six yards away on a ledge of rock!" cried Mr. Andersvik. "That's impossible!"

"Poor Arkol," she said again. "But that's only the start. Are you willing to be dead?"

"No," he cried. "I don't believe it. Don't touch me. I can't be dead! I have years of work in front of me. Thord must be given a good start. Freya must be provided for. There's the housing committee and the graveyard committee. I am going to extend the business. I haven't made a will."

His sister soothed him. She spoke to him with all the tenderness and kindness that in the old days had persuaded Mr. Andersvik that, for example, he must really not be so pompous, he must learn to laugh at himself a little; that he must give Freya a more generous house-keeping allowance, she was having to pinch here and patch there—it was a shame, him with all that money and all these pretensions.... Now Mr. Andersvik sensed a new depth in his sister's concern. He bowed his head. He yielded to her wisdom, there on the bridge between the dead and the living. Anne kissed him on the mouth, and so sealed his death for him.

Arkol crossed over the bridge then.

In darkness the dead man returned to the dimension he had left. Time is a slow banked smoulder to the living. To the dead it is an august merciless ordering of flames, in which the tormented one, in Eliot's words, must learn at last to be a dancer.

*

His fellow-councillors were sitting in the council chamber. There was a new member seated in the chair he normally occupied—his brother Wistan. The provost was making some kind of formal speech. "...welcome our new councillor, Mr. Wistan

Andersvik, to this chamber. We welcome him doubly in that he is the brother of the late councillor Arkol Andersvik, who died in such tragic circumstances a month ago. The late councillor was a highly valued member of this assembly. His wisdom and his humanity will be greatly missed. Some said that maybe he was over cautious in this matter and that, but my reply to that was always, 'Arkol Andersvik is a true custodian of the public purse....'A more prudent man never walked the streets of this burgh. We trust, indeed we know, that his brother will be in all respects a worthy successor. He will bring imagination to our debates where the lamented elder brother gave us abundant practical sense. I will ask you, fellow-councillors, to be upstanding as a token of our respect for that good man who was taken so suddenly from our midst...."

They stood there, a lugubrious circle, and Wistan stood among them. Arkol felt for the first time the pain of the wound in his head. He cried out that they had taken a murderer into their fold, a brother-killer; but no one heard him. They passed on to the next business on the agenda.

*

Arkol shook himself clear of that flame. Darkness beset him again for a while (he did not know how long); then, far on, a new flame summoned, a white splash of time. He eddied like a moth towards it....What shuttered place was he standing in? Light sifted through slatted window blinds. Or course he soon recognized it: it was his shop. The clock ticked on the shelf, spilling busy seconds into his timelessness. It was a quarter past ten in the morning, and still the door hadn't been opened to the public. So, it had come to this. How had Freya ever allowed it! She ought to have sold the business as a going concern. It had been a small gold-mine. Plenty of folk would have given a handsome price for "A. Andersvik—Novelties, Presents, and Souvenirs."

The key shrieked in the lock. The street-door opened. A familiar shadow stood there, carrying a heavy bucket.

Arkol saw in the light from the street that there were no longer any painted pebbles or sealskin on the shelves. In their place were pieces of baked hollowed-out clay, garishly decorated. So

Wistan had set himself up as a potter? The shop was a sham-
bles—it reeked of burnt earth.

"You killed me," he said sternly. "But you're too loutish and
lazy to enjoy the fruits of murder. How dare you ruin a good
business! Filthying my shop with your mud and fire!"

Wistan set his bucket of clay beside the warm kiln. He moved
over to the bench. He began to knead a lump of clay with knuckles
and fingers. He was humming happily to himself.

Arkol came out of that flame singed and trembling, and glad
of darkness.

*

He stood on Celia's pier in the first light of morning. . . . (Time
here was, as always, surely, a limpid invisible burning.) The old
women arrived with their cats and basins while the fishermen
(just back from the west) handed up the steps baskets of haddocks. It was a famous place for gossip and opinion and elegy.
Gulls, savage naked hungers, wheeled between the boat and the
pier.

They were speaking about a death.

"Accident," Maisie Ness was saying. "That makes me laugh.
You can't shoot yourself by accident. He was in trouble, if you
ask me. He was on the verge of bankruptcy. So I heard. There
was nothing else for him to do but shoot himself."

"Well," said Andrina Moar, "he isn't that much of a miss. The
swank of him! The strut of the creature along the street!"

Not one face on Celia's pier stilled with sorrow for the dead
man. Instead, the women, old and young, began to tear at Arkol's
death like gulls among fish guts.

The haddocks gulped and shrugged in their baskets: dying
gleams. Cats mewed. Sea and sky and stone was an asylum of
gulls. The voices went on and on in the sunlight.

The darkness wrapped him away, trembling, from the slanders of the living.

*

He emerged into fragrance and sweetness. A peaceful green
rectangle sloped down from the hill to the clustered roofs of
Hamnavoe: his garden. What man was that sitting on the bench
under the sycamore tree? It was, again, Wistan. Years had passed.

229

Wistan's face was thin and sick and grey. Was he perhaps on the point of accomplishing his suicide by alcohol (an end that Arkol had more than once prophesied)? Then Arkol saw that Wistan was somehow injured—his right hand (the one that had pulled the trigger) was white and thick with bandaging. Wistan looked very seedy indeed in that net of green wavering shadows. (So Freya, out of the foolish kindness of her heart, had taken the creature into her house, for cure or for death.)

Freya came out of the kitchen into the sunlight. There was an extra decade of flesh and capability on her now. She was carrying a tray with salves and bandages on it. Wistan looked up. Blackbirds sang here and there in the bushes. It was a marvelous summer morning. The man and the woman smiled at each other. But immediately the shadow fell on Wistan's face again.

Freya set down the tray on the bench. She bent forward and kissed him on the forehead.

The ghost stirred in its flame.

"So, dearest," said Freya, "this is one of your black days, is it?..." She knelt on the grass and began to undo the bandage on Wistan's hand.

There was a passionate outpouring of song from the rosebush at the bottom of the lawn.

"It *was* an accident," said Wistan in the shivering silence that followed. "The gun went off in my hands. But, dear, he'd done such terrible things, anything he could think of—you know—to make me eat dirt, that sometimes I think..."

"We've been through all that before," said Freya the comforter. "I know. You've told me hundreds of times." She kissed the scarred hand. "There, if it helps you. Of course it was an accident. Just as you didn't mean to put your hand in the kiln last Friday. You were aiming for the seal that day. You might as well argue that *I* killed Arkol. If I didn't particularly want him to die, that was just because I'd got used to him. I realize that now.... You wedged the gun into his arms—that's all you have to reproach yourself with, love. It was nothing. It was clever of you, in fact. It saved a lot of trouble, a lot of fuss and anger and suspicion."

Wistan closed his eyes. Freya began to spread the unguent over his charred palm.

Freya said, after another blackbird interlude, "I don't think now, looking back, that I ever really liked Arkol. The meanness of him, the arrogance! That horrible flesh lying beside me all night and every night! But you, dear, the first time I ever saw you..."

The ghost smouldered in the garden, among the sievings of birdsong. It glowed. It reeked. It longed to be anywhere, in any darkness, away from this incestuous place. Then it remembered, and acquiesced in the stake. The flames thickened. The ghost burned terribly. Yet it forced itself to look while Freya wrapped Wistan's wound in new bandages, swiftly, delicately, tenderly; and even afterwards, when the man and the woman enfolded each other on the long bench.

If only a ghost could die.... It bore into the darkness terrible new scorchings.

*

Arkol came to a room that had a stale smell in it. It was the study where he had sought to improve his mind with good music and books. A reproduction of Van Gogh's "Sunflowers" hung over the mantelpiece. Freya, it seemed, had sealed the place off like a mausoleum. The dust whispered to him from shelf and record-player, "What good was it to you, after all? You went through life blind and dense and hoodwinked. Here we are, Chopin and Jane Austen and Shelley, and we tried to tell you many a wise and many a true thing, but it only served to bolster your self-importance. Go and look for some peace now, poor ghost, if you can...." No one ever entered the study. *Hamlet* was lying on the table, just as he had left it the day before his murder, and *The Oxford Book of English Verse*, open at "The Grecian Urn." The ghost bent over the gray page. The poem was, as never before, a cold pure round of silence; a fold; a chalice where, having tasted, a man may understand and rejoice.

*

Arkol passed deeper into the charred ruins of his life. In another room a youth was sitting at a table, making notes of some kind. Thord had grown into a pleasant-looking young man. Bits

231

of *Hamlet* drifted through the ghost. "Thy father's spirit...He took me grossly full of bread...Avenge his foul and most unnatural murder..." The ghost smiled, in spite of its pain. As if this ordinary youth could ever be roused to such eagle-heights of rage, assoilment, passion! What had Thord done with his life? Arkol had had high hopes of the shy eager boy with his pile of science fiction books on his bedside table. Thord, he had thought, might well become a physicist, or a writer, or even a seeker among the stars. The ghost bent over the warm shoulder. Thord was filling up a football pools coupon. On the door-hook hung a postman's cap. To this favour the clever little boy had come: knocking at doors with white squares of gossip, propaganda, trivia. It did not matter. The ghost drank the beauty of his son's face—and saw, without rage, how like his mother he was now. He longed to linger out his time in this flame. But, shadow by slow shadow, he was folded in oblivion once more.

*

This was the rock, right enough. Coldness and heaviness and poise lay across the ghost, a gun-shape. It oppressed him. He wished he were free of it. Another man was walking on the loose stones of the beach fifty yards away. The man stooped and picked up a stone or a shell every now and again. The man uncorked a flask and tilted it towards his mouth. A sleek head broke the grey surface—a seal, with large dark brimming eyes. The ghost whistled, but no smallest sound was added to the wash of the waves, the sliding of stones, the click of a bolt. There was another louder whistle farther along the shore. Suddenly the bay was musical with seals; they clustered about the off-shore rock; their sea-dance was over, they clambered awkwardly on to the stone. "Come on, my beauties."...Whitman's song came on the wind:

> *I think I could turn and live with animals,*
> *They are so placid and self-contained.*

A line of Coleridge flowered: "he blessed them in his heart."... The ghost raised an invisible hand seaward. He greeted the clean swift beautiful creatures of the ocean. He acknowledged the long wars of man against that innocent kingdom. He whispered for forgiveness. Then he turned calmly to face the blaze and the roar.

*

The day began with streams of blood. All the village followed the white-robed priest and the heifer whose horns were hidden under wreaths and clusters of blossom. Children danced and shouted. The throng of people disappeared beyond the last house of the village.

The only man who did not go to the ceremony sat in his cell and waited. The door had been open since first light.

He heard, after a long loaded silence, a whisper on the hillside, a fierce flailing of hooves, a surge and a spattering; then a wild ecstatic cry.

Presently the folk returned to the village. The lonely celebrant went with his red arms into a small house at the shore. The village street was soon empty. Family by family, purified, was eating its morning meal.

Not long afterwards the prisoner was summoned out to the village square.

A court of some kind was assembled and waiting. The square brimmed like a well with light. People of all ages sat here and there. Arkol was invited to station himself beside a sun-warmed stone.

The interrogator faced Arkol. Four people sat apart from the others, against the wall of the pottery-maker. Arkol took them to be a panel of judges. They consulted together. Occasionally one looked across at him and smiled.

The interrogator began with a reading out of the statement that Arkol had originally made: "trust of the townsfolk...quest for truth and beauty...intend to get to the bottom of this..." The interrogator was interrupted every now and again by wondering laughter.

The older men and women sat in their doorsteps. Children—hidden voices—shouted in the gardens behind the street. The sound of the sea was everywhere. A young man went round the people in the square carrying a tray with a pitcher and tankards. An old man nodded approval over the white blown fleece of foam. An old woman shook her head reprovingly at all the raised tankards.

The voice of the interrogator—austere, measured, and melodious—reached into the bright morning. The villagers were rather bored with the proceedings, on the whole. Arkol could tell by their faces that they would much rather have been down at the fishing boats, or on the hill with their sheep, than wasting the day with such a trivial case. But at the end, he supposed, the villagers would have to give some kind of a verdict in the square.

Some young folk had got out of it by bathing. Arkol could hear shouts along the beach and the splash of bodies in the surf. There were mocking harplike cries, then a sudden silence. A young man, gleaming with sun and water, passed hurriedly through the square and entered a small steep alley. Children shrieked at the sea drops that shivered and showered over them. Voices from the rocks called for the insulted one to come back. A girl with wet hair appeared at the mouth of a seaward close. "We're sorry, Ardol," she called. "Please come back. Please."

"Silence," said the interrogator sternly. "Go back to the sea. We are considering an important case."

The girl withdrew bright hair, bright shoulders.

The case suffered no more interruptions. The interrogator paused upon this phrase and that: "...a word or two about Wistan." "I...am not a skinflint, I hope." An old man laughed above his ale. Arkol smiled ruefully.

A boy called from a hidden garden that he had caught a butterfly—he had—but it had wriggled out of his fingers and was free in the wind once more.

What intrigued Arkol more than anything that morning were the faces of the four judges who, he supposed, would finally decide whether his application should be granted or no. They sat on a long bench in front of the interrogator. It was as if old woodcuts and frontispieces and dead music had trembled and quickened. These were the jurors: a man with wild hair and a wild mouth; a young woman who in spite of merry mischievous eyes looked rather prim; a man with a russet beard and a scar at one ear—long lank hair over a lank dark cheek, a velvet jacket, lank fingers: the hollows and shadows scattered whenever the man smiled, which was often.

There was silence in the square. The reading of the statement was over.

The cup-bearer had spread a white cloth on a long trestle

table. He reappeared in the square now, carrying a tray with steaming fish on it, and bread. He set the tray on the table. He began to arrange seats.

"The statement, it is a tissue of lies," said the hollow-cheeked juror in a foreign accent. All the jurors nodded. They looked at Arkol and smiled.

"The wonder is how he ever managed to escape," said Van Gogh. "I took him for a typical moor-dweller as soon as he arrived here last night."

"He is a hero," said a girl in a doorway who was feeding a baby at her breast.

The bathers came up from the sea, white-shrouded and shivering. The girl whose face had been glimpsed for a moment between the houses looked anxious now. Her companions tried to reassure her. They went in an agitated troop up one of the alleys.

The cup-bearer carried from the inn a huge pitcher—both his arms were round it—some wine slurped over on to the cobblestones. An old man cried out in alarm. But the pitcher was safely deposited at last among the fish and the bread.

"As one of the villagers," said a man who was leaning against a wall smoking a pipe, "I think he must at least do this before we give him the stones to build a house—he must alter the account of his life so that it comes a bit nearer the truth."

The villagers shouted their approval.

"You can't eat or drink with us, you understand," said the interrogator to Arkol, "or stay here in this village, until you have paid your debt to the truth. You must revise your statement in certain important respects. You will be given pen and paper. Now that you've crossed the bridge and been through the fire, I think you may enjoy doing it."

The villagers turned away from Arkol. They began to gather round the table. The bathers, all but two, came down the alley and joined the others. Mugs and pieces of bread were passed round—there was a mingling of courtesy and banter. Three seats were empty.

Arkol sat on a sunlit step. He poised his pen over the paper. He wondered how to begin.

The children's voices drifted down from the hillside. They

were filling baskets with blackberries. Pure echoes fell into the square. The children shouted that they would not be home till sunset.

The lovers who had quarreled on the sea verge stood in the mouth of the close. They were tranquil and smiling now. They moved into sunlight. Folk rose up at the table to let them pass on to their places.

Arkol wrote. Phrases with some beauty and truth in them began to come, with difficulty. He longed to sit among the villagers, and share their meal. But the feast was eternal. He hoped that he might be able, before it was over, to present to the elders the poem of his life.

THE SEVEN POETS

(In Memoriam S G S)

Finally, after very much suffering, the earth fled from cities and machines.

Yet the war had, in its dreadful way, fused mankind together. The peoples were one, in woe and horror and destitution.

A simpler species rose out of the ruins, no less intelligent, but with their faces set against science and the ruthless exploitation of the earth and its resources. "Progress" was a word they uttered like a curse.

On the fringes of the vast deserts of ruin left by the war, they lived in small villages of not more than 250 people. (It was forbidden to exceed that number: if a village was shaken with sudden fruitfulness one year, certain young people chosen by lot had to hive off and form a new community higher up the river, in the next valley, nearer the mountain snow.)

So the earth became an intricate delicate network of villages, each self-sufficient but aware of all the others. There was no possibility of war between neighbouring communities. The making of arms was forbidden; even a boy seen sharpening a stick was rebuked. The animals ranged unmolested in their separate kingdoms. Men kept their dominion over cattle, sheep, horses, swine, poultry, fish; because it was held that men had a very ancient relationship with these creatures, a sacred bond.

*

It can be said, with justice, that a great deal of excitement went out of the human story once this pastoral system was established. Men considered boredom to be a small price to pay for their new tranquility. In fact there was little boredom. The simple village system had within itself endless variety.

There were however a few restless men here and there who

237

could not endure the life of the villages. Allowances were made for them. They were called "the wandering ones." They had freedom to travel wherever they chose. If they wanted to stay in a village and help with a harvest, that was good. If they stopped till the last of the snow had gone from the mountain pass, that was good. If they passed through the village at night like a furtive shadow, and drank out of the well thanklessly, and were gone in the morning, that was good also. There was no need for them to thieve—they were welcomed and fed wherever they went. I know; I have been one of those wandering folk all my life.

*

I have never found the village system dull and repetitive, though I must have visited upwards of five thousand villages in my time. Always there was the cluster of houses, with the occupation carved or painted over each lintel—"Shepherd," "Blacksmith," "Baker," "Fisherman," "Vinter," "Weaver," "The House of the Old Men," "Shoemaker," "Priest," "The House of the Women and Children," "Poet," and the three "Houses of Lovers."

A village in China is very different from a village in Greenland or Africa. The legends over the doors are in a variety of scripts; so are the offered foods and the dances in the village square and the faces of the people in the sun.

It happened that, wherever I went after the age of forty (being then too old for the delectable House of Lovers), I chose to stay in the house of the poet. You may say "a strange choice," and so it was. In almost any other house I would have been better fed and more comfortable; in the "House of the Old Men" I would have heard more entertaining lies; in the "House of the Vinter" my head would, night after night, have been transformed into a happy bee-hive. But it was the poet in every village that fascinated me; they were so various, so unlike, so unpredictable.

The main duty of the poet was to write a masque, or chorus, or group of poems, for the villagers to perform in midwinter. Those entertainments were in the main naive, and crudely performed; but the villagers entered into them with deep enjoyment, and so the poets were honoured people in the communities, and never lacked for flowers and wine.

Most of them were honest workaday craftsmen. But here and

there I stayed overnight, or maybe for a full week, with an extraordinary poet. In Spain, in a village high on a mountainside, the poet read me his new work. Rehearsals were about to start on it as soon as the grape harvest was in. In was an uninspired piece, and the man knew it. He poured some of the tar-smelling wine of the hills into two cups. We drank in silence. He was one of those that wine makes morose. At last near midnight he said, "I think often of the boundless power of words. A Word made everything in the beginning. The uttering of that Word took six days. What is this poetry that I busy myself with? A futile yearning towards a realization of that marvelous Word. What is all poetry but a quest for the meaning and beauty and majesty of the original Word? (In most languages the poet is "the maker.") Poets all over the world since time began have been busy at the task of re-creation, each with his own little pen and parchment. We do not know the great poetry of the past—the libraries are dust. But I think that Shakespeare in his lifetime made perhaps the millionth part of a single letter of the Word. Will the complete Word ever be spoken for the second time? When it is, stranger, than the world will be perfect again, and time will have an end...." He looked at his manuscript. "This is my contribution to the Word—such a sound as a speck of dust might make falling on grass—no more." He sighed among the harsh wine fumes. He did not speak again. When the flagon was empty he went to his bed. I was glad to leave the house of that gloomy man before dawn next morning, breakfastless. From the vineyards the harvesters greeted me in the first light.

They would enjoy the masque two weeks later, whatever the only begetter thought of it.

In a Mexican village the poet had done nothing for twenty years. "The bird inside me has stopped singing," he said. He was quite cheerful about it. The villagers bore him no grudge. The bird had stopped singing, there was nothing more to be said. The poet in the next village had to compose two entertainments each year, one for the songless village. "I say to them," said the once-poet, "'I gave you many fine poems before the bird stopped singing. They still remember these poems in The House of the Old Men. Why not perform them again, with the dances and tunes to go with them?'...But no, they refuse to do that. There must be a new entertainment each year. It is a sign of death, they say, to repeat a masque. These endless repetitions, they say, the worship of the husks of dead art—that was one symptom of the sickness of pre-Village Man."

I left him with the wish that the bird inside him might soon start singing again. He laughed, delighted at the possibility; but then shook his head.

In a Swedish village the poet was a great heretic. His poems and plays were all about machines: tanks, tractors, motor-cars, aeroplanes, the internal combustion engine. "These great times will come again," said the young blond visionary. "Next time we will know how to use them without danger to ourselves. There must come an end to this cutting of corn with scythes, and sailing out into the teeth of the fishing wind with only a patched sail! That is barbarism!" A hundred years ago he could not have said such a thing; he would have been ritually strangled if he had whispered a tenth part of it. Even in some villages today they would see to it that his mouth was stopped. But in all the villages in that part of Sweden the people have arrived at such a mildness of the spirit that they are tolerant of their poet. They take part in his midwinter drama, in which the heroes are made of metal and have oil for their blood, but they manage to do it in such subtle ways that the drama, far from being a noble vision of the future, is reduced to burlesque, and becomes by implication a celebration of the pastoral simplicity they have attained. "The truth is," said this poet to me, "they have not sufficient talent to perform my work properly."

Once I came to a village in an African jungle. The poet, a little old withered man, made many poems every day, sometimes as many as ten. They were all about the praying mantis, its wisdom and beauty and power. He clicked with his teeth, made deep clonking noises with his tongue against his palate. "Praying mantis, my delight, my brother, you wise one..." He had never composed a poem on any other subject. I could imagine, in the darkness of that jungle, the village performers declaring all one night the joy that the universe felt for that stick of an insect.

Somewhere in Siberia, one spring, I stayed several nights in the house of a poet. This man did not compose in any language. He repeated a few poems to me—not one word was familiar;

there was a syllable now and then that seemed to come out of the speech of the people. (You will have to believe me when I say that I have a fair knowledge of many languages, having been on the roads since I was a boy.) I listened to his theories late into the night. I only partially understood what he was trying to do. There was some kind of kinship, it seemed, between the speech of a people and their natural surroundings. Birds, winds, waterfalls, the coil of a river, the shape of a hill, even the hush of falling snow, moulded speech. "That is why the speech of this village is subtly different from the way they talk in that village twelve miles back, where you stayed last night. It is a matter of the utmost fascination. Human speech cannot be left to itself— it will wither—its roots are deep in the elements, our tongues take nourishment from the splash of a salmon in the river, the black howl of blizzards, the thunders and glories of the Siberian spring. So, in my poems I am steeping speech in elemental sound. This is a powerful, mysterious, and dangerous art. It will be the death of me before long." He was so absorbed in theories about his art that I was poorly fed and sheltered, day after day. As I was leaving the village, having thanked him at his door for the veiled but stimulating vistas he had opened for me, I met The Blacksmith at the end of the street. "Tell me," I said, "how is it possible for his masques to be performed? People can neither speak them nor understand them."

"That is true," said The Blacksmith. "I used to take part in the mid-winter masque when I was young—now I stand among the audience. Always we feel that we are one with the earth. We understand the silence of stones. We reaffirm our kinship with fish and stars."

*

Once, when I was younger, I nearly died among ice. Why I wandered so far north I can't remember—a young man must always be tempting providence.

I had no food in that white wilderness for three days, or maybe four. I remember biting my right hand like a wolf and sucking the warm blood. ("Better you than the wolves," I said to myself.) I expected such a grey savage death.

Instead it was a small befurred man with a face genial as the sun who found me. In a very short time I was sitting in his ice-house, among a cluster of ice-houses. There were no legends over these doors, for the villagers could not read or write.

They spoke a language I did not understand, too.

My rescuer gave me to know that I should spend the night in his house. Obstinate as ever, I shook my head. I made signs to him—striking an imaginary harp, kissing an imaginary pipe and making my fingers dance. At last he understood. His smile was broader than ever. I would rather pass the night in The House of the Poet than with him. He was not in the least put out.

A boy took me by the hand and led me through a squat white labyrinth of a village to a house exactly the same as all the others. Inside the smells of blubber and fish-oil were dreadful. I discovered, to my deep surprise, that the poet could speak several languages. He had been "a wandering one" in his youth. He had gone through Scandinavia and Central Europe, he had lingered among the isles of Greece for a while; then he had walked eastwards, through Persia and India, intending to get as far as Japan. But while he was being entertained by a village in the Himalayan foothills, word had come to him that he was wanted back home. The poet in his village on the shore of Baffin Bay had died; it was for him now to make the songs of his people. I interrupted him—how had this news come to him? The poet in the Indian village had told him, he said. All true poets all over the world have this gift of divination—an exquisite network of sensibility binds them together. (I had not known this before.)

Meantime the igloo grew more and more uncomfortable. People were crowding into it—men, women, children, even infants. The air got steadily hotter and ranker. There was no room to sit—we were crowded shoulder to shoulder. Others stood in the freezing night outside. All waited patiently for the poet to begin.

The word flowered out of a long deep silence.

I did not understand it, of course, The mouth cried, whispered, sang, whistled, shouted. There were seven poems in the recital. At the end of each one the villagers showed their delight with silence and sun-looks. Nowhere had I seen happier faces.

At last the recital was over; it must have been an integrated group of lyrics. They went away as mildly as they had come, leaving only that intolerable fish-stench behind, and a silence enriched.

I said to the poet when we were alone again, "These are happy poems, surely." "All poetry is gay," he answered. "Are they love poems?" I asked. "One is," he said.

> "The young man says, 'Come into my hut.'
> The girl answers, 'I have a bird for a lover.'
> The man, 'I will hunt that bird. There will be
>   red drops in the snow.'
> The girl answers, 'No.
> For the bird is to take me under his wing into
>   the north.
> His nest is on a black cliff. You will never find
>   us.'

"There is the hunting poem then.

> The boy says, 'Tomorrow I will hunt for the
>   first time.
> Beware, walrus. Beware, reindeer.
> I am coming to play at arrows with you.'
> At the end of the snow
> The great bear stood, who does not like the
>   game of arrows.

"Then there is the poem of the whale.

> The whale grew tired of eating little cold
>   fishes.
> It swallowed the sun.
> Then fell the black time, winter.
> The people said, 'Must we always stumble
>   about in blackness?
> The stars are too feeble.
> We want our children to play among the beau-
>   tiful snow crystals.'
> They hunted down that whale.
> They filled a hundred lamps from his belly.
> Just when the last lamp was empty
> The sun peeped at us over a low rim of ice.

243

Dead whale, drowned hunters, devoured sun.
Inside this circle all dances are made.

"There follows the aurora poem.

'Come, children, into my house of crystal.
Come, the feast is set.
Here kings sit and eat, and heroes, and the
bravest hunters.'
We are bidden, night after night,
To feast in that house of marvelous shining.
But we linger here sick,
Growing old, filled with regrets, in hovels of
snow.

"My own favourite is the poem of the women.

'Go away, man.
I will not open my door to you.
Quench your fires in the snow.
I will never leave the dancing children.'
The witch moon kissed me as I slept.
I am her blood-servant now.
She has put a sign on my doorpost.
Now many hunters come. All are welcome.

"Did you not see how the old men smiled at the poem of
childhood?

'I am a salmon.'
'I am a bear-cub.'
'I am a reindeer.'
'I am the moon.'
'I am the hole in the ice where ivory is.'
'Stop your games.
Three hunters are coming to teach you the
trade—
Winter, Age, Death.

"You understand, stranger, these translations I am making for
you are poor things, withered leaves plucked from the tree of

ose lazily, as if to get a better view of the horizon.
s in its flank, the two boats full of men, it seemed
re of. Another harpoon, flung by Isbister, skidded
ing hide and raised a little silver fountain from the
r away, a thin voice came shivering over the water:
.! Come back...!"

le seemed to hear this voice. It turned for a second
its reading of the horizon, and it seemed to Bronsky
of the first boat that a light of understanding broke
ast blunt forehead. Then it plunged. Two hundred
water hit the *Fergus* and the *Odins*. The *Fergus* was
d. Wallace, who was on his feet, braced and ready
er harpoon, was flung in an arc athwart in the sudden
of water. The other was swamped. From the *Odins*
en heads bobbing among whirls of green water and
e.

ou, come back!" came the insect voice from another

ns survived the massive onset. Only Leask was thrown
ver seen again. The five other boatmen were flung
other, a tangled web of flesh, leather, hair, iron. At
huddering boat, they managed to disentangle them-
wick the bow-man had a red-flowing wrist wound
ne's harpoon.

me it occurred to them that shipmates were drowning
g in the sea, it was too late. Not an arm or head was
The *Fergus* turned slowly, upside down, as if it too
g, blindly, the six who had manned her.
ce came again, flawed, across the sea of whale-fare
ing. The skipper of the whaling ship was beside him-
ge and anxiety. The five survivors in the *Odins* could
ogether the urgent words: even if they had cared to.

our language. (I remember grove
ends with the winter poem.

> I don't mind winter.
> I listen to stories.
> I make love.
> I don't mind winter n
> My eyes, some mornir
> Will be caught like tw
> Tell me, poet
> The cruelest things th

"Somber songs," I said. "Ye
like wine, cup after cup."

"Wine," said the poet, and s
and rages in the House of the
wanderers. Here in the far nort
have only poetry. The word w
seems to be the futility, pain, id
to the pure essences. And I ar
make cups that remain beautif

In that latitude there is a n
poet tried to give me some id
in the ultimate darkness. I co
Since—as in the lyric—this
can never enter the House o
nation of the poet builds abc
beauty, their primitive words
mony, and there they kept a tr
year.

Now, thirty years later, I find
mountains of Scotland.

The w
The h.
quite
off its
sea. Fr
"Put al
The
or two
at the t
across
tons of
overwh
to cast a
surging
could b
chunks
"I tol
world.
The (
out, and
upon ea
last, in tl
selves. N
from som
By the
and freez
to be see
was seek
The v
and drow
self with
not piece

"The old bastard!" said Isbister. "It was him that launched us against the whale. A foolish order—a piece of criminality. And because we have had a lean trip. This monster whale was to make up for everything. Them in their grand houses, in the town of Dundee, the whale-masters, they would be pleased—they would pay Surfax a bonus. Not a penny for the likes of you and me. And for that hellish nonsense, seven men are drowned!"

The others in the *Odins* said nothing.

Meantime the great whale, as if indeed it had glimpsed some good thing under the horizon, a mate of a legion of plankton-locating birds, was surging rapidly into the east. It was possessed by a huge pulse, the sea fell away from the beast in white throbbing furrows. (Or perhaps it was the tickle of the harpoons that had stung it into a splendid rage.) It sundered the ocean where it fell, and fell, and fell.

How could they have ever thought to see such magnificence plumbed for oil, sawed and salted into steaks, its head made a network of bones for some museum in Dundee or Glasgow?

"You bloody crazy old fool!" Isbister cried in the direction of the whaling ship, towards which the *Odins* edged now with hesitant striking oars.

Macpherson did not row. His head was down on his saturated knees, his shoulders were convulsed.

"Now, Isbister," said Marwick, "now, man, there's been overmuch trouble this voyage. We volunteered to man the boats. That's the truth. Be glad you're alive!"

The Highlandman sobbed, over and over again, "I have lost him that I loved better than hawk or horse. He is drowned. He is lost indeed, forever."

By this time they were close enough to read the name *Swede Boy* on the whaler's prow, and (when they swung their heads round) to fix on the intent white face at the rail.

The quiet horizon, miles off, quivered like a struck string. Their quarry had broken through the line. It was gone.

Michael Surfax, skipper of the *Swede Boy*, whaler out of Dundee, said (and his voice, close by, was dull as pewter now), "I ordered you, not once but four times, to turn back."

"It was too late," said Marwick, shipping his oar.

"Did it not occur to you," said Mr. Surfax, "to take the *Fergus*

247

in tow? What are you thinking of? She is undamaged, as far as I can see."

There was silence for a full minute between the whaler and the whaler's boat; except for Macpherson, who said, "Seven brothers I had, none dearer than him!" And his blunt fingers across his eyes blittered with other water than what dripped from the oars.

Isbister said, in a voice of complete awe, "Turn round then. We are to fix a line on the *Fergus*. Mr. Surfax has said it."

When they were half-way back to the upturned *Fergus*, Marwick saw a dark swan-neck arch out of the green water. It was followed by an unrecognizable blur—a grey mask between frozen hair and frozen beard. The mask uttered a few distinct syllables of pain or wonderment; then the half-ghost was dragged under again by the weight of water in its clothes and boots.

Marwick's oar yearned towards the slight broken swirl.

Isbister said, "We are sent not to pick up corpses, but to fetch the *Fergus* back. Mr. Surfax ordered that."

Between the Faroes and Shetland Michael Surfax wrote, with considerable fluency, several letters in his cabin.

1

"To Sir Malcolm McPhallin-Gray, merchant, in the port of Dundee, Scotland.

"Dear Sir, the *Swede Boy* had had, thus far, but a moderate trip. We stalked whales between Greenland and Newfoundland, to no avail. Iceland waters yielded us two, but one old and diseased, that I thought better to abandon. I have had the usual stirrings and murmurings from the crew, mainly (as has happened before) on account of the food, but they can see plain enough that I eat the same food as themselves. There is one Orkneyman, Isbister, that will not sail with me again. We struck a fine beast two days after midsummer, in golden waters. The flensing knives were sharp, we turned that sea red, barrels bulged at the end of the day. Then, for a week, nothing. 'Has every whale in the sea,' I asked at the supper table, 'gone to an assembly of whales off Spitzbergen?' The length of the board, not a man laughed. I think it my duty to give them a cheerful countenance, it leavens somewhat their labours and discontents.

"Then, sir, into my glass next morning swam this king of whales, a Behemoth, larger than any my eyes had ever beheld. I balanced prudence with daring. If we struck him, and held him, and wore him out, it would be the most famous cargo of whale ever to enter the port of Dundee. I knew that I, and my men, would share in the overplus of profit, but I reasoned more that it would be a shining honour to your family and firm and whaling-fleet. Two boats, *Odins* and *Fergus*, manned with volunteers, were sent against the huge placid sea-dome. (Sir, the creature seemed marked for death; ready, passive, and acquiescent.) The first harpoons were flung, and they adhered. Still the whale seemed asleep. The two boats circled her closer. I saw then what I dreaded, for I had seen it before, always as a prelude to disaster. The creature seemed to heave up, and hang, as if it had drawn a vast breath. I cried through the trumpet of my hands, again and again, for the boats to return. They heard me, surely, but the lust of blood and money was on them. They drew closer, more barbs were flung. Then the whale subsided, with a mighty displacement of water, wherein, I regret to say, *Fergus* was swamped, with the loss of all hands. But later I contrived to recover the boat, virtually undamaged. *Odins* somehow rode the wave, and suffered the loss of one man only, William Leask. We did not attempt any pursuit of the whale, being grieved by the loss of so many fine men. The knowledge that their lives were adequately insured, upon their signing on, must prove some satisfaction. We have fading hopes of another strike before the end of summer. Joshua Wharton of the *Reprieve,* whose path crossed with *Swede Boy* three days since, assured me there is a school, and many unattached whales, hereabouts. I live in hope. But the men are very wretched, some of them ill with scabs and complaints of the stomach, and speak only of Hamnavoe and home. The man Isbister I spoke of, the Chartist, I had to isolate below deck; where he still lies, darkling, and promises nothing in the way of obedience, loyalty, and honest labour...."

2

"To Mistress Maria Leask, in Clouston, Stennis, in the Orkneys.

"Your man is dead. I will not soften the blow. I think he said once to me he had five young children at home. It is pitiable in the extreme. William Leask died with credit to further the comfort and well-being of his family. He died in front of an enormous whale, that not Samson nor Hercules could have subdued. Six young men besides were lost that same hour. Be assured, Mistress Leask, for your loss you will have as much money as ever you have seen. My intention is to come and see you, poor woman, in Stennes, as soon as *Swede Boy* anchors in Hamnavoe harbour...."

3

"To the Russian consul in Leith, Scotland.

"Sir, A young Pole from the port of Danzig, by name Joseph Bronsky, is cast away on a whaling voyage near the coast of Greenland. The body was not recovered. Have the charity, I beg of you, to acquaint his relatives. Some monies owing to the deceased will be forwarded to them, along with his sea chest...."

4

"Dear Williamina, how I am to put this letter together, is a matter of anguish and confusion to me. I cannot conceive how it will affect you, who must read it. The one of us is dead and drowned, and that one not I. How came it, my dear woman, that all of last winter and spring you would not or could not choose between him and me, and even on the day of our setting sail from Hamnavoe, your eye went uncertainly between us, full of pain and love. In moments of common sense I would say to myself, 'Why, Michael Surfax, you are old, your beard is grey-flecked—you must not think a fine young woman like Williamina would prefer you to Laurie, who is as handsome and heart-winning a lad as ever the parish of Sandwick put forth. No, Michael, but I think she loves you just a little now because you are a man of reputation, a man with a command and money, a rock in the uncertainties of life. It will not last, Michael. She is a young beautiful woman. Laurie is Laurie. You, Michael, are but a step or two from tombstone and skull....' But then I would reason, that a woman's heart does not feed on common sense. Perhaps, after all, the dice would come down in my favour, and in the end Laurie would have to look elsewhere for a bride. The goodness and innocence of the boy! The week before the departure of the whalers from Hamnavoe, he arrives at my cabin door, shy and smiling. 'Mr. Surfax,' says he, 'please take me on this one voyage with you, if you can. I am much in love with a girl in Hamnavoe, I want to marry her before Yule. But I am a poor man. She can't still make up her mind. If I were to return from the Arctic with a little pouch of gold and silver, perhaps the precious coins would be a kind of shadowy sign of the love I feel for her. Please let me make my mark in your book....' This Laurie said, standing just inside my cabin door. He could not know anything of the storm he had set raging in my breast. My immediate impulse was to say, 'No, Sinclair, my crew was completed yesterday. I am busy. The *Swede Boy* sails in four days. Goodbye....' Instead I told him to come back in an hour. He was back in fifty minutes, a faint smell of rum on his breath. 'Why, Sinclair,' I said, 'you're a lucky man. It seems there's room for another crewman after all. Be here seven o'clock sharp in the morning. Get your gear together at once. No time for farewells. The woman will keep, if she's any good....' Laurie nearly wrung my hand off, with relief and gratitude.

"Williamina, I am telling you all this, exactly as it happened. It is your due. Also, I wish to have the situation as clear as possible in my own mind, and writing (I have found) is a purifying fire.

"Laurie proved a good whaleman. He was liked by all our ship's company. He worked well and cheerfully. I had no fault to find with the lad.

"It proved to be, however, only a middling season.

"When, on the fifth day of July, a vast whale was sighted near Greenland, I was certain that, if the boats were to be launched, Laurie must be set in charge of one, he being a young man of resource and daring. I took him aside. I said, 'Now, Sinclair, it's no good playing around with a whale like that. Go right up to her, put the harpoons in, then wait for the whale-storm to blow itself out. There'll be enough bounty money in it to buy a whole harem of brides.' Our young friend smiled. He followed his five comrades into the *Fergus*, that soon bristled with harpoons.

"Whaling is a game of dice. Whalemen must take chances, or they starve. In this case they—Laurie also, as well as myself— underestimated the cunning and resource of the beast. It lay against them, it drowned seven of the twelve in a vast wave. Laurie was not seen again.

"Love too is a game of dice. But when there is only one player, how can he lose? I am half-a-year older since last I saw you, my dear. I have a heart greatly troubled. I need you now, if never before. Time runs out, but my love has not wasted by a single grain...."

5

"... In honesty I should tell you, it had been a hundred times better if Albert and Tom had bidden at home with you on the croft of Troddle. They were but poor hands at the whaling. Albert and Tom were in a small boat that was overset by a whale. Men die instantly in such intensities of ice. In due course, you will get guineas in accordance with the insurance pledged. Many an Orkney woman has anxious summers—year after year—till the whaling fleet returns. Keep your remaining boys at home. They are safer with ploughs than with harpoons, be assured. You may watch the corn patch growing, from now on, in peace."

A WINTER LEGEND

The princess was a prisoner for fifty-one years in the high tower. Yet she did not grow older by a wrinkle or a grey hair from the first day of her imprisonment.

She did not know what became of her brother, the prince. He had been taken that same day, in the palace garden, by the soldiers, and dragged away crying through the tall gate.

"The king and the queen are both dead," said a strange stern woman to the princess as she led her that day up three hundred and sixty-five circling steps to the high tower. "A council of grey men rules the land now."

The woman with the key said, "Eat these worms and grass-blades—they're all you're getting to eat. Eat them, or you'll die...." As soon as the wardress had gone away, the princess looked at the long cold worms and pieces of shriveled grass on the plate. She was almost sick with horror. She pushed the plate away from her.

The wardress came back just before it grew dark. She said, "I see you haven't eaten your good dinner. There's no more food until you eat the worms and the grass."

Then she said, "The sun's down. It'll soon be dark. Don't think you're going to get a lamp or a candle. You aren't. No blanket either. You must sleep on the cold floor. The council has given orders."

The wardress lingered by the door. "The council," she said, "has had pity on your sick brother. He has a job in the palace garden, helping the twelve gardeners. He carries water up from the river. He brings dung from the stables. He's so slow and weak the head gardener has to beat him every now and then. The head gardener is a strong bad-tempered man."

The princess said nothing. She was glad it was dark, so that her torturer couldn't see her tears.

"Perhaps," said the evil voice in the dark shadow of the door, "you'd like to know what happened to your father and mother, the former king and queen? I'll tell you, they were drowned in the sea. Huge stones were tied to their necks and feet, and they were lowered out of a boat. They were sunk with all their finery on them."

At that the princess wept. Her sobs echoed through the cold high cell. The wardress laughed—it seemed she liked the music of grief. Then, with a shrieking of hinges and locks, she closed the door of the tower.

The princess wept for a long time, until she had no more tears left.

When she lifted her head from her knees, she saw that a new moon was shining through the narrow slit of window; it brimmed the cell with silver light.

The princess was very tired; no wonder, after the turmoil and horror of the day just past. "How can I sleep, though, in a cold place like this without a blanket?" Her maid Isabel always, every night, had brought to her bedside a little plate of sweets. Now, heavy with sleep, oblivious, she stretched out her hand and put into her mouth what was on the plate at her side, and ate it. She startled awake with a cry—she had swallowed the worms and the grass! Horrors! Yet her mouth and throat were all sweetness, as though she had sipped honey and wine.

The princess lay down. "I might as well *try* to sleep." The stones of the floor were warm, as though they remembered an age of sun-soaking in the royal quarry. They accepted the soft flesh of the princess as kindly as rose petals.

The princess thought, on the edge of sleep, "How strange, the moon should have vanished an hour ago from the window. It's still there...." Enchanted with sorrow and moonlight, the princess fell asleep.

Day after day, month after month, year after year, the princess lived in the tower like an unfading flower in a pot. The same things happened over and over. The same wardress came about noon with a plate of worms and grass; she said a few hurtful things to the girl and went away again. The princess had nothing to while away the time: no book or harp or embroidery frame.

She tried to remember the stories her nurse had told her in her childhood, and found to her joy that she could remember them all: all except one, a winter legend that was a white confusion in her mind. Without those stories she might have withered. Not only did she tell them to the spider in the corner of her cell; she set them to music, she sang them to the blackbird or the thrush that came from time to time and perched on the narrow window ledge, cocking a bright eye at her. After she had sung a story, the bird sometimes would answer with a pattern of immaculate pure thrilling sound. "Oh," cried the princess then, "thank you, bird. I wish I could sing as sweetly as that!"

Sometimes, when her throat was dry with recitation or song, the princess would try to picture the people in this story and that: their faces, their clothes, their gestures and movements. Then, behind her closed eyes, the story became a slow wonderful wordless dance, a masque. Each story had its own quite different ballet. Once she tried to remember the forgotten winter story; it remained a cold confusion; but when she opened her eyes she saw that a white butterfly had come in through the window and was drifting from wall to wall of her cell. She tried to take the butterfly in her fingers but it rose, fluttered, drifted out again. She cried a little; the butterfly was a more beautiful dancer than the dancers who moved through her ballets. "Perhaps it'll come again, and stay with me for a while."

Those dancing people in the stories—she tried to fix them so that they wouldn't drift and fade. She chipped a piece of stone from the wall one day. She scratched the childhood stories on the stone floor: the lion, the full moon, the witch, the fish-girl, the boy with the silver penny, the dragon, the simpleton, the wounded soldier, the frog, the apple-tree, the talking statue, the chimney-sweep, the seal-king. She had always been good at drawing (so her drawing master had said in the old days) but never had she drawn as well as she did now in the loneliness of her cell. Every single line that she scratched indicated something singular or important about the character, and how he or she stood in relation to the other characters within the circle of the story.... The princess was making of her prison a magic cave.

Months merged into years. The princess thought certain things were very strange in this place. For example, it had been a summer day when she had been dragged here and locked in; it remained summer; every day the golden finger of the sun wrote at the same level across the wall; there was never a day that a bee or a rose-petal didn't come drifting in through the high narrow slit of a window; the bright eye and song of the bird never failed either. What had become of spring and autumn and winter?

And she never got dirty. Every morning in the palace she had been bathed and scented by her ladies. She knew that people got dirty; she had seen the thin hungry unwashed faces from the city slums at the palace gate before the guardsmen rode at them with lances and scattered them. "The poor are dirty," she thought, "because they live far away from fountains...." No water was ever brought to her prison. Yet when she looked at her hands, her legs, her sides, they were as lustrous as if she had just stepped out of the river. Sometimes she touched her face (for she had no mirror). Her fingers could detect no flaw or etching of time. "Perhaps," thought the princess, "the dew comes in and clusters about me while I'm asleep."

Yet, as the months and the years passed, she saw the deepening nets of age on the wardress's face and hands. The creature would stand wheezing for a long while in the cell door before putting down the daily plate of worms and grass-blades. Now she had not enough breath to hurt the princess with evil news; she could only squinny and sneer, and turn, and go away grumbling. The wardress was growing old, she was slowly breaking up.

One thing the princess *did* notice—her clothes were wearing out. She looked one day, and there was a hole in the elbow of her blue silk gown. With kneeling on the floor drawing with the stone upon stone her stockings had gapes in them at the knees. Here and there were shreddings and unstitchings. The dust of the long long summer was working itself into the fabric; her dress hung on her, a soiled frayed thing.

In the old royal days she had seen the moon rounding out to the full, and then shrinking, and then vanishing into the House of Darkness. In this cell, at night, the moon never darkened. Always, over her sleep, the silver mask stood guard at the high narrow window: a gondolier, a fat smiling Chinaman, an old woman over fading cinders. The scratched stories on the stone were washed with moon enchantment.

How many years passed? The princess reckoned that fifty-one years must have passed since that guardsman had put the hood over her head and tied her hands behind her. If she had no calendar to tell her the exact count of time, her clothes said a little. They hung from her in tatters; the blue had long faded into a dull gray. They were so filthy they seemed only to sully her firm fragrant flesh. "Perhaps soon," she said, "I'll have to live naked in this place!"

Next morning, she heard a wheezing and a choking in the corridor outside her cell. The key screeched in the lock. The door opened. The shriveled wardress stood there with her plate of sweet-tasting worms and luscious grass-blades.

"If you please," said the princess, "could I have a needle and thread to darn my clothes?"

Five minutes passed before the old one could find breath to speak. Meantime a leaf drifted in through the window; the princess noticed, astonished, that it wasn't a summer leaf, it was yellow and brittle.

The old woman said in a voice like a rusty knife, "Needles, thread.... Your next dress, milady, will be your shroud. Worms and grass to eat—you should have been a skeleton long ago! Why are you not out of your mind with loneliness and heartbreak? It's too bad, too bad.... Well, you slut, make the most of this feast. You're getting no more. Winter's here. I'll never climb that stair again!"

The old woman put a white mad look on the princess. Then she turned, the key shrieked in the lock; the girl heard her feet fumbling uncertainly down the darkling stair.

Never had the princess experienced such a night of intense cold and darkness. The long summer was over at last. The stone floor on which she lay, unblanketed, was drained of its long-stored sun. The masked moon had gone at last from the station at the window-slit. Winter, a black bony hand, clutched at her heart; her clothes were hardly more substantial than spiders' webs.

She endured the longest coldest most miserable night of her life.

*

Dawn came with a single snowflake; it undulated, a grey moth, past her window. Then the flakes came in a flurry and a flock; at last in dense ceaseless driven hordes.

As the princess watched, a lost snowflake came hovering into her cell. She had not seen snow for fifty-one years. She reached up on tiptoe, to grasp it before it drifted on to the floor and died.

She had it in her fingers. She opened her hand. It lay there, a fragile silver key!

The princess fitted the key into the rusty lock of her cell. It turned with a little silver sound. The door creaked open.

The stone stair spiraled down, twelve turnings and three hundred and sixty-five steps. As she went down the last web-thin rags fell from her in the dark airs that moved everywhere in the tower.

She would never never go back to that cell, now that winter had got into it. She would rather suffer the insults and gross looks of the guardsmen in the barracks-yard outside. A white glimmer, she walked along a corridor towards the great outer door of the tower.

The square opened before her, transfigured with snow, and empty. There was no mark of hoof or foot or wheel in the white thick-blanketed yard. Where had all the soldiers gone?

From a bare branch a single bird, a robin, looked down on her. Its throat was a songless tremor.

And now the swift-moving hands of the snow spun and wove about the princess a seamless vesture. Soon she was no longer a chaste statue in the barrack square. Her arms were sheathed in heavy flocculence. Her bosom was a white powerful curve.

The robin chirped from the bare tree, "Follow me, I'll show you where your brother is...." It flew away into the incessant wavering blizzard.

The princess yearned after the bird, but her feet had become rooted in a snowdrift. She threshed with her arms. She was suddenly free of the ground! She staggered in the air, she whirled, she was flying over barracks and guardhouse. Her new wings beat like a bell in the silence.

Below in the palace garden, the robin was perched in the heart of a rosebush. Its breast seemed like one of the scarlet blossoms. Scalloped in snow, the roses were more beautiful than in the lucency of high summer.

The fountain beside the rosebush was frozen silent arches.

The princess glided down on the printless garden. The red-breast said in a bleak voice, "This is your brother, this root, briar, rose. I'm sitting in his hair. One day in autumn the gardeners turned on him at last. Their pruning hooks and spades struck him, time after time. He died; they buried him. They hid him from the savage sun. I carried a seed in my beak and dropped it on his grave."

The princess covered her face with her webs, and wept. "Swans usually don't care about such unimportant things," said the little shivering bird. "Swans think proud beautiful deathless thoughts."

The swan-princess uncovered her face. Indeed it was the beauty of her brother's change that had touched her heart, not the cruel edges that had been suddenly turned on him.

What was the matter with the palace? It stood there silent as a morgue. No winter music drifted from the gallery of the great hall. Where were the court ladies in their muffs and furs, moving perilously and soundlessly through the drifts? The lake did not ring with the noise of iron on ice. From the basement kitchens came no chef's curse and little scullery-maids' tremulous tearful answer, nor any enchanting tangle of cooking smells to thaw, later, the winter out of cold high-bred bones.

The swan-princess looked, and she saw that here and there the roof of the palace showed only naked rafters.

And the wrought-iron gate through which the poor folk from the slums of the city had shaken thin white fists that last sum-mer—that was festooned with tattered rose-petals of rust....

The robin chirped, "The revolution wiped it all out. They've all gone into stories. You and I, we're changing too."

"I see," said the princess. "I'd like to see my father and mother now, if you please, before I'm closed up in a book."

The small bird leapt out of the rosebush and disappeared into high mazes of snow.

With a slow heavy clap of wings the swan-princess followed.

The great bell-beat, hung high, at last rose above the snow cloud, and the sun dazzled her with burst after burst of winter brightness. Far below, the little bird was a quivering dot, lost from time to time in fringes of snow-cloud. The swan surged on effortlessly. Splendours showered from her pulsing wings, a slow folding and unfolding.

Once the vast snow-cloud that seemed to cover creation split silently open. Through the chasm the princess could see a tract of the land her father had ruled—a hunting forest, a river. But something was wrong. Great gaps had been torn in the forest, and the scars were more than could have been wrought by axe or fire. The wide river, once so bustling and populous with trade, went on towards the sea heavy and black as treacle.

"This is the last winter of time," said the swan-princess.

The cloud chasm closed up again, and she was left with the sun and, far below, the hesitations and spurts of the questing robin.

The smell of the sea was suddenly stronger than the fragile incense of snow. The robin dipped, dropped, disappeared. The swan-princess stooped.

Plunging down through the dark heart of the snow-cloud, she heard the ocean. She stooped again, perilously. She flew across flung veils of spindrift. A rising wave washed her feet.

There, on a stone of the beach, hung the robin, quite exhausted after its endless arches of flight across the last winter. The swan-princess dropped down on the sea margin. The heart of the little bird seemed to be quivering in its throat.

At last it cried, "Look, swan, now, quickly! Here comes your father."

A slow wave rose, hung, glittered, fell wounded on the wide beach, ended its reign in a hundred wondering whispers.

"The queen now," panted the little bird. "Look, look!"

A smaller wave stooped, curtsied, sang, spread itself in torn white fringes over pebbles and sand.

The two waves mingled their seethings and sighings, sweet unending sea voices, and withdrew.

"Life," said the robin, "doesn't last very long, does it? It's a very brief story."

The swan-princess rose, hovered, tried to follow the two torn waves. But all those innumerable strands and drops were mingled inextricably with the ocean; for other intertwinings, other deaths and renewings.

The snow fell thicker. Time passed. The little bird was quilted in white. Its voice became a frozen crystal.

"Once upon a winter..." The swan-princess sang at the shore the lost legend. A silver key turned in her throat. Silent, unmoving, she was gathered into the pure crystal of time.

AN EPIPHANY TALE

There was once a small boy and he was deaf and dumb and blind.

He knew nothing about Christmas. All he knew was that it got cold at a certain time of year. He would touch a stone with his fingers. His fingers burned with frost!

One day the boy was sitting on his mother's doorstep wrapped in a thick coat and scarf against the cold.

A stranger came and stood above him. There was a good smell from the stranger's hands and beard. It was different from the smell of the village people; the fishermen and the shepherds and their women and children and animals. The man smelt of sunrise.

The stranger touched the boy's ear. At once he could hear all the village sounds—the sea on the stones, his mother at the hearth baking scones, the seagulls, and the children playing in the field.

"No," his mother was saying to the stranger, "I don't want to buy a pan or a fork from your pack. No use speaking to the boy— he's deaf as a stone. Look, I'll give you a scone to eat. We're poor. I have no money to buy a thing."

The boy didn't understand what the stranger and his mother said. The interchange of sounds seemed to him to be more won- derful than anything he could ever have imagined, and the most wonderful was the stranger's voice.

It said, "Thank you for the bread, woman."

Soon the stranger was no longer there. He had taken his rich silk smell and his clanging treasure away. The boy sat on the doorstep as the multitudinous harp of the world was stroked again and again. His mother kneaded dough on the board and stoked the peat fire.

Then the doors of his ears were closed once more. He laughed, silently.

Another smell drifted across the boy's nostrils, different from anything he had known. It was like incense of darkness, a circling of bright swift animals.

The second stranger touched the boy's eyes. They opened. The things he saw all at once amazed him with their beauty and variety. A few flakes of snow were falling on the dead ditchgrass. Gray clouds huddled along the sky. A cat crossed the road from a fishing-boat below with a small fish in its mouth.

Two people were arguing in the door. The white strenuous kind face must be his mother's. The black smiling face belonged to the stranger. Both were beautiful.

The boy's looked into the gloom of the house. The flames in the hearth were so beautiful it gave him a catch in the breath.

Clearly his mother was refusing to have anything to do with the objects the stranger was spreading out before her: soft shining fabrics, ivory combs, a few sheets with music and poems on them. The boy did not know what they were—each was marvelous and delightful in its different way.

At last his mother, exasperated, took a fish that had been smoking in the chimney. She gave it to the black man. He smiled. He tied up his pack. He turned to the boy and raised his hand in a gesture of farewell.

The boy's mother shook her head: as if to say, "There's no point in making signs to this poor child of mine. He's been as blind as a worm from the day he was born."

Then, to her amazement, the boy raised a blue wintry hand, and smiled and nodded farewell to the second stranger.

For an hour the boy's eyes gazed deep into the slowly turning sapphire of the day. His mother moving between fire and board; the three fishermen handing a basket of fish from the stern of their boat to half-a-dozen shore-fast women; the gulls wheeling above; the thickening drift of flakes across the village chimneys; a boy and a girl throwing snowballs at each other—all were dances more beautiful than he could have imagined.

Then the luminous stone dulled and flawed. Between one bread dance and another, while his mother stood and wiped her flame-flushed brow at the window, she became a shadow. The boy was as sightless as he had ever been. He laughed, silently.

*

It was the most wonderful day the boy had ever known. And still the day wasn't over.

He was aware of a third presence at the door, lingering. This stranger brought with him smells of green ice, flashing stars, seal-pelts.

The mother, at her wits' end now, mixed with those smells of the pole her own smells of flour and butter and peat-smoke. The boy knew that his mother was angry; the smells came from her in fierce thrusting swirls.

It was enough to drive the most importunate pedlar away, but the man from the far north stood mildly at the threshold. The boy could imagine a bland quiet smile.

His mother's anger never lasted long. Another smell came to the boy's quivering nostrils: ale. His mother had poured a bottle of ale for the stranger, to refresh him for his journey. And now the smells of ice and fire and malt mingled gently in the doorway.

"I wonder," thought the boy, "what they're saying to each other? The same beautiful things as before, I expect. Their hands and their mouths will be making the same good shapes."

It seemed a marvel to him that his ears and his eyes had been opened both in one day. How could any human being endure such ravishment of the senses, every hour of every day for many winters and summers?

The winter sun was down. The boy felt the first shadow on the back of his hand.

It was the time now for all the villagers to go indoors for the night. But this day they didn't go straight home. The fishermen and their wives and children came and lingered on the road outside the boy's door. He could smell the sweet milk breath of the children, and the sea breath of the men and the well-and-peat breath of the women. (Also he could smell the ashen breath of one old villager who would, he knew, be dead before the new grass.)

The villagers had come to stare at the stranger. The aroma of malt ebbed slowly. The boy felt the stone shivering; the stranger, having drunk, had put down his pewter mug on the doorstep.

Then he felt the touch of a finger on his locked mouth. He

opened it. All his wonder and joy and gratitude for this one festival day gathered to his lips and broke out in a cry.

His mother dropped her baking bowl on the floor, in her astonishment. The bowl broke in a hundred pieces.

The old man who was soon to die said he had heard many rare sounds in his life, but nothing so sweet and pure as the boy's one cry.

The youngest villager was a child in her mother's arms that day. She remembered that sound all her life. Nothing that she heard ever afterwards, a lover's coaxing words, or a lark over a cornfield, or the star of birth that broke from the mouth of her own first child, no utterance seemed to be half as enchanting as the single incomprehensible word of the dumb boy.

Some of the stupider villagers said he had made no sound at all. How could he?—he had never spoken before, he would never utter a word again. A mouse had squeaked in the thatch, perhaps.

The stranger left in the last of the light. He joined two other darkling figures on the ridge.

The villagers dispersed to their houses.

The boy went indoors to the seat beside the fire. How flustered his mother was! What a day she had had! Her baking interrupted by three going-around men—her best blue china bowl in smithereens—her poor boy stricken with wonderment in the shifting net of flame shadows! She had never seen him like this before. He touched his ears, his mouth, as if his body was an instrument that he must prepare for some great music.

And yet, poor creature, he was as dumb and deaf and blind as he had ever been.

The boy sat and let the flame-shadows play on him.

The mother washed her floury hands in the basin. Then she crossed the flagstone floor and bent over him and kissed him.

He sat, his stone head laved with hearth flames.

ANDRINA

Andrina comes to see me every afternoon in winter, just before it gets dark. She lights my lamp, sets the peat fire in a blaze, sees that there is enough water in my bucket that stands on the wall niche. If I have a cold (which isn't often, I'm a tough old seaman) she fusses a little, puts an extra peat or two on the fire, fills a stone hot-water bottle, puts an old thick jersey about my shoulders.

That good Andrina—as soon as she has gone, after her occasional ministrations to keep pleurisy or pneumonia away—I throw the jersey from my shoulders and mix myself a toddy, whisky and hot water and sugar. The hot water bottle in the bed will be cold long before I climb into it, round about midnight: having read my few chapters of Conrad.

Towards the end of February last year I did get a very bad cold, the worst for years. I woke up, shuddering, one morning, and crawled between fire and cupboard, gasping like a fish out of water, to get a breakfast ready. (Not that I had an appetite.) There was a stone lodged somewhere in my right lung, that blocked my breath.

I forced down a few tasteless mouthfuls, and drank hot ugly tea. There was nothing to do after that but get back to bed with my book. Reading was no pleasure either—my head was a block of pulsing wood.

"Well," I thought, "Andrina'll be here in five or six hours' time. She won't be able to do much for me. This cold, or flu, or whatever it is, will run its course. Still, it'll cheer me to see the girl."

*

Andrina did not come that afternoon. I expected her with the first cluster of shadows: the slow lift of the latch, the low greeting, the "tut-tut" of sweet disapproval at some of the things she saw as soon as the lamp was burning....I was, though, in that strange fatalistic mood that sometimes accompanies a fever, when a man doesn't really care what happens. If the house was to go on fire, he might think, "What's this, flames?" and try to save himself: but it wouldn't horrify or thrill him.

I accepted that afternoon, when the window was blackness at last with a first salting of stars, that for some reason or another Andrina couldn't come. I fell asleep again.

I woke up. A gray light at the window. My throat was dry— there was a fire in my face—my head was more throbbingly wooden than ever. I got up, my feet flashing with cold pain on the stone floor, drank a cup of water, and climbed back into bed. My teeth actually clacked and chattered in my head for five minutes or more—a thing I had only read about before.

I slept again, and woke up just as the winter sun was making brief stained glass of sea and sky. It was, again, Andrina's time. Today there were things she could do for me: get aspirin from the shop, surround my greyness with three or four very hot bottles, mix the strongest toddy in the world. A few words from her would be like a bell-buoy to a sailor lost in a hopeless fog. She did not come.

She did not come again on the third afternoon.

I woke, tremblingly, like a ghost in a hollow stone. It was black night. Wind soughed in the chimney. There was, from time to time, spatters of rain against the window. It was the longest night of my life. I experienced, over again, some of the dull and sordid events of my life; one certain episode was repeated again and again like an ancient gramophone record being put on time after time, and a rusty needle scuttling over worn wax. The shameful images broke and melted at last into sleep. Love had been killed but many ghosts had been awakened.

When I woke up I heard, for the first time in four days, the sound of a voice. It was Stanley the postman speaking to the dog of Bighouse. "There now, isn't that loud big words to say so early? It's just a letter for Minnie, a drapery catalogue. There's a good boy, go and tell Minnie I have a love letter for her....Is that you, Minnie? I thought old Ben here was going to tear me in pieces then. Yes, Minnie, a fine morning, it is that...."

I have never liked that postman—a servile lickspittle to any-one he thinks is of consequence in the island—but that morning he came past my window like a messenger of light. He opened the door without knocking (I am a person of small consequence). He said, "Letter from a long distance, skipper." He put the letter on the chair nearest the door. I was shaping my mouth to say, "I'm not very well. I wonder...." If words did come out of my mouth, they must have been whispers, a ghost appeal. He looked at the dead fire and the closed window. He said, "Phew! It's fuggy in here, skipper. You want to get some fresh air...." Then he went, closing the door behind him. (He would not, as I had briefly hoped, be taking word to Andrina, or the doctor down in the village.)

I imagined, until I drowsed again, Captain Scott writing his few last words in the Antarctic tent.

In a day or two, of course, I was as right as rain; a tough old salt like me isn't killed off that easily.

But there was a sense of desolation on me. It was as if I had been betrayed—deliberately kicked when I was down. I came almost to the verge of self-pity. Why had my friend left me in my bad time?

Then good sense asserted itself. "Torvald, you old fraud," I said to myself. "What claim have you got, anyway, on a winsome twenty-year-old? None at all. Look at it this way, man—you've had a whole winter of her kindness and consideration. She brought a lamp into your dark time: ever since the Harvest Home when (like a fool) you had too much whisky and she supported you home and rolled you unconscious into bed.... Well, for some reason or another Andrina hasn't been able to come these last few days. I'll find out, today, the reason."

It was high time for me to get to the village. There was not a crust or scraping of butter or jam in the cupboard. The shop was also the Post Office—I had to draw two weeks' pension. I promised myself a pint or two in the pub, to wash the last of that sickness out of me.

It struck me, as I trudged those two miles, that I knew nothing about Andrina at all. I had never asked, and she had said nothing. What was her father? Had she sisters and brothers? Even the district of the island where she lived had never cropped up in our talks. It was sufficient that she came every evening, soon after sunset, and performed her quiet ministrations, and lingered awhile; and left a peace behind—a sense that everything in the house was pure, as if it had stood with open doors and windows at the heart of a clean summer wind.

Yet the girl had never done, all last winter, asking me questions about myself—all the good and bad and exciting things that had happened to me. Of course I told her this and that. Old men love to make their past vivid and significant, to stand in relation to a few trivial events in as fair and bold a light as possible. To add spice to those bits of autobiography, I let on to have been a reckless wild daring lad—a known and somewhat feared figure in many a port from Hong Kong to Durban to San Francisco. I presented to her a character somewhere between Captain Cook and Captain Hook.

And the girl loved those pieces of mingled fiction and fact; turning the wick of my lamp down a little to make everything more mysterious, stirring the peats into new flowers of flame....

One story I did not tell her completely. It is the episode in my life that hurts me whenever I think of it (which is rarely, for that time is locked up and the key dropped deep in the Atlantic: but it haunted me—as I hinted—during my recent illness).

On her last evening at my fireside I did, I know, let drop a hint or two to Andrina—a few half-ashamed half-boastful fragments. Suddenly, before I had finished—as if she could foresee and suffer the end—she had put a white look and a cold kiss on my cheek, and gone out at the door; as it turned out, for the last time.

Hurt or no, I will mention it here and now. You who look and listen are not Andrina—to you it will seem a tale of crude country manners: a mingling of innocence and heartlessness.

In the island, fifty years ago, a young man and a young woman came together. They had known each other all their lives up to then, of course—they had sat in the school room together—but on one particular day in early summer this boy from one croft and this girl from another distant croft looked at each other with new eyes.

After the midsummer dance in the barn of the big house, they walked together across the hill through the lingering enchantment of twilight—it is never dark then—and came to the rocks and the sand and sea just as the sun was rising. For an hour and more they lingered, tranced creatures indeed, beside those bright sighings and swirlings. Far in the north-east the springs of day were beginning to surge up.

It was a tale soaked in the light of a single brief summer. The boy and the girl lived, it seemed, on each other's heartbeats. Their parents' crofts were miles apart, but they contrived to meet, as if by accident, most days; at the crossroads, in the village shop, on the side of the hill. But really these places were too earthy and open—there were too many windows—their feet drew secretly night after night to the beach with its bird-cries, its cave, its changing waters. There no one disturbed their communings—the shy touches of hand and mouth—the words that were nonsense but that became in his mouth sometimes a sweet mysterious music—"Sigrid."

The boy—his future, once this idyll of a summer was ended, was to go to the university in Aberdeen and there study to be a man of security and position and some leisure—an estate his crofting ancestors had never known.

No such door was to open for Sigrid—she was bound to the few family acres—the digging of peat—the making of butter and cheese. But for a short time only. Her place would be beside the young man with whom she shared her breath and heartbeats, once he had gained his teacher's certificate. They walked day after day beside shining beckoning waters.

But one evening, at the cave, towards the end of that summer, when the corn was taking a first burnish, she had something urgent to tell him—a tremulous perilous secret thing. And at once the summertime spell was broken. He shook his head. He looked away. He looked at her again as if she were some slut who had insulted him. She put out her hand to him, her mouth trembling. He thrust her away. He turned. He ran up the beach and along the sand-track to the road above; and the ripening fields gathered him soon and hid him from her.

And the girl was left alone at the mouth of the cave, with the burden of a greater more desolate mystery on her.

The young man did not go to any seat of higher learning. That same day he was at the emigration agents in Hamnavoe, asking for an urgent immediate passage to Canada or Australia or South Africa—anywhere.

Thereafter the tale became complicated and more cruel and pathetic still. The girl followed him as best she could to his transatlantic refuge a month or so later; only to discover that the bird had flown. He had signed on a ship bound for furthest ports, as an ordinary seaman: so she was told, and she was more utterly lost than ever.

That rootlessness, for the next half century, was to be his life: making salt circles about the globe, with no secure footage anywhere. To be sure, he studied his navigation manuals, he rose at last to a ship's officer, and more. The barren years became a burden to him. There is a time, when white hairs come, to turn one's back on long and practiced skills and arts, that have long since lost their savours. This the sailor did, and he set his course homeward to his island; hoping that fifty winters might have scabbed over an old wound.

And so it was, or seemed to be. A few remembered him vaguely. The name of a certain vanished woman—who must be elderly, like himself, now—he never mentioned, nor did he ever hear it uttered. Her parents' croft was a ruin, a ruckle of stones on the side of the hill. He climbed up to it one day and looked at it coldly. No sweet ghost lingered at the end of the house, waiting for a twilight summons—"Sigrid...."

I got my pension cashed, and a basket full of provisions, in the village shop. Tina Stewart the postmistress knew everybody and everything; all the shifting subtle web of relationship in the island. I tried devious approaches with her. What was new or strange in the island? Had anyone been taken suddenly ill? Had anybody—a young woman, for example—had to leave the island suddenly, for whatever reason? The hawk eye of Miss Stewart regarded me long and hard. No, said she, she had never known the island quieter. Nobody had come or gone. "Only yourself,

Captain Torvald, has been bedridden, I hear. You better take good care of yourself, you all alone up there. There's still a greyness in your face...." I said I was sorry to take her time up. Somebody had mentioned a name—Andrina—to me, in a certain connection. It was a matter of no importance. Could Miss Stewart, however, tell me which farm or croft this Andrina came from?

Tina looked at me a long while, then shook her head. There was nobody of that name—woman or girl or child—in the island; and there never had been, to her certain knowledge.

I paid for my messages, with trembling fingers, and left.

I felt the need of a drink. At the bar counter stood Isaac Irving the landlord. Two fishermen stood at the far end, next the fire, drinking their pints and playing dominoes.

I said, after the third whisky, "Look, Isaac, I suppose the whole island knows that Andrina—that girl—has been coming all winter up to my place, to do a bit of cleaning and washing and cooking for me. She hasn't been for a week now and more. Do you know if there's anything the matter with her?" (What I dreaded to hear was that Andrina had suddenly fallen in love; her little rockpools of charity and kindness drowned in that huge incoming flood; and had cloistered herself against the time of her wedding.)

Isaac looked at me as if I was out of my mind. "A young woman," said he. "A young woman up at your house? A home help, is she? I didn't know you had a home help. How many whiskies did you have before you came here, skipper, eh?" And he winked at the two grinning fishermen over by the fire.

I drank down my fourth whisky and prepared to go.

"Sorry, skipper," Isaac Irving called after me. "I think you must have imagined that girl, whatever her name is, when the fever was on you. Sometimes that happens. The only women I saw when I had the flu were hags and witches. You're lucky, skipper—a honey like Andrina!"

I was utterly bewildered. Isaac Irving knows the island and its people, if anything, even better than Tina Stewart. And he is a kindly man, not given to making fools of the lost and the delusion-ridden.

ANDRINA

*

Going home, March airs were moving over the island. The sky, almost overnight, was taller and bluer. Daffodils trumpeted, silently, the entry of spring from ditches here and there. A young lamb danced, all four feet in the air at once.

I found, lying on the table, unopened, the letter that had been delivered three mornings ago. There was an Australian postmark. It had been postmarked in late October.

"I followed your young flight from Selskay half round the world, and at last stopped here in Tasmania, knowing that it was useless for me to go any farther. I have kept a silence too, because I had such regard for you that I did not want you to suffer as I had, in many ways, over the years. We are both old, maybe I am writing this in vain, for you might never have returned to Selskay; or you might be dust or salt. I think, if you are still alive and (it may be) lonely, that what I will write might gladden you, though the end of it is sadness, like so much of life. Of your child—our child—I do not say anything, because you did not wish to acknowledge her. But that child had, in her turn, a daughter, and I think I have seen such sweetness but rarely. I thank you that you, in a sense (though unwillingly), gave that light and goodness to my age. She would have been a lamp in your winter, too, for often I spoke to her about you and that long-gone summer we shared, which was, to me at least, such a wonder. I told her nothing of the end of that time, that you and some others thought to be shameful. I told her only things that came sweetly from my mouth. And she would say, often, "I wish I knew that grandfather of mine. Gran, do you think he's lonely? I think he would be glad of somebody to make him a pot of tea and see to his fire. Some day I'm going to Scotland and I'm going to knock on his door, wherever he lives, and I'll do things for him. Did you love him very much, gran? He must be a good person, that old sailor, ever to have been loved by you. I *will* see him. I'll hear the old stories from his mouth. Most of all, of course, the love story— for you, gran, tell me nothing about that...." I am writing this letter, Bill, to tell you that this can never now be. Our grand-

273

daughter, Andrina, died last week, suddenly, in the first stirrings of spring...."

Later, over the fire, I thought of the brightness and burgeoning and dew that visitant had brought across the threshold of my latest winter, night after night; and of how she had always come with the first shadows and the first star; but there, where she was dust, a new time was brightening earth and sea.

THE FEAST AT PAPLAY

Thora, the mother of Earl Magnus, had invited both the Earls to a banquet in Holm after their meeting on Easter Monday, and Earl Hakon went there after the murder of the holy Earl Magnus. Thora herself served at the banquet, and brought the drink to the Earl and his men who had been present at the murder of her son. And when the drink began to have effect on the Earl, then went Thora before him and said, "You came alone here, my lord, but I expected you both. Now I hope you will gladden me in the sight of God and men. Be to me in stead of a son, and I shall be to you in stead of a mother. I stand greatly in need of your mercy now, and I pray you to permit me to bring my son to church. Hear this my supplication now, as you wish God to look upon you at the day of doom."

The Earl became silent, and considered her case, as she prayed so meekly, and with tears, that her son might be brought to church. He looked upon her, and the tears fell, and he said, "Bury your son where it please you."

Then the Earl's body was brought to Hrossey, and buried at Christ's Kirk (in Birsay) which had been built by Earl Thorfinn.

—*Orkneyinga Saga*

In the morning Sverr the fisherman came up from the shore to the Hall of Paplay and called in at the kitchen door, "Hello, there. I have this basket of haddocks." Gudrun the housekeeper appeared. "Hello, Gudrun," said Sverr. "Here is the fish."

"Don't take your sea-stink into the kitchen," said Gudrun. "Wait here at the door."

Ingerth called from her loom, "Who is there, Gudrun?"

"Sverr the fisherman," said Gudrun. "He has a basket of haddocks, lady. He wants paid for them now."

"My mother-in-law is in the chapel," said Ingerth. "Tell the man he'll be paid after Mass."

"I've a good mind to take the fish away," said Sverr. "Fishermen can't wait. We could easily sell them among the hill farms."

"The lady Thora will pay you as soon as she comes in from the chapel," said Gudrun. "Just sit at the door for half-an-hour or so. It's Easter Monday—I hope you've been to the church yourself."

"Some folk have to earn their living," said Sverr sourly, and sat down on the stone at the door, beside his basket of fish.

Gudrun went back to the kitchen and sat on the fireside stool. The floor about the stool was strewn with red and white and black feathers, and from a rafter three dead naked chickens hung by their claws. Gudrun picked up a fourth chicken and began to pluck it. Feathers swirled about her feet like snowflakes. She heard someone calling outside, "Gudrun, Gudrun, I've come with the pig. Do you want him killed now?"

It was John the herdsman. He carried a young fat placid boar under his arm.

"Yes, kill it," said Gudrun. "But do it away from the door. We don't want blood everywhere."

Sverr was still sitting beside his basket of haddocks. The fish slithered feebly one on another, and gaped, and choked slowly in the dry April air.

John set the bewildered piglet on its feet in the yard. He took a knife out of his belt and pushed the blade into the pink throat. The beast squealed. It ran and staggered, and the blood welled out of it. It stood still, then shook its head in a sad puzzled way. Blood spattered on the paving-stones. The boar's eyes clouded, it keeled over, and it died in floods of gore.

"It will make a very tender pork pie," said John the herdsman. "What's happening out there at all?" said Ingerth from her loom.

Gudrun hung the fourth chicken from the rafters by its feet. She took a straw basket from the recess and went out into the yard. The two men, Sverr and John, were playing some kind of a game on the pavement, tossing flat stones into a circle scratched on the furthest flagstone. Gudrun crossed over the field to the mill. She had to bake a great quantity of bread and cakes for the feast that evening. The two greatest men in Orkney were to be the guests at the table: the Earl Magnus (Thora's son) and the

Earl Hakon. She would have to excel herself. Thank goodness, some of the farm girls would be coming in the afternoon to help in the kitchen. The ale, she thought; the ale at least will be very good. She had made it a month ago, in the cold hard air of March, always the best time for brewing. The ale had been seething gently for three weeks in barrels beside the kitchen fire. The earls would be glad of Gudrun's ale after their journey from the island, at sunset.

The little bell above the chapel at the end of the Hall began to nod and cry, and the bronze mouth brimmed with sound. *The Lord is risen! The Lord is risen! The Lord is risen!*

Ljot the stable-boy tugged at the bell-rope. The upsurge lifted him to his toes, again and again.

The Mass was over. A tall woman came out of the church, and after her a few farm women. She walked purposefully towards the door of the Hall. The priest told the stable-boy to stop ringing the bell so hard—he would have his arms out of their sockets, he would crack the bronze. The women from the farms smiled. Sverr the fisherman and John the herdsman threw their splintered stones into the grass and rose to their feet as the woman approached. "The Lord is risen," said the lady Thora, the widow of Erlend Earl of Orkney, to the two men. They mumbled a greeting to her. Thora passed into the Hall. "The Lord is risen," she said in the interior gloom and coldness.

Ingerth, working at her loom, did not reply.

Gudrun crossed back over the field from the mill carrying a basket of new meal on her shoulder. "A good Easter to you," she greeted the women who were returning now from the Easter service to this croft and that fishing bothy. They raised their hands and answered, "And to you too, Gudrun."

The lady Thora put a silver piece into the palm of Sverr's hand. "Thank you, my lady," said the fisherman, "it is too much." His tarry fist shook with greed and joy.

"No," said Thora, "but I have never seen such firm bright haddocks."

Gudrun set down her oatmeal on the table. The kitchen was hot and full of the smells of blood and strangulation. The ale seethed gently in the barrels and gave out a sweet smell. Gudrun added some peats to the fire. "Outside," she said to the thin black cat that was stretching itself beside the new flames. Gudrun took a sharp knife and went out to the yard to gut the fish. The cat, smelling the dead salt creatures, ran after her, mewling faintly.

The Hall precincts were empty now, except for the boy Ljot who was sitting in the grass looking up at the shriveling silent bell.

Gudrun listened at the door between kitchen and hall. Her mistress was saying to Ingerth, whose loom still clacked and birred inside, "It was a beautiful Mass."

Ingerth, her daughter-in-law, wife of Magnus the earl, said nothing.

"The Lord is risen," said Thora in a hurt voice. "Does that mean nothing to you? Of course it means nothing, if one does not see all the actions of Christ's life in the events of every day. Today in the island of Egilsay your husband and his cousin—the two earls—who have been on bad terms for years, they are holding a meeting. They are making a treaty. Does that mean nothing to you? Orkney that has been bleeding to death for many winters, that is dead in fact and laid in a hollow rock, Orkney is to be resurrected again this very day. Does that mean nothing to you?"

"I am dead also," said Ingerth. "I am dead here in your house. I lie dead every night in my bed. I think I will never come to life again. All that talk means nothing to me."

"The bread was broken in the church this morning," said Thora. "Here, tonight, in this very room, it will be broken again: the bread of peace. Does that not gladden your heart?"

"Nothing gladdens the heart of a married virgin who is growing old," said Ingerth, and sent the shuttle flying again with fierce clackings.

Soon, from the kitchen fire, came the smell of baking bread.

Five farm girls came in the afternoon to help Gudrun in the kitchen and the house. One swept the floor of the main chamber; one scrubbed the great table; one ran and fetched for Gudrun, a little salt from the stone in the cupboard, a few dock-leaves from the ditch to keep the fish cool; one watched the fire anx-

iously, bringing in peats from time to time and stirring the flames;
Solveig would have been better biding at home—she stood between the hearth and the kitchen bench gossiping like a bird
all afternoon, yet Gudrun did not reprove her because it was
such a special day: Easter Monday, and in the evening, here in
Holm the feast of the reconciled earls.

The girls murmured and giggled to each other from time to
time, passing with broom or salt or flame or fish-oil.

"...and so I just said to him," said Solveig. "'Peter,' I said,
'you needn't bother coming back here, I don't want to see you
again, what about the silver ring I gave you, what about my three
pearls found in the oysters, what have you done with them, drunk
them most like, now I know it only too well, you've been coming
here all winter to this house for only one thing, but now I've
had enough, you can go some other place, what do you take me
for, a simpleton,' I said. And the last I saw of him he was going
round the corner of the pigsty like a kicked dog, but the ale-
house had the story the same night, and the brute was getting
pots of beer for telling it over and over again...."

"I am glad to be here today," whispered little Una to the lady
Thora as she passed her in the main doorway. Una was carrying
in bits of greenery for the garnishing of the fish once they were
baked.

"It is Easter again," said Thora to herself as she walked in
her thick coat through the fields towards the shore. "The whole
world is alive and astir with resurrection. Look at the new grass
in the ditch, how young it is and full of sap, and the wild flowers
everywhere, and the birds dropping back among the islands from
the fires of Africa."

She passed some peat-cutters, a man and two women, on the
hill. "Bless your ladyship," said the woman humbly as the lady
of the Hall went past, but the man turned his back and sank his
blade viciously into the soft spongy turf. "Get on with your work,"
he whispered to the woman. "Do you want to be warm next
winter? It's all right for her—she gets her peats cut and dried
for her, yes, and set on the fire, yes, and the ashes raked in in
the morning. She can walk about in the sun if she wants to. But

the likes of us, we have to work our guts out for everything we have...." He spat on his hands. The two women clucked at him reprovingly.

"The very light is renewed at this time of year," said Thora to herself as she walked on towards the shore. "The air is no longer shroud-grey. There's a brightness in the wind. And the stars are not so fierce as in winter. There's a sweetness in that great wheel as it goes through the sky on an April night."

A man ploughing behind an ox in the field below raised his hand and shouted, "A good Easter, my lady," Thora stopped and answered, "And to you too," and passed on down to the beach where a few fishermen were sitting beside their sheds working with hooks and creels.... Behind her, in a fold of the hills, Tolk the ploughman fell to cursing at his ox; but even the cursings sounded new-minted, and they diminished at last to a few remote bright fragments.

Thora stood with her feet among the weeded washed rocks. At her approach the fishermen had turned their backs, not out of discourtesy but because they were shy in the presence of the great lady. They knitted their creels and baited their lines with great concentration. A lamb fluttered among the dunes; the ewe called to it from the edge of a low crag.

"At this time of year," said Thora to herself, "new life appears everywhere on the earth—lambs, calves, grice, nestlings. The new creatures come trooping through the door of summer. Heaven has ordained everything with great wisdom. Only man, the prodigal, is littered at all seasons of the year. How strange that is. Christ, as if to emphasize his manhood, chose to place his death at this time of birth and quickening; but at once, three days afterwards, he asserted his godhead by bringing out of death this thing that is so much more marvelous than birth even—resurrection.... Halcro," she called to the oldest fisherman, "thank you for the haddocks. Sverr brought them to the Hall. They are good fish. A good Easter to you all. I am expecting Earl Magnus and Earl Hakon from Egilsay round about sunset."

"They will come by road, my lady," said Halcro. "I heard there are horses waiting on the shore at Tingwall."

That, thought Thora, was how they would come indeed. She was standing among her fishermen at one end of this large island that was called the Island of Horses—Hrossey. Earl Magnus and Earl Hakon would, after their kiss of peace on the island of Egilsay, cross over in a small boat to the shore of Tingwall. Their squires would have been waiting since morning with the horses. Tingwall and Paplay were at opposite ends of the Island of Horses. The earls would have a long ride from Tingwall to the shore of Firth, then across the flank of Wideford Hill to the village of Kirkwall with its little church of St. Olaf. They would stop there most likely for refreshment—a cup of wine and some honeyed bread—with the priests, then on again along the sea-banks above Scapa Flow, until in the thickening light they saw below them the Hall of Paplay with its festive lights and flames.

"There will be happiness in Orkney now," said Thora to the old man.

Alternatively the two earls might sail from Egilsay, past the flat island of Wyre, then between Gairsay with its one hill and the long sprawl of Shapinsay, and avoiding Kirkwall and the priests sail through The String and drop anchor in the sheltered bay at Inganess. There they could get horses at a farm, and ride between the heather and the little bird-haunted hill lochs. In either case, the final stage of the journey would have to be by horse.

The lady Thora thought for a while, between the shining April sea and the ploughlands, of the skill and toughness and patience of the island generations. Hundreds of years ago men had come hungry to these islands, easterlings, and they had hauled up their longships here and at a score of other bays and inlets, and they had turned their salt sinewy hands to the earth. They had hewed cornerstones and set them here and there along the shore. They had dug little fields out of the heather. In summer they turned their axes against the dark folk who lived among the hills. Harvests came, a good one this year, an indifferent one that year; and their beasts multiplied and their beasts dunged the earth and their beasts were struck down before winter. The families made alliances, quarreled, schemed; and love blossomed here and there, erratic and marvelous. Somehow that Scandinavian tribe learned to live at reasonable peace, the farmer on the hill with the farmer at the loch-side (though the women at the hearths were forever stirring up jealousies and ambitions and old an-

gers). Or if a field here or there was desperately disputed, the
litigants took it to the district assembly, and generally abode by
the verdict of the men sitting solemnly on the side of the little
hill. There were occasional spear-storms and corn-batterings;
but in spite of that life had gone on, with new fields dug out of
the hill year after year, and new poems sung to the harp, and
new innocent eyes opening to the sun. There was a feeling of
slow continuous ripening, generation by generation, as of corn
wavering sunwards through a long summer of history. The time
of the great Earl Thorfinn—grandfather of Magnus and Hakon—
seemed now, looking back, like a golden harvest, with all the
sanctity and song and heroism that were in the islands at that
time.

After the death of Earl Thorfinn it was as if a chill wind blew
in from the sea, and the sun shrank. The horses reared their
hooves at the grey sun beyond the equinox. Winter came early
with its frosts and fires; that is to say, looking at these matters
in the long perspective of history, for the past two generations
life in the islands had not been so agreeable as it had been up
to then. Spite, anger, upset in every island, in every district, in
every household—a sense of stagnation and loss, of a honey-
comb broken and the sweetness draining away.

What had happened? Some argued that it was simply a loss
of independence and identity. The king of Norway had asserted
all too successfully his overlordship of the islands (as he had not
dared to do in Earl Thorfinn's time), and to emphasize it had set
up two puppet earls to squeak and gesture at each other; for he
knew that a single strong ruler in Orkney could, with a cynical
half-nod eastwards, plough his own furrow and fill his own barns.
So much was true: the lady Thora knew well enough how it had
been with her own husband Erlend, yoked impotently in the
earldom along with his brother Earl Paul. In those days the yawls
had begun to rot along the shore. But matters had got much
worse under the double rule of Magnus Erlendson and Hakon
Paulson—war had broken out—all Orkney was sundered into
two hostile camps, and foreign mercenaries rode through the
cornfields all one summer—there was everywhere a sense of
hopelessness and futility.

If misfortune goes on for too long—if stones drift over the

mouth of springs and people no longer have the will to shift them—then one has a sense of other than purely political forces at work; a veiled mysterious cipher has entered the equation; Fate has taken a hand in the game.

As year on year of murder and bad faith and anarchy succeeded one another, it seemed that an evil winter indeed was deepening over everything. The islanders trembled at the approach of the black solstice. They knew well enough in theory how the disorder could be cured: if they had a single strong earl standing in the door of his palace up there in Birsay, guarding the heraldry and the music and the lawbook and the looms inside.

But now events had passed out of their control. They could do nothing about the evils all around them. Fate was working out its own dark inscrutable design, which seemed to be the death of Orkney. The mere mention of the word "Fate" increased the hopelessness and helplessness.

Indeed (thought Thora as she walked back home through the fields) the ancient faith continues to be strong here in the north. Men acquiesce too easily still in the orderings of Fate. They have had Christianity for more than a hundred years and they are not comfortable with the new religion. It has not entered into the bloodstream of the tribe at all. Well, today in Egilsay, the new faith was being put to the test. The Orkneymen would see soon enough what a miraculous strength would flow from this meeting of enemies in Egilsay. It would be finally proven to them that it is Christ that rules the universe, not Fate.

Even a pagan might feel on a day like this that the islands were astir with hope and expectation and promise. The Lord is risen. The dove is fallen and furled in Egilsay now, thought Thora. The meeting is over. The horsemen are on the road to Paplay.

As she drew near the Hall she saw two of the farm girls— Gudrun's helpers—bringing the slaughtered piglet from a hook on the courtyard wall to the fires inside. The beast had a dark gash at its throat....

At the shore, the crew of *Godspell* still sat among the creel-stones and twine. It was the first afternoon that year that they had been able to sit out of doors.

"She's a good kind lady," said old Halcro reverently. "God help her."

"A fine sight it'll be," said his son Harald, "the two earls on the road, and all the gentry of Orkney riding behind them. From the ale-house door we might get a glimpse of them."

"There'll be music and feasting till all hours," said another fisherman.

"I'll tell you what the best sight of all would be," said a young fisherman called Ward. (His father had lost all his fields and his steading in the troubles, and Ward had had to beg the fishermen for a place in their boat.) "I'll tell you what the best sight of all would be—one horseman on the road tonight, a hard solitary silent man."

The fishermen looked at Ward and shook their heads. They did not know what he was talking about.

In the Hall kitchen the preparations were almost over. There was a heap of baked haddocks on a platter at one side of the fire; on the other the huge pot of chicken broth steamed. One of the girls turned the young pig on the spit. The first of the ale had been poured into a silver jug and it had a tilted cap of froth. Gudrun's face was flushed. The lady Thora entered from the main chamber. Her hair hung loose. Some new idea must have occurred to her in the middle of her toilet.

The sun had been down over Hoy for ten minutes or more.

"Solveig," said Thora, "you've done little but chatter nonsense all day. Go out and listen for the sound of hooves. They'll be riding between Gaitnip and Deepdale. It's a calm evening. You'll be able to hear them miles off."

Solveig put on her shawl and went outside.

The pig on the spit rained drops of its own burning fat into the fire.

"Una," said Thora, "have you set the ale-horns, a dozen of them, on the table?"

"Yes, I have," said Una, "and I polished the silver bits round the rims too."

"Well, don't stand there gaping—carry the goblet through," said Thora.

From the main chamber came the slow irregular clack of the

shuttle. The lady Ingerth had been at her weaving all day, and still she sat at the loom in the fading light, plotting intricacies of form and colour. She mingled scarlet thread with black thread and grey thread. It was uncertain yet what the web was meant to represent.

"The priests in Kirkwall are keeping them," said Thora. "That's what it is. Meantime the fish is getting cold. Magnus said they would be here before sundown, for sure.... Gerda."

"Ma'am," said Gerda.

"Go out and stand on the howe. You have good eyesight. See if you can see them."

"It's getting dark, ma'am," said Gerda.

"Just do what I say," said Thora. "Keep your eyes on the road. If you keep looking you'll see a thicker moving clot of shadows on the hillside. That will be them."

Gerda took her flushed face into the darkening wind outside.

"There's two or three good ale-houses between Tingwall and here," said Gudrun, between innocence and mockery.

"Earls are not blacksmiths and poachers," said Thora. "Earls don't go into ale-houses."

Solveig Rattle came back out of the night, shivering. "There's no sound of horses on the road at all," she said. "I crouched there five minutes with my ear to the ground."

The loom fell silent next door.

"I've heard," said little Una to Broda, breaking the new bread with her fingers and arranging the pieces on a platter, "I've heard that Earl Hakon is a terrible man. Of course I've never really set eyes on him. But they say he's fierce and black as a wolf."

"That's nonsense, Una," said Thora. "Earl Hakon is a very gentle courteous person. You'll see that for yourself before the night's done. Broda, my hair."

"Maybe, Una," said Solveig, "he'll take you on his knee."

"O for the love of God," shrieked Una. "I would die!"

Gerda came back, cold and grey-faced. She squatted beside the fire and held her hands out to the blaze. "The road's empty, ma'am," she said. "There's nothing moving in the darkness but a cow and a few fishermen going from the beach to the ale-house."

"It could be," said Gudrun, "that the meeting took longer

than they thought. Maybe they didn't get away from Egilsay till late."

Broda stood on tiptoe behind Thora. She pushed the comb into the burnished coils of hair and fastened it with a pin.

"That's possible," said Thora. "That's likely, in fact. They were hard and difficult, the things they had to discuss. If only Magnus and Hakon had been there themselves, the two of them, it would all have been so much more simple. But there were men in Egilsay today—Sighvat Sokk for example, and Hold Ragnarson—awkward difficult creatures at any time—supposed to be councillors—they couldn't counsel a cock to crow...."

"There will be a wish-bone for everybody," said Gudrun to Una and Broda. "Don't quarrel about it."

Through the open kitchen door the first star shone above the hill.

"Whatever delay there has been," said Thora, "Magnus and Hakon are coming to Holm. Nothing will stop them. It was a promise. They'll come, I know it. They'll come if it should be midnight."

"This pig will be a cinder long before midnight," said Gudrun. She took her forearm across her shining brow.

The dog set up a sudden fearful unending hullabaloo at the gate: until the stable-boy ran out and silenced him.

"Listen," said Una.

The women stood about the open door. They tilted their heads. They touched their fingers to their ears. They heard breathings in the night, a distant whinny and snicker, thuds on the soft turf, the bright faint chime of harness. A troop of horsemen was abroad. A horn blew. As if the rising sea rolled stones upon rock there was a sudden outbreak of clops and splashes—the horsemen were crossing the burn half a mile away. The women heard Ljot calling, "This way, this way—follow the lantern." The night was one jangling snorting onset then, though the hooves fell muted again on the grass of the park: a tumult of thuds and breathings, coming closer. "This way, my lord," said Ljot—"take care of the duckpond." Iron on stone: the cobbled courtyard was loud with men and horses. "The stable is over here," cried Ljot. "I'll hang the lantern in the rafters. There's plenty of hay. There's water in the trough over there."

"It's them," cried Solveig, clapping her hands. "They've come!"

"Come back inside, all of you," said Thora. "Shut the door. Gudrun, see to the ladling of the soup. I don't want any carry-on tonight between women and horsemen. Remember what day it is. When I sound the bronze, that will be the time to put the fish on the plates. Una, come with me, please."

Thora opened and closed the door between kitchen and hall. Una followed her. Ingerth had left the loom and was pacing unquietly between the hearth and the table.

"Your husband is here," Thora said. "Get ready. I should put on something gay—that yellow gown for example...." She passed on, followed by Una, into her bed-chamber.

The clatter of hooves lessened in the courtyard as the horses were led one by one from the troughs to the flickering stable. To the girls watching from the kitchen, the yard was a throng of noisy shadows. One tall shadow detached itself from the clamour. It moved, slow and hesitant, towards the stone heraldry of the main door. A fist rose and fell.

Ingerth in her sombre dress stood behind the loom and did not stir in the direction of the vibrant oak.

Thora, fixing a silver brooch to the shoulder of the red magnificence swathing her, came breathless out of her room towards the summons, followed by Una.

"Welcome," she said. And pulled the heavy door open.

A solitary figure reeled in, and stood there, rooted, shaking his head slowly in the light. Thora and Ingerth recognized, through the ale-stupor and the mask of fatigue, Hakon Paulson, the second of the two expected guests.

"I've come, Thora," he said. "I'm here."

"You're welcome, Hakon," said Thora. She moved towards him anxiously. He bent his barley-reeking head. Thora kissed him on the cheek. "A good Easter to Earl Hakon," she said.

"From Egilsay to here was a long hard journey," said Hakon thickly. "I've had one or two rough journeys in my time. This was the worst."

"Sit down, Hakon," said Thora. "You're very tired."

Hakon took his axe from his belt and laid it on the table. He sat down with tipsy suddenness in the high chair. His face was

carnival red among the torches. "Yes," he said, "I'm tired. There
was a lot of business to do in Egilsay today."

"So," said Ingerth. The shifting fire-reflections went over her
and filled with shadows her cheeks and temples and throat. Her
face fluttered slowly in the fire-and-torch-light. Her black eyes
never left Hakon's face.

"I came as quickly as I could," said Hakon. "We had trouble
with the horses. One cast a shoe. They turned their heads away,
anywhere but in this direction. The horses did not want to come
to Holm. One broke his leg on Wideford. They had to finish him
off."

"Hakon," said Thora, "it looks to me that you've ben cele-
brating early."

"No," said Hakon, "but I do not like killing. The horse—it
was Sigrud's gelding—he stumbled on a loose stone on the side
of Wideford. We had to kill him. That kept us back."

There was silence in the Hall. From the kitchen came the
clatter of pots and the cold swift orders of Gudrun to the farm-
girls. Little Una stood at the door between hall and kitchen,
waiting for the word to bring in the soup.

"The dinner is almost ready," said Thora. "You must be hungry, Hakon."

"No," said Hakon. "I want to drink."

"Una," said Thora, "tell Gudrun that we do not want the soup
or the fish just yet. Tell her to fill a jug with the oldest strongest
ale—the stuff she brewed for Christmas."

Una disappeared into the hot clattering kitchen.

"So, what is keeping Magnus so long out in the stable?" said
Thora.

Una came from the kitchen carrying the silver goblet. She set
it carefully on the table before Thora. Thora tilted the jar into a
cup. The ale went over thick and frothy and dark. She handed the
cup to Earl Hakon. "Magnus is not in the stable," said Earl Hakon.
"Magnus is in Egilsay." He drank till the beard on his upper lip
was dark and soaking. He noticed Ingerth standing between the
loom and the hearth fire. "Madam," he said, "your husband Earl
Magnus is in Egilsay. Magnus couldn't come to Holm tonight." He
drank again. "This is very good ale," he said.

"It is all one to me," said Ingerth, "where he is."

"Una," said Thora, "put some more of the ale into the earl's cup."

Una poured out of the jug. Her hand shook. The horn shook. Some ale fell on Hakon's fist.

"You stupid girl!" cried Thora. "Have you never learned to pour straight out of a jug!"

Una's lower lip quivered and she set the empty jug on the table. "I'm sorry," she whispered to Earl Hakon.

"No," said Hakon, "but it was my arm that was shaking. What's your name, girl?"

"Una."

"You are a very pretty girl, Una. I'm sure you're a great help to the lady Thora. It was my fist that was shaking and so some of the ale got spilled."

"Yes, lord," said Una.

"Una," said Thora, "the jug is empty. Ask Gudrun to fill it up again from the same barrel."

"Yes," said Una, and lifted the empty jug from the table.

"Tell Gudrun," said Thora, "that we will not be needing food after all. Tell her the girls are to carry the food to the men in the stables."

"Keep coming back with the ale jug," said Hakon. "You are a good girl."

"So Magnus is staying tonight in Egilsay," said Thora.

"That's right," said Hakon. "In Egilsay. Magnus is staying tonight in Egilsay."

"What house, I wonder?" said Thora. "Will he be sleeping in some farm, or at the priest's house?"

"No house," said Hakon. "I wish that girl would hurry with the ale. He is spending the night in the fields."

Una came back with the goblet and set it on the table, and stood looking with wide eyes at Earl Hakon.

"Go back to the kitchen," said Thora sharply to Una. "The earl and I have important things to talk about."

"You are a very sweet pretty girl," said Hakon. Thora poured ale into Hakon's cup. Una went back into the kitchen. Ingerth twisted her ring, a glittering golden snake-writhe on her finger: she looked at Hakon indifferently.

From the yard and the stable came sounds of laughter, a

mingling of bright and dark cries. The women were offering fish and bread and cheese to the men who had ridden from Egilsay. A woman broke the chickens into hot pieces. A woman put a knife into the roast pig. There were cheers when a girl crossed the yard with her arms full of ale-horns. The horses nuzzled the hay. Solveig shrieked twice. There were volleys of dark and bright cries.The main barn of Paplay was a house of laughter.

Earl Hakon put the ale cup to his mouth and emptied it with several strong workings of his throat. "This is very good ale," he said."I congratulate you. I'll tell you something. I am not a coward but I was terrified to come to this house tonight. What were we talking about?"

"Magnus in Egilsay," said Thora.

"Magnus is not staying in any house," said Hakon. "Magnus is spending the night under the stars."

"It will be cold for him," said Thora. "He did not take his thick coat with him."

"No," said Hakon, "he is not needing any coat. Magnus will never need another coat. but I need more ale."

"So," whispered Ingerth. "It is the dark bride."

"Hakon," said Thora, "I think you've had plenty of that ale. You would be better off with something to eat."

"No meat," said Hakon. "I carved flesh in Egilsay today. I was hellishly sick after it."

"Your axe is clean enough," said Thora.

"It was Ofeig's axe," said Hakon. "I didn't do anything personally, if you understand. Lifolf the cook, he did it. You know Lifolf the cook? We put Ofeig's axe into his hands. Lifolf carved the meat."

There was another long silence in the hall: the man building round his day's work a labyrinth of drunkenness—an old woman stumbling down dark hints and guesses to a simple central event (a fire on a stone, a lustration, a dove-fall). Ingerth looked at the web in the loom. It was grey lamb's wool, lightly woven, a half-finished summer coat: that would never now be worn.

Hakon poured a cup of ale for himself with a steady hand.

"Still you haven't told me what happened in Egilsay today," said Thora.

Hakon drank deeply.

"A man died," he said. "That's what happened. A man died."

"Well," said Thora, "that's always happening. Men die. Never a day but a man dies in this island or that. So long as this dead man in Egilsay was shriven and given heavenly bread for his journey, then he's happy enough, I'm sure. So long as he's lying in the church in Egilsay, between the font and the altar, all's well with him. The living weep—a mother, a widow, children weep—but there's worse things than a good death."

"There were no children in this case," said Ingerth.

"The dead man," said Hakon, "he is not in the church. He is in the fields. He is lying under the stars. I told you."

"It is a work of mercy," said Thora, "to give the dead sanctuary and burial. What were you all thinking of in Egilsay today? There is more ale in the jug. Were you all so busy with peace-making that you had no time to carry this poor man who died into the kirk?"

Hakon kneaded his eyes with his fists. He bent his head on the table beside the ale jug. A convulsion, like a slow ponderous wave, passed through his body, from chest to knees. His face streamed. He opened his mouth. He yelled once like a beast under a branding iron.

"Well wept, butcher," said Ingerth.

Thora lifted one huge trembling fist from the table and stroked it. "Well now," she said, "when you think of it there's worse places for a dead man to lie than the fields. But still I would be better pleased if the wounds and the silence were laid before the altar in the kirk of Egilsay. It isn't much for an old woman to ask."

Hakon whispered that he would send word to the priest and people of Egilsay in the morning. He sat up. He said in a firm voice that he was very tired. He said he must be on his way now. He thanked them for the fire and the ale. But still he sat where he was.

Thora touched him on the shoulder. He rose blindly to his feet. She kissed him again on his shivering mouth. She lit a candle from one of the wall torches. She called him "son." She led him through the far door to the bed-chamber beyond.

The byres and the barn and the stables round the courtyard brimmed with laughter and shouts and songs.

"The filth," said Ingerth. "The scum. The beast."

On the half-finished cloth in the loom could be seen now, in the torchlight, a sun, a cornstalk, a cup.

FIVE GREEN WAVES

1

Time was lines and circles and squares.

"You will go home at once to your father," said Miss Ingsetter, rapping her desk with a ruler, "and tell him I sent you, because you have not prepared the mathematics lesson I told you to prepare. Now go!"

A rustle went through the class room. The pupils looked round at me, wide-eyed. A few made little sorrowing noises with their lips. For it was a terrible punishment. My father was a magnate, a pillar of authority in the island—Justice of the Peace, Kirk Elder, Registrar, Poor Inspector, a member of the Education Committee itself. He was, in addition, the only merchant in the place and kept the shop down by the pier; even before I was born he had decided that his body would be a credit to him— he would go to the university and become a minister, or a lawyer, or a doctor.

Now, this summer afternoon, while blue-bottles like vibrant powered ink-blobs gloried in the windows and the sun came four-square through the burning panes, my stomach turned to water inside me.

"Please, Miss Ingsetter," I said, "I'm sorry I didn't learn the theorem. I promise it won't happen again. I would be glad if you punished me yourself."

The bust of Shelley gazed at me with wild blank eyes.

Her spectacles glinted. Down came the ruler with a snap. "You will go to your father, now, at once, and tell him of your conduct."

The bright day fell in ruins about me. I crossed the floor on fluttering bare feet, and was soon outside.

"You, Willie Sinclair," I heard her shouting through the closed door, "stand up and give us the theorem of Pythagoras."

A red butterfly lighted on my hand, clung there for a moment, and went loitering airily across the school garden, now here among the lupins, now there over the flowering potatoes, as if it was drunk with happiness and didn't know on what bright lip to hang next. I watched it till it collapsed over the high wall, a free wind-tipsy flower.

Inside the classroom, the formal wave gathered and broke.

"...is equal to the sum of the squares on the other two sides," concluded Willie Sinclair in a sibilant rush.

"Very good, Willie," said Miss Ingsetter.

Despised and rejected, I turned for home.

2

The croft of Myers stands beside the road, looking over the Sound, and the hill rises behind it like a swelling green wave. Sophie, a little bent woman, her grey shawl about her head, was throwing seed to the twelve hens.

She smelt me on the wind."Hello there," she cried. I muttered a greeting.

She peered at me. "And who might you be?" she said.

I told her my name.

"Mercy," she said, "but you've grown."

Our voices had roused the old man inside. He was suddenly at the door, smiling. Peter's face was very red and round. He had been a sailor in his youth. The backs of his hands, and his wrists, smouldered with blue anchors, blue mermaids, blue whales. "Come in," he cried.

It was like entering a ship's hold, but for the smells of peat and kirn and girdle. I breathed darkness and fragrance.

They ushered me to the straw chair beside the fire. I had hardly got settled in it when Sophie put a bowl of ale between my hands. The sweet heavy fumes drifted across my nostrils.

Peter sat filling his pipe in the other straw chair. The old woman never rested for an instant. She moved between the fire and the window and the bed, putting things in order. She flicked her duster along the mantelpiece, which was full of tea-caddies and ships in bottles. The collie dog lolled and panted on the flagstones.

"And tell me," said Peter, "what way you aren't at school?"

"I got sent home," I said, "for not learning the lesson."

"You must learn your lessons," said Sophie, setting the fern straight in the tiny window. "Think what way you'll be in thirty years' time if you don't, a poor ignorant fellow breaking stones in the quarry."

I took a deep gulp of ale, till my teeth and tongue and palate were awash in a dark seething wave.

"And tell me," said Peter, "what will you be when you're big?"

"A sailor," I said.

"If that wasn't a splendid answer!" cried Peter. "A sailor. Think of that."

"My grandfather was a gunner on the *Victory*," said Sophie. "He was at Trafalgar. He came home with a wooden leg."

"That was great days at sea," said Peter. "Do you know the ballad of Andrew Ross?"

"No," I said.

A hen, shaped like a galleon, entered from the road outside. She dipped and swayed round the sleeping dog, and went out again into the sunlight.

"Woman," said Peter, "get the squeeze-box."

Sophie brought a black dumpy cylinder from under the bed, and blew a spurt of dust from it. Peter opened the box and took out a melodeon.

"Listen," he said. A few preliminary notes as sharp as spray scattered out of the instrument. Then he cleared his throat and began to sing:

> *Andrew Ross an Orkney sailor*
> *Whose suffering now I will explain*
> *While on a voyage to Barbados,*
> *On board the good ship* Martha Jane.

"That was the name of the ship," said Sophie, "the *Martha Jane.*"

"Shut up," said Peter.

> *The mates and captain daily flogged him*
> *With whips and ropes, I tell you true,*
> *Then on his mangled bleeding body*
> *Water mixed with salt they threw.*

"That's what they used to do in the old days, the blackguards," said Sophie. "They would beat the naked backs of the sailors till they were as red as seaweed."

"Damn it," said Peter, "is it you that's reciting this ballad, or is it me?"

> *The captain ordered him to swallow*
> *A thing whereof I shall not name.*
> *The sailors all grew sick with horror.*
> *On board the good ship* Martha Jane.

"What was it Andrew Ross had to swallow?" I asked.

"It was too terrible to put in the song," said Sophie.

"I'll tell you what it was," said Peter, glaring at me. "It was his *own dung*."

The sickness began to work like a yeast in the region of my throat. I took a big swallow of ale to drown it.

Peter sang:

> *When nearly dead they did release him,*
> *And on the deck they did him fling.*
> *In the midst of his pain and suffering*
> *"Let us be joyful," Ross did sing.*

"He was religious," said Sophie, "and the captain was an atheist. That's the way they bad-used him."

> *The captain swore he'd make him sorry,*
> *And jagged him with an iron bar.*
> *Was not that a cruel treatment*
> *For an honoured British tar!*

The house took a long dizzy lurch to starboard, then slowly righted itself. My knuckle grew white on the edge of the chair. The good ship Myers burrowed again into the fluid hill.

"Mercy," said Sophie, "I doubt the boy's too young for a coarse ballad like that."

> *Justice soon did overtake them.*
> *When into Liverpool they came.*
> *They were found guilty of the murder*
> *Committed on the briny main.*

"High time too," said Sophie. "The vagabonds!"

Soon the fateful hour arrived
That Captain Rogers had to die,
To satisfy offended justice
And hang on yonder gallows high.

I stood erect on the heaving flagstones. "Going be sick," I said.

"The pail!" cried Sophie, "where's the pail?"

But she was too late. Three strong convulsions went through me, and I spouted thrice. The flagstones were awash. The dog barked. Then the cottage slowly settled on an even keel, and I was sitting in the straw chair, my eyes wet with shame and distress. Not even Andrew Ross's sorrow was like unto my sorrow.

Old Sophie was on her knees with a wet clout and a bucket.

Peter patted me on the shoulder. "Don't you worry," he said. "You're not the first sailor that's been sick on his maiden voyage."

3

Below the kirkyard the waves stretched long blue necks shoreward. Their manes hissed in the wind, the broken thunder of their hooves volleyed along the beach and echoed far inland among cornfields and peat bogs and trout lochs, and even as far as the quiet group of standing stones at the center of the island.

I made my way shoreward, walking painfully along a floor of round pebbles. One had to be careful; Isaac of Garth, going home drunk and singing on Saturday nights, was in the habit of smashing his empty bottles on these rocks. He had done it for so many years that the amphitheater of pebbles above the sand was dense with broken glass—the older fragments worn by the sea to blunt opaque pebbles, the newer ones winking dangerously in the sun. If one of the sharp pieces scored your foot, you might easily bleed to death.

There was no one in sight along the wide curve of the beach, or on the road above. In the kirkyard the grave-digger was up to the hips in a grave he was making for Moll Anderson, who had died at the week-end.

Quickly and cautiously, under a red rock, I took off my clothes—first the grey jersey with the glass button at the neck, next the trousers made out of an old pair of my father's, and finally the blue shirt. Then I ran down to the sea and fell through an incoming wave. Its slow cold hammer drove the air out of my lungs. I thrashed through the water to a rock thirty yards out and clung to it, gasping and shivering. "Lord," I thought, "suppose Miss Ingsetter or my father saw me now!" A shred of cloud raced across the sun, and the world plunged in and out of gloom in a second. And then, for an hour, I was lost in the cry and tumult of the waves. Shags, dark arrows, soared past my plunging face. Gulls cut gleaming arcs and circles against the sky, and traversed long corridors of intense sound. Seals bobbed up and down like bottles in the Sound, and grew still every now and then when I whistled. For a brief eternity I was lost in the cry, the tumult, the salt cleansing ritual of the sea.

The grave-digger paused in his work and, shading his eyes beachward, saw me stumbling out of the waves. He shook his fist at my nakedness. The sand was as hot as new pancakes under my feet. I ran wild and shouting up the beach and fell gasping on my heap of clothes. I lay there for a long time. From very far away, on the other side of the hill, a dog barked. The rockpool shimmered in the heat. The music of the grave-digger's spade rang bright and fragile across the field. Suddenly three words drifted from the rock above me: "You naked boy." I looked up into the face of Sarah, Abraham the tinker's daughter. She rarely came to school, but whenever she did she sat like a wild creature under the map of Canada. She was sprawling now on the rock with her legs dangling over. Her bare arms and her thighs, through the red torn dress she wore, were as brown as an Indian's.

Sarah said, "I come here every day to watch the boats passing. When the sun goes down tonight we're moving to the other end of the island. There's nothing but the hill and the hawk over it. Abraham has the lust for rabbits on him."

The tinkers have curious voices—angular outcast flashing accents like the cries of seagulls.

She jumped down from the rock and crouched in front of me. I had never seen her face so close. Her hair lay about it in two blue-black whorls, like mussel shells. Her eyes were as restless as tadpoles, and her small nose shone as if it had been oiled.

"Sarah," I said, "you haven't been to school all week."

"May God keep me from that place for ever," she said.

With quick curious fingers she began to pick bits of seaweed out of my hair.

"What will you do," she said, "when you're a tall man? You won't live long, I can tell that. You'll never wear a gold chain across your belly. You're white like a mushroom." She laid two dirty fingers against my shoulder.

"I'm going to be a sailor," I said, "or maybe an explorer."

She shook her head slowly. "You couldn't sleep with ice in your hair," she said.

"I'll take to the roads with a pack then," I said, "for I swear to God I don't want to be a minister or a doctor. I'll be a tinker like you."

She shook her head again. "Your feet would get broken, tramping the roads we go," she said.

Her red dress fell open at the shoulder where the button had come out of it. Her shoulder shone in the wind as if it had been rubbed with sweet oils.

She stretched herself like an animal and lay down on the sand with her eyes closed.

I turned away from her and traced slow triangles and circles in the sand. I turned a grey stone over; a hundred forky-tails seethed from under it like thoughts out of an evil mind. From across the field came the last chink of the grave-digger's spade— the grave was dug now; the spade leaned, miry and glittering, against the kirkyard wall. Two butterflies, red and white over the rockpool, circled each other in silent ecstasy, borne on the stream of air. They touched for a second, then fell apart, flickering in the wind, and the tall grass hid them. I turned quickly and whispered in Sarah's ear.

Her first blow took me full in the mouth. She struck me again on the throat as I tried to get to my feet. Then her long nails were in my shoulder and her wild hair fell across my face. She thrust me back until my shoulder-blades were in the burning sand and my eyes wincing in the full glare of the sun. She dug sharp knees into my ribs until I screamed. Then she raveled her fingers through my hair and beat my head thrice on the hard sand. Through my shut lids the sun was a big shaking gout of blood.

At last she let me go. "Next time I come to the school," she said, looking down at me with dark smiling eyes, "I'll sit at your desk, under the yellow head of the poet." She bent over quickly and held her mouth against my throat for as long as it takes a wave to gather and break. Her hair smelt of ditch-water and grass fires. Then she was gone.

I put on the rest of my clothes, muttering through stiff lips, "You bitch! O you bloody bully, I'll have the attendance officer after you in ten minutes, just see if I don't!"

As I left the beach, walking slowly, I could see her swimming far out in the Sound.

She waved and shouted, but I turned my face obstinately towards the white road that wound between the kirkyard and the cornfield. The salt taste of blood was in my mouth.

4

The grave-digger had finished making Moll Anderson's grave. He was sitting on the shaft of his barrow, smoking a clay pipe. As I turned in at the gate he wagged his beard at me, for he did not associate this shy decently-clad boy with the naked insolence he had seen running out of the sea half an hour before. I wandered away from him among the branching avenues of tombstones—the tall urns and frozen angels of modern times; the fiery pillars with the names of grandfathers on them; the scythe-and-hourglass slates of the eighteenth century; and the lichened leprous tombs of a still earlier age. This small field was honeycombed with the dead of generations—farmers with stony faces; young girls rose-cheeked with consumption; infants who had sighed once or twice and turned back to the darkness; stern Greek-loving ministers; spinsters with nipped breasts and pursed mouths. I stood on the path, terrified for a moment at the starkness and universality of shrouds; at the infinite dead of the island, their heads pointing westward in the dense shoal, adrift on the slow tide that sets towards eternity.

My dreaming feet brought me to a low tombstone set in the east wall:

HERE LIES BURIED
A FOREIGN SEAMAN,
OF UNKNOWN NAME AND NATIONALITY

WHOM THE SEA CAST UP ON THIS ISLAND,
JUNE THE SIXTH, 1856

*"Though I take the wings of
the morning, and flee to the
uttermost places of the sea."*

I closed my eyes and saw a little Basque town between the bay and the mountains.

The feast of Our Lady of the Sea was over. The nets and the oars had been blessed. The candles were still burning in their niches among the rocks.

Now the young people are dancing in a square that lies white and black under the moon.

The musician slouches, as if he were drunk or half asleep, against the fountain. Only his hand is alive, hovering above the strings like a vibrant bird.

The young people are dancing now in long straight lines. The partners clap their hands and bow to each other. They shout; the dark faces are lit up with a flash of teeth. They move round each other with momentarily linked arms. They incline towards each other, their hands on their knees, and stamp their feet. It is all precision, disciplined fluency, a stylized masque of coupling.

Older men and women sit gossiping on the doorsteps. Occasionally they sip from tall glasses. One, a fat man with a yellow beard, looks often through a gap in the houses, at a ship anchored in the harbour.

An old shawled woman stands alone, in the shadow of the church. No one speaks to her; the seal of separation is on her. She is the guardian of the gates of birth and death. In this village she comes to deliver every wailing child, she goes to shroud every quiet corpse. Her eyes are in the dust, from which all this vanity has come, and to which it must return.

The hand over the guitar moves into a new swirling rhythm. Now the square is all one coloured wheel, a great wavering orange blossom.

Suddenly there is an interruption. A tall bearded sailor appears at an alley-opening and walks slowly across the square.

The guitar falters. The dance is frozen. The old dark woman raises her head. The officer points to one of the dancers and crooks his finger: he must come, immediately, the ship is sailing tonight.

The seaman—he is only a boy—turns once and looks back. A girl has raised her apron to her face. The yellow-bearded man rises from his doorstep and makes a gesture of blessing: "Lady of Waters, guard him this day and all days till the sail returns to the headland."

Above the village a cross stands among the stars. Through a long silence comes the sound of the sea. The last votive candle gutters and goes out among the rocks.

The little town of moonlight and music will never see that sail again. Her voyage has ended on a northern rock. All her sailors have vanished down the path of gull and lobster, scattered in a wild Atlantic storm. One broken shape only was lifted out of the seaweed. Curious hands have carried the nameless thing in procession across the fields. They have clipped the rags from it and combed its hair, and covered the crab-eaten face. And though there was no priest to sing Latin over it, a Calvinist minister said, "All flesh is grass, and the glory of flesh is as the flower thereof"—the orange-blossom of Spain and the little blue Orkney primula, whose circles of beauty are full and radiant for a short time only; and then, drifting winterward, or broken with June tempest, lay separate shining arcs in the dust...

My slow circuitous walk had brought me to the new gaping hole in the earth. The grave-digger was still sitting on his barrow. He bored a sidelong glance into me and said: "There's only one way of coming into the world, but ah, God, there's two or three ways of going out."

"That's a fact," I said.

"Would you like," he said, "to see what a man *truly* is?"

Not understanding, I gave a quick nod. He groped with his hand into the small hill of clay beside the open grave, and brought out a skull. Carefully he wiped it on his moleskin trousers. "That's you," he said, "and me, and the laird, and Frank the idiot. Just tha."

He laughed. "There's nothing here to make your face so white. It's as harmless as can be, this bone. It's at peace, and not before time. When it lived it had little rest, with its randy eyes and clattering tongue. This skull belonged to Billy Anderson, Moll's grandfather. He was twice in jail and fathered three illegitimate bairns. O, he was a thieving, drunken, fighting character, and it was a good day for him when we threw him in here. Wasn't it, Billy?" he said to the skull, blowing smoke into its eye-hollows. "Wasn't it, boy?..." The skull grinned back at him.

From the other side of the loch the school bell rang the dismissal.

Over the hill from the village, like a procession of beetles, came the mourners.

5

After I had finished my lessons that evening, I was summoned into the shop.

My father was sitting at the counter between a barrel of paraffin oil and a great dark coil of tobacco. There was a jar of sweets at his elbow. Over his head hung jerseys and scarves and stockings, with price tickets on them. The lamp swung from the hook in the ceiling, smoking a little. There was always a good smell in the shop.

"It's thee, John," he said, raising his head from the ledger for a moment. "Sit down, boy." he counted the sticks of toffee in a glass jar and then said, "How did thu get on at the school today?"

"Fine," I said.

"I've been thinking about thee," he said, "what to make o' thee, once thee school-days are over."

He gathered up a handful of coins, and rang them one by one back into the till. Then he marked the ledger on his desk with a pencil.

"There's no future in this shop, I can tell thee that," he said. "The profits are getting smaller every year. The reason is, the folk are leaving the island. They're going to the cities and the colonies. Not a month passes but another family leaves.

"And then they send to the mail-order places in the south for their clothes and their ironmongery. A great lot of them do that. They forget that we depend on each other for our livelihood in a small island like this.

"And there's debts too," he said. "For instance, Mistress Anderson who was buried this afternoon died owing more than six pounds. So it'll be a poor inheritance for thee, this shop," he said.

He licked his pencil and wrote more figures in the ledger. His hair glittered fraily in the lamplight.

"I had a word with Miss Ingsetter this afternoon about thee," he went on. "She called at the shop after school for some fly-papers. She seemed surprised thu weren't home yet. . . . I made a point of asking her about thee. She says thu're an able boy, good beyond the general run at reading and writing and history. Not so bright at the mathematics. Sometimes thu're inclined to be inattentive and dreamy, she says. At times, only at times. But there's no harm in the boy, she said, and he's by no means stupid. And it's my opinion, she said, he ought to go to the grammar school in Kirkwall for a secondary education, once he turns twelve."

"I want to be a sailor," I said.

"The dreaminess," he said, "you take from your mother. . . . After the school comes the university. That'll cost money, a power of money. Still, I'm not barehanded, I haven't neglected to pro-vide for things like that. With a degree in thee pocket, thu could enter *the professions*. Think of that."

"It's the sea I have a hankering for," I said. "Uncle Ben said he could get me into the Saint Line, any time I wanted."

"The ministry is an honourable profession," he said. "There isn't a lot of money in it, but you get a free manse, and I can tell you old MacFarland doesn't spend a fortune on food. He gets a hen here and a pound of butter there and a sack of tatties from the other place. On his rounds, you understand, his visitations. Cheese at the Bu, and fish from Quoys, and a fleece for spinning from Westburn, all for nothing. And nobody can say the work is strenuous."

"Supper is ready," my mother sang out from the kitchen.

"Now doctoring is strenuous, there's no doubt about that. They haven't a moment to call their own. They can't even be sure of a night's sleep. There's always somebody thundering at Doctor Leslie's door after midnight with the toothache, or a pain in the guts, or a hook's got stuck in their hand. It's no wonder he's taken to the drink lately. But, putting all that aside, medicine is a fine calling. Plenty of money in it too if you can get them to pay their bills."

"I spoke to Mother," I said. "She would like fine for me to be a deep-sea captain. She's going to write to Ben."

"The law," he said, "is a different thing. Not that there's anything wrong with it, if you understand, but there's a shady side to it, there's a certain amount of trickery about it that makes the ordinary honest man wonder sometimes. You can hardly open a newspaper without seeing some lawyer or other in trouble for embezzling his client's money, and carrying on. You'll hear a couple of them arguing a case like mad in the courts, and then, half an hour later, there they'll be walking down the street together cheek by jowl ... John," he said, "never go to law if you can possibly help it. Not but what there aren't honest lawyers too."

He unscrewed the lid from a bottle of black-striped balls. He took out a couple between his fingers and handed them across the counter.

"If there's one place I have a longing to see," I said, "it's Japan."

He suddenly withdrew his hand and dropped the black-striped balls back into the jar.

"Not before your food," he said, licking his fingers. "I forgot. ... Then there's teaching—"

"Are you coming for your supper," chanted my mother impatiently, "or are you not?"

Outside the dog began to bark. There was a clattering of hooves and wheels over the cobbles. The poultry squawked like mad in the yard. "Mercy," said my father, running to the door, "it's the tinkers. *The hens!*"

I followed him out, into the moonlight. The tinker's cart was opposite the door now. Abraham sat on the shaft. He cracked his whip and cried to the grey pony. In the cart sat Mary his wife with an infant slung behind her in a tartan shawl. Sarah walked alongside with her arms full of wild lupins.

They were going to the other end of the island where the rabbits were thick, to camp there.

"Giddap!" cried Abraham and cracked his whip. "That's a fine dog you have there, Mister Sigurdson," he shouted to my father. "I'll take a half-pound of bogey roll, and I'll pay you when I come back along next week."

"No," said my father sternly, "you'll pay now, for you owe me sixteen and six already."

"Hello, Sarah," I said. She stood on the road and looked at me through the dark blue congregated spires of lupins.

"Are you seeking a tin pail, mistress?" yelled Abraham to my mother who had come out and was standing at the corner of the house guarding the hens.

"Yes," she said, "I'll need one when you come back by next week."

Suddenly my father was furious. "We need no tin pails!" he shouted. "There's plenty of tin pails in the shop!"

"Next week-end, mistress," cried Abraham. He stood between the shafts and cracked his whip. "Giddap!" he yelled. The wheels rolled in crazy circles over the cobbles and stars streamed from the pony's hooves. There was a sudden wild *cluck-cluck-clucking* from inside the cart as it moved off. Sarah stood looking at us, smiling through her screen of lupins.

My father went back into the shop, muttering. My mother stood at the corner of the house and watched them out of sight. "One of the hens is missing," she said. "I darena tell thee father. He would have the police at them for sure."

A wave of purple blossom rose in front of the moon and showered over me.

Soon the racket died away at the far end of the village. Sarah's mockery sounded from a distance of three fields. I turned back into the house. My face was wet with dew and petals, and the moon raged above the mission hall wilder than ever.

"The very idea!" cried my father from inside the shop. "A sailor! A tin pail! *The thieves!*"

Time was skulls and butterflies and guitars.